**monsoon**books

# THE RED THREAD

Dawn Farnham was born in Portsmouth, England in 1949. Her parents emigrated to Perth, Western Australia, when she was two. She grew up a sandgroper, barefoot and free, roaming the bushy suburbs and beaches with her friends. In the 1960s she, like so many other young Aussies, left on a ship for London, aged seventeen. In the Swinging Sixties she met and married her journalist husband, moved to Paris, learned French and travelled round Europe in a Volkswagen Beetle.

As a foreign correspondent, her husband was posted to exotic locations and they lived in China, Hong Kong, Korea and Japan in the 1980s and 1990s. During this time she raised two daughters and taught English. Back in London she returned to school, doing a BA in Japanese at The School of Oriental and African Studies (SOAS) and a Master's Degree at Kings College.

She and her husband now live in Singapore where she is a volunteer guide at the Asian Civilisations Museum. It is in this thriving port city-state that she found her muse and began to write, finding particular pleasure in Singapore's colourful and often wild past. This is her first novel.

# The Red Thread

A Chinese Tale of Love and Fate
in 1830s Singapore

## Dawn Farnham

**monsoon**books

Published in 2007
by Monsoon Books Pte Ltd
52 Telok Blangah Road
#03-05 Telok Blangah House
Singapore 098829
www.monsoonbooks.com.sg

ISBN-13: 978-981-05-7567-0
ISBN-10: 981-05-7567-X

Cover photograph copyright©National Museum of Singapore,
National Heritage Board.
Maps on page 6-7 courtesy of National Archives of Singapore,
National Heritage Board.

Printed in Singapore

12 11 10 09 08 07          1 2 3 4 5 6 7 8 9

*This book is dedicated to the story of Singapore and to the energy, variety, resilience and enterprise of all Singaporeans, past, present and future.*

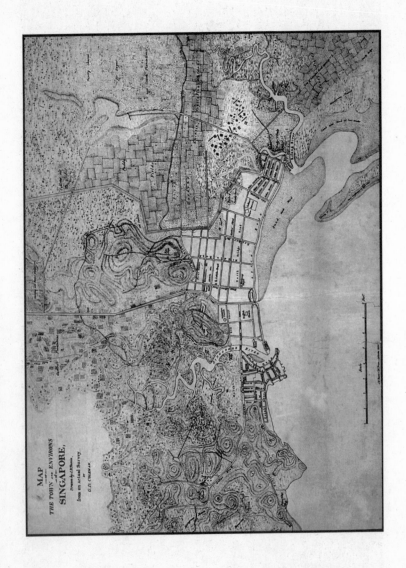

ABOVE: *Map of the town and environs of Singapore. Drawn by J.B. Tassin from an actual survey by G.D. Coleman, 1836.* RIGHT: *Detail of the town.*

# Glossary

| | |
|---|---|
| *Ah ku* | Polite Cantonese term for Chinese women brought from China to Singapore to work as prostitutes |
| *Ang mo* | A Hokkien term literally meaning 'red hair' that is used to refer to Caucasians |
| *Baju panjang* | Popular in the nineteenth century among *nonya*s, it was a loose, calf-length tunic, with sleeves tapering at the wrists that was worn over a *sarong*. A more conservative precursor to the shorter *baju kebaya* blouse popularised in the early twentieth century |
| *Bangsal* | The Malay word for shed or jungle lean-to |
| *Batik* | A wax-resist dyeing technique used on textiles, especially *sarong*s, and the name for the textiles it has been applied to |
| *Cha-li* | Betrothal gifts from a groom's family to a bride's family usually contained tea, money, cakes, poultry, sweetmeats and wine but the gift of tea was such an important part of this ritual that the gifts became known collectively as *cha-li*, or 'tea presents' |
| *Chandu* | The Malay word for processed opium ready for smoking |
| *Cherki* | Card game popular in the Peranakan community |
| *Chinchew* | Chinese middlemen who traded regionally, travelling from port to port |
| *Chunam* | A fine stucco based on very pure or shell-lime, used for the highest quality finishes, often to external walls and roofs |
| *Jamu* | Traditional herbal medicine from Indonesia and Malaysia |

| | |
|---|---|
| Munshi | A degree in South Asia, that is given after passing a certain course of basic reading, writing and maths. The word munshi also became the name of a profession after munshies were hired as clerks in the government in British India |
| *Orang laut* | The Malay term *orang laut* means sea people. Historically the *orang laut* were principally pirates |
| *Pak chindek* | Wedding master of ceremonies who would accompany the groom and help him with the many marriage rites |
| Peranakan | Descendents of intermarriages between early Chinese male settlers in the Straits Settlements (Penang, Malacca and Singapore) and local Malay women. This Chinese sub-ethnic group adopted some cultural traits from the Malay community, as seen in their cuisine, dress and language, but also adopted many European customs thus elevating their social standing in relation to the *singkeh* or China-born immigrants. Also known as Straits Chinese. The men are known as Baba, the women as Nonya (or Nyonya) |
| *Sampan* | A relatively flat bottomed Chinese wooden boat. In Cantonese the term literally means 'three planks' |
| *Sangkek um* | Wedding mistress of ceremonies who would accompany the bride and help her with the many marriage rites |
| Tao | Chinese character often translated as 'way' or 'path'. It is based on the understanding that the only constant in the universe is change |
| *Tongkang* | Bumboats, lighters or sea-going barges used in the Malay Archipelago for transporting goods from ship to shore and vice-versa |
| *Towkay* | Chinese merchant |
| *Wayang kulit* | Shadow puppets that are prevalent in Java and Bali |
| *Wu wei* | Important tenet of Taoism that involves when to act and when not to act. The aim of *wu wei* is to achieve a state of perfect equilibrium |

# Prologue

'An invisible red thread connects those who are destined to meet,
regardless of time, place or circumstance.
The thread may stretch or tangle but will never break.'
—The Legend of The Red Thread

The wind tasted red. Pu-erh tea, sorghum liquor, dark vinegar and schisandra.

Red aromas on the air. Smoke of aloe's wood and dragon's blood. Incense in the mind.

Their skin felt seared by cool rays, brushed by the wet silk of the sun's sleeve.

Thunder rolled far away, its growl rippling and fading beyond their ears. Red *chi* dragons playing.

Eyes, pinpricks, rising and falling on the enchanted swell, filled with hues. Squinting light.

The coolies sat, hushed, flushed.

Two crimson suns moved in the coral sky, one rising astern and the other dripping into the blood-red sea ahead of the junk. Land and sky blurred into all the shades of fire.

So it was true.

The slanted sails were redder than the sea, the colour of vermillion seals, stretched and straining on the wind. Scarlet pennants on the top gallants of the masts danced in the gusting breeze. The captain stood like a mandarin on the high prow, his long robe stained magenta.

No sound could be heard now, save the groaning of the heavy rigging, the sigh of the wind and the deep splashes of the unnatural sea.

The junk had left China from the port of Amoy and headed down the southern coast past the Zhenyantou pillar of rock, which stuck like a white needle straight out of the sea. Junks had followed this route for thousands of years. The captain's maps were ragged copies of copies of the charts of maritime passages of long-dead Chinese sailors. The sea deepened where the Pearl River emptied into it, as the junk followed the Kwangtung coast, before turning south to pass east of Hainan Island.

Here a storm had caught the ship, testing its crew to the breaking point, each man holding fast to ropes, to spars, to life, as best he could.

When it calmed, bodies were dropped overboard into the deep sea, cooked rice in their mouths against hunger in the underworld, heads and arms wrapped in white cloth covered in twisted, red cloud-shaped characters that were talismans against their return as vengeful demons. Flames licked the joss paper hell money burning in the brass censer on the fore deck. Smoky sandalwood swirled round the beams and ropes of the rigging, the breath of the dead mounting skywards.

The captain carried a stock of these funereal items in a chest in a storeroom far from his cabin. In his years in this pig trade, he had used them at least once on every voyage. If it wasn't storms it was sickness. The coolie agent in Amoy was supposed to weed them out, but some made it past him, desperate to be taken, for there was hope on the ship and none on the land. Each man touched his amulet and gave silent thanks for his life. Copper cash, mirrored pa kua, carved peach stones, small Buddhas or tiny Kuan Yin, the compassionate ones; whatever it took to ward off evil.

Some of the ballast had been used to weigh down the corpses; their feet were tied to the ingots of pig lead. One ingot per pig was all the captain allowed, which meant that the bodies sometimes stood to attention in the water a little longer, the shrouded heads bobbing in a line in the ship's wake as the junk pulled away. But he and the crew were used to it.

The coolies' eyes were fixed on the blue paper-cuts of Zhong Kui, powerful queller of demons, which a crewman was busy pasting to the masts. Or they watched as the sailors purified the ship, sprinkling the decks and rails with realgar wine. Finally the captain poured a cup of the ruddy liquid over the bow as an offering to the Dragon King of the South Sea and his duty to the dead and the ocean was done.

He would have liked a rest, but not yet, for now he must navigate his ship between the long and deadly reefs and shoals of the Xisha Archipelago and the coast of Cochin China. At a small bay near the promontory of Cape Varella, he dropped anchor and waited until morning.

From here the junk must leave sight of land and head out across the open sea to the twin dragon horn peaks of Tuma Shan, the island the Malays called Pulau Tioman. This route, though perilous, would be safer than the pirate-infested coasts of the South China Sea. His ship was large and carried cannon: attack was unlikely, but this was pirate season. An old friend had perished in these waters only last year, cargo taken and thirty-three of his crew dead or sold into slavery. They'd been no match for the sixteen boats rowed by cut-throats who emerged swiftly from the dense mangrove swamps off Pahang, cutting them down as they drifted, windless. Better to take his chance with the pirate chief who had taken residence on Tioman. For trade in sea cucumbers and bird's nests—goods the Chinese prized—he offered a haven to the big junks from his own fleets, which regularly plundered the islands of the surrounding seas. For this reason the captain displayed prominently on the foremast a large and ornate *kris*. It had been given to him by the Raja of Pahang, to whom the chief owed some kind of allegiance.

It was always a risk. These islands could change hands at any time, but everything in these seas was a risk. This was the price they all paid for profit. In the green waters of Juara Bay, the ship dropped anchor for the night, the watch armed and ready despite the chief's assurances, for his human cargo was as attractive as silk or opium in the slave market at Endau. This night, though, passed quietly, only the snores and snuffles of his little piglets disturbing the peaceful swishing of small waves on the shore. The captain took on fresh water and, as the dawn crept up the sky, set sail for Point Romania and the vicious rocks of Pedra Branca. Here, where the South China Sea meets the Straits of Singapore, the five towering curved vermillion sails swung sharply to his order and the junk swept due west into the lowering sun.

The captain had seen the sky signs as they headed south. He knew his passengers were as superstitious as only ignorant Chinese coolies could be. It was near the mid-month, and here on the Equator the full moon chased the sun from east to west. At this time, he knew, the moon might appear aflame right in the middle of a clear blue sky. He deemed it wise to calm fears and avoid trouble by giving an explanation they would understand.

'The dragon is chasing the flaming pearl. It is a good sign. One of the special sights of the Nanyang, the southern seas. Here are the Vermillion Hills, where the red phoenix, bird of peace and wisdom, guards the quadrant. She has brought this ship through its perils.'

The men were reassured; the captain was the man who had saved them from the deadly storm. They were alive; the flaming pearl was the jewel of good luck, the magic granter of all wishes. It meant hope, potential for the new life they were beginning in the fabled Nanyang, a place where their fortunes would be made, the coolie agents at home had assured them. They would be guarded by the gentle phoenix, sovereign of the feathered world, the bird that never dies. The towering ring of fire surrounding the ship told them it was true.

'Nuts.'

Zhen turned and murmured to his friend. Qian looked at him quizzically.

'A pretty speech from our admiral, eh? He is a sage.'

Qian shook his head, not understanding. Sometimes Zhen could be infuriatingly cryptic. Zhen smiled.

'Once there was a monkey keeper handing out nuts. He said to the monkeys, "Three every morning and four every evening." The monkeys were all in a rage. "All right," said the keeper. "Four every morning and three every evening." The monkeys were all delighted. The captain, doubtless unawares, had harmonised with the monkeys' perspective. You see? These coolies are the monkeys. Say the right words, and they will believe anything. Tell 'em we're floating on the elixir of immortality, and they'd all jump overboard.'

Qian smiled, but in his heart he was like the monkey coolies. He wanted to believe that they were secure in the bosom of a benevolent power, not merely drifting like so much flotsam and jetsam on the surface of this ruby sea.

The colours began to change as they pursued the setting sun. The persimmon moon gradually became a saffron moon. Even the captain, with his long experience in the South Seas, had not seen such light. The flying fish that dashed along beside them flashed coral, apricot, peach. When the sun had fallen below the horizon, the sky and sea turned slowly from pale rose to purple; the rising amber moon was now their sole companion, before and aft, lighting both the way back to China and the way forward, to their new home.

Not until the moon was high in the darkened sky did it turn a pearl white and throw its silver light over the sea, bathing the waters around the hull in a pale, translucent glow. The junk slid its two great anchors into the depths. The men from the east had arrived in Si Lat Po.

Zhen and Qian leaned over the rail and gazed at the harbour. All around lay the paper-cut silhouettes of ships. A forest of masts bathed in moonlight spread to the shore. On each craft, the lights of the night watch flickered like fireflies, the dark sea glittering like a starry mirror of the Milky Way. Zhen whispered the words of a long-dead, homesick poet:

'Athwart the bed
I watch the moonbeams cast a trail,
So bright, so cold, so frail,
That for a space it gleams
Like hoar-frost on the margin of my dreams.
I raise my head
The splendid moon I see,
Then drop my head
And sink to dreams of thee
My homeland, of thee.'

Qian felt tears caught in his throat. Despite his relief at this safe arrival and the flickering beauty of the scene before his eyes, thoughts of his family filled his mind. He said the poem again in his head. This same moon hung like a bright eye over his village, casting its hard, white gaze on a place of walking dead, of decayed and rotten fields, a wasteland where parents abandoned their babies and sold their daughters into slavery for a pittance. He had seen things he could not speak about, monstrous hunger turning men into fiends. He thought of his wasted mother, his desperate brothers, his young, sickly sisters (at least they had not yet been given up) and his father's grave. He thought of how all of them had placed their hope in him, the scholar, and sorrow overwhelmed him.

His reverie was interrupted abruptly by Zhen, who nudged him and pointed to the west.

The billowed white sails of a schooner leapt from the curtain of darkness like a fox spirit from a wood. The burnished prow cut through the dark waters of the roads. His thoughts of home disappeared as they watched this fairy craft approach, drop anchor and lower sails. The watch was set. Between the junk and the schooner a glittering ribbon of silver formed a watery path.

A small figure moved forward to the bowsprit. She had watched as the schooner neared. She had never before seen such a monumental vessel. The heavy carved wood and the thick trunks of the masts made the schooner look plain and puny.

In the glow of the moon it looked unreal, like a dream of wizard's invention, too huge for mortal men. Charlotte raised a finger and traced the outline of the moon with its misty white halo.

A thunderclap of voices erupted from across the water, and she started, becoming suddenly aware of hundreds of eyes turned upon her.

For a brief moment Charlotte froze, then shrank back into the shadows.

From the high deck of the junk, Zhen and Qian stood looking down on the foreign ship. The men pushed and shoved to get a glimpse of this woman who stood so brazenly in the open night. Was she a ghost? A loud murmur went round the ship.

Qian, the smaller of the two men, turned to his companion. 'Ma Chu, the Sea Goddess; she is like Ma Chu, no? She has appeared at the moment of our safe arrival. She's greeting Ch'ang O, the Moon Goddess.'

Zhen shook his head. 'No, blockhead, she *is* the Moon Goddess and I am Yi, her husband. She wants to hold me in her tender embrace.'

He stepped up higher onto the ship's rail and, leaning precariously over the edge, threw out his arms. 'Ch'ang O, my little lady of the moon. I'll come soon darling.'

The words were rough, slang and full of innuendo. The ship erupted in laughter.

From the shadows Charlotte saw the man step into a pool of pale light and hold out his arms towards the schooner. Strange sounds fell on her ear, and she heard the roar of laughter roll over the water. She could just make out his silhouette, and she guessed that this laughter and his gesture were aimed at her. Astonished, she remained in the shadows, watching, until Mr Dawson came suddenly to her side.

Mr Dawson had paid her the most exquisite and pointed attentions since he had come aboard at the Cape. She had learned that he was taking up an appointment with the British and Foreign Bible Society. During his many years in Asia he had tried a handful of professions, but none had served him well. His employers had been difficult and overbearing, his capacities unappreciated. He reckoned that God could not be more difficult than the directors of the East India Company.

Now, Charlotte was much more intensely curious about the junk.

'Where does it come from, this ship?'

'China.'

He was from Bristol and pronounced it 'chainarr'. He waved vaguely to the East. 'The cargo is human mostly. They are called coolies.'

China? Charlotte knew little about China. It was a mystical land of silk and tea. Her aunt possessed a Chinese bowl covered in designs of charming pagodas, pretty gardens and crooked bridges, exotic birds and graceful ladies with parasols. What did he mean, human cargo?

'Are they slaves?' she asked.

'No, but as good as. They are labour for the plantations and tin mines or in the town. For at least a year they must work to pay back their passage. Then they are free, so it is said, but by then most of the wretches are indebted from gambling or addicted to the opium which the bosses sell them. The Chinaman loves these pursuits, you see, and cannot give them up.'

He shrugged. 'Some make good, I suppose. They say there are merchants richer than royalty who came here with nothing.'

She detected a note of bitterness in his voice.

He looked down at Charlotte. 'Never fear, you will have little to do with this kind of rabble. We all stay well apart. In Singapore each race has its own living place.'

She feared he might put a comforting hand upon her shoulder. She was, on this occasion, glad of his loquaciousness and interested in the information he had imparted, but she knew he was as addicted to the sound of his own voice as, apparently, Chinamen were to gambling. This fact, added to the sourness of his breath, made conversation with him more a trial than a pleasure. As he was about to continue, she quickly curtsied, thanked him and, wishing him good night, went below.

Charlotte turned uncomfortably in the narrow bunk. The proximity of the Chinese ship seemed to have a physical effect on her; the air was stifling and now, so close, she was anxious to see Robert, who she knew would be waiting for her. Abandoning rest, she found her box of lucifers, lit the candle and took out Robbie's last letter.

*Dearest Kitt,*

*I have extraordinary but good news. I have been promoted from my position at Johnstone & Co in a most unexpected manner. Actually promotion is hardly a word for what has happened, as I am no longer employed by Mr Johnstone at all. In the absence of a proper police force, the state of affairs in the settlement has been worsening over the past several months, with gang attacks and robberies becoming so frequent that people dare not sleep at night. So much so that the strongest remonstrance was made to the East India Company's officials in Calcutta. The government there has been forced to pay attention to this matter, which they'd much rather ignore. They have grudgingly agreed to the permanent appointment of a head of the police force.*

*Now, my dearest sister, you must sit down, for have you not guessed it? It is I, your brother, who has been asked to take up this post, to my surprise and, I must say, delight. I had so tired of clerking. I have been told that this unusual step was taken because of the good terms I am on with the mercantile community here, both European and native, and equally because I am not a military man, clanking about in uniform and spurs. Of course, I am also affable and charming, etc., etc.*

*The better news is that, while this post is not so well remunerated as I would wish, it comes with a good-sized residence. You are almost nineteen, and your education finished, and so you must come at once to live with me here in Singapore. I have written also to Aunt Jeannie that she is to arrange your passage, to be paid for from father's inheritance. As you know, I will come into this only when I turn twenty-two, but I cannot think there will be any objection. Grandmère will most assuredly be glad to see the back of both of us, though Aunt Jeannie may be saddened. She has been as much a mother to us as she has been allowed, and I am sorry to grieve her. But there is nothing else for it. I fear to wait. Grandmère has been casting around to marry you off to some oaf or other almost since I left. Out here your prospects will be considerably better, for while your looks, as you are aware, are wanting, women of your age are as rare as hens' teeth, and there are plenty of up-and-coming and much better oafs to choose from!*

*I do not mean to alarm you with talk of gangs and robberies. We shall be entirely safe. Where safer than with the head of the police force! Singapore is a warm and healthy place and now has such elegant buildings, thanks to Mr Coleman's splendid architecture. From the governor's mansion on the hill to the streets of the Chinese town, everything here will delight you. Although our group of* orang putih *(white people) is small, yet we are a jolly band.*

*Voyage safely chère soeur.*
*Your loving brother, Robert.*

A steward had brought some tea. She opened the box with the robe she had kept for this reunion. After the months of this voyage, her other clothes were now practically in tatters. Everything was so difficult on board a ship, in particular *la toilette*. She brushed her hair and began to arrange the yellow ribbons.

Charlotte and her brother had been raised in Madagascar, where her father ran the school and orphanage of the London Missionary Society. When the violence against white men began there, he had sent his children to his mother and sister in Scotland, his homeland. They travelled under the protection of one of the young missionaries, Father Michael, who was carrying reports back to London. He and their mother would follow soon, he had told them. She remembered her parents' faces as she and Robert left those childhood shores: her father stoic, her mother's face streaming with tears, too filled with misery even to wave as their tiny figures became mere specks. They had never seen either parent again. On that journey to Scotland, she and Robbie had at first cried but Robbie, bold young boy that he was, soon came to think of this as an adventure, dogging the crew and climbing about in the rigging. He grew tired of her tears. She thought her heart might shatter. Only the presence of Father Michael, endlessly patient and kind, saved her and gave her some peace.

For a very long time she had been angry at her parents, resentful of her forced exile in this town of granite, her obligatory presence in the cold stone church where she silently cursed the god who had so indifferently robbed her of mother, father, love. Gradually, as she grew up, this feeling had been replaced with sadness and longing for what she and Robbie had missed. She no longer cursed God, for she felt that this meant that she was also cursing her mother and father, and even Michael, who had been her saviour. Though she could not find Him in her heart, she had learned a grudging appreciation for those good souls who did.

Charlotte put down her brush and took a deep breath. Though perilous, this voyage had been happier than that childhood one so long ago. She smiled. Soon she would be with Robbie.

The moon was still dropping from the night sky and the sun sitting below the horizon when Charlotte stepped warily onto the deck and opened her parasol. This, she felt, might accord her some measure of privacy from the eyes on the junk, but it seemed the men were still asleep, as there was no movement. She lowered the parasol. Now she could see what a mighty thing this Chinese ship was. The wood glowed red, redder as the dawn crept up the sky. The bow was a little lower than the stern, which stood fifty feet above the sea. The sails were lowered, but she could see they were a faded vermillion. The stern was square and carved with images she did not understand. Two great eyes adorned either side of the bow. An enormous rectangular keel, honeycombed with holes, hung massively in the smooth water, little eddies forming as the ship swung gently. Two anchors, fixed to the sea floor, kept the ship stationary. Pennants with strange symbols fluttered on its masts. Viewed from such close quarters, the ship was overwhelming, dwarfing the schooner on which she stood.

'Crimoney!' she whispered.

'They are magnificent, aren't they?'

The captain had strolled to her side.

'We call them junks, from the Javanese *djong*, I believe, which the Portuguese turned into *jonc*. The Chinese doubtless call them by some other name. I have seen many but never grow tired of them. For flatness of sail and handiness, their rigs are unsurpassed.'

He traced the outline of the ship with his hand, almost a caress.

'Do not be fooled by the busy superstructure. Under the water they are very sweet. The deep rudder and forefoot keep the ship windward. In the hell storms of the China Sea and on blue water, they are the finest vessels afloat, I think. But don't tell the Admiralty.'

Charlotte smiled. The old captain was something of a heroic figure, and she had come to admire him immensely over the long months of this voyage. Having discovered that Charlotte knew how to sail small craft, he was delighted to talk to her of nautical things.

'Her passengers may find you interesting, my dear, so I think we may move a little further inshore.'

He had heard of the incident the previous night. He liked this unusual young woman who, alone, had made the long and occasionally dangerous voyage with a quiet and gritty stoicism. In times of need she had been helpful and unflappably useful to the other passengers. In periods of calm he often found her studying a book of the Malay language and was delighted to help her, for he had spent years in these waters and spoke it fluently.

'Actually we have been signalled to go in closer and given permission to disembark.' He pointed to the staff in the distance bristling with flags. 'This Chinese ship will soon move round beyond the fort to unload at Telok Ayer Bay.'

A painted bird with outstretched wings and serpentine tail feathers covered the entire surface of the stern. A fabulous creature with faded plumage of red, black, yellow, green and white, it had a curved back like the crescent of the moon, sharp eyes like the sun; those eyes watched the schooner sail smoothly round the junk.

Now human eyes were watching too and, to her annoyance, she found herself searching to see who had called out, but the faces lining the length of the ship were a mass of brown and black. Modesty, she knew, should have sent her below, but since the schooner was pulling rapidly away, she felt bold enough to withstand the gaze of those alien eyes—even, if she were truthful, to rather enjoy it.

'Kitt Macleod, you have become a hussy,' she murmured to herself.

The shoreline came clearly into sight. As the sun shot its opal rays over the horizon, she turned and caught her first real view of the settlement. A pang of recognition. Her breath caught in her throat. The green, thickly wooded hills, the low, red-roofed houses, the sandy shoreline and the turquoise waves, reminded her of Toamasina, the island port of Madagascar, her birthplace. She felt the breeze of this eastern isle like a welcoming kiss.

Robert had written her amusing letters about this small settlement. Charlotte had laughed, but in between the lines she read of sad loneliness, of long nights far from her, from their deep affection for each other; she had shed tears for him. Now she smiled. This soft dawn would bring her to him and to her new home. She forgot the Chinese ship and went below to make her final preparations.

The coolies had stirred when the schooner drew anchor, and they moved to see this sleek little ship, with its white sails, move gracefully towards shore. All hoped to catch a glimpse again of this Ch'ang O of the western seas, as she had now been named. Superstitious and afraid, they felt she might be an extra good omen in Si Lat Po, this land of no winters, of tigers, snakes and barbarians. Zhen did not step forward this time, but watched silently as the foreign woman glided past. He could see her quite clearly from his vantage point at the stern. Her dress was white, with a wide, pale gold sash. The top was tight-fitting, with a kind of puffed sleeve. She was slender. The skirts were large and of some gauzy material. She looked as if she was standing in a cloud. Her hair was long, black, like Chinese hair, held back by shining gold ribbons that floated below her waist; her features were delicate. Despite the morning heat, she looked as cool as moonlight on a river. He was surprised; he had heard that people from the Western lands were red and coarse.

He could not make out her eyes. Then she turned and looked to shore. Within a minute she had disappeared, and the schooner grew smaller.

Zhen grinned and turned to Qian.

'Her robe a cloud, her face a flower ...
Meeting on the dew-edged roof of paradise.'

They were lines from Li Bai's 'Song of Pure Happiness'. With him, Zhen carried two books. In one he had copied all his favourite poems. Waiting in Amoy for the coolie ship to leave, he and Qian had discovered a mutual love for this ancient, reckless, romantic and drunken poet and his steady and loyal friend, Du Fu. Zhen had deliberately changed 'moon' to 'dew' to give a sensual liquid overtone. 'Playing the game of clouds and rain' had been the poetic allusion to lovemaking between men and women since time immemorial.

'Perhaps Yi will meet Ch'ang O again.'

'Perhaps, but don't forget how Li Bai ended up. Up ended, trying to capture the moon in the river, poet no more.'

'Yes, but it was a fine death. Drunk on poetry and wine.'

They both laughed, but a small tic began to twitch alongside Qian's right eye. He knew from their long conversations that he was the Du Fu to Zhen's Li Bai. Perhaps that was why they had formed such a strong bond. Surely he would not mix himself up with these *ang mo gui*, these foreign devils whom no one could understand.

He sighed. There was always something dangerously Taoist about Zhen. He had grown to love him, though. Despite the miseries of their journey, Zhen stayed resolute and cheerful. At those times, the words of Du Fu's ode to Li Bai came to him: 'caught in a net, how is it you still have wings?' When he had said this, Zhen had told him a story.

'There was an old farmer who had worked his crops for many years. One day his horse ran away. Upon hearing the news, his neighbours came to visit. "Such bad luck," they said. "Maybe," said the farmer. The next morning the horse returned, bringing with it three other wild horses. "How wonderful," the neighbours exclaimed. "Maybe," replied the old man. The following morning, his son tried to ride one of the untamed horses, was thrown and broke his leg. Again the neighbours came to offer their sympathy for his misfortune. "Maybe," answered the farmer. The day after, military officials came to the village to draft young men into the army. Seeing that the son's leg was broken, they passed him by. The neighbours congratulated the farmer on how well things had turned out.

"Maybe," said the farmer.'

They turned back into the ship. Like the rest of the poor hopefuls on board, they must ready themselves for the task of survival which loomed precariously ahead. They could see boats of every possible size and shape, flying from the shore like hornets out of a nest and racing towards them.

Almond eyes bobbed along the water line as the *sampan* cut swiftly across the harbour. Charlotte's hair was full of the wind. A mist of salty spray flew up from the bow, showering her face. She did not care. She could see the rim of low bungalows along the beach front and the big trees on the plain; the governor's residence on the hill; the fluttering of flags on the flagstaff. The fort stood low on the opposite side of the riverbank. Then she saw Robbie, standing on the jetty and her heart leapt. She waved and Robert waved.

In a flash she had arrived. A journey of 10,000 miles had ended in a minute. Robert pulled her from the boat and hugged her tightly, trembling from this feeling of profound happiness. Charlotte, overcome, held him too, smelling him, filling her empty places up with him, this brother she loved so well. Finally he released her, and they began to laugh. Arm in arm, they made their way into the bungalow. The rest of the day passed in a whirl of news of Scotland and the voyage, Robert's unusual appointment and the discovery of her future home. As evening drew in, Charlotte, exhausted, prepared for bed. She went out onto the verandah, which faced the sea. A pleasant breeze cooled her face. She looked out over the roads, but the great junk had disappeared.

# 1

'I found out I was a half-breed bastard when I was ten,' Charlotte said. 'Before that I lived in Madagascar, where I suppose everyone was a half-breed bastard of one sort or another and no one had the slightest idea.' She laughed lightly. 'What a lovely house you have, Miss Manouk.'

Charlotte's hostess smiled.

'*Alamah*, for goo'ness sake, don' be silly-billy, my name is Takouhi. I too am so-called half-breed, although no one can call me bastard, since my father and mother marry. He, Armenian Dutchman. She, Javanese. It is like this in the world, I think, but George tell me not like that in England. George say maybe no half-breeds in England, but lot of bastards. He is Irishman, so I think he know this. Sometimes I don' understand what George say.'

She pronounced his name softly, like the French. This was said in the gravest of tones but broadest of smiles. English was not her favourite language, though she enjoyed some of its colourful expressions.

'My parents, too, were married,' Charlotte went on, 'but that did not make any difference to my Scottish grandmother. My mother was mixed blood. A pirate father, French, and a Creole mother from Mauritius, so she told us. Everybody was so mixed up on the island. My grandmother was ashamed of us, it was as simple as that.'

The three da Silva girls sat, wide-eyed, silently listening to this conversation. They did not know where this Madablasta place was, but it didn't matter. They had no idea where America was, or England. India, Java, China: all mysteries. Mr Coleman had told them that Ireland was the biggest country in the world, inhabited by green folk, that he himself had been green but had faded after a long absence from those shores. Their exasperated father had assured them that this was just one of Mr Coleman's jokes. Everyone in Singapore was from somewhere beyond their horizon. They were used to it.

Boldly, the youngest, Isabel, ventured, 'How is that possible, Miss Macleod? Since you are her granddaughter, she must love you, surely?'

For the Misses da Silva, any new addition to their meagre acquaintance was welcome, and Charlotte, freshly arrived from Europe, was an object of benign curiosity. Gossip formed the central pillar of their lives in this small settlement, and a fresh source was too good to resist. Their own father had been widowed often, and their lives in a house full of brothers and sisters from several mothers were full of occasional rancour but more often of raucous affection. Isabel and her twin sister, Isobel, whose mother was English, were light-skinned, light-haired and blue-eyed. The elder sister, Julia, was a shade darker in every way: skin, hair and deep brown eyes. Her mother, a mixture of Portuguese and Indian blood, had died when she was five.

Charlotte smiled at the three girls. Julia was twenty, pretty and quiet. She was soon to be married to Lieutenant Sharpe of the Madras Native Infantry, which was permanently billeted in Singapore. Isobel and Isabel had had the bad luck to resemble their mother, who sat, rather squatly, by their side on the wide sofa. Charlotte could not know it then, but almost no sign of the aquiline good looks of da Silva *père* had been passed on to them. They were all, however, so friendly and agreeable, and Charlotte was happy to like them all very much.

'Well, Miss da Silva, perhaps she did, in her way. It was just that she was so intent in knocking out of us what she called our "island ways". You know—speaking native and being lazy. She made us learn proper English and French and go to church. Robert, my brother, had to go off to school. We had never been separated. It was hard for a time.'

Her voice broke slightly, but she quickly recovered.

'But we had a lovely aunt, Aunty Jeannie, who had never married, and she cared for us so it was not so bad,' she abruptly finished.

Takouhi, alive to changes in feeling, quickly changed the subject. They had been chatting for hours, and she now offered to show her companions over her house. This proved the ideal suggestion, and with general assent, they prepared to set off. Few of the ladies present had had the opportunity to see this magnificent residence, and they attributed this visit to Takouhi's brief but growing affection for Charlotte.

'Takouhi Manouk is George Coleman's friend,' Robbie had told her at breakfast that morning. 'I wrote to you about him. He does all the architectural work and building here, makes the roads, builds the bridges, drains the swamps. Not much he doesn't do, really, when you think of it. I think you could say that this is Coleman's town. He's Irish, but I suppose it's not his fault, ha ha. Anyway, he has built a beautiful house for Takouhi, and you should meet her. Her name means "queen", I think, in Armenian. They are Armenians, the Manouks, from Batavia. Her brother is immoderately rich.'

With this abbreviated introduction, Robert had placed her in a smart two-seater open carriage with great wheels, pulled by a little Sumatran horse, and sent her off. She had protested that she had hardly seen him, it was too soon, but Robert was adamant. He was busy today. Tomorrow he would show her the town. She needed to meet people, have friends. There were not many women of her sort in Singapore.

She wondered what 'sort' that was: young or poor or unattached? Perhaps all three.

So off went the carriage, away from the bungalow on the sea side and up High Street. The driver was a wiry Indian with skin the colour of deep mahogany. He wore a blue-and-red turban, pushed jauntily back off his brow. His lower regions were clothed in a white dhoti, but he was bare-chested except for a sash thrown over one shoulder. He smelled vaguely of cloves. She felt strange but not uneasy about being in such proximity to naked male flesh and shot glances at him out of the corner of her eye. He looked straight ahead, impassive. At the courthouse they turned right and passed in front of three large, elegant white houses with green shutters and red roofs surrounded by luxuriant gardens. In one rose the crimson-crowned head of the flame of the forest. Charlotte recalled playing in the dense shade among the grey buttress roots of this lacy-leafed plant in Madagascar. This road ran along the edge of the plain, and beyond its expanse she could see the sapphire blue of the sea and the masts of the ships.

She felt a sudden upsurge in spirits. Here was a place intensely familiar, yet brand new. It was a frontier. Perils lay beyond, perhaps, but promises too. She felt a mantle of the past slipping from her shoulders and, for the first time, she was willing to let it go.

It was ten o'clock in the morning and the heat was already wilting. The parasol shaded her but did nothing to stop sweat trickling down her neck. The street was deserted. The only noise to be heard was the squeaking of the big wheels on the carriage and the sonorous buzzing of a thousand cicadas in the shrubberies. Fiery air shimmered on the plain.

A few minutes later, she caught sight of another large, columned building at the end of the plain; then the carriage turned left, and a gleaming white house came into view. Charlotte had never been to Pall Mall, but she had seen pictures, and she thought this house would not have disgraced it. The two storeys of the house were fronted by a great porch supported by six slender fluted columns, topped with scrolls in a neo-classical style. A deep frieze supported the long triangle of the roof front. On this, in foot-high, exquisite Celtic script were carved the words: 'Tir Uaidhne'. Charlotte recognised the lettering from the books of Scottish myths and fables in her grandfather's library but had no idea what the words meant. She liked it, though: a house with a mysterious name.

Half-columned bays projected from the sides of the house into the gardens. Unlike the other houses she had seen, the shutters on this house were white and the roof tiles green. Surrounded by tall trees and palms in a myriad of verdant shades, the house had an air of undeniable coolness.

Like an emerald isle in an emerald sea, thought Charlotte, remembering that Coleman was an Irishman.

Before the porch, a mass of bushes covered in tiny white flowers spilled frothily onto a lawn. As they turned in to the gate and drew up in the deep shade of the porte-cochere, a woman descended the marble steps and put her hands together in greeting.

Charlotte had never seen such a woman. She wore a silk *sarong*, which played about her ankles as she moved, a shimmering garment in hues of lime, gold, brown, tan and black, a tumbling profusion of geometric and floral designs. Over a tight bodice she wore a plain tunic in pale green, of a material which was gossamer fine. The borders of the tunic and sleeves were filigreed lace, and it fitted her body like a glove. The jacket made a deep V-shape over her tiny waist. She wore no shawl. Her jet-black hair was drawn up into a loose chignon and held with a simple gold lacquer pin. The colours so matched her light brown skin and black eyes that she seemed almost unreal. On her feet she wore open sandals so delicate they seemed to be made of diaphanous threads. Then Charlotte noticed that the skin from her toes to her ankles was covered in fine coils and tendrils of black and brown vines and leaves, as if she had stepped from a magical autumn garden. This was so fascinating that Charlotte knew she was staring and had to drag her eyes away.

'Come,' said the vision, seemingly unmoved by her inspection, and took her hands. Up they went into the great hall. Charlotte had no time to crane her neck before they reached a sitting room on the side of the building. A wide bay window overlooked a grove of trees, with leaves which drooped prettily in pinkish–purple tassels. There, on a long sofa of pale yellow silk, sat Mrs da Silva and her three charges. Seven other ladies were also present, seated apart on pale green, damask-covered chairs. They all rose when Charlotte entered.

Without ado, Takouhi had introduced them, and Charlotte had curtsied to each in turn. She took in only a blur of green and gold robes, white organza, pretty eyes with a pink *sarong*, sallow skin, red hair and freckles, black curls on a bulky frame, and fragile paleness.

The room was relatively cool, the shutters of the windows thrown open to catch the breeze. It was a high-ceilinged room of elegant proportions, entirely white, with pale yellow silk curtains. An unusual, low black table stood before the sofa; it had a shiny lacquered surface and stocky legs in square geometric shapes. A large round bowl of pure translucent white stood in the middle, filled with greenish–white jasmine flowers which imparted their faint sweet scent to the air. The sofa itself was a shape unlike anything Charlotte had seen, the back a series of undulating curves that scrolled outward at the arms. A long sideboard of glowing teak, carved with floral and vine motifs, stood against a wall. An English Georgian silver tea service stood on a side table with the pale green porcelain tea cups and saucers. Chased silver platters held small pastries. Two pretty young Javanese boys dressed in white cotton *sarongs* and short green jackets served. They wore green and white *batik* head scarves and had long, feathery eyelashes.

Charlotte marvelled at the unexpected elegance of her surroundings and the extraordinary group of women seated around her.

No more remarkable assembly than this could surely be gathered in any other drawing room in the world, Charlotte thought. She was glad she had come. Sipping her tea, she began to pay attention to the women gathered around her. Fair-haired and porcelain-skinned Charlotte Keaseberry was from Boston. She had met and married her English missionary husband in America. At first she had been excited by the prospect of serving God in heathen climes, but the heat had worn at her and, although by nature resolute, she secretly longed for the bracing air of New England. There were no children; she had miscarried twice.

'It is a common story in the tropics, my deah,' she said laconically in her nasal Bostonian drawl, the slow deliberateness of which Charlotte liked. 'One must live with it, the will of God but I admit, at times I question the purpose of these mysterious ways.'

The older women nodded, but some of the younger ones looked startled and a little embarrassed. Mrs Keaseberry, whom they met infrequently, if at all, was a person of open and frank opinions.

Dark and curly-haired Mrs Johannes van Heyde was of Dutch extraction, with liberal doses of Indian and Malay through her maternal grandparents. Mrs van Heyde always used her husband's name. Her own first name was a mystery to everyone but her beloved. She spoke only broken English. She was more at home in Malay or Hindustani, she said through Takouhi, who translated.

'Malay,' she said forcefully in English directly to Charlotte, 'bes' one.'

'True,' said Takouhi nodding her head slightly. 'Malay best for here. You go munshi. I help.'

Charlotte nodded in return, although she had no idea what or who was munshi. She had started to learn Malay on the ship from England. Robert had told her how important it was. 'English is fairly useless here except between white men. Malay is the lingua franca of the South Seas. Without it, nothing gets done.'

He had arranged for a copy of *Marsden's Grammar* to be sent to her. She had, to her surprise, found it easy, even familiar. There were faint echoes of the native language she had spoken in Madagascar. Now, listening to the ladies, she began to hear those distant rhythms.

The van Heyde house traded extensively with Takouhi's brother,

Tigran, in all the multifarious merchandises of the South Sea islands. Of her eight children, only three had survived. Mrs van Heyde's eyes had softened when Mrs Keaseberry spoke of lost children.

The white organza clothed the plain-faced, young frame of Lilian Aratoun. She said little but twice asked Takouhi whether her brother, Tigran, was well, and when he would be visiting Singapore again.

Meena Shashtri wore a green and gold *sari*. She had been widowed after her third child had been born. Her husband, for whom she had not much cared, had had the good manners to die and leave her in charge of the family fortunes, of which she took prodigiously good care. She spoke good, clear and very correct English in clipped but lilting tones.

It was the owner of the lovely eyes and the pink *sarong*, though, who had the most intriguing tale. Sharifah Kapoor had been part of the old sultan's harem, brought here from Rhio—the islands to the south, she explained for Charlotte's benefit. Though the sultan had grown so fat he rarely went near the women, his wife would often fly into rages and take sticks to the pretty young girls. After a particularly vicious attack one day, thirty-one of them agreed to run away. One early morning they made their way out of the harem at Kampong Glam which was, in any case, poorly guarded. They turned up at the police station and appealed for mercy. Despite angry objections from the sultan, the governor, having seen the state of their backs, arms and faces, granted them freedom. Many went off with merchants, some to be concubines in the Chinese houses, but Sharifah had gone to live with her now husband, Kapoor, a policeman who was Robert's top sergeant, his *jemadar*.

Red-haired and freckled, Elizabeth Scott was a well-developed thirteen-year-old. She was a bonny creature with a fiery look which seemed to increase the heat in the room. She burned very easily in the sun and, like Mrs Keaseberry, went everywhere with a bonnet and a parasol. This last information she had imparted with an air of superiority, as if a tendency to burn in the sun were a sign of good breeding. She had the singular distinction, much appreciated by her and some of her acquaintances, of being the niece of Captain William Scott, the harbour master, himself a cousin of the famous author, Sir Walter. She had dressed this morning in a shade of fuchsia which merely added to the overall picture of a furnace. She said little, but when she spoke, Charlotte could hear her strong Scottish accent. She and her elder brother had arrived only a few months ago, after the death of their mother, to reside with their uncle. Despite her predisposition to dislike everything Scottish, Charlotte felt sorry for the girl's situation which so closely mirrored her own.

Evangeline Barbie perfectly illustrated why few white women cared for the tropics. She was thin from frequent fevers, her skin ravaged by the harshness of a life spent in the service of the natives and of God in regions ruder and lonelier than Singapore. She had married once, but he had died regrettably young. Now in her fifties, she was resolutely cheerful. 'One must make ze best of zings,' she said with a brittle laugh.

Annie da Silva, though herself English, was entirely at home in Singapore. The fifth Mrs da Silva had been born and bred in India, had never been to England and didn't care to go. She had met her husband in Calcutta and, though he was her senior by more than twenty years, was very happy to be rid of that city, which she considered unhealthy, and to live in the cleaner climes and breezier town of Singapore. She took care of her twins and Mr da Silva's younger children, and had little to do with the rest of the brood, who looked after themselves. She hadn't expected twins, she had explained, and loved the name Isabel, which was her mother's, so had simply named them both a variant of it. Neither she nor the girls seemed to find anything odd about this, and the girls rather enjoyed the confusion it generally created.

Charlotte's gaze now rested on Takouhi Manouk. She was the coolest-looking woman in the room. The Europeans were trussed up like wheat sheafs in their skirts and petticoats. Charlotte herself felt like a heap of poufs and appreciated keenly the inappropriateness of their dress in these climes. Mrs van Heyde, though dressed sensibly, in similar fashion to Takouhi, with a blue and white *sarong* and loose white jacket, managed through her size to look hot and fussy, and she dabbed constantly at her brow with a handkerchief. Takouhi's Javanese slenderness made her seem to waft like a zephyr through the room. Her high cheekbones gave her a regal air; her skin was light brown and perfectly smooth; her black eyes turned up slightly at the corners; her lips were full and sensuous. When she smiled, Charlotte could see that her eyeteeth came to a point, like a cat's. No, not a cat, thought Charlotte, but something feline. Her gestures and speech were slow and purring. A lynx, yes, that was it. Like a tawny lynx. Charlotte thought her the most graceful and beguiling woman she could ever hope to see.

Takouhi came from a wealthy family in Batavia. Her brother, Charlotte learned from Miss Aratoun, was the *taipan* of Batavia, the richest merchant in the Dutch East Indies. Robert had said she was Armenian, but Charlotte was not sure where that was and did not dare ask even Lilian Aratoun, although she was most curious. Takouhi's father had married a Javanese princess. This information thrilled Charlotte. She had met George Coleman—Irishman, surveyor and architect—in Batavia and had moved to Singapore, where he had built her Tir Uaidhne, this house. She had pronounced the name 'Teeroowain' but did not elaborate on its meaning, to Charlotte's disappointment.

For their part, the assembly inspected their new arrival and would have been surprised to know that in some northerly drawing rooms Miss Macleod was not considered a beauty. For many Scottish ladies, her skin was not pale enough, her hair too black, her nose very slightly snub. Her eyes were her best feature, a violet blue, but there was something too direct in her gaze. Her figure was reckoned to be fair but somewhat too thin. And she had that impossible name. All those French bits. Not just plain Charlotte Macleod, but Charlotte Toussaint de la Salle Macleod. It was not seemly for a good Protestant Scottish girl. But then again, her background was unsavoury. What could you expect?

In Miss Takouhi Manouk's drawing room, however, the collective opinion was one of benign and affectionate approval. The rigorous and critical class system of Europe was, like the mail, a dangerous year away by sea.

Mrs Keaseberry summed it up in her Bostonian drawl. 'Singapore's a man's town, my deah, and we women so few that we must all get along as well as possible, no matter our skin colours or stations. All that matters very little here.'

Indeed she had discovered the meagre extent of her possible acquaintance. Apart from the women in this room, there were few other European or Eurasian women with whom she could expect to have regular intercourse. The wives of the government officals and merchants numbered no more than fifteen, few of them young. The greatest number of young women were among the da Silva daughters, daughters-in-law and granddaughters. She realised that what Robert had said was true. Her sort—youthful, white, of acceptable social standing and of marriageable age—was rare. She was not sure how she felt about this.

Returning from this remarkable visit to an empty house seemed an anticlimax. She had not known what Singapore would really be like, but this colourful and intimate kaleidoscope of people and languages was the furthest thing from her expectations. To know Takouhi Manouk alone was, she felt, worth the journey. She had received a swarm of invitations, and when finally she had stepped down from Takouhi's carriage, she longed to tell Robbie. However, she soon was glad of the silence. She struggled out of her hot dress and rinsed quickly, ladling water from an earthenware jar over her hot skin. In her camisole she lay back on her bed in the shuttered, darkened room. She began to think about the last two days since her arrival in Singapore, and then, within minutes, she was fast asleep.

# 2

By the time Zhen and Qian began descending the rope ladder, it was late afternoon. They were anchored in a large bay. Smudgy islands, dark and indistinct, lay like sleeping dragons along the horizon. Since dawn, the junk had been surrounded by boats, more arriving as the sun rose, giving the harbour the appearance of a floating fair. At each fathom the junk gained bulk until she slowly trailed into the bay surrounded by a dense mass of boats. The captain stood atop the quarter deck surveying the scene.

For many of the coolies it was good to hear voices speaking their language, asking for news, calling out names. The merchant boats were haggling for trade, assuring the captain of best price, best quality. In addition to human cargo, the junk carried porcelain and earthenware, paper umbrellas, vermicelli, dried fruits, joss sticks and joss paper, raw silk and nankeens, medicine, tea and ornate roof tiles. The junk's owner had ordered a return shipment of guns, opium, gambier, sapanwood, red sandalwood, saltpetre, dragon's blood, elephant teeth, pepper and cloves.

The captain, who had been many times to Si Lat Po, listened imperiously to the din but would deal with the only men he trusted: the biggest coolie agent in Singapore, Guan Soon, and Inchek Sang, the richest merchant. They had all known each other since Malacca days and had come to Singapore immediately after its founding, at the call of Raja Farquhar, the first resident of the new settlement and former governor of Malacca; Farquhar was a man they knew and trusted from long acquaintance.

The attractions of Singapore were manifold, but first and foremost was its status as a duty-free port. No ship which docked paid port duty; no cargo which landed was taxed; no transaction attracted fees.

Nothing stood in the way of the freedom and profit of trade. This made Singapore unique. As a consequence, honest and dishonest tradesmen, steely ship's captains, pirates, cut-throats, wily country traders, fishermen and farmers, missionaries, ne'er do wells, the poor labouring masses of the surrounding lands and merchant princes all flocked to its verdant shores.

The wide *tongkangs* bumped against the junk, and the captain watched the coolies being unloaded. He had been involved in the pig trade for years. Incheck Sang asked him to look out for likely candidates to work for him and made it worth his while. The rich merchant *towkays* needed a big force of docile labourers for their gambier and pepper plantations and tin mines, for the turnover was high, but occasionally they also needed smart, strong workers, and the captain kept his eye out during the voyage. He had noted Zhen and Qian from the beginning. They were two of only three who could read and write, and the third looked sickly. He would talk to Incheck Sang later, for now they would go, like all the rest, to the *kang* coolie houses in Gu Jia Chue, the Water Bullock Cart Chinese town. He was looking forward to some amusements in town, a good meal and maybe a visit to the women at the *ah ku* whorehouses, or some gambling.

First, though, he would go to the new temple he could see on the beach side. A Hokkien temple. Better than the Fuk Tak Chi temple, which was built for bloody Hakkas and Cantonese. He spat a gob over the side. He would go to the temple of his own people and make offerings to Ma Chu, Goddess of Heaven, Goddess of the Sea, and give thanks for a safe journey. He had lit incense to her shrine on the poop deck of the junk and, throughout the morning, all his cargo had proceeded slowly past the shrine to make their thanks. Now he contemplated the lighters as, heavily laden, they made their way to shore. Over 200. Profits would be good.

The disembarkation was slow. Zhen and Qian watched as each skinny, brown coolie, with his bundle of rags, stepped up over the edge of the lighter and walked unsteadily down the gangplank, over the stones onto the beach. The sun was searingly hot, and both men wore their wide-brimmed straw hats. In his hand Zhen carried a yellow cloth. From time to time he opened it out and wiped his face. Qian had seen this cloth once on the ship. It carried the black printed outline of three peaches, and the characters for 'peach garden'. When he had asked about it, Zhen had said his father had given it to him as a good luck token. This made sense; the peach was a symbol of longevity, and the three peaches represented the great Lord Guan Di, God of War, and his bond brothers, Zhang Fei and Liu Bei, symbolising loyalty and friendship, all things his son might need in a new land. But from their conversations, Qian had discovered that Zhen, though penniless like himself, had other reasons for leaving China. He suspected that Zhen had been in trouble with the authorities. Zhen was always circumspect on the subject, and he asked no more. However, he knew that Guan Di and his boon companions were used as a spiritual glue for the forbidden Tian Di Hui brotherhood society in China, which had vowed the overthrow of the Qing dynasty. Qian sighed. He was sure Zhen was involved with the brotherhood. He did not like it, but realist that he was, Qian knew that these ties could be useful here in Si Lat Po, where they knew no one.

Finally, their turn arrived. Zhen had helped Qian descend the rope ladder from the ship, for the latter had a slight limp and a weakness in one leg, the result of a bout of sickness as a child. He was easily able to negotiate the gangplank. Nevertheless Zhen preceded him in case he needed to hold onto him as the plank trembled. Zhen had felt a strange protectiveness for this skinny fellow the moment they had met on the road to Amoy. Qian reminded him somewhat of his youngest brother, the runt of the litter, second child of his father's fourth wife, who had died in childbirth. Zhen's mother had raised this boy as her own, teaching him her Beijing dialect.

They joined the throng squatting along the road, all patiently waiting for what came next. Now that Qian was on dry land, his spirits lifted and he began to take an interest in his surroundings.

Hills, covered with a profuse and smothering array of vegetation, surrounded the bay, an arc of sandy and gravelly beach lapped by clear waves. Fishing platforms dotted the shallow waters. At the western end he could see mangrove swamps and coconut palms. A large house on a hill stood surrounded by numerous trees of varieties beyond his meagre knowledge. He was sure he could see monkeys and bright-winged birds flitting and skipping through the jungle growth. At the eastern end, the way they had come, lay a number of buildings, the most prominent of which had a large, double octagonal red roof and projected out over the water.

The main street was home to a variety of houses and shops, mostly of two storeys, some well built, some ramshackle, some with verandahs and some which fronted directly onto the street. There was an ancient wooden attap-thatch building. Up the street stood a building with square, pagoda-like towers and small green domes projecting above the upper floor. Qian had no idea what this building could be for. Beyond that, he could make out a smaller Chinese temple.

Men of every shape and hue moved up and down the beach side, carrying trays and poles laden with goods and foodstuffs the likes of which they had never seen. One fruit seller passed by with a large prickly fruit which smelled strongly of urine and rotten eggs. The coolies, not generally sensitive to even the most hideous smells, nevertheless covered their noses against this violent stench. The multifarious population of the beach side seemed to barely notice it.

Along the length of the beach, big craft and small had drawn up on the sand, unloading their catch. Buyers for the fresh fish came and went in a steady stream. Dark-skinned men were sorting and mending fishing nets. Other lighters disgorged coolies. Agile, wiry men jumped out of small, sleek, almond-eyed craft and made them secure, quickly offloading their cargoes in straw bundles or rattan baskets. Clacking, thumping, voices calling, ducks quacking, dogs barking: the din of commerce.

The middle of the bay was dominated by the temple, close to which the coolies had been gathered. Qian could read the black and gold plaque that hung over its entrance: 'Thian Hock Keng' (the Temple of Heavenly Happiness). He could see it was newly built, the green of its gleaming roof tiles glinting in the lowering sun, and his heart rose. The heavy perfume of incense wafted over the walls and mingled with the fish, vegetable, fruit and cooking smells and the heat of the dusty street.

'Zhen Ah,' he said, turning to his companion. 'A temple for our people here; it is a good sign, don't you think?'

'It's a sign that there's money in the place, anyway. It looks like it was built by the fat cats. Always sucking up to the gods. We shall have to see how we can get our hands on some of it and become fat cats ourselves, eh? It's lively, all right. Have you ever seen men like them?'

They stared at a gathering of merchants. Blue, silk-gowned Chinese, white turbans on thick, black beards, long moustaches and high hats on red hair, a green-and-brown skirt on a short, fat-framed man. Red-coated, dark-skinned soldiers and ships' officers in blue and white strolled by. Ruddy-skinned, orange-haired sailors mingled with darkly bearded shopkeepers and long-queued Chinese. Around them a din and clamour of incomprehensible language mixed with general calls of hawkers and tradesmen. They laughed, amazed; there was too much to take in.

A doe-eyed bullock harnessed to a heavy water cart pulled up dustily, and the bullock keeper began filling up tubs which the coolie overseer passed around the thirsty men. All the men stared at the handler, for they had never seen an Indian man before. He was a lean, dark Tamil, his skin as black as ebony and he was wearing a small, jaunty turban of brilliant orange and loose trousers of a similar hue. He flashed a smile of red-stained teeth at the gaping crowd and spat a squirt of red juice on the ground. His bullock dropped a steaming deposit. The bullock keeper pocketed the coins the overseer passed him, and with a 'yup yup' moved the cart and his muscled companion on down the beach, squishing the hot pats into the ground. The pungent smell of cow dung assailed their nostrils.

A pale-skinned man dressed in black approached the group, leading a small pony. From the box attached to the animal's back, he took out a slim book. Holding it up, he began to address the group of coolies, who eyed him with alarm. He took off his wide-brimmed hat to mop his brow, showing his yellowing teeth in a grim smile, then began distributing books to the men. The overseer gazed impassively and said nothing. Zhen and Qian looked at one of the books. It was written in Chinese, but as far as they knew, they and only one other were literate. On the cover page were the crossed lines of the number ten, but strangely wrought, the downward stroke being longer than the horizontal. When the man had left, the overseer simply said,

'I dunno what this book is for, but every time a ship comes, they give them out. The paper comes in handy for wiping your arse.'

He began mustering them into groups, and a big, shaven-headed man with a pocked face ordered them to move off. They walked away from

41

the harbour, along a dusty street of closely packed houses, goods spilling out onto the pavement. Awnings projected out into the street, closing the sky above. Red, black and gold shop signs hung from every façade, huge characters advertising their names and wares. Children spilled from doors and played in the rubbish-strewn street. They stopped to watch the men go by. Living cadavers sat crouched on low chairs, sucking on soup and noodles. A Chinese barber had set up his stool in the shade of a ramshackle wooden building. A line of customers crouched, waiting.

Zhen ran a hand over his head and face and felt the prickly growth. A shave would be wonderful. A bath would be heaven. All the coolies stank of sweat, their clothes stiff with dried seawater.

Two imposing, dark-skinned men with fierce, dark eyes, massive red turbans and great black beards walked slowly by, eyeing them. The overseer and his coolie group instinctively moved aside to let them pass.

'Police,' the overseer called to the group, pointing to a building on the corner of the bayside street they had left. 'That's the police station. Stay away from them and do as you are told; there'll be no trouble.'

The town was small, and just two streets later they shuffled into a dilapidated building, the *kang* coolie house. Seeds sprouted in the walls of the narrow building. Saplings struggled for life along the parapet. Spidery ferns clung to every crack, as if the jungle were determined to take back its territory. Dark, slimy stains ran the length of the façade. The upper floor was shuttered. There was an air well towards the middle of the building, and another at the very back, next to the kitchen. Here was a chipped stone bench with two clay stoves covered in soot. Wood was stacked under the bench; bent and beaten iron woks and crusty utensils hung from the scorched, greasy yellow walls. In the back well there was an open stall with a stinking bucket, black and brown lumps encrusted on its side. Insects spawned on the dirt-strewn surface of a shanghai jar filled with stagnant water. Hollow-eyed, bony-chested men lay on shelves on either side of the squalid passage, unmoving as the newcomers passed.

Pock Face pointed to two shelves at the back of the building, one above the other, close to the waste and slops cupboard. It was better than the ship only because it was not rocking. The smells of stale cooking oil, stale air, stale sweat, shit and opium fumes were overpowering. A feeling of hopelessness stole over Qian. He sat on the low shelf, drew up his legs and stared at Zhen. His left eye began to twitch.

Zhen took a look around, scratched his chin and said quietly,

'*Aiya*! Still the mind, you big girl. Remember the farmer. Tomorrow we will go to the temple and speak to the gods and anyone else who might be around for a chat. I'll have a word with Pock Face tonight.'

He sat at Qian's side.

'Take the top shelf, rats have further to run.'

# 3

When Charlotte awoke it was late afternoon. She could hear movement in the house. She was bathed in sweat and flung open the shutters to the verandah. Air wafted over her. She went out again to the big earthenware water jar, took up the ladle and began to pour the cool water over her body, slip and all.

'That you, Kitt?' called Robert.

'Who else?' she called, happy he was home.

'Will you nae join me on the sitooterie, Miss Macleod?' It was their grandmother's term for a verandah or a gazebo or any place where you 'sit oot', and it never failed to reduce them to giggles.

Laughing delightedly, she wrapped a large cotton cloth around her and went, trailing watery footsteps across the wooden floor, into the front living room. He was seated in a big rattan chair on the verandah, which looked over the fort and out to sea. The awnings on the riverside were all down against the sun. She plopped wetly into the seat beside him.

'You look cool. Auch, it's been damned hot today and I've been on horseback most of it. This job is turning out to be tough.'

He smiled as he said this, though, and she knew he enjoyed policing more than anything he had done before. He told her he had been investigating the mauling of two unfortunate Chinamen by a tiger not more than a mile from the settlement; and he talked of two other Chinamen found on the same road with their throats cut. There had been a murder at sea, the captain of a brig which had sailed two days before. Two sailors had attacked the captain while he was asleep and thrown his body overboard. The second mate was also missing. The trial would be held in the next few days.

'Robert, this place really is rather wild, isn't it?'

'Kitt, my love, you don't know the half of it.'

As they chatted, a handsome middle-aged Indian turned the corner of the verandah and began to approach.

'Stop *jemadar*,' said Robert in Malay. 'I think my sister is not dressed to receive company.' The man immediately turned his back and began to retreat.

'The police office is around the corner and is generally stuffed full of men from morning to night. Poor Kitt, you will have to put on a dress when you come to the sitooterie!'

This set them off in a fit of laughter again. When it subsided, finally, Charlotte rose and went indoors, and Robert called to Azan, the Malay boy who was their servant, to bring them lime juice drinks.

After she had dressed, he showed her the police office, a large room on the river side of the bungalow next to the sitting room. Seven men were sitting in it and rose and bowed when she entered. Most were young Malays and Indians. Robert introduced Charlotte to the group generally, and particularly to Jemadar Kapoor, whose wife she had met today. He was one of Robert's best policemen and spoke excellent English.

Back outside, on the verandah, Robert said, 'You see it's quite separate from the rest of the house. We go in at the steps and front door, and so we are quite private. Sometimes one or more men may be sleeping in the office, but this should not alarm you. Actually it is safer that way. All my men are either Indian or Malay, and there are two English sergeants whom you'll meet later. There are no Chinese, for we fear they are all more or less involved with the secret societies here.'

He told Charlotte briefly of the Chinese *kongsi*, a sort of fraternal brotherhood that looked after the needs of the Chinese coolies. This was laudable and necessary, he said, but he suspected that they were also somewhere behind the increasing number of robberies taking place in the town, in Kampong Glam and out where the dhobi washermen lived, by the freshwater stream. Only a week ago, the dhobi village had been attacked and hundreds of clothes stolen. He and some men had followed a trail of washing into the jungle, but it soon petered out, and no one had been arrested. Policing here was a matter of good relations with the community, members of which, in turn, gave him and his men information.

The image of Robert following a trail of underclothes through the jungle was amusing, but Charlotte hid her smile, for she saw how serious he was.

'Everything is based on trust. Heavy-handedness will not work. My men use a soft approach, and I believe we have gained the respect and cooperation of most of the law-abiding community of all the different races. If things get very bad, of course, I can call on the military, but that would really be a last resort.'

Charlotte was glad to hear Robert talk so enthusiastically about his job. His eyes grew bright and his face animated. He clearly loved this work and the men he worked with.

They re-entered the bungalow at the door next to the office. Charlotte's room was directly in front, behind the sitting room. On the left, a long hall led to back steps and a covered outdoor passage to the kitchens and servants' rooms. Here lived Aman and Azan, the two Malay servants, and Mo, their Cantonese cook. They had a separate washing and closet area and a small garden where Mo grew ginger and garlic. When the wind blew in certain directions, the smell of night soil wafted from this corner. On either side of the corridor were smaller rooms. One of the rooms on the right was Robert's bedroom, and one was a storeroom. Two others were empty but for two low cots; they sometimes served to accommodate low-ranking officials of the East India Company who might be passing through the settlement. The whole building was of brick, surrounded on three sides by a deep verandah.

Their own washing and waste cubicles were situated at the back of the verandah. Washing consisted of a large earthenware pot of water, kept filled by Aman from the bullock carts which plied a constant trade around the town and drew the water from the reservoirs made from the springs on the riverside of Bukit Larangan. The governor's residence stood low on the top of this hill. The porous earthenware, constantly covered by a wooden lid against mosquitoes and other pests, kept the water cool and fresh. When it rained, they used the water gathered in two large containers beside their quarters. The front verandah extended out on brick posts over the water, which at high tide lapped and gurgled under their feet. A short jetty jutted off the verandah. At the back were two large, handsome angsana trees and a pretty grove of prickly-trunked nibong palms. To the west was the fort, the river and the Chinese town and to the east, a view along the seafront and out over the harbour and the roads. It was not Miss Manouk's magnificent residence, but Charlotte loved it just as well.

Especially now, as the evening drew in and the sun shot pink and purple hues over the masts of the ships, across the waters of the harbour to the luxuriant hills across the bay. The estuary waters were filled with large rocks, with little rivulets running between the fissures like green snakes. The reefs and rocks made it difficult to enter the mouth of the river, and it took great skill to manoeuvre the boats to and fro.

'Kitt, I have something to tell you,' Robert said and stopped.

Charlotte was struggling with her chicken. The fiery sauce it had been cooked in was taking her breath away. After every small mouthful she took a spoonful of rice and a big drink of water.

'Crimoney, Robbie, do you think we could ask the cook not to make it so spicy? How do you manage it?'

Robert was gazing into the distance. He was not as striking as herself. He had more of their father in him: his brown eyes and sandy-brown hair, which he wore long, gathered in a tail. It was not in the least fashionable, but he did not seem to notice. He was good-looking in a gentle sort of way, taller than her but not tall, compact and strong.

He looked at the spoon that she was waggling up and down. 'Auch, I have no control over any of that sort of thing. Perhaps you can sort it out, no?' he trailed off.

He was actually glad she had not heard him. He poured himself a glass of claret, and after Charlotte retired, Robert wrestled with his conscience. He did not like to keep secrets from her but really, what was he to say about Shilah? Sooner or later his sister would find out that he had been living with a woman here until the day before her arrival. The men would not talk, of course; many of them had native *nyai* companions. Hundreds of slave women and boys from the islands turned up at the Bugis marketplace every season. It wasn't mentioned. In a place like this, for someone like him there had been, until recently, simply no possibility of marriage. He lacked the means to support a family. The company frowned on it, and the truth was Robert had, at present, no desire to settle down with a da Silva daughter or such like. At least not yet. Shilah was too intoxicating.

47

She was the unwanted child of an Indian convict woman, dead at an early age, and a white man who had long since left the settlement. As a little girl she had been taken in by George Coleman's household, cared for and taught to read, cook, sew and clean. When she turned fifteen Coleman offered to find her a husband. By then, however, she had seen Robert, who spent a good deal of time at the Coleman house, and conceived a longing for him. One evening she had stolen into his bed at the riverside bungalow. She was dark-eyed, soft and yielding, and she was a virgin. He had simply been unable to resist her.

Robert had come to the settlement as the lowliest uncovenanted clerk. He had shared a room with two other bachelors on Malacca Street and, being of affable nature, had made friends easily. He enjoyed the society of the European settlement, the occasional amateur dramatics, the cricket games on the plain, the dinners and billiard evenings. The only real problem was female companionship. In the few European or Eurasian families, marriage was the only thing on offer, and not to young agency clerks with no immediate prospects. The Chinese merchants kept their daughters locked away like gold dust. The Malays and Bugis lived in kampongs with their wives and children. The Indians were mostly a floating population of men, soldiers, convicts or moneylenders, just like the thousands of Chinese coolies and, indeed, like the British agency clerks. The Chinese and mixed-blood prostitutes in Chinatown were outnumbered at least ten to one. This mathematical equation and a lecture by Dr Montgomerie on the diseases to be obtained in that quarter had left him dubious as to its pleasures. Privately, he had been advised to get hold of a native bed-servant, a *nyai*, as it was termed.

However, Robert had not tried to find a *nyai* in his first years in Singapore. Though widespread, the practice was distasteful to him, perhaps because his own mother had been a so-called 'native' woman. Somewhat drunk, and anxious to be rid of his nineteen-year-old virginity, in the company of his friends, he had let himself be led to the room of an *ah ku*, a Chinese prostitute. She spoke no English, and his Malay at that time had been rudimentary. They had barely been able to communicate, and later, whilst certainly relieved, he had felt somewhat grubby. Since then he had thrown himself into the life of the community, taken up the study of Malay with the munshi and, apart from the very occasional transgression, had not returned to Chinatown.

Shilah was something entirely different. She spoke English, she was untouched and obviously in love with him. As soon as he put his hand to her soft breasts and kissed her lips, he was lost.

This had been going on for months and he had said nothing to George, to whose home she disappeared after each encounter. Well, tomorrow he would have to find his courage and speak to George. Coleman was not a disapproving man, and honesty was the best policy with him. Nevertheless, Robert was nervous.

He poured himself another glass of claret, looked out over the twinkling lights on the darkened bay to vague firelight at Tanjong Rhu and felt a headache coming on.

# 4

Early the following morning, before the gun, Robert dressed and left the bungalow. The steps to the street gave a view over the river to the town. He stood briefly and contemplated the boats, so closely packed they looked like a swarm of beetles. The tide was out, and many of them sat crookedly on the gravelly bank at the centre of the river. On the north bank, close by, was a low building used for government business, a fives court attached to its western side. Beyond and above that rose the classical lines of the courthouse, with its wide space leading to the quayside. This had been one of George's first commissions, illegal as it turned out. A private house, unsanctioned by Raffles, who had reserved this bank of the river for official buildings, it had been so splendid that it had been allowed to stand. Robert knew little of architecture, but even he could see that this building, with its deep eaves and shady verandahs, its arcades and columns and elegant central tower with the double cupolas, was a work of some refinement. Its precincts were cool and perfectly adapted to the tropical climate. The company had leased it these last fifteen years or so for the court and government offices, and Mr Church, the resident councillor, was in negotiations to purchase it outright for the administration.

Nearby, on the riverbank, was the elegant landing stage, with its steps and columned arches and, peeping over that, the inelegant roof of the post office and the master attendant's office.

A short walk from the police bungalow would take Robert directly to the offices of the governor and Mr Church for discussions about public safety and policing issues, or just to sit in its shady corridors for a chat with a glass of brandy. This suited Robert, for he was not one for memoranda, and preferred to deal directly on every issue. He was in no doubt that it was as much his easy and amicable relationship with

Governor Bonham as his competence that had secured him his present position.

Policing was not on his mind at this moment, however, and with a quick glance at the rows of slumbering godowns and houses on Boat Quay, he turned heel and made his way to Number 3, Coleman Street. George, he knew, was also an early riser, but he had given Aman a note to take to his house last night. Robert was never sure how many nights George spent at Tir Uaidhne, and Coleman could be tetchy about unwanted intrusions, even from his friends.

He strolled behind his bungalow along the beach side road, enjoying the stiff cool breeze and the view. Fishing boats sat on the seabed, and the tangy smell of low tide mingled with the ricy, fishy odours of cooking from the boats. Naked children scuttled about on shore, gathering up driftwood, bare-breasted women suckled their babes. The children waved. Sometimes he envied these sea gypsies with their lives of freedom. When they were hungry, they fished; any surplus they sold for rice or cloth, and for the rest of the day they basked in the sun or under the mangrove trees, or swam like little fish until hunger aroused them to labour again.

'Obeyed as sovereign by thy subjects be
But know that I alone am king of me
I am as free as Nature first made man
Ere the base laws of servitude began
When wild in woods the noble savage ran.'

These men always won the boat races held every year on New Year's Day. Racing sailors like no one on earth, they were never beaten. They were born, lived and died on the sea. He could think of worse lives.

Their *sampan panjang* were craft of extraordinary elegance and lightness. He had once sailed in one and fallen in love. Nothing equalled the pace they set, each man like a part of the boat itself, the sustained pitch of excitement as they cut the water, waves sweeping over the gunwale and the bodies of the men baling. Ballast was a few bags of stones. The men leaned out windward for balance; the sails boomed with long forked poles. Yet there was hardly a sound of their speed, merely a quivering slithery sensation, as if they were propelled not by wind but by a silent watery hand. It was beyond beauty, the clean-cut rip through the water and the sharp, curling wake behind. Robert, completely overcome, bought one for himself, naming it *Sea Gypsy*, and it was the sleekest, loveliest of boats.

He waved back cheerily then, turning, cut directly across the plain. He could see lights in the three great houses which lay behind low walls and luxuriant gardens.

As he entered Coleman Street, Robert rather envied George the honour of a street named after him, but since the Irishman had laid them all out, he had to admit that it was reasonable. In company George referred to it laughingly as 'me road', and to his friends it was G.D. Street. Three houses owned by George stood in this street, and, passing the Reverend and Mrs White's and Mr and Mrs Wood's houses, he turned into the open, pillared gate of Number 3, passed under the seven-bayed porte-cochere and over the cool green and white Malacca tiles of the porch and pulled the doorbell. This was a mere formality, as the doors stood open, and he made his way into the entrance hall.

There he stood, waiting, and within a minute, Coleman himself, dressed as he usually was in loose trousers and a *kurta* of soft Indian cotton, emerged from the inner hall.

'For Gaard's sake, Robert! What on earth can ye be wanting advice for at this time of the morning?'

He ran his hand through thick, wavy brown hair, which he wore longish over his ears, and looked quizzically at his guest. His Irish accent was as strong today as when he had left Drogheda twenty-five years ago.

'G.D., you must help me, for I have not the faintest idea what to do. This is personal. Policing is no problem but this, really, I've done something— .' He trailed off. He looked as if he might burst into tears at any minute.

George took pity on him and threw an arm round his shoulder. 'There, there, come on, up we go.'

Coleman smiled and led his young friend across the hall, up the stairs, through the sitting and dining rooms and finally out onto the wide upper verandah, where lounging chairs and tables were in abundance. Calling for coffee, Coleman indicated two high-backed rattan chairs covered in cushions, and they sat.

A platter of fruits, chunks of prickly pineapples, furry mangosteens and juicy pieces of giant pomelo arrived on the table, carried in by a pretty Tamil girl in a soft pink *sari*. Coleman preferred women around him and always tried to employ female servants whenever possible. This girl was the daughter of servants of one of his most important colleagues, Nanda Pillai, one of the most indispensable men in the settlement, in George's opinion, whose brick kilns were his main supplier of building materials.

'These young Indian lasses, they're quiet and loyal. As they grow older, I always try to find them husbands from the convict lines. The Indian convicts are the most reliable men in the entire settlement,' he explained when asked.

George Dromgold Coleman was not only the surveyor and architect of Singapore; he was Superintendent of Public Works and Overseer of Convicts, thousands of whom formed the cheap labour pool needed to carry out the East India Company's road and building contracts, as well as his own private commissions.

He also had the best coffee in Singapore, which he got directly from Sumatra, Toraja and Java through Tigran Manouk, Takouhi's brother. George raised his cup. 'To Baba Budan who stole the bean that so many fortunes are built on.' This morning he had asked for beans from the high fields of Mandheling, in western Sumatra.

George was always full of stories. He was very well read, had a personal library, was a frequent contributor to John Armstrong's library and reading rooms on Commercial Square as well as a patron of the library at the institute and part-owner of the only newspaper in Singapore. Robert, who would rather do anything than read, nevertheless liked to listen to what Coleman called 'tales of woe and wonder'. The story of how an Indian holy man smuggled the fiercely protected coffee beans out of Arabia was one of them. For a moment they both sat, silently savouring its richness and breathing in the aroma; then he addressed his friend.

'Well, Robert, what seems to be the trouble?'

'I think I've done something you won't be pleased with.'

Coleman raised an eyebrow but said nothing. Robert swallowed another gulp of coffee and in a strangulated voice began. 'About two months ago I came home one evening, and when I got into bed there was a young native woman already there. She's young and lovely, and I'm afraid I was unable to resist. She apparently has feelings for me, and I like her a great deal, but I think any kind of marriage would be out of the question. Since Charlotte has come, she can no longer visit me and, really, I've come to you for some advice.'

The words tripped over each other as they fell off his tongue, and when he stopped, he felt drained.

Coleman looked at him sardonically. 'Well, now, that's an unusual case, is it not? Can't think of any of the other bachelors in the settlement who are sleeping with young native women, can you?'

Robert said in a small voice, 'No, I know, but George, this girl, it's ... Shilah.'

Coleman put down his cup with a bang.

'Shilah? Our Shilah, here in the house? Two months, by the saints, and you haven't been to tell me! Why, she could be pregnant by now. Did you think of that?' His voice had risen.

Robert stood up and looked out in the half light over the balcony, past Tir Uaidhne and towards St Andrew's Church.

'Auch, George, don't yell at me I beg of yer, for I want to do the right thing. She came to me. I know that's no excuse, but I'm a young man, and really that sort of thing has been sorely lacking. You know I don't like to go to the *ah ku* women.'

He turned and faced Coleman dolefully. George shook his head.

'Well, sit down. We'll discuss this calmly. What's done is done. The girl's as much to blame; I offered to find her a decent husband.'

He poured them both some more coffee and sat in thought. Robert, relieved, said nothing and watched him warily.

'She'll stay here with me for the moment,' Coleman said finally. 'I'll speak to her and get Dr Montgomerie to look her over. If she's pregnant, then you have to decide what you want to do about it. Takouhi knows someone who can fix that. After that, if you still want to continue in this, then I think, if you want to be fair, you have to set her up somewhere. Does your salary run to a small place? I've almost finished a nice row of houses on Middle Street, on a plot of land I've leased. Perhaps I could let you rent one of the upper rooms cheaply. But think this out carefully. If you want to get married in a few years, better think what you'll do then.'

Robert was glad he had come. Coleman was always a reasonable and pragmatic man. At the moment he could not think of giving up Shilah, and to establish her in Kampong Glam was a good idea. His inheritance was but a few weeks away, and, while it was not large, money would not be wanting. Any child could be got rid of. Shilah was young, only sixteen; there was plenty of time for that if they were still together later on. He looked over at George with gratitude.

'George, how can I thank you?'

Coleman looked at him severely. 'You can thank me by making this unfortunate young woman happy. She was raised with no parents and doubtless has a large store of love to offer you, the lord knows why. This is the only home she has ever known. At the moment you are crazy to get your hands on her, but life has a way of setting traps. Don't let her down when you no longer have any use for her. Yer know, Robert, just because she's a parentless half-blood doesn't mean she doesn't aspire to marry you or that you should reject it out of hand. But that is up to you.'

George suddenly rose and approached the edge of the verandah. Robert looked over and saw Takouhi at the upper window of the house opposite. The dawn was almost upon them, and birds were busily twittering and flitting amongst the trees and shrubs and in and out of the pagoda-like birdhouse. Her black hair fell over her shoulders, and she waved and smiled at them. At her side was a young girl, pretty, with shoulder-length brown hair. This was Meda Elizabeth, George's daughter. Coleman blew them a kiss. Not for the first time, Robert was struck with how strong and affectionate this relationship was.

Coleman was not conventionally handsome, but he was a manly figure, tallish and broad in the shoulders. His nose was somewhat long and his lips thin, but that did not matter much. Everything was in his eyes, which were a hazel–green, surrounded by deep wrinkles. They seemed in perpetual good humour, even when he was not. He delighted in the ridiculous and had a love of wit and repartee. He was a great favourite with almost all the Europeans, young and old, and the English-speaking Chinese. His thorough knowledge of Bengali, Tamil, Hindustani and Malay gave him an easy relationship with those communities as well. He had built virtually every road, quay and canal in the town. He had surveyed the island and drawn up its first accurate map. He had filled in the swamps and opened up the jungle. He had almost finished construction of the only two solid bridges in the town: one over the Singapore River and the other on the Rochor. He had built the houses of almost every important European, Peranakan, Malay and Chinese family, the rows of shophouses, the princely mansions and the godowns of the rich merchants. Over fifteen years, his tireless industry had made Singapore the most elegant town in the British East.

Only once had Coleman talked to Robert of his relationship with Takouhi. She had been ill with fever, and while Dr Montgomerie and Mrs White had attended her, he had sat with George in the drawing room of Tir Uaidhne.

'She is a woman full of grace and passion, Robert. I have no idea what I should do without her.' He had sat slumped on a chair, his head in his hands.

'I've offered marriage, you know, but she will not. Just says, today we are together. It is wonderful. Gets these dark moods, you know. It's the marriage to that old Dutch pig when she was just a girl. By the saints, a bad man can ruin a good woman, crush the trust and love out of her. He was a brute. She wasn't to blame.'

Coleman stopped abruptly and looked quickly at Robert. By the time Dr Montgomerie descended the marble staircase with good news, he had pulled himself together. Robert had not known what to make of this or what to say, and the subject had never come up again.

Now Robert thanked his friend and left. He was grateful. On his walk back to the bungalow he went over Coleman's words about marriage in his head.

'Really, George is not thinking straight on that score,' he said to himself.

'Why, there's no comparison between George's situation and mine. Shilah's a simple servant girl, and Takouhi Manouk is the educated and cultivated sister of the wealthiest man in the East Indies. George is rich and powerful, a man who does as he pleases. I'm a policeman, serving the government. My conduct is constantly under scrutiny. And what about

Charlotte? What would her prospects be with a native sister-in-law. No, it's impossible.'

At heart, Robert was a simple soul and with this issue settled in his mind, he felt better than he had for days. He was looking forward to taking Charlotte on a visit to the town. There was no reason to trouble her with this matter, which, after all, was his personal business.

As he arrived back at the bungalow, fat drops of rain began to fall.

# 5

The men in the coolie house had passed an uncomfortable night. The perpetual comings and goings, the sounds of sickness, coughing and moaning were all interminable. The fetid smell of the toilet buckets hung chokingly in the air. Qian couldn't wait for the night to end. In his exhaustion he had slept but he woke constantly, dripping with sweat in the humid atmosphere. He would rather have slept outside, but the doors were barred. Thank all the gods, Zhen had spoken to the pock-faced guard, and they had some kind of agreement that they could go to the temple tomorrow.

Hanging his head over the edge of the cot, he whispered, 'Thunder boy, are you awake?' He had given Zhen this nickname when he had seen the thunder character for his name. This was not his real name, but an assumed name. Zhen had told Qian that he had been given it by a lady friend because of his extraordinary sexual prowess, but Qian did not believe him. Qian had learned something of Zhen's Taoist philosophy, knew he had spent time in a Taoist monastery and that thunder was one of the eight *kua*, the elemental forces that made up the hexagram of the *I Ching* oracle. But it didn't matter to Qian. His own nickname, given to him by his elder sister when he had been a sick young boy, meant 'modesty', and Zhen had made fun of him for its girlish overtones. Qian did not mind this, either.

Zhen grunted, turned face upwards and yawned. 'Morning, miss, is it daylight?' he mumbled between stretches. Qian put on his straw sandals and climbed down from the cot. He ran quickly along the narrow corridor to the air well and looked up. Nothing but a gloomy light was visible but, to his delight, it was raining. He ran quickly back and waved to Zhen to come.

In the air well, the rain fell with raging force, bouncing off the stone walls and gurgling down a drain that was rapidly becoming overwhelmed. They looked up, and the water streamed off their faces and over their bodies, soaking them within seconds. Zhen motioned to Qian to wait and ran back to the kitchen area. When he returned, he called to Qian to take off his clothes. The rain was so strong he had to yell over its din. Pulling him to the side, he rubbed his back with the wood ashes and oil he had mixed in a bowl and put a big dollop in Qian's hand. Then he tore off his own filthy clothes and rubbed himself from head to toe in the mixture. Qian rubbed his back, and then they both stood, faces upturned to the force of the rain as the dirt ran away down a hole in the floor. They stamped on their dirty clothes.

For the first time, Qian saw Zhen's body. In comparison his own looked puny, although he was not weak. Zhen's arms and shoulders were strong and muscular, his chest broad and smooth narrowing to a flat abdomen and slim waist; his limbs were long and well shaped. To Qian's eyes, he was as perfectly formed as a man could be, and Qian felt momentarily envious. He noticed the pale red, blue and black tattoo of Guan Di on Zhen's chest. On the road to Amoy, where they had met, eating, not bathing had been their first priority. On the junk no one undressed, no one washed—unless getting doused by volumes of seawater or standing in the rain could be considered washing. For the moment they were both lost in the happiness of this unexpected and refreshing downpour.

Other men were coming now, and before they could be swamped by human bodies, they scooped up their clothes and ran naked, whooping and laughing, up the corridor and jumped on their wooden cots.

As they dried off with small cloths, Qian watched the play of muscles under Zhen's back and buttocks and, to his horror, found himself becoming aroused. He rushed to throw on his only other cotton trousers and loose top and sat back against the wall, quietly drying his queue. Zhen had noticed nothing and, dressed now himself, was hanging up their wet clothes around the cots, where they steamed quietly. His face was strong jawed, his forehead unblemished and perfectly formed, but there was something indefinably pretty in his face too, his lips perhaps. They all combined to make him a good-looking man, and Qian knew Zhen turned women's heads. Qian's own forehead was bumpy, and he knew his ears were too pointed, making him look a bit like a weasel. Zhen's eyes were not so narrow as his, more almond-shaped, but in moments of anger they became dark slits, making him appear hard and cruel.

Zhen set off to the kitchen for soup, rice and tea, which the coolie bosses supplied until the men could be moved on to work either on the island or, in most cases, in the tin mines of Malaya or further afield. Qian contemplated his slowly dwindling erection and what it could mean. He wasn't a virgin; he'd been with several women. He hadn't enjoyed it very much but doubted any young man did in the beginning, especially with the wrinkled old crones who sold their services in the nearby village. He shook the mental image of that encounter out of his head, and by the time Zhen returned, had recovered his poise.

Having finished their meal, they attended to each other's hair. Since they had met they had both discovered a common concern with their personal hygiene. Zhen was almost obsessive. His father had been a practitioner of Chinese medicine, a scholar who had taught his son to read and write and given him knowledge of plants. Health and cleanliness had been drummed into his brain since he was a boy. Until his father had fallen under the spell of opium, Zhen had been his apprentice, choosing the roots and leaves, blending the herbs, mixing the potions. The night before, he had picked up a broom and booted two coolies into action to clean up the hallway to his satisfaction. Now from his sack he took a porcelain bottle of a green, oily mixture and, having unpicked their long queues, they both combed a small amount through their hair. This concoction had served to keep them both free of the awful hair bugs which infested other men. Relieved that touching Zhen's hair in this mindless routine had no physical effect on him, Qian relaxed. Finally, when they had finished replaiting, Zhen rose.

At the door, Zhen shook Pock Face, who was sitting on the floor dozing.

'Oi, it's late. Get up. We are going to the temple to give thanks, remember?' he said, holding his yellow handkerchief balled in his hand.

Pock Face grunted and stretched. Then, taking a large key, he unlocked the front door. They stepped gratefully out into the fresh air of the street. Zhen knew that Pock Face couldn't have made the decision to let them out and calculated that someone higher up might be waiting for them at the temple.

After a few minutes they found themselves before its doors. Pock Face motioned them to enter, and they stepped up over the great log which formed the entrance, went between the Fu lions and into the inner courtyard. Rain fell steadily, but the large, ornate double-roofed incense holder gave off a heady perfumed smoke. This temple was tiny compared to the great Kaiyuan Temple in Quanzhou, but it smelled like home.

A large statue of the Sea Goddess, Ma Chu, golden and red, stared down on them impassively through her beaded headdress. Her faithful companions, red-faced wind-favouring ears and green-faced thousand *li* eyes, stood on either side of the altar. They lit incense and gave thanks for a safe arrival.

When they had finished, a small figure appeared from the back of the temple and approached. Dressed in loose black trousers and a white jacket, he held his hands in front of his waist, fingers intertwined but for the index fingers, which were bent and connected at the first knuckle, and the thumbs which were touching each other. It was a *kongsi* brotherhood sign for peace. Zhen drew his right arm across his chest, making the sign for heaven by holding the thumb, index and middle finger pointed upwards, the two others remaining curled against his chest. He bowed and motioned Qian to do so also. Then all three went into a side room of the temple. Pock Face slumped down by the door and immediately fell asleep.

'Welcome, brother,' the man said to Zhen and looked quizzically at Qian.

'I am Zhuang Zhen of the Green Lotus Kongsi in Zhangzhou,' Zhen said. 'This is Lim Qian, from Yangshan village in Quanzhou prefecture. He is not a brother yet. We seek the protection of the *kongsi* here and your help to find work in Si Lat Po, where we know no one.' Zhen took from his cloth sack a paper, unfolded it and handed it to his interlocutor.

'I see,' said the man examining the paper, then eyeing them both shrewdly. Their first names were made up, of course. He knew this. Almost no one used their given names. *Singkeh* newcomers often sat around on the junk inventing names for themselves. He had known *singkehs* who called themselves dog-ugly, donkey, banana-head, stone-balls or monkey's arse. It had something to do with their feeling of impermanence here. Make money, go home, throw off the name, the temporary identity and, at the same time, jettison the fears and loneliness of this enforced exile.

'I think we can help you. You can both read and write?' They nodded. 'Good, good. First must come the initiation ceremony for your friend, and you must swear again also. Until then nothing can be done for you. Do you agree?'

He looked at Zhen. Taking back his paper, Zhen looked directly at the man.

'We are in the coolie house, it is not a clean place, is there no other until this matter is sorted out?'

The man looked back at him steadily. They were all alike, these bloody *singkehs*; give them half a chance and they wanted more. Even if this one had interesting credentials, he would have to discuss this with his superiors. But he had to be a little wary. From the paper he had seen that Zhen had been a feared *honggun*, red rod, chief disciplinarian of his guild, albeit probably a small one if it was in Zhangzhou. The Heaven and Earth Society here was a widespread confederacy of many thousands. It was the only resort for the penniless Chinese workers who turned up each month. The *kongsi* was like a piece of China far from home. It offered them a temple, comfort and work, medicine when they were sick and assurance of a decent burial. Without it they would perish. It connected them to people who spoke their language, knew their villages. Here in Si Lat Po, the Ghee Hin Kongsi, the main branch of the society, was much more powerful than any local guild. For twenty years it had operated with efficiency and impunity under the headman, Inchek Sang.

Still, it paid to be careful, and he was a careful man.

'I am a *hujiang*, tiger general. You know very well I must speak to my superior. For now the coolie house; maybe in a few days you will go to the plantations, work there until the ceremony, then we see. This is not my decision.'

He called Pock Face, who came running at a trot, rubbing his eyes, and instructed him, 'Take good care of our friends.'

He gave Pock Face some coins. 'For some food and refreshment. They will stay at the coolie house, but find them cots near the street. Tonight they may go out with you, but do not leave them alone. We do not wish them to get lost.' He looked fiercely at Pock Face, who shuffled uncomfortably.

Zhen and Qian bowed and followed Pock Face back to the street. The rain had stopped, and the heat had begun to rise. Pock Face looked at his two companions with renewed respect. Coins for some good grub, out on the town. Whatever this fellow had said had had some amazing effect. Qian, too, couldn't believe their luck. He wanted to quiz Zhen, but that would wait.

They wandered along the bayside towards the market area, with its distinctive red double octagonal roof. On its outskirts they stopped an itinerant hawker carrying his stove, bowls and ingredients slung from two poles. Pock Face ordered noodles, and they squatted, eating and looking out over the sea and its continuously moving ships and boats, along the crowded street and into the market building bustling with tradesmen and wares. Qian felt as if a great weight had lifted from his shoulders and, as they slurped their noodles, which tasted of home, he realised the extent of his emotion and gratitude towards Zhen. A dark-haired, dark-eyed woman wrapped in a cloth of purple and yellow came sauntering by, carrying a tray of fruit and nuts on her head. They gawped at her. For the first time in many months, they ate their fill. Even Pock Face was enjoying this unexpected feast, and they chatted amiably about home, basking in the clean salt air from the sea.

Then Zhen saw her: the black-haired Ch'ang O from the barbarian ship. She was with a white man. They were wandering about the marketplace, and the man was pointing out things now and then and talking animatedly. From time to time he put out his hand for hers and led her somewhere else. Zhen watched them with narrowed eyes, an odd heavy feeling in his chest. For a moment he thought she looked in their direction. He thought they might come towards him, willed them to do so. More than anything else at that instant, he wanted to see her close up. But they turned and left the market.

'Snatch the joys of life as they come and use them to the full
Do not leave the silver cup idly glinting at the moon'

He watched the place where she had been for a long time.

# 6

Incheck Sang sat alone, cross-legged, on a large tiger skin in the middle of the room. Strewn around this skin on which he slept were coffers and chests of varying sizes. Other than these objects, the room was bare. This was his sanctuary and his treasury. The only other person who ever set foot inside this room—and then only under his fierce gaze—was his eldest daughter. She came in to clean the room, change his clothes and bring him food. He entrusted these duties to no one else, not even his wives. The windows were barred, behind shutters which were rarely opened. The only air that penetrated came from a band of open decorative porcelain bricks that ran around the room on three sides under the ceiling. It was humid and hot, but Sang did not mind. Sometimes he would open one of his chests and draw a long, curved fingernail over its silvery contents. The little finger on one hand was missing from the knuckle, the stumpiness of this finger emphasising the length and boniness of the others. He had cut it off himself after a spectacular loss in the gambling den, as a painful reminder to stop this obsessive habit. It had made no difference. Gambling was in his blood.

Sang was cutting his toenails. He was a superstitious man. After each snip he would dexterously pick up the clipping with his long fingernails and place it carefully in a dull metal box which sat atop the tiger's head. When the job was finished to his satisfaction, he closed the box, took a small key on the long cord around his neck and locked it. Opening a silver embossed chest, he placed the box inside and locked it. He was a small man, bird-like and wrinkled. His face drooped slightly to one side, the results of a stroke he had suffered five years before. He was over seventy years old, but his eyes were clear and his mind was sound. He wore a long black coat with a silk skullcap. His beard and droopy moustache were grey, and real. The thick black queue attached to his head was not.

The captain from the Amoy junk, an old colleague, was waiting for him in his entrance hall, together with Ah Liang, his chief clerk, and Guan Soon, the coolie agent. Locking the door carefully behind him, Sang crossed the open courtyard with large pots of bamboo, went through the ornate central hall and out into the open yard. The two men were seated in the entrance hall, chatting amiably. When they saw him they sprang to their feet and bowed low.

'Come,' he commanded. They followed him into a room he used as an office on the side of the entrance hall.

This room contained a desk and several hardwood chairs, elaborately carved and inlaid with veined marble. Sang's chief clerk was also present.

They sat. Sang did not call for tea, but looked at the two men he had known for years.

'How many men do you need, sir?' Guan Soon asked respectfully.

The men talked about labour and numbers; then Guan Soon left, and they turned to filling the captain's orders for his return journey. Most of the captain's needs could be filled from Sang's own warehouse, but some items required negotiation. Opium was controlled by the European houses. This would be no problem as Sang was a man the British trusted to regulate the affairs of the Chinese community. The captain was in no hurry. He would be trading as a *chinchew*, sailing from port to port in the region, picking up goods from the local Chinese until the trade winds changed to carry him back to China four months from now. There was a woman in Palembang he would like to see again.

Before the captain left he said, 'Don't know if it's of interest, sir, but there are two men on the ship who are hardy-looking and can read and write; they actually sat around spouting nonsense poetry.'

The captain looked as if he wanted to spit, but rapidly thought better of it.

'In case you're interested, sir, these are their names.' He passed a paper across the table.

Sang eyed him, looked at the names and passed the paper to his chief clerk.

'If they are interesting, you will be paid.'

When the captain had departed, Sang looked at his clerk. Ah Liang was a small, fat man with droopy eyes and crooked yellow teeth. He was the master of the Ghee Hin Kongsi, keeper of the seal and rule book, and collected subscriptions from the large membership. Sang trusted him most of all the brotherhood. He looked after all of Sang's business and most of his private affairs. Sang had brought him from Malacca; Liang owed his livelihood and his success to Sang, and he'd never forgotten it. Thanks to Sang he had a house, a Balinese wife and two Sumatran concubines, sisters he had bought at the slave market a few years ago. Sang envied him his three sons, all married, and his five grandsons. There had been a time when Sang had thought to marry his young daughter to one of Ah Liang's sons, but they were all mixed blood, and he wanted a pure Chinese for his daughter, one who could speak the language, fresh blood from home.

After discussing business, Sang tapped the names of the two coolies the captain had written on the paper with his yellowing fingernail.

'Find these two and look them over. Let me know what you find out.'

He dismissed Ah Liang and, rising, made his way to the garden courtyard.

There he called his old wife, and she came and sat beside him. 'Second daughter is fifteen,' he said. 'It is time to marry her. If something happens to the son, there is no one for the ancestral rites. He must take my family name.'

His wife nodded; she was glad he had raised the subject. She detested the child of the second wife as much as she detested the second wife. But this was an important decision. There had been no sons born alive to either, and her own daughter had married a man who had pocketed anything he could get his hands on: the daughter's jewellery, two chests of silver and five chests of opium, and run off within a year. Sang had hunted high and low, brought all his money and influence to bear, but the man had either disappeared up some river somewhere or was lying, with his money, on the bottom of the sea. The first daughter had never been able to marry again. It had left an ache in her heart, and her mother took out her anger on the second daughter.

Sex was of little interest to Sang, who had taken no concubines, an expense he deemed unnecessary. He had reluctantly married his second wife when he was fifty-three and she was seventeen. His first wife, a second cousin, he had met as a young man on a visit back to China, through the matchmaker, the usual channels, and he had fallen, he supposed, in love. He had, contrary to custom, brought her from China, for she had no close family living. The second was a mixed-blood daughter of a Chinese headman of the tin mines in Perak and his Malay wife. He did not like her much. She was polluted. But pure-blood Chinese wives were not to be had. There had been the birth of the daughter, then miscarriages and a stillbirth. Finally, out of desperation he had adopted a boy from an impoverished Chinese couple in Batavia, who was now his son. He was twelve, and Sang's heir, but he was not absolute pure blood either. He hardly knew his adopted father and was terrified of him. As Sang grew older he became more and more obsessed with the duties owed to him in his afterlife. More than ever he wanted a Chinese son-in-law, one who would take his name.

'Husband, remember the first daughter's man. Choose well.'

Sang did not like to be reminded of that terrible time, but he knew she meant well. He still cared for her and on rare occasions shared her bed.

'Yes. Tell second wife.'

His old wife said nothing but smiled slightly. No matter how much she hated these other women, she longed for grandchildren, which she fully intended to bring up as she saw fit. She would consult the fortune-teller today.

# 7

Mrs Keaseberry was in her garden when Charlotte called. She was sweating in her long-sleeved dress and her overly large, floppy-brimmed hat. She rose from the low stool she had been sitting on and, removing her gloves, apologised for her rather dirty state. The house was a pleasant but plain building near the corner of Brass Bassa and North Bridge Road. The garden, however, was like a small corner of paradise. In every space and on every level of the surrounding wall were pots of orchids, small and large, pink, white, orange, long-lipped, spotted and plain. The whole was shaded by the outspread branches of a massive *tembusu* tree. Orchids scrambled up the trunk of a tall areca palm.

'My passion,' Mrs Keaseberry explained unnecessarily. 'My children, I suppose.'

They moved into the house, where a *punkah* immediately began to move to and fro in the ceiling.

'*Terima kasih, jamu,*' she called, and a little giggle emanated from the verandah. 'The *punkah* boy is also one of Peach's pupils.'

Mrs Keaseberry was referring, Charlotte knew, to her husband, Benjamin Peach Keaseberry, and fleetingly felt the affection reflected in the use of his middle name.

'He teaches the boys printing and bookbinding. Peach has one of the printing presses here, and we can get quite busy. His office is down on the square. We can visit it later, my deah. Peach is now with the London Missionary Society. We have been learning Malay with the munshi for quite a while. The mission chapel is across the way, a poor building I'm afraid, but it suffices for the moment, and there is a small school.'

Charlotte told Mrs Keaseberry of her father who, too, had been with the London Missionary Society and had died in its service. Then quickly she changed the subject.

'Who is the munshi, Mrs Keaseberry? I hear about him from everyone.'

'Why, my deah, the munshi is the most extraordinary and wonderful man we have in the whole of Singapore. He came with Raffles and Farquhar, knew Crawfurd. He knows everything there is to know about this place. He is a most lovely man. Though he is a devout Muslim he is helping Peach translate the Bible into Malay.'

'Yes, I want to do that, learn Malay. Also, I think I can be of some use teaching English if it would be permitted. Robert said that Mr Moorehouse and Mr Dickinson at the institution would probably welcome people to help them with the Chinese boys.'

'Certainly, my deah. It pays to keep busy here, and Peach says there is always so much to do.'

They were taking some refreshments when the da Silva twins dropped by, calling a loud 'hello' and rushing without ceremony into the sitting room. Charlotte was surprised by the way the Europeans were happy to leave their doors open to all and sundry. In the police bungalow, too, there always seemed to be people roaming unannounced. Groups of native people, men and women, sometimes congregated in their pirogues along the sea front to stare at her, but when she waved to them, they fled. Robert called them *orang laut*, sea gypsies, people who had lived here hundreds of years before Raffles and Farquhar set foot on the island. They fished and lived around the mouth of the river, over on the Rochor and Kallang rivers, the unexplored backwaters of the interior, on the islands of Brani and Blakang Mati and around the temenggong's village at Telok Blangah, west of the town. Robert showed her his boat, *Sea Gypsy*, and she had been thrilled. Sailing was a pastime they both shared.

The Misses da Silva had somehow learned that Charlotte was here and had walked over from their large house on Beach Road. They were keen to accompany the two ladies on their tour of the town. There had been talk of visiting the new Chinese temple at Telok Ayer. They were as happy as puppies, and Charlotte was delighted to have such gay company.

When Mrs Keaseberry had donned her hat and raised her parasol, they set off on foot along North Bridge Road. Charlotte, too, had opened a parasol, welcoming the shade. The twins paid no attention to the sun and went bareheaded, although Mrs Keaseberry tutted.

Their path took them along the edge of the former institution gardens to the building works of Mr Caldwell's house, which Coleman was completing; the site was full of half-naked Malay and Indian labourers. Mrs Keaseberry told Charlotte that the trustees of the institution had recently disposed of a large parcel of land in nine lots between North Bridge Road and Victoria Street.

They turned into Victoria Street, crossed the small bridge onto Hill Street, then walked along the edge of the stream down to North Bridge Road. The water of the stream was clear, and the sound of water over rocks was pleasant and, somehow, cooling. Through the big trees they could see St Andrew's Church. Occasionally they passed Chinese men holding up umbrellas or carrying goods on long poles. Charlotte noticed their unusual dress: loose-fitting trousers and jackets which fastened with a kind of toggle to the neck.

They passed Tir Uaidhne, where small groups of men worked in the garden, crossed over Coleman Street and walked along the side of a series of buildings with unusual, curved roofs, which Charlotte Keaseberry told her belonged to Inchek Sang, the most miserly and godforsaken man in Singapore. Arriving at the river, they made their way over Monkey Bridge. It creaked and groaned, and its wooden planks rattled as they went gingerly across.

'It should be demolished. Some fellow called Jackson built it years ago. It wasn't much good then and it's a good deal worse now.' Mrs Keaseberry spoke with annoyance. 'Peach says it will collapse at any moment. Thanks be that George Coleman has almost completed his new bridge up the river by Hill Street. You can see it from here. You would think all these rich merchants in town could have long since afforded a decent bridge, since it benefits the whole community but they and the government are close to their silver when it comes to the common good. Every man for himself here, my deah.'

All the ladies, including Charlotte, looked wary and were glad when the short distance was negotiated.

Charlotte contemplated the river, which now stood open to her gaze. The southern side was fully built with godowns and long corridors on the quayside; she saw merchandise and men in unceasing motion. For its entire length, Charlotte could see not one woman. *Tongkangs, sampans*, sailboats, rowboats and pirogues filled the river idly, waiting for the tide to turn, for it was low, and a large, gravelly bank showed at its centre. The activity was less evident on the north side. After the Chinese compound, Charlotte could see Mr Hallpike's shipyard and blacksmith's, with its anchor poles in the river. Sounds of sawing and banging emanated from this untidy collection of wooden buildings. The riverside here was hardly contained, and muddy-banked. Next to this was the customs house and post office. Stone banking began again at the steps of the arched, covered landing stage. Behind rose the roof of Mr Coleman's courthouse. The police bungalow was hidden by trees and the curve of the river. The noise and bustle of the tight-knit town here stood in the starkest contrast to the quiet, rural peace of the European side.

Negotiating several steps, they moved onto Boat Quay, where they saw Robert and Mr Francis, proprietor of the local public house and hotel on Commercial Square, as well as an inn in Tavern Street. He invited them to join him later in the refreshment hall of the hotel and took his leave. They moved along the bustling curve of the river, skirting bales and baskets filled with cloths, fruits, squawking ducks and turkeys, iron goods and guns, greeted by most of the merchants. With a dignified tilt of the head, Abraham Solomon was introduced to Charlotte. She thought him quite magnificent in his Old Testament turban and robes and his great white beard. He was a Jew who had but shortly arrived from Baghdad. Mr Duthie, owner of one of the biggest agency houses in Singapore, together with Dr Mongomerie, were also strolling along the quay and stopped to be introduced to Charlotte. Around them milled sellers of vegetables, soup, a strange jelly made of seaweed which the da Silva girls called *agar-agar*, long-poled food hawkers, buffaloes and water carts. There were coolies and boatmen waiting to be hired. All this assortment of males stared and gawped at the women as they passed. Charlotte felt uncomfortable, but it seemed to have no effect at all on her companions.

A little bridge spanned a slightly smelly canal, where rubbish had gathered. The backs of the houses which curved along this waterway looked rickety, with numbers of sooty spaces, giving the whole area the appearance of a mouth filled with decaying and stumpy teeth. Robert explained that there had been a fire, and a lot of the wooden buildings had disappeared. George was gradually replacing them with brick.

A Chinese man of medium height and a pleasant demeanor was sitting outside his godown and rose as soon as he saw them. He was dressed much like the coolies she saw around her, but his clothes were finer. The short dark blue jacket was fastened to the neck with toggles of knotted silk. Instead of trousers he wore a skirt, and on his feet, not sandals, but high-soled shoes. If this were not extraordinary enough, on his head and over his queue he wore a tall, black shiny top hat. As he moved from the shade he opened a yellow, oiled-paper umbrella against the sun. Her companions did not seem in the least amazed at this sight, and Charlotte quickly presumed that this was his standard dress.

'Come, you must meet Baba Tan. After Incheck Sang, he is the most influential man in the Chinese community, and he speaks English uncommonly well.'

Charlotte curtsied charmingly and Baba Tan, in the best English manner, shook hands with Robert, raised his hat to Charlotte and, looking exceedingly pleased, greeted them all warmly. His English was very good, and Charlotte would have liked to speak more to him. She was delighted when he offered to take them all on a tour of the new Chinese temple at Telok Ayer Street, which he and other rich *towkays* in the town had helped finance. The da Silva girls were not very interested in ancient Jews or old Chinamen. They were keeping their eyes peeled for some of the regiment officers or the more handsome young agency house clerks who might be in the town. Both girls, despite their commonplace looks, were well aware of how much their rarity was worth, for their mother had discussed it at length. She was looking out for men with prospects, they knew, but with the choice so wide, both hoped to get the best-looking man they could find.

'How fascinating everyone here is, Mrs Keaseberry, don't you think?'

Mrs Keaseberry looked surprised. 'Fascinating? Yes, I suppose so. It is so difficult to understand the Chinese mind, though. Even when we can speak English to them, it is another world, my deah. Well we have so little to do with them really. The Malays are different; they have a soul.'

This statement interested Charlotte. Did the Chinese not have a soul? What could she mean? She wanted to pursue the subject, but Robert had stopped in front of a big old house, somewhat dilapidated, which stood next to the fort. Mrs Keaseberry and the girls had disappeared into a shop selling Chinese silk, Indian cotton, English cloth and fine ribbons. Charlotte, too, would have liked to go in, but Robert, rather boringly she thought, insisted on his lecture.

'This is Tanjong Tangkap, it means "capture point". It is Mr Johnstone's house and godown, and everyone calls it that because it is placed so well to capture all the captains as they come into the river for trade. Mr Johnstone is one of the oldest residents of the settlement and has been a good friend to me. When I worked for him he was fair and hospitable. Now that I do not, he is still gracious and kind.'

Charlotte eyed the musty, dilapidated building with a jaundiced eye.

While they waited for the others, Robert told Charlotte of Raffles' and Farquhar's landing and the establishment of the colony, the first agreements and finally the purchase from the previous fat old sultan and the temenggong, his chief minister; he spoke also of the way clever Crawfurd, the second governor, had managed to get them to agree to it.

'As Munshi Abdullah tells it, Crawfurd wanted to fix the colony for the company once and for all. The previous agreements had meant that the place could not grow, for it was not secure, and people were reluctant to take out land leases when it might revert, at any moment, back to the sultan. So Crawfurd held back the stipends which they were paid as compensation for the island and told them the money had not arrived from Calcutta. Finally they were so desperate that they agreed to sign the document of permanent sale. Was that not clever of Crawfurd?'

'I'd say it was rather underhanded.' Charlotte was quite annoyed by this story.

'Well my dear sister, that is business in this part of the world. Neither the sultan nor the temenggong would indulge in trade which is beneath them, yet they are not above the piracy which takes the lives of many good men and makes the seas even more dangerous.'

Robert sounded irritated. 'These royal potentates are absolute rulers in their fiefdoms. They are an indulgent lot, lazy and greedy. They give no benefit to their own people, who are oppressed and taxed into virtual slavery. Even the munshi agrees that this is so. He is harder on them than any of us. Why, the present sultan's run off in disgrace with his catamite or some such.'

Charlotte was dismayed at the storm she had caused and, laying a hand on Robert's arm, said, 'Crimoney! Forgive me, Robbie; I am very new here. I don't understand everything, but rulers everywhere oppress, do they not? I heard that the Chinese headmen here also use the poor men who come from China in the big ships. Do not we also take advantage of the natives for our benefit throughout the empire? Mr Hume and Monsieur Voltaire— '

'For heaven's sake, Charlotte.' Robert interrupted her. 'This is not the place for philosophical discussions.' He softened his voice. 'This is a frontier town, not Marischal College. My job is to understand and keep the peace as well as I am able.'

Charlotte said no more but thought it rather hypocritical of Robert to criticise the sultan and lay no fault of exploitation at the doors of the other communities. After morning lessons in her grandmother's house, she had often been left to her own devices. Her cousin, Duncan, would come and see her and take her sailing, a pursuit her father had taught his children in Madagascar. She would go for long walks on the hills around Aberdeen. This semi-solitary existence was not unpleasant. She did not care much for the company of the silly Scottish lasses she met at lunches and tea parties, all giggles and gossip. She had also spent hours reading in her grandfather's extensive library, and this had framed ideas she knew few women were privy to. She had thought she might talk of these with Robert. The sudden realisation came to her that there might be few people in Singapore with whom such ideas could be discussed. Robert himself had altered, was more serious, even had a stronger Scottish accent than when he had left Scotland. When she had taxed him on this, he had merely answered,

'Almost everyone here is Scots. Why, most of India is Scottish; it serves well.'

She thought of her Aunt Jeannie and her cousin, Duncan, with whom she had spent hours in such talk. Even her grandmother, though strictly Kirk, had indulged the family in intellectual debate. Her beloved husband had been a professor of Greek, a scholar and polemicist. Robert, too, when he was down from university, played a central part in these debates. Charlotte realised at that moment, and to her surprise, that she was grateful to her Scottish family for the expansion of her mind. Had they stayed in Madagascar, no matter how hard their father might have tried, they might have been what Robert now despised: ignorant and lazy. Whether they were happier for not being so, she was not sure.

These musings were interrupted by the arrival of the other ladies. Isobel da Silva showed her a pretty muslin, which she had bought. Charlotte realised that she must turn her attention a little to her wardrobe and, as she questioned the girls on materials and tailors, they made their way down by Mr Johnstone's gloomy godown, to Battery Road. The sea on their left was filled with ships and boats transporting goods to the long jetties of the godowns along the seafront.

The sun was, by now, so hot that Robert proposed a short stop at Mr Francis's refreshment rooms, and they made their way along the edge of the elegant little square to a shuttered building on the corner of Kling Street.

Here, in the cool ground floor, they sat as Mr Francis placed orders for lime juice for Charlotte and Mrs Keaseberry, pineapple juices for the girls and a cool India pale ale for Robert. John Francis was a Cockney who had served as a ship's mate for many years, before settling down in Singapore to open the first public house, in Tavern Street. His language was a little rough and ready, but Charlotte liked him. Since his tavern was meant for the ships' crews who ebbed and flowed like the tide, his rough ways did not offend the majority of his clientele. His hotel often took in sick sailors for a pittance which, in the absence of any hospital, was an act of some charity.

Refreshed, they made their way along the north side of Commercial Square towards Malacca Street. Here, Charlotte noted the first women she had seen in the town. Two dark-haired Indian women were sauntering around the square arm in arm, dressed in pretty pink and green saris. As they passed, Isobel giggled and whispered something to her sister. Mrs Keaseberry threw them a hard glance and they stopped.

'Ladies of the night, my deah,' she said with a moue.

Of course, thought Charlotte. This is a port.

Charlotte found much to admire in the interesting architecture of the square. Most of the houses were three-storey buildings ornately decorated with shutters, porcelain tiles and painted eaves. The architecture of the town was unusual, and she had asked Robert about it. He had merely said that, as far as he knew, it was Raffles who had decreed that all the buildings should be uniform and ordered Coleman to ensure that they all be fronted by a five-foot way to allow shelter from the sun and the rain. 'Proper smart chap, that Raffles.' For the rest she should speak to George Coleman, who 'knew bally everything about architecture and much else besides'.

Just beyond the auction rooms they stepped into the building which housed Mr Keaseberry's mission press. A dull thump-thump could be heard coming from a back room.

Robert hailed Benjamin Keaseberry—a tall, thin man with a slightly florid complexion—and his companion with a loud 'Greetings, gentlemen.' Mrs Keaseberry went up to her husband, who took her hand, and greeted the other man somewhat coldly, Charlotte thought. Having curtsied to Mr Keaseberry she was introduced to Mr Coleman.

So this is the man who knows bally everything and has the heart of Takouhi Manouk, thought Charlotte. He took her hand lightly and bowed slightly.

'Miss Charlotte Macleod, by the saints, Robert has not been telling lies.'

He had a way of looking directly into her eyes which was very seductive.

'Welcome to our little world. As sure as the Pope's a Catholic, we shall be best friends.'

The da Silva girls both kissed him warmly on his cheek, for they had known him all their lives. He was a favourite at their musical soirées, where he sang Irish songs in a pleasant baritone.

Mr Coleman was at the mission press to pick up personal items of printing and, when pressed by the da Silva girls, revealed that they were invitations to a ball that he would be giving in honour of a visit by Takouhi's brother and to which, they, much too young, were not invited. After a great deal of pouting they convinced him to relent, and he confessed that they might be on the guest list.

He explained to Charlotte that he was interested in the printing process as part-founder of the settlement's newspaper, the *Singapore Free Press*, although this journal was printed on its own presses in Battery Road.

'It's only four pages long, and there's some rather drear commercial stuff which the others insist on. But it gives the settlement a voice in a time when the lordships in Calcutta pay little interest to what goes on here. I fear there is not profit enough for them in Singapore. Only the Chinese and Arab merchants make the fortunes. So they rather see Singapore as a glorified fishing village or a repository of convicts. Yet we are frugal. The government lives off the vices of the population, taxes only the gambling, liquor and opium farms. There are no port duties, no tax on trade. We have a chamber of commerce but no hospital. We have crime aplenty but no one willing to subsidise the police force. So we rail and bemoan our sorry lot. Directly beside a letter groaning about the state of our thoroughfares, there's an editorial against the imposition of carriage taxes, which are to go to improve them. Free trade, that's the clarion call. So the lord must take care of the rest. Is it not delightful, Miss Macleod?'

Mrs Keaseberry looked on disapprovingly at this bantering tirade for although she agreed with the sentiments, she had never warmed to Mr Coleman's sense of humour, nor could she countenance his habit of dressing like the natives. She had even seen him in a turban. It was too much.

Coleman smiled wryly, took possession of his bundle and departed with a wave.

They made a tour of the premises, and Mr Keaseberry explained enthusiastically and somewhat at length the working of the press and the merits of Koenig and Bauer's steam-powered single machine and Applegarth and Cowper's four-cylinder machine versus the older Stanhope iron-frame lever press. When they took their leave. Charlotte's head was spinning and the da Silva girls looked as if they might cry. Mrs Keaseberry had declined the remainder of the tour and stayed to help her husband.

Stepping outside into the sunshine, the three women looked at each other and suppressed a desire to laugh until they had moved very quickly across the pretty leafy square. The girls then ran gaily into a handsome shophouse directly across from the mission press, which was the dispensary of Dr da Silva and the place of work for his mercantile interests, as well as of Thomas Crane, his son-in-law by marriage to Maria, one of his many daughters. They occupied the upper rooms.

Dr Jose da Silva was a man of some sixty years, tall and slender with thick silver hair and a patrician face. Charlotte could see that he was attractive and was no longer surprised at the remarkable number of wives he had possessed. He greeted them distractedly. Although he cared for all his children, since there were some twenty of them, he often had trouble with their names.

He had been a ship's surgeon on board a Portuguese man-of-war and had fallen, by chance, into the merchant business when an enforced stopover in Singapore had turned his language skills into an opportunity he could not afford to miss.

In the face of the north-east monsoon, a Portuguese and a Spanish vessel, bound for Macao and Manila respectively, could not proceed with their voyage and were detained in the harbour for four months. Wishing to sell their cargoes to meet expenses, they consulted Dr da Silva and he agreed to act as their agent and help sell the cargoes at auction. This proved so successful that some fifteen years on Dr da Silva was a very wealthy man.

Maria Crane had come down to greet them and invited them to lunch after their visit to the Chinese town. She was a pretty dark-haired, almond-eyed woman, a daughter of her father's second wife, a Portuguese Chinese whom Dr da Silva had taken as a wife in Macao. Her motive in extending this invitation was not entirely altruistic. She had several unmarried brothers for whom Charlotte was entirely suitable. Since he had taken up his post of police chief, she had also had her eye on Robert as a potential match for one of her daughters, sixteen-year-old Teresa. Though she had not wished to extend the invitation to her twin stepsisters, she could see no way of avoiding it.

When they departed, the small party headed towards Telok Ayer Street, where Robert had arranged to meet Baba Tan outside the Chinese temple.

As they went along, Charlotte could only wonder at the extraordinary variety of goods on offer at the small shophouses. Each shop they passed held a powerful appeal: the boot makers, oil shops, locksmiths, ivory carvers and jewellers as fascinating as the ship's chandlers and the paper lantern seller. Down side streets, Charlotte could see carpenters and coffin makers, soap sellers and opium shops. Every tiny space along the side roads contained stalls as well, with men selling vegetables and dried fish, small goods, thread, pickled plums, kajang mats and baskets. The speed of fingers on the clacking abacuses was mesmerising, the noise of it like the incessant chirping of crickets in the jungle. She saw a man writing the picture language with a black brush on white paper. The streets rang with hammering and calls, everywhere around her the incessant clatter and chatter of these wondrously industrious people.

The clamour died down as they went along the bay but, suddenly, a clear strong voice rang out into the air.

'*Allah O Akhbar*! The call to prayer,' said Robert, 'from the mosque in South Bridge Road.'

He led her to the shrine built by the Chulias from south India, traders and money changers, who were Mohammedans and followed a god called Allah. This building was small but exquisite, rising like a lacy green multi-tiered miniature palace, surrounded by pierced balustrades, topped by tall minarets. He greeted the guard outside, who rose in *salaam*, and they moved past and stopped in front of the Chinese temple.

As they stood waiting, Charlotte took in the lovely curve of the bay and its occupants. Here were some women, at least, Malays, around the fishing boats. Children, too. She had seen the Malay women in the market and noticed that they and their men alike seemed to chew what Robert explained was betel. The peppery leaf was wrapped round ground cinnamon, sometimes cloves or other spices. Some people liked to add tobacco. Inside there was a slice of crunchy areca nut. The whole was a mild stimulant. He had not especially enjoyed it, and prolonged chewing left the mouth red and the teeth blackened. The practice was so commonplace that one simply didn't notice it after awhile. Chinese men never chewed betel, he added, or the women who came from China. But amongst the wives and daughters of the local Chinese it was de rigueur. Charlotte could not immediately make sense of these fine distinctions and chose to let the subject drop.

She turned her attention to the roofs and walls of the temple. Fierce dragon creatures with curled tails and long tongues adorned each curved roof angle, a mirror beset with flames in the middle of the roof over the main door. Tree-like carved pillars rose on either side of entrance doors which were painted with fearsome men richly dressed in robes of gold and black. The black doors on either side of the main façade were decorated with images of writhing, golden dragons with long sharp teeth and bulging eyes.

The twins thought them hideous, but Charlotte found them provoking.

Baba Tan suddenly appeared from a side street and joined them, apologising for his lateness. He motioned them to enter the temple between the two stone lions. A heady smell of incense assailed them as they stepped inside. He explained the legend of the temple's principal deity, Ma Chu, Goddess of the Sea and Queen of Heaven. As a young girl from a maritime province, she had been distinguished for her chasteness and devotion to Buddha. He did not explain who this Buddha was, but Charlotte presumed some higher god. Ma Chu had miraculous powers of prophesy and was deified. She became patroness of seafaring people. Every Chinese man or woman who travelled on the sea invoked her name before departure and gave thanks on their safe arrival. Charlotte thought her rather haughty and distant behind her headdress of glassy beads.

Giving some coins to an old man in the corner of the temple, Baba Tan presented some bundles of incense to his guests and showed them how to light each stick and place it in the urn. Charlotte found the scent of the sandalwood enticing. Now she understood Robert's references to the 'perfumed Orient'. The spices of the market, the aroma of cooking, the scents of incense and oils: these were the perfumes of the East. Charlotte was quickly falling in love with this wonderful town, as varied and facetted as a fabulous jewel.

To the right and left of the goddess stood other figures, her constant companions: two huge carved figures with grotesque faces. The green-faced one pointed to his ear, the red-faced one had bulging eyes.

According to Baba Tan they symbolised the virgin's all-seeing and all-hearing powers. Before the goddess stood two gigantic imitations of wax candles, eight or ten feet long and painted red, and three or four great false joss sticks. Baba Tan explained that, during festivals, oil lamps are placed inside them and give a fine effect.

On the altar before the goddess stood immense brass incense urns, porcelain vases and flower ornaments and, under the table, stone carvings of a tiger, tigress and cub. It was customary, Tan explained, in a land of tigers, to offer incense to the tiger spirit to induce him to keep away from humans. Charlotte thought this rather charming if somewhat ineffectual. If Robert was to be believed, it didn't seem to help the poor Chinamen of the interior who, he claimed, were carried off with regularity.

Before each of the three deities Baba Tan pointed out two short wooden sticks both having a flat side and a curved one. He explained that these were the *puey*, the oracle blocks. Before a man set off on any enterprise, he consulted the virgin or the other gods to intercede on his behalf with the higher deities.

Baba Tan took up the sticks in front of the God of Medicine. He threw them in the air, and they both landed with their flat sides uppermost.

'Lucky side, gods are pleased. If the other way, the business must be given up. If the blocks land one flat side, one curved side, this is best omen of all. Most lucky sign.'

Tan offered the sticks to Robert and Charlotte but they politely declined. Charlotte was not sure why, but this ritual felt a bit like the voodoo she had seen a little of in Madagascar. Nevertheless, she thought, she could see little difference between this and the adoration of Jesus or praying to Mary.

Really, she thought, at bottom humans just can't rely on themselves. What we can't control we relinquish to the gods and, if we fail, it's their fault.


As Baba Tan began to lead their group into another courtyard, Charlotte noticed a group of Chinese women enter the temple. The sight of women was so unusual, and their silk costumes so attractive, she dropped back to watch them light bundles of incense. A great fog of pungent-scented blue–white smoke swirled round the courtyard.

Then, as the smoke moved here and there, she saw two Chinese men emerging from an opposite courtyard. She turned her head in their direction, and one of the men suddenly stopped walking and gazed towards her. As his dark, hooded eyes met hers, she felt her heart give a sudden thump; her eyes widened, and blood rushed to her face. She put her hand to her throat, but when she tried to move her legs, she found she could not. The incense seemed to thicken around her, enter her brain, befog her mind. She stood like this, seemingly for a long time until she heard Robert call to her. His voice broke what she could only think of as a kind of spell, and she turned and quickly rejoined her party. She could make no sense of her reaction and, saying she was somewhat hot, fanned herself lightly and gathered her composure, quietly listening to Baba Tan explain one of the fearsome-looking idols with a long red tongue.

Zhen had just finished his talk with Ah Liang, the master of the *kongsi*, who had agreed that, until the ceremony of initiation, he and Qian should go with other coolies to one of the *bangsals* run by the *kongsi* and work at the headman's gambier and pepper plantation. Ah Liang had assessed this young man and felt that, though he was healthy and clever, he might just be too headstrong to be an obedient son-in-law for his master. His friend, Qian, was much more suitable material, more timid and malleable. He would make his recommendation, but what Sang might do he could not say. Sang was a gambler and not always predictable.

When he saw Charlotte through the clouds of incense smoke, Zhen could not believe his eyes. He stopped so abruptly that Qian walked on several steps before realising that his friend was not beside him. Turning back, he too noticed the foreign woman and, guessing what his friend was thinking, pulled at his sleeve.

Zhen paid him no attention. Her eyes had widened when she saw him. Even through the swirling billows he could see they were a deep violet blue, the shade of a late evening sky. He had seen her confusion and was glad that his face showed no emotion. He took a step towards her but she turned suddenly and disappeared. Qian pulled again at his sleeve and he looked down at him.

'Are you crazy?' he hissed.

Zhen turned and left the temple without a backward glance.

# 8

Charlotte was glad to return to the bungalow. Lunch with Mr and Mrs Crane had been pleasant, with some unusual Portuguese dishes. Robert had, at first, seemed uninterested in young Miss Crane but appeared to warm to her after a while. She was a pretty girl, with deep chestnut wavy hair and large brown eyes, which she used to excellent effect, raising and lowering her long lashes whenever Robert addressed her. Charlotte was amused by this as well as by Isobel and Isabel's obvious annoyance. She had not observed it before, but clearly there was some interest in Robert on their parts as well. How they thought they could divide him up was a mystery, but she was determined to rib him about it when she got the chance.

Now, in her room, lying on her bed with the shutters closed, she turned her attention to the encounter at the temple.

What on earth was the matter with me? she thought. There are Chinamen all over the town. Why should this one have any effect? The incense probably, disturbs the brain.

But she did not find these thoughts convincing. Gradually she began to remember the night she had arrived, the young man calling to her from the junk. Had it been him? She grew tired and the moonlight, the man, the junk all became a swirling dream as she slumbered.

When Robert returned for dinner she was refreshed, and they passed a pleasant evening. He told her of a robbery which had occurred at one of the European houses.

'Auch, really it's their own fault. Why, you can walk through almost every European house on the beach at Kampong Glam at certain times of the day without meeting a single inmate or being challenged. The Chinese thieves know this. They carry fictitious notes, you know. If they meet someone they present a note and get told the person does not live there, and off they go, having made a good observation of the house. If not, they pocket whatever pretty baubles, clocks, watches and jewels they can see and depart scot free. Other times it's their own servants that are the thieves.'

A tiger hunt was to be organised, for attacks were getting more frequent. A man had broken into the godown of Mr Balestier, the American consul, and a body had been found floating at the foot of Coleman's new bridge works. The corpse turned out to be an American crewman from one of the opium clippers in port who had been reprimanded and fined by Mr Balestier. He seemed to have broken his neck in a fall from the window. Two houses had been broken into in Kampong Glam. A Chinese gang of men had attacked and released some Chinese prisoners working on a road site. Two had been recovered; the rest had fled into the jungle.

'Such a lot to do with so few men. Can't ask policemen who are paid a pittance to go off searching in the jungle. We must do our best. I shall try to speak to the Chinese headman, although I suspect him of turning a blind eye. Only the Chinese can keep these gangs under some kind of control.

'Tonight I have a class with my men. I'm teaching them to read, you know, for until they can read and write I cannot promote them. We'll talk about patrols. But I don't expect any man to stand up to a gang of armed thugs. Also, I may be out late tonight. I want to check on the police station out on the road to Hurricane House. It's good to drop in on them to see if they're paying attention.'

Charlotte was alarmed. 'Is it not dangerous, Robert, going alone? Is it far from town?'

'A mile or two. Auch, well, I shall take Jemadar Kapoor. He is an excellent shot. We shall take our swords, and I have a pistol. I may stay the night at Hurricane House, at the plantation of Captain Scott. He is the harbour master; you met his niece. There is a peon here on duty, so you need not fear. If you like, tomorrow morning he can bring you out there. William's plantation is worth a visit.'

'I think I would like that very much. Now I must go to bed. When that gun goes off I never feel like getting up.'

Yawning, she rose and kissed Robert resoundingly on the forehead.

Robert poured himself a small glass of whisky. There was the sound of footsteps on the verandah, and George appeared around the corner. He sat down and took a whisky with his friend.

'Come walk with me. I've news for you,' he said.

They left the verandah and strolled out in front of the courthouse. George looked up at the building.

'You know this was almost the first house I built here in Singapore. I designed the residency house on the hill entirely in the hope that Raffles would take it up. I waited here for four months for him to come from Bencoolen.

'That was a time, I can tell you. I stayed for a while with a man called Nicholson, a trader. He'd been in the East a long time. We shared a basic attap house along the beach. It was my first time here, and the view was like magic. Anyway, he had this little dark *nyai* who swept up, did the domestic work and shared his bed. He was like a damn rabbit. There was no sleep until the nightly ritual of huffing and grunting had been completed. The fact that I was a plank's width away from them didn't seem to bother him. Then he'd snore like Thor. You'd have thought that'd be the end of it, but Nicholson was a generous man, and apparently had ordered his young woman to cater to his guests. She'd come in completely naked and get into bed and start— well, you know. No matter what I said to Nicholson, or what he said to her, in she'd come every night and we'd go through this ritual until it became comical. "*Tuan*, I come play jolly-jolly," she'd say.

'Can you imagine? Nicholson called the act of bliss and wonder between a man and a women "jolly jolly". So, I'd say "no jolly jolly", which made no difference. She'd get into bed, me pushing her out and insisting "no jolly jolly" like a demented child, Nicholson's snores practically drowning out my words.'

Robbie was laughing, and George looked at him.

'Well, so I understand what you're getting at Robbie, of course I do. I'd met Takouhi by then, so this creature was of no interest at all. My head was filled with her.'

George looked down at his shoes, and Robert detected a slight embarrassment, as if he'd said more than he had intended.

'Anyway, I was saved by Bonham, who was in a humbler position then. He took me in, and I've been grateful to him ever since. Thank the Lord, Raffles liked my plan. Even gave me a commission for a garrison church. I had designed the residence in brick and tile, but Raffles had it made up in wood and attap. That was common in those days. I've added to it greatly over the years, changed the wood for brick and so on. It's really a pleasant house now.

'When I came back from Java I built David Napier's house next, but this building was my first real design. The first time I turned my hand to something new and unusual, yer know, something classical but which suited our tropical climate. It was truly born in Singapore. Maxwell wanted the grandest home in the settlement, and I enjoyed building it, sure I did. Maxwell never lived in it, for this part was reserved for government buildings. Somehow he had wangled a lease. Smart devil, he rented it back to the administration before it was even finished for five hundred rupees a month. None of my business that. It did the job though for me. It impressed the merchants enough to get me plenty of commissions. I hope it will stand hundreds of years. I'm well proud of it, and for a long time now I believe it has given our young town a certain class.'

Robert said nothing. When they reached the landing stage they stopped and contemplated the far bank. The glow of red lanterns and yellow oil lamps reflected brightly in the river. A ramshackle theatre had been thrown up out over the river near Monkey Bridge, and the high-pitched whine and clashing cymbals of a Chinese opera could be heard. Cheering and clapping erupted occasionally.

'That's the powerhouse. We may be the wheels on the carriage, but the engine is over there, driving us forward like Mr Stevenson's *Rocket*. Then I came here, the river was a meandering mess of swamps and marsh. Still is up river round the sago factories.'

He stood silently for a moment, and Robert grew curious. After Raffles had died so suddenly, his wife Sophia had published a book of memoirs of her husband, a collection of his copious correspondence. In the face of Singapore's evident commercial success, this had had the remarkable effect of lifting him out of the obscurity into which he had fallen, and he had become an instant celebrity, his deeds re-evaluated by the East India Company, memorials commissioned. Robert knew that

George had been asked to submit plans for a Raffles memorial but that, in the end, the public subscription had gone to improve the institution, a project close to Sir Stamford's heart. This information, and Crawfurd's success with the temenggong and the sultan, formed the sum total of his knowledge about Singapore's past.

'George, what was Raffles like?'

Coleman looked at him and smiled. Such curiosity in Robert was unexpected.

'Raffles was not an easy man. Ambitious, but that's not unusual. He was very short in stature, and short men can be difficult. Raffles was governor at Bencoolen then, but he had been Lieutenant Governor of Java for five years during the brief British administration. Well, anyway, Raffles felt his position keenly, I'm sure. Bencoolen was given up for Malacca a few years later, after the Dutch and English drew a line on the map. North is yours, south is mine. That sort o' thing.'

George looked at Robert. He wasn't sure how much history he was interested to know.

'Left Farquhar in charge, told him to make it all work on nothing and then gave him hell. Farquhar was a great man, had the touch. Without him, no one would have come, for every man who traded—Malay, Chinese, European—knew him and liked him. Flint, Raffles' brother-in-law, was here then, always in Raffles' ear, though he was far away in Bencoolen.'

Coleman pointed to the fort. 'His house was there where the fort is now. Big building on a nice high hill, best bit of land in the place. Flint was made harbour master by Raffles, who legitimised his monopoly of the lighter trade and the port services. No goods arrived from the ships except by lighters, and all ships needed water and supplies so, of course, he grew rich. By the saints, he was a nasty character, dishonest and untrustworthy, greedy, sly. Took Crawfurd to get him out, point out fraud, make him sell his boats, make things fair. Great days, he was furious.

'Raffles never saw the advantages of the river. Ordered the godowns and jetties built on the beach. Hopeless. It was either mud flats or monsoon swell banging the boats around. Made it impossible to land goods. Most people saw the obvious role of such a naturally sheltered river and started to build on it, even though it was a lake at high tide. When he came back he made such a lot of trouble for Farquhar because of it and then quietly revised his plans. I know because he consulted me, amongst others, and we saw the advantages of the river all right.'

He lit a small cigar and stood looking at the quay.

'I recommended filling it up on the south side, and Raffles agreed. Perhaps he took too much to himself, I don't know, but he was the decision maker after all, and history isn't written by coolies.'

Coleman smiled wryly and looked at Robert.

'By the saints, I still remember the effort it took to fill in the land, pick and shovel, Chinese, Indian and Malays labouring for one rupee a day. Whatever is written after I'm long gone, it was other men than Raffles who built this town, no matter what his madame says. It was a great and exciting enterprise. Where we stand was the temenggong's *kampong*. Look at it now. Soon I shall have completed the new bridge and will open up the road in Kampong Chulia.'

He extinguished his cigar underfoot.

'Perhaps it is fair to say that Raffles was a clever man, energetic certainly. It was said he could write one letter while dictating two others! His attempts at economic reform in Java were muddled and ill-conceived, though, to be fair, he had little time to see them through. I suppose he was a man of ideas; carrying them out was his shortcoming. He was not cut out for administering a fledgling colony, despite his letters to Milady Somerset. Farquhar was, Crawfurd was, Bonham is. Really, Raffles was at his most petty in his attacks on Farquhar. Well, all water under the bridge now. Fortunately he spent little time here and departed soon enough that no harm was done.'

Robert had never heard Coleman so voluble.

'Bejasus, I love this town, I really do. For a man on his mettle the possibilities are great. Singapore is like no other place in the empire. It will survive not through imperial patronage, for we shall surely have none. Not a single taxpayer in all his vastness needs fear that he shall pay for us. No, by God, we shall thrive entirely by our own efforts and industry.'

Robert knew what he meant. Singapore had given him the chance to make his name and fortune. Fatherless and without influential relatives, a man such as himself would have stood little chance anywhere else. Its very newness, its simple imperatives, its total lack of importance to the powers in India and back home: all these things meant men like him had a chance.

They wandered back to the fives court and sat on a stone bench facing the river. George lit another small cheroot and they sat in companionable silence. When George had finished, he flicked the cigar away and turned to Robert.

'Well, lad, Shilah's not pregnant, yet. Seems like a blooming miracle to me. I've had a talk with her and so has Takouhi. She seems adamant that you're the one.'

In fact Coleman had tried to frighten her off. He had explained what she could expect from this relationship with the white policeman. She could not expect marriage; she must put that thought out of her head. As for children, they would have to be got rid of or raised in some out-of-the-way place. Eventually he would certainly take a white wife. Takouhi, too, had tried to change her mind. But there was nothing for it. So she had given Shilah a bottle of neem oil and told her how to use it.

'There you have it, lad. So next week we should go over to Middle Road and look at some of my new houses. In the meantime, do me the favour of leaving her alone. She won't be pleased, but she knows she can't be coming over to your bungalow and, as sure as sure, I don't want to see your ugly face skulking around my place. Within a fortnight everything should be settled. Can you do that, Robbie?'

Robert beamed. 'Auch Aye, I can, George.' And grabbing Coleman's hand he began pumping it up and down. George slapped him on the back and, waving, began to make his way back to what was, nominally and literally, his street.

# 9

Long before dawn a group of a dozen coolies were gathered together and began a march out of the town. The track took them along South Bridge Road, past the jail, over the canal and across a rickety hump-backed bridge. Turning onto a wide street, they had their first glimpse of the European town. The path followed the contour of the hill, then branched off into the jungle. Here a guard gave them some bamboo twine to tie on their straw shoes for, he told them, the going would get a little rough.

A *little* rough, thought Qian after only ten minutes.

Rain overnight had made the ground muddy, and they all slipped from time to time or tripped over the ropey roots of the trees. Everyone was slick with sweat in the humidity. Fat raindrops dripped noisily, hoots and calls erupted, sticks cracked, and the forest breathed a hot, fetid breath.

Going over and under trunks of trees, zigzagging through swamps and standing water, they slapped constantly at insects. One of the guards showed them how to put mud on their hands and faces to protect themselves from this pestilential barrage and how to tie their trousers tightly to their legs to keep off leeches. The two beaters in front slashed incessantly at the undergrowth or into the puddled water to frighten snakes but, nevertheless, they saw several long green shapes slither slowly, seemingly fearlessly, away. One guard killed a sleeping six-foot-long snake, black and mottled, with his long-handled axe. Holding it up over a stick, he told the coolies that this was the most poisonous snake on the island, after the sea snakes, which were all deadly. Later he pointed out a massive python fast asleep on a small hillock, its middle engorged with its last dinner.

When they crossed rivulets, the guards would check on both sides of the muddy banks for crocodiles.

Qian realised that such a track was impenetrable for police, soldiers and white men. Out here, the Chinese ruled unchallenged. From time to time they passed other men coming and going, carrying baskets on their heads or slung from shoulder poles. Zhen was silent, although the other coolies chattered to each other to keep up their spirits. The sun had got up in the sky, and the humidity was rising as steam from the jungle floor. After a couple of hours they were called to stop, and a group of men appeared through the trees in a clearing. Hearing the noises, a pack of dogs rushed out, barking and snapping. Confusion was finally allayed, and the men called for them to proceed.

The group was motioned to sit under the shade of a jackfruit tree, and pumpkin and roasted potatoes were brought out. Water was passed around in dirty cups which smelt of liquor. The guards went off to eat their meal with the owner and, as the men ate and dozed, Qian took a look around.

'This place is damn well guarded,' he whispered. Dozens of shields, several iron tridents, twenty or thirty daggers and six or seven pairs of white men's trousers were stacked against the wall inside an outhouse. The trousers looked as if they'd just been laundered and taken either from the dhobi or a white man's house.

'Been some thieving too, by the looks,' muttered Zhen.

A scrawny man emerged from the wooden house and addressed them, staring at them through rheumy eyes. He was Teocheow and spoke with a thick accent, using some words the Hokkien group did not understand.

'Brothers, you are welcome here. This place is called To Tang Leng. It is far from the *ang mo* settlement. Here your brothers will help you, teach you the work and supply you with your needs. This is a plantation of gambier and pepper which you will tend. Food will be supplied to you, and there is liquor and opium at the *kangkar* stores. You can go there once a week. There are some women there also. Others will work on the opium farm, which is an hour from here. Soon there will be the initiation ceremony, where you will pass through the Hung Gate and swear loyalty to the *kongsi*. Is there any man here who does not wish to swear?'

He waited a few minutes, then smiled thinly.

'Well, go with the brother; he will show you where you will sleep.'

He turned and went back into the hut.

Most of the men seemed happy to have things settled. Work, grog, women; this they had understood. It was better than they had imagined. They would work off their year and soon be able to save some money for their families back home. In a few years they would return to China.

Zhen and Qian looked at each other. They wandered to one side of the compound to take a piss. Zhen took aim at a large red ant.

'Did you see how they mark the trail?' he asked.

Qian was surprised by the question, for he had noticed nothing in the exhaustion and difficulty of the march. He shook his head.

'If you look carefully along the ground, there are painted rocks about every ten feet or so. On this trail they are coloured red. My guess is that different trails have different colours. Sometimes, too, the big trees are stained with three red lines high up, like those over there. Didn't you notice anything, sweetheart?'

Qian looked up and saw the mark on the tree trunk but refused to rise to Zhen's joshing.

'Well, we shall bide our time and learn what goes on here. The boss men seem to have everything organised to make sure these stupid coolies never leave. When they are sick on grog and opium they will never return to China, unless it is in the afterlife.'

They joined the others and made their way to a large attap-covered building, where rough cots were set out. Baskets of rice were stacked at one end, raised off the floor. Their first job was to put the rice into rat-proof wooden containers near the cook house. They all set to work.

'Never mind, ah,' Zhen confided to Qian. 'Soon the ceremony will be held, I shall meet the headman and we shall get out of this god-awful backwater and into the town where the real money is made.'

And where a woman with violet eyes is waiting, he thought, but this he did not voice. The prospect of an improbable liaison with this foreign woman had begun to occupy his thoughts and, despite himself, his dreams. From his book of poetry he read often now the verses of his favourite Taoist poet, who could contemplate the empty wind but still find a place for love, the old refrain, the eternal wellspring of passion, as old as time itself, made new in every new lover's heart.

'A lovely maiden roaming
The wild dark valley through
Culls from the shining waters
Lilies and lotus blue
With leaves the peach trees are laden
The wind sighs through the haze
And the willows wave their shadows
Down the oriole-haunted ways
As, passion-tranced, I follow,
I hear the old refrain
Of Spring's eternal glory
That was old and is young again.'

He suspected he was in danger of becoming passion-tranced.

# 10

Monkeys watched from the tree tops as the group made its way along the track. Wild almond and cinnamon, red-headed flame of the forest, the spiny-spiked toddy palm, glossy *pong pong*, pagoda-shaped *pulai*, dense- domed *jambu laut*, the fabulous columned *jelutong*, stretching high into the sky and a myriad of other trees spread on either side. The arms of the *tembusu* trees closed the sky overhead forming a cool canopy.

Charlotte, Miss Scott and her brother, together with Takouhi, were seated in a gharry pulled by two sturdy ponies. These were led by one of Captain Scott's Indian syces. Robert, Jemadar Kapoor and Mr Coleman rode their horses alongside. From time to time Coleman would make a comment, and the group would burst into laughter.

They had spent a pleasant morning and lunch with Captain Scott on his plantation. His house stood amidst orchards of spice trees and groves of purple cocoa, rambutan, duku, mangosteen, durian and graceful betel-nut palms. The road ran out abruptly at his gate and beyond lay impenetrable jungle.

He was an amiable old man and had made them all welcome. One of his own chickens had been killed and prepared; rice, a mild green curry, pickles and yams had been served.

The previous evening Robert had checked on the police post on the far side of the road and found the two peons fast asleep. He rebuked them mildly, for he did not know what they would have done had any attack taken place. Sometimes he felt it was a losing battle with his tiny band.

Captain Scott had his own weapons. In this isolated place he was well aware that he had to look out for himself. After a discussion with Robert, he had decided it was no place for the children, and it was agreed to take them into the town to board with Mrs Whittle at her school and receive what education they could. Laurie would attend the institution which Mr Coleman was extending. Captain Scott, though a kindly man, was a bachelor and had found the children trying. He was not sorry to see them leave.

Charlotte had been pleased by the unexpected arrival of Mr Coleman and Takouhi, and they had driven out of town on the new road. Near the town, gangs of convicts were still working on filling in the sides, creating ditches and stabilising the centre with broken rocks and pebbles. They stopped from time to time while George addressed the headman of each of the groups. Charlotte was surprised to see how fit and lean these men looked despite their hard labour.

To her enquiries, Coleman said, 'Good food, decent living conditions and a hope for a better life. These men are sent from India for years of penal servitude. Bejaysus, for most of them have stolen from hunger or such like. Sure, and poverty can make criminals of us all. The Calcutta government dumps them on us, but I don't mind, I do not. I can make use of them very well and teach 'em trades. They police themselves, and many stay and marry local brides. The Indian convict women work in service and are snapped up for marriage.'

He waved to a contingent that was resting by the roadside, smoking.

'Robert recruits the men for his new force, for they're as reliable as you'll find here. The troublemakers or hard types are whittled out and generally made to see the error of their ways. When they work in the outer areas like this lot, they have their own huts and strong fences to keep out the beasties, and I leave them to themselves. There's little chance of rebellion, as the old Indian caste system ensures a complete lack of unison and cooperation. It works a rare treat, and when I feel like a good curry I invite myself, for Takouhi doesn't care for it.'

Takouhi shook her head and wrinkled her nose. She smiled at George as if he was a foolish child stating the obvious, and said something in Malay. To Charlotte she said, 'George very ignorant man and silly-billy.' They all laughed.

'Yer know, she's just learnt that word. Underneath her exotic looks beats the heart of a true Armenian, which wouldn't be so bad, but there's a touch too much Dutch. Her tastes run to the most dreadful bland. It's a constant source of trouble between us.'

Takouhi was dressed today in a white and brown *kebaya* and *sarong* with loose leather sandals on her tattooed feet. Takouhi had told Charlotte this was *mehndi*, the art of staining with *pachar*. She did not know the English name. George said it was called henna and, with a wink, that the sight of it on a maiden's skin made men wild. Charlotte could imagine this to be so, for it exerted a strange charm even for her.

Although it had rained, the track was reasonably passable and now, on the return journey, had dried off well enough to make going easy. Robert pointed out some graves off the roadside as they passed by. The Chinese graves were particularly interesting, with their horseshoe shapes and large mounds. Further along they passed a Sumatran burial site with simple longhouse-shaped tombs. From time to time they saw trees wound with coloured threads, enshrined with flowers and incense: temples to invisible spirits and ghosts of the land.

Suddenly the horses grew restless, stamping their feet and tossing their heads. Monkeys screeched urgently across the tree tops, and the small group turned their eyes upwards in alarm. The sharp cracking sounds of rapid movement rustled through the undergrowth. Their heads turned as each new noise erupted around them. Then, the jungle fell ominously silent. Jemadar Kapoor whispered tersely to Robert.

Robert addressed Charlotte in French.

'*Ecoute-moi bien*, you must stay very calm and in a minute may have to see the children stay quiet. We think there is a tiger in the vicinity.'

Charlotte's hand flew to her mouth, and her heart began to beat wildly. She held herself under control with great effort and put her arm around Elizabeth Scott, who looked bewildered. Coleman dismounted and explained to Takouhi, who calmly moved over to sit squashed up next to Laurie. Charlotte whispered to the children and put a hand over Elizabeth's mouth. Fortunately the youngsters made no sound, Laurie contenting himself with looking around curiously. The men drew their weapons and waited. The horses continued to shuffle and whinny.

From the shadows at the roadside about a hundred feet away, the animal appeared. The *jemadar* handed the reins of his horse to Robert, dropped to one knee and took aim at the tiger. The tiger looked in their direction but paid them scant attention and padded into the middle of the road. Here, he flopped down noisily and emitted a low groan, followed by a great yawn.

Coleman whispered to Robert, 'He looks fat; I think he has eaten, for there's plenty of wild boar in the jungle round here. Perhaps if we shoot in the air he may be scared off. Otherwise we may be in for a long wait while he has his nap.'

Before they could decide what to do, a sudden commotion in the jungle caused the tiger to jump to his feet. He gave a deep, ferocious growl. Within seconds chaos erupted. The horses pawed the ground and reared into the air. Coleman's horse pulled his reins and started at a gallop back down the path. The tiger gave another great growl and began loping towards them. Elizabeth screamed, and Charlotte and Takouhi looked at each other in terror. Laurie, demented child, stood up and began waving at the beast. Charlotte pulled him down. It was all George and Robert could do to control the ponies and keep the carriage still. The Indian syce ran to hide behind the carriage.

Kapoor gripped his rifle and fired at the animal, but his shot was wide. It served, however, to stop the tiger in its tracks. Then, to their collective amazement, a wild-looking man, hair flowing round his face and shoulders, jumped out onto the path and took aim. The tiger, sensing danger, turned and jumped as the shot bit into the road. In a flash he had had enough and with another roar fled into the jungle. The sounds of his crashing retreat could be heard for several minutes.

The wild man stood checking his rifle ruefully. Coleman called to him.

'Carroll, for gawd's sake, you're a lousy shot. *Tu tires mal,*' he added in Irish-sounding French. 'Ladies and gentlemen, may I present Mr Carroll, a Frenchman from Canada, tiger hunter and all-round mad ol' blaggard.'

In the carriage, the passengers simply stared. Charlotte thought Mr Coleman must be as mad as the tiger hunter. The men, however, laughed with relief, and Kapoor sent the syce to retrieve George's horse, which had stopped not far back and was now chewing absently on the verge.

Carroll was a big man, over six feet tall, dressed in a green *batik* jacket and black cotton trousers. On his head he wore a flea-bitten hunting cap with several feathers poked into the brim. Grey, stringy hair flowed about his shoulders, and a thick beard fell to his waist. Halfway up, this mass of hair was drawn together with a large gold ring. Below the ring hung little plaits of different sizes. Shouldering his rifle, he approached the carriage. The children's eyes goggled. Charlotte, calmer now, surmised from his musky odour that any washing that took place on his person was purely at the whim of the rain.

Robert had heard about Carroll and was pleased to meet him. He had brought several dead tigers into the settlement. He had hunted in Canada for twenty years and feared no creature except humans. His arrival in Singapore was a mystery; where he lived in the jungle was a mystery, and rumours about him abounded. He made a good living, for the governor paid a hundred dollars for bringing in a dead tiger, and then Carroll sold the flesh, pelt, bones and all the rest to the Chinese or Indians, who paid highly for an animal which guaranteed sexual potency, strength and long life. There would be money for many a year, for tigers swam over the strait from Johore to hunt pigs, deer and Chinamen and would be doing so after Carroll was dead and gone.

The men exchanged a few words, and then Coleman mounted his horse, bid farewell to the Canadian and set off down the track to check on his convict labour force. Kapoor put the trembling syce on his horse and took the reins of the ponies. Robert walked some distance behind, talking with Carroll. Monkeys called shrilly in the forest.

As they came within sight of the settlement, Carroll left them and disappeared into the undergrowth. Robert was quiet, deep in thought, for he had been alarmed by their conversation. Carroll had told him that there were large groups of Chinese in the interior. He thought they might even have a large fort up towards the Seletar River, with five to six thousand men. Robert decided he would speak to the governor, but what they all could do about it he had no idea. Not for the first time, Robert felt how precarious was the European position in this town.

# 11

When they got back to the settlement the children were left with Mrs Whittle, and Takouhi and Charlotte made their way to the institution. Their route ran the length of the freshwater stream, past the church and the end of the plain. Here, the carriage went up over a charming stone bridge at the sea's edge, where a mighty banyan tree stood, and followed a curved drive to the entrance. The building had been recently rebuilt and extended by Coleman and his men from the unfinished original building which had been a tumbledown eyesore. Covered in jungle and stagnant marsh, it had become a hide-out for thieves. In this condition it had lain for some ten years, offering newcomers to Singapore the surprising aspect of an ancient castle ruin. Now the jungle excesses had been cleared, and palms and trees occupied its vast grounds. The far wing was still under construction, and the chinking and clinking of stonemasons could be heard. It gleamed white with *chunam*, its shutters freshly green. A low fence ran round the sea side, and it looked over a grassy space to the sandy beach and, from there, a view to the to and fro of small boats, the ships at anchor, the glittering sea and islands. Beyond the institution, large houses and luxuriant gardens lined the length of Beach Road: princely mansions which George had erected a few years before, occupied by the richer merchants of the town. The sea breeze was delicious after the closeness of the forest. Charlotte could hardly believe the episode with the tiger had occurred less than an hour before. This town was full of surprises.

As they arrived, the women turned to see Coleman gallop over the bridge. Jumping from his horse, he approached the carriage. Putting his hands round Takouhi's slender waist, he lifted her lightly. Without a word she lay a hand on his shoulder as he held her just a moment. When she smiled down at him, he released her gently to the ground.

Charlotte could clearly see the deep tenderness between Takouhi and George. A palpable aura of unassuming romance surrounded them. She was momentarily envious. She recalled, suddenly, the encounter in the temple and the face of the young man. Surely something had happened then. But what?

Coleman turned to Charlotte, bowed and held out his hand to help her down.

'One of life's little pleasures, and you never know when the tigers'll get you. Except for the dance floor, whenever else do you get the chance to hold beautiful ladies without impropriety?'

He gave a wink but was careful to hold her hand only briefly. Charlotte found herself wishing he had lifted her, too, wanting to feel his hands on her waist. Ashamed, she flushed slightly. Though she had no idea what George had said, Takouhi noted Charlotte's discomfort, stepped up and took her hand. Charlotte guessed she was not unaware of the effect that George could have on women.

'*Alamah*, George, you silly-billy, go away.'

Coleman made an exaggerated flourish and bowed extravagantly. Leading his horse, he disappeared around the building.

They entered the cool precincts of the institution, and Charlotte again looked in admiration at the elegant art of Coleman's designs. They mounted the broad staircase and strolled along the tiled corridor where the shutters were all thrown open to admit the breeze. Soon they arrived at a room which gave a wide view over the sea. Takouhi drew her gauzy silk shawl over her hair and knocked very lightly on the open door.

At the sound a man looked up and smiled widely: Munshi Abdullah bin Abdul Kadir. He had, Charlotte saw, the physiognomy of a Tamil from southern Hindustan and was dressed in the style of Malacca Tamils. He was spare, with a slight stoop, his complexion bronze, his face oval with a high nose and a lightly bearded chin. One eye squinted outwards a little. George had told Charlotte that he had the vigour and pride of his Arab heritage, the subtlety of his Hindu mother, but in language and sympathies he was Malay.

Putting down his pen, the munshi rose and greeted them, hands together in a *salaam*. In English he bade them sit and called a young boy to bring tea. Introductions were made, and he agreed to take on

Charlotte as a Malay pupil.

'Munshi, everybody so sorry about family in Malacca.'

This was in English, but Takouhi added some sentences in Malay, and bowed her head.

She had already told Charlotte that the munshi had lost his wife and a daughter in childbirth not long ago. He could no longer bear to live in the house where they had died, so he had sold everything at a great loss and moved permanently to Singapore.

'There is pain in this but, praise be to Allah, they await me in paradise. This is the balm for my heart. Now I have my new house in Kampong Malacca, my children are with me, my son is a good scholar and helps me teach. There are many blessings,' the munshi responded.

To Charlotte's consternation a large tear slid down his cheek. She herself began to feel tears well, and Takouhi dabbed her eyes. For a few minutes they all sobbed very quietly and without any embarrassment.

'My word, Abdullah, you certainly have a way with the ladies.' It was George, and beside him was Mr Moor, the headmaster of the institution.

The munshi wiped his face with a large handkerchief and rose from his chair.

'How do you do?' Mr Moor greeted the ladies. 'Pleathe allow me to show you the thchool.'

'Moor studied for holy orders,' said George. 'He'd have made a fine preacher, don't you think?'

The munshi shook his head at these antics. Coleman and Moor both grinned at Abdullah and then, gathering in the ladies, began a tour of the institution.

Mr and Mrs Moor and their three children occupied several rooms in the western wing. He took care of fourteen boys who boarded at the school. Below these apartments were the Chinese schoolroom and a printing room. The central body of the building was divided into rooms for teaching Malay and English (on the ground floor) and a library and meeting room (on the second). The headmaster explained that there was an upper school, with some fifty boys who came from Calcutta. There were also over a hundred Chinese, more than half of whom were Christians, thirty Kling and fifty Malay boys. A Bugis class had been abandoned for lack of students. Invitations to the Malay chiefs to send their sons had come to nothing.

He was delighted at the suggestion that Charlotte should help his wife and the Reverend Stanford in teaching the English classes.

Removed a small distance from the main building and sheltered by trees was a large attap shed for play, with a gymnasium, a small fives court and a quoit ground. Some of the boarders were running about the grounds, but the shed was deserted, for the school was open from nine in the morning until two in the afternoon.

They stood for a while watching the comings and goings of bullock carts gathering stones from a hillock behind the school. Mr Moor explained that the trustees had advertised that anyone leasing land near the school and wishing to erect substantial buildings could freely take stones from this hillock.

'There is a great dethire by everyone here that Coleman's buildinth should be emulated so that Thingapore can prethent a civilithed fathe, as Mr Raffelth wished.'

Takouhi looked at him and then George. Coleman grinned. Charlotte hid a smile behind her hand and thanked Mr Moor graciously. She was looking forward to helping such a man.

# 12

Zhen and Qian were sick of work on the plantation: chopping and gathering vast quantities of wood to heat the water for boiling the gambier, tending the damn stuff, then distributing the lees as fertiliser for the pepper plants. The fire was so intense you couldn't get within twelve feet of it. It was hot and exhausting work, and they had both had more than enough.

At the end of the first week they had been guided to the *kangkar*, the three-hutted settlement where they could get the local palm toddy and opium. The women were kept in a shaky hut in the forest. After a couple of drinks of *arrack*, which they both found unexpectedly tasty, Zhen and Qian had gone to investigate this place, where men were crouched in a line. Three would go in at once. Inside the dark hut, the reek of dirt and sex was overpowering. Three women were lounging against the wall waiting. They were naked and filthy, their eyes as vacant as those of dead fish. One looked to be pregnant. Qian had never seen women like these, very black, with squat noses and large breasts and hips. He had no desire to touch any of them and, looking at Zhen, was relieved to see that he, too, was appalled at the condition of these creatures.

The smell of opium and alcohol hung heavy in the hut. The third man who had entered was put off by his companions' disgust, and they all left. Nobody could tell them where these wretched women came from, except that they had been sold as slaves at the Bugis slave market.

When they heard that the accounts-keeper at one of the opium farms had died, Qian volunteered to take his place. He feared all the backbreaking labour on the gambier farm would kill him. Zhen simply stepped up to the headman, looked him in the eye and said he was going too. The headman—a small, thin addict with a constant cough—merely shrugged. They plodded through the jungle for an hour until they came to the opium farm.

Zhen had seen opium aplenty. He had tried it but he knew that it was a hard mistress. His father, clever pharmacist though he was, eventually became addicted, and this, in the long run, had brought misery and bankruptcy to their family. Opium was the reason he and his brothers had sought out the *kongsi*, the reason his mother's health had been ruined from hunger and worry, the reason he was here. Now, if he could, he would grow rich on it. The irony was not lost on him.

While Qian settled down to the quiet business of learning the organisation of the accounts, which seemed to be in poor order, Zhen learned the process of making the cooked opium, *chandu*. He was told to place the raw, gummy opium in a pot with water to cover it. This was boiled until it liquefied, and then he was set the task of straining it through gauzy cotton to remove the twigs, dirt and little stones. This strained mixture was set aside, and the impurities were reboiled and strained until all opium had been thoroughly removed. He learned that a hundred grams of raw opium could give seventy-five grams of *chandu*. Then the men sat around the pot of purified opium as it bubbled slowly over a low flame until all the water had evaporated and only a thick black paste was left. Now the *chandu* was ready to be rolled into cannonballs for shipment to the town or distributed to the *kangkars* throughout the interior.

This work was so easy that they fell into a sort of rhythm with the other six men on the farm. Supervision was minimal. Since the previous account-keeper had died, no one had visited the farm, and the men, taking advantage of this, had been stashing small bundles of *chandu* in the jungle. Qian saw this in the accounts but could not stop it, and Zhen did not care.

At the end of a few days, the temptation to share several pipes with the other men was overwhelming.

In a jungle clearing a little way from the huts, the men lay on their sides in a circle while they 'kicked the gong around'. One was designated the *chandu* chef, and he skillfully rolled and cooked each of the *yen pok* pills. He warmed the pipe to exactly the right temperature, inhaled deeply and passed the pipe along.

Each *yen pok* pill lasted about one to three minutes; they consumed about ten. Qian initially felt a shock at the bitter taste, but the smoke was sweet and pungent. He felt a loosening in his muscles and, as the pipe passed around, it loosened tongues as well. Men who barely said a word all day began to talk of their villages and the heroic deeds they had performed there, tales real or imaginary of the foes they had vanquished, the number of women they'd had. Even Zhen suddenly began to babble incoherently about some women he'd known and the poems he had written. Then the men drifted off into dreams.

Qian, who had smoked very little, awoke suddenly, befuddled by his surroundings. Men on either side of him were snoring. It was evening. A low growl came from the jungle, and he froze with fear. Frantically looking for Zhen, he knocked the man next to him, who awoke. In an instant a huge tiger had padded into the clearing. Qian could smell its musty odour, hear its rattling breath. To his horror, the tiger seized the leg of one of the sleeping Chinamen in its jaws and crunched down, dragging the man into the jungle. The victim awoke with a curdling scream, and all the other men leapt up. Qian was frozen with fear as men rushed around grabbing sticks and cudgels from the camp. The tiger did not reappear, and no one was going after it to try to save the hapless victim, whose screams could be heard receding into the darkness. Zhen grabbed Qian, and they ran back to the huts and began to light fires around the encampment.

The next morning, one of the guards came to check the camp. When he called, Zhen came to the door of the hut and explained what had happened. The boss simply shrugged.

'Ready yourselves; get the accounts together. Master Liang's man will come today.'

He called for tea and food, and the men emerged slowly from the hut and began the business of the day.

Within an hour, a small group of men walked out of the jungle. One of them went into a hut with Qian, and when they came out some time later, he said to the men,

'This man, Qian, is the new headman here for now. You obey him.'

The man handed Qian some pieces of red paper with black writing.

After they had left, Zhen went up to Qian, who handed him a paper and distributed two others. The final one, destined for the man who had been the tiger's dinner, had been discarded. The notices told them the initiation ceremony would take place in eight days.

'Well, well, headman, eh, you girlie. How did you wangle that?'

'No need for such amazement, my thunder friend. I'm learning fast. We both know people from my village. I told him that the dead guy kept lousy accounts which I have been putting in order and that I have now stopped the pilfering which was endemic until I arrived. Then I mentioned that you, with enormous bravery, had saved the other coolies from the tiger. I also asked him to give our compliments to Master Liang, whom we both met in the temple at Guan Soon Street and that we are looking forward to seeing him again at the initiation ceremony.'

Zhen looked at his companion appreciatively, held up the red paper and made the *kongsi* sign for heaven with his hand. Qian made a circle with this thumb and first finger and kept the other three straight as Zhen had shown him. Heaven and earth. They both laughed.

# 13

Mr Coleman was holding a ball. An invitation had been handed in by George's Indian syce. The date was fifteen days hence, and everyone was invited, including Robert's two European policemen, William and Thomas, and three of the Indian *jemadars*. Robert told Charlotte that Coleman's soirées regularly outshone the governor's and that almost everyone of any consequence was likely to attend. To repeated questions he said he thought that the temenggong might put in an appearance, the governor certainly, and also Colonel Murchison, head of the regiment, most of the Europeans, some important Indian merchants and the leading Chinese and Arab merchants. Several ships were in port, and he thought that most of the officers would also be invited. This information simply put her into a state of high nervousness.

'Women will be in dreadfully short supply. The ideal opportunity for you to pick up a husband, *chère petite soeur*. George likes to throw the local lads and lasses together now and again. Not being married himself, he's very keen on the wedded state.'

He grinned at her and left.

She wanted to kick him and could not comprehend his blasé attitude, especially since the invitation had been accompanied by an announcement that the only dance of the evening would be the three-step waltz and that the services of the famous Count Papanti had been engaged for dance instruction. Charlotte had no idea how to perform this dance, considered scandalous by her Scottish relatives and, to the best of her knowledge, neither did Robert. Perhaps he already knew about this Papanti fellow. She shook her head and made her way across the plain to Tir Uaidhne. Here she received the information she needed.

It would be a very big ball, maybe a hundred people. Takouhi's brother, Tigran, was coming over from Batavia in his ship. Count

Papanti was passing through Singapore, visiting Marie Balestier, wife of the American consul, and Charlotte Keaseberry, both old friends of his patron, Mrs Otis of Boston, who had recently introduced the waltz to America. Dance instruction would be held at George's house for several evenings before the ball. Charlotte was quite thrilled at this news, for she had heard of the 'wicked' dance sweeping Paris and London where, for the first time, men and women danced in each other's arms.

They would need new clothes, Takouhi announced. Up they went to Takouhi's elegant bedroom, where a huge four-poster bed draped with gauzy netting was covered in an array of silks, satins and chiffons the colours of the rainbow. Charlotte thought this a beautiful room, with its curved bay windows overlooking a grove of palms. To one side stood an English desk of inlaid walnut. On the other, a low cabinet of drawers above which hung a painting. At least she thought it was a painting, but when she went up to it she found it was made of cloth, stained with pigments. Swirling shades blended witchingly together to depict a woman of great beauty standing amidst clouds and foam, fabulous fish and sea creatures at her feet.

'This is Loro Kidul, Queen of the South Seas. New sultans must make her first wife. Very powerful goddess.'

Takouhi spoke in hushed tones and, putting her hands together, bowed before the image. A long wooden dish lay on the cabinet under the painting, filled with jasmine flowers and small candles.

'This made by *batik*, don' know English word. Put wax then colour. Mmm, difficult. I show you another day. Like my *sarong*, yes?'

Charlotte nodded, yes; she had seen these cloths in the market, marvelled at their intricacy.

Takouhi turned to the bed and took Charlotte's hand. 'Please choose. My brother send these for me last ship. My tailor make for you. Today we spend all day for this. By Hanuman's tail, it be fun. On this day I also wear European dress. I like sometimes very much. George always help me. He has paper with pictures. He know we like to make new dress.'

She went into a large closet and emerged with several magazines. One was in French and had colour plates of the fashions in Paris. Takouhi, she knew, had a passion for French things and had begged Charlotte to teach her and Meda the language.

They pored over the magazines, Charlotte translating with Takouhi repeating the words and laughing a silvery laugh. When Meda came home from school, she squealed with pleasure to see Charlotte, and her mother had to reprimand her for such noise, but soon they were all again laughing at French words, wrapping themselves in the stuff which lay scattered around.

Even Evangeline Barbie had agreed to dress up for the occasion, albeit somewhat more modestly than the present fashion decreed. And she had strictly refused to waltz. Evangeline was cook and housekeeper to the Reverend Jean-Marie Baudrel, head of the Catholic mission in Singapore, and Reverend John Lee, the padre of the Chinese mission, as well as those members of the church who passed through and required shelter.

Charlotte accompanied her to the Catholic chapel after her final fittings, and they chatted excitedly.

The chapel was a plain wooden building in the middle of a large piece of ground in Brass Bassa Road. The parochial house occupied a corner compound at nearby Church Street. This, too, was built in wood and raised on brick pillars. Around the chapel and its little schoolhouse, the jungle had been cleared, but there were many little groves of coral trees, yellow kassod, saga and tamarind.

Today, Evangeline was acquainting Charlotte with the workings of the schoolhouse. Charlotte had grown to like her, for they could converse easily in French and, despite her own lack of interest in any religious curriculum, she was happy to help teach the young boys their letters.

The last weeks had been quite hectic. Charlotte's Malay studies with the munshi had been most successful. He was a wonderful and patient teacher and a man of infinite good grace and temper.

She practised with Azam and Asan and improved quickly. Even Robert was surprised at her swift progress.

Munshi Abdullah was pleased to have found a student, so rare, who was interested in the poetics as well as the practicalities of Malay. Once the traders and agency clerks had mastered enough to carry on business, they came to him no more. Together, Charlotte and Abdullah talked of poetry, and she showed him a small book of Shakespeare's sonnets, which he took home to read. He confessed them very difficult to understand and showed her some Malay *pantun*—quatrains which were similar but, he felt, easier to grasp.

He set her a task to translate one. She spent several nights saying it quietly to herself:

> '*Laju laju perahu laju*
> *Lajunya sempai Suraya*
> *Lupa kain, lupa baju*
> *Tetapi jangan lupakan saya*'

Eventually, after much work, she had decided not on a literal but on a poetic version to show to the munshi:

> 'Speed, speed, swift boat upon your way
> The pace for Surabaya's set
> Forget your coat or wrap you may
> But me I pray do not forget.'

He had been delighted. Charlotte was more than happy to have found someone to share her love of language and was sorry when their time came so rapidly to an end each day.

In addition, the munshi was a wonderful teller of tales. He had been Raffles' scribe, present at all Singapore's most important moments.

He had laughed when he told her how Raffles had advised him to take up some land in Commercial Square which could but increase in value.

'Poor scared thing that I was, I felt I could not afford it for lots were selling for up to twelve hundred dollars and, in any case, I did not believe that Singapore would become so densely populated. You see what a poor thing I am, no foresight whatsoever. How would I pay? I thought, but no money ever changed hands. How would I build a stone house, when no house was required? How would I manage to return to Malacca? All these silly worries. So I made a bad mistake.'

At the Catholic chapel, Charlotte was drawn to the Reverend John Lee, a handsome Cantonese who had been educated in Penang. He was a charismatic preacher, there could be no doubt, and he was responsible for a great number of Chinese conversions. He had an aura of invincibility, as if faith really could move mountains. His gentle manner reassured her, had she been in any doubt, that it was not only the Malays but Chinese men, too, who had a soul.

Hundreds of Chinese coolies went to mass on Sunday, and a small chapel had opened recently at Bukit Timah to tend to the needs of the growing flock in the interior. Father Baudrel had proposed a new church, and an appeal for funds had gone out. The French community was a tiny, close-knit group and she liked her time at the chapel, speaking French and occasionally learning some Chinese with the boys who boarded with the priests.

As Charlotte and Evangeline were teaching one afternoon, a sudden clamour arose from the garden and two Chinese men rushed into the chapel, bleeding and covered in dirt and mud. Evangeline and the children cried out, and Father Lee came from the sacristy to find a chaotic scene. Water was sent for, and the women began to tend the men's wounds as Father Lee interrogated them. The children were all taken to the parochial house by one of the older Chinese boys.

'They say they were attacked. Thirty or forty men came out of the jungle with *parangs*, knives and sticks, and set about the farm. They have killed three others, and these two fled. Two or three days ago they say. The attackers burnt everything to the ground.'

Father Lee was simply translating as the men spoke. Now he looked up at Father Baudrel, who had just entered the chapel.

'Reprisals against the Catholic Chinese, most certainly. We interfere with the power and control of the Chinese societies over the plantations of the interior. How can we protect these poor souls?'

In response to a message, Dr Montgomerie and Robert soon arrived and joined Charlotte at the chapel. Dr Montgomerie had the patients moved to the parochial house. After talking to the fathers, Robert and Charlotte left to make their way back home.

'Nothing to be done by my men, of course,' Robert told Charlotte. 'I may station some peons out at Bukit Timah with some weapons, but really what can we do against such numbers in the jungle? I have told Father Baudrel that these men who convert are placing themselves in danger. If possible they should try to seek work in town, or at least very near town. The far-flung areas are impossible. This situation will only get worse as time goes on, mark my words.'

As they were passing Tir Uaidhne, they called in and were invited to stop for refreshments. Talk invariably turned to the ball, now all but a few nights away. Robert, who had matters of violence on his mind and who had had more than he could bear about this wretched ball, left the ladies to their pleasures and made his way back to the courthouse for a word with the governor.

Yet the ball stayed on his mind; he couldn't rid himself of this nuisance. The dance instruction evenings with M. le Comte Papanti had been unbearably irritating. Robert was a fair dancer when it came to quadrilles, but this waltz was a difficult proposition. The man had to guide the woman, and he had stepped on Charlotte's toes so often she had smacked him with her fan. The ladies and the officers of the regiment seemed to have grasped the thing right away, and Colonel Murchison and Coleman were positively annoying as they swept their partners round the hall. The count, to Robert's horror, had insisted on showing him personally. '*Avanti, Roberto*!' He shuddered at the memory of holding this perfumed little man in his arms and cringed as he saw how the ladies fairly swooned when the count guided them through the steps. Even Charlotte had not seemed immune. Evangeline, sensible woman, had refused the instruction but was happy to play the waltz melodies on Coleman's piano. Coleman had given out the latest music sheets from Herr Lanner and Herr Strauss to the regimental band. There was nothing for it, Robert knew he would have to dance at the ball and now, as he made his way, he directed a kick at a stray dog which happened across his path. What a bother it all was, and no Shilah either. He had kept his word to George and not been near her. Fortunately, the rooms in the house at Middle Road were almost ready, his birthday and his inheritance were only a week away.

Leaving his horse with the boy, Robert climbed the curved staircase of the courthouse to Bonham's office on the first floor, its three windows overlooking the river.

The quality which Robert valued most of all in Bonham was

his broadness of mind, for he had cast aside, as far as he dared, the monopoly of patronage to men of the East India Company. From this he and Coleman had benefitted in their appointments to government positions. Without him, Robert knew, no matter what their merits they would have been passed over.

Today Bonham looked unwell and had a glass of white liquid on his desk.

'Church's d— d— d— dinner last night,' he replied on enquiry. Indeed Mr Church, the resident councillor, was noted for his poor dinners, a fact so widely known, even in Calcutta, that it had been an insurmountable obstacle to his promotion.

They sat amiably for some time and discussed the attacks, as well as the spate of robberies on the sultan's compound at Kampong Glam. Piracy was another issue preoccupying the governor's mind. In this way, the afternoon passed and eventually both Robert and Bonham repaired home.

Later, around five o'clock, Robert and Coleman together with a couple of young clerks met at the fives court on the riverside. It was their custom once a week to have a game, which usually attracted an audience of curious onlookers.

After this, the men wandered home to bathe and take dinner. A stroll or ride around the plain was a common activity in the cooler evening, with groups gathering on the beachfront at Scandal Point to rattle over the news and affairs of interest. The European contingent in the town was no more than two hundred and all were known to each other. As the light fell and the oil lamps were lit, they turned for home. The bachelors might yet get together for billiards at one of the grander houses or seek out companionship in the Chinese town.

Amateur dramatics was popular, but no plays had been put on for some time. Robert had formerly been feted as one of the best low comedians in town, but upon taking charge of the police the governor had hinted that his days on the stage should probably come to an end. Neither he nor Church could think that private theatricals and the midnight watch for Chinese thieves could go together. For most of the Europeans sleep came early, for the gun at Government House would be waking the town at five o'clock the next morning.

# 14

Inchek Sang and Baba Tan were drinking tea in the baba's elegant courtyard. The rich carving of the wooden doors, lattice windows and red and gold furniture contrasted with the cool water pool near which they were seated. This was a Peranakan house. Baba Tan was the first child of a *baba* father and a *nonya* mother. With no women permitted to leave China, Chinese merchants who settled in Malacca and, later, Penang, had married non-Muslim local women and begun families far from their homeland. Although they endeavoured to marry their daughters to Chinese men, this had not always been possible, and Peranakan intermarriage was the norm. This centuries-old mix had produced a hybrid culture of which Sang did not wholly approve. There might have been little direct Malay influence for several generations, yet the women of the house continued to dress in Malay fashion passed down by their mothers and to chew the betel, a habit which no pure Chinese woman would have countenanced.

The food that Sang was served was a mix of Chinese and Malay tastes, which he did not like. Occasionally he picked up a peanut or some other delicacy, but the spices of the *nonya* cuisine were repugnant to him. Even the baba language was difficult to understand, a mélange of Hokkien and Malay words and grammar. Sang was used to it by now, after long years in Malacca and Singapore, but he did not like it any the more.

Baba Tan, fully aware of Sang's prejudices, made a point of calling for spicy *nonya* food whenever he came to visit. The women of the house were confined to the upstairs rooms. However, they had a spyhole in the roof over the entrance, through which they could check on visitors, and they always looked this old man over. With his withered skin and grey beard, his claw-like nails and his old-fashioned clothes, he was a sight they could gossip about for hours. Tan's wife had met Sang's two wives on occasions at the temple or in the market. She felt sorry for them, having to be cooped up with such a man. She knew he did not care much for his daughters, who she suspected were ill-used. Everyone knew of the scandal of the first son-in-law. There was a sickly adopted son who looked like he might drop dead any day.

In a *nonya* house, daughters were valued, of the highest order, for, unlike in China, they would often remain in their parents' house and bring into the home new Chinese men, new blood: men who could speak the language which they could not, who could continue the ancestral customs of the old country and who, most importantly, would be malleable and obedient to the ways of the Peranakan lifestyle. Healthy, smart but poor Chinese young men were the ideal choices.

Nonya Tan was a happy woman, for she had no sons. This fact had, at first, saddened her, made her feel unworthy. She had feared her husband would take a second wife but to her surprise he had not. She knew he had a concubine in Kampong Glam, but she made no fuss, for she was glad that there were no sons and no other wives to usurp her authority in the home. She had given her husband four daughters, all pretty and healthy. She was the ruler of her home and, on his death, would become the matriarch, for foreign sons-in-law counted for very little. Love had not been an issue between them; she had been sixteen when they had married. They met on their wedding night, and those early years of unhappiness in the house of her husband's family, with her tyrant of a mother-in-law, she preferred to put behind her. Since then, husband and wife had grown gradually to like each other, sharing the responsibility for their daughters and the family finances.

Now she was very happy, for she knew that her husband and this old man were discussing marriage partners for their daughters.

'Well, Lao Sang, how shall we proceed with this matter? I have heard of the two young men, Zhen and Qian.'

Sang nodded but said nothing. He had heard from Ah Liang of the exploits at the opium farm. These two might turn out to be good choices, but until the ceremony of initiation tomorrow he would not commit to either. He put a long fingernail against his cheek and scratched lightly. Tan shuddered slightly internally. Really these geezers and their ancient ways. Whenever he looked at the old man he was reminded of a shrivelled corpse. Tan himself was only thirty-four.

'Baba, you will allow me first choice. Age has some privileges. It may be wise to bring them into town to work for us for a while. In a few months we should be able to judge which is better suited to our families. This one called Qian is keeping accounts at one of my farms. He can work at my godown for a time. The other you can bring to your shop. After a time we can exchange them. Are you agreeable to this arrangement?'

Baba Tan nodded his head. It seemed reasonable. After all, he had yet to meet either of these two men. And Sang was a wise old bird. He was right to be cautious after the awful business of the first son-in-law. This was an important step; better to go slow. Tan loved all his daughters but especially the eldest, who was pretty and very smart. He had been unable to resist teaching her to read Malay and English and some Chinese characters that he could remember. It was unusual, he knew, but he could not understand why women should remain ignorant of everything except domestic chores. His own marriage had not suffered for his wife's lack of education, for she was a canny housekeeper, but she had been a timid person and this he did not want for his own children.

His concubine was a beautiful girl purchased at the Bugis slave market. The colourful and numerous Bugis fleet of distinctive *prahus* arrived to great fanfare on the south-east monsoon every June, bringing a vast array of marine and island produce, the lifeblood of trade in Singapore. They also brought slave girls and boys captured amongst the thousands of islands of the archipelago. The English authorities frowned on slavery in theory but had done little up till now to stop it.

Her house was in Kampong Glam, and he had been careful to make sure that she and their two sons would have money after his death. These sons could not inherit his wealth, of course, nor carry out ancestral rites, but they would be taken care of and would eventually work in his business. He made sure to keep his two households well apart, for he had seen what evil came about when other men tried to keep everything under one roof. Jealousy, cruelty—even murder, though that was extreme. Usually everyone was just miserable, and the first wife generally bullied the second and subsequent wives or concubines ceaselessly. The bullying was echoed by the first wife's children, who cruelly picked on and tormented the concubines' offspring.

'Very well, Lao Sang, let us proceed this way.'

'*Hao, hao,* good. Tomorrow there is a ceremony. Their loyalty will be assured.'

Baba Tan raised his hand in slight protest. He knew of these goings-on in the jungle, but it did not serve his purpose to know too much. The English speaking Peranakan Chinese had, through long association, won the trust of the European administration in the town. None of them cared to get too close to the activities of the powerful *kongsi*. To know was one thing; to be involved, another. Tan knew the real need for such associations as a control mechanism and a lifeline for the *singkehs* and was grateful that they were run, very efficiently, by others. All the Peranakan families preferred their role as middlemen, taking neither side but reaping substantial rewards for their deep knowledge of the cut and thrust of local conditions. The British administration depended on them almost entirely.

'Well, baba. Reluctant to face realities, as usual. You know it is an interesting situation. Should I will it, I could wipe all the Europeans from this place with one word. I have the control of thousands of men. You see how powerless are the white men to deal with even small bands of robbers.'

This was talk that Tan had heard before. Sang liked to boast and flex his muscles.

'Of course, you are right. But what would it serve? Fortunes are to be made only with the English trading power and network. They open the world to us. It was so in Malacca, and more so here. The English do our donkey work by bringing opium and weapons. Everything we trade yields profit. I find them easy to deal with. But you are most certainly correct that a word from you could put an end to all this. We are fortunate that you are a wise man.'

Sang rose, placated.

'Well, well. They serve our purpose for the time being. On the matter of sons-in-law, we shall speak again when we have had time to examine the two men.'

After he had left, Nonya Tan came to her husband.

'You heard our discussions. That old fool, Sang, how he weevils on.

As if any of this would be possible without the English. Well, well, we shall see what these two men are made of. I know it is not customary, but would it not be worth letting first daughter take a brief look at them? If there is not much in the choices, it would be best if she could like one of them. It may help her happiness.'

His wife looked at him in surprise. He was getting soft in his old age. She had never heard of such a thing. But she could see his point. Their own marriage had been so miserable at the beginning. It would be a happier home if her daughter could care for the man she was going to marry.

# 15

The day of the initiation ceremony had arrived. Zhen and Qian joined a band of some thirty men and made their way across country, with some difficulty, since rain had fallen all night. Much of the land they crossed had been completely cleared of forest, but great swathes of thick-bladed grass had sprung up where the trees had been cut. It was the typical pattern that, as the soil became barren and the trees were all felled, the gambier and pepper farmers moved on and cut down the next part of the jungle. Zhen was not sure how big this place was, but a lot of it seemed to have been used up. At one point they skirted the burnt-out buildings of a plantation settlement. Zhen was curious to know what had happened there, and addressed one of the guards.

'It is a question of territory. A rival gang run by the *ang mo* has tried to challenge the power of the *kongsi*. This is what happens.'

Zhen was surprised. The white men had a *kongsi* here? Quite interested, he tried to find out more, but these guards knew nothing. He decided he would raise this with Master Liang when he had the chance.

They continued for many miles. At times along the way, they met men with black masks who guided them. Finally, at about four o'clock in the afternoon, exhausted from the terrain and heat, they arrived at an encampment. A pack of dogs came rushing, barking and growling, along the jungle path, until a man came out of a hut and called them off. In the centre of a large clearing stood three large, temple-shaped buildings each at least 180 feet in length, flags and pennants fluttering atop their roofs and walls. Inside and around the huts, men swarmed like maggots. Zhen recognised the flags of the seasons, the flags of the ranks. Others he did not know.

Around the perimeter of the huts, deep trenches twenty feet wide had been dug. As the group approached, planks were laid down. When the men had crossed to the other side, the planks were lifted away. On the far side the guard called them to halt. He pointed out small signs which indicated a maze of holes covered with loose brushwood and dried banana leaves. The top was strewn with earth so that it looked like firm ground. These holes were eighteen feet deep, the guard warned, and anyone not knowing about them would certainly fall in.

When Zhen and Qian looked briefly inside the first hall they saw hundreds of lamps burning. On all sides men were smoking opium; the air hung blue with fumes. Round the outside were piles of pointed wooden stakes, and inside were hundreds of shields, daggers and wooden spears.

The guard led them to a wooden shed to one side of the hall, where food and water were laid out on rush mats.

'Wait here. The ceremony will take place this evening, when everyone will be here.'

Over the next three hours their shed filled up with two dozen other men who had been brought in from the farms. Zhen began to realise the extent of the plantations throughout the interior. It was all so much bigger than he had expected.

Inside the hut it was swelteringly hot, for there were only small openings in the sides. By nightfall, the noise from the main halls had become deafening. A huge crowd of about 600 men had gathered inside, eating, drinking grog and smoking opium. Then, suddenly, gongs sounded, drums were beaten, and the men fell silent and sat themselves in rows.

The initiates were told to unbraid their queues and were then led from their hut by three men carrying red flags with white borders. On the flag was written one word: *ling* (warrant). It meant that the flag empowered this vanguard to bring initiates into the lodge.

The initiates were gathered, seated at the door of the building. This was the Hungmen, the Hung Gate, the first of three they would pass through on their symbolic journey. Inside, by the flickering light of a hundred candles, they saw a great altar covered in red cloth with a picture of Guan Di, God of War, in the centre, stern and red-faced, holding a double-edged sword. On his left was his squire, Zhou Cang, and on his right, Guan Ping, his son, holding the god's seal wrapped in a cloth.

In front of this picture in the middle of the altar was a large peck of rice, covered with a red paper and black calligraphy. The peck contained a multitude of flags, which Zhen knew were those of the commander in chief, the sun, the moon, the five founders and the tiger generals. The altar was covered in an assortment of objects: copper coins, bundles of joss paper, pagodas, a sword and a white censer filled with joss sticks.

Directly in front of the altar on a large chair sat the headman of the lodge. He was ancient, almost corpse-like, yet dressed in his red and black robes, with the paraphernalia of office spread around him in this place full of incense and opium smoke, he had a strange power. His eyes glittered. On his right and left stood his officers and eight men with drawn swords.

Chanting, the master of ceremonies sanctified the grounds and the items on the altar, beckoning the spirits to bear witness. The initiates were ordered to kneel with their right arms and shoulders bare and the bottoms of their left trouser legs rolled, a symbol of the union of man, heaven and earth.

Elaborate role-playing began, as the master and the first vanguard re-enacted the lives of the heroic founders of the Tian Di Hui in China. At length, the newcomers were each handed lit joss sticks and ushered by the vanguard through the Hung Gate, where they were met by the master of ceremonies. Next they were led through a series of questions and answers. They swore they had no living parents; they had come to swear eternal brotherhood. Twelve oaths were read to them. One by one they vowed never to divulge the secrets of the society and extinguished their joss sticks in a bowl of water. Their place in the society was explained to them, and they were introduced to the leaders of Ghee Hin Kongsi, the most powerful branch of the Tian Di Hui in Si Lat Po.

Zhen recognised Master Liang, next to the headman. As his turn came to bow before them, Liang bent and whispered something into the headman's ear. He peered carefully at Zhen and Qian but made no other sign.

The next stage of the ceremony followed: as they passed through the next gate into the Hall of Loyalty and Righteousness, guards tapped them on their backs with large flat knives. More icons of the Hui were on display here. Twelve more oaths were taken. Qian's head was swimming, and he was having difficulty taking everything in. Zhen said nothing but looked straight ahead. Finally, they passed into the third hall, the City of Willows, symbolic of the Heavenly City, where twelve more oaths were sworn. They had completed the thirty-six oaths.

Only the Red Flower Pavilion which housed the tablets of the five founders of the Tian Di Hui awaited them. One by one they crossed the ditch which formed the inner perimeter. The Red Flower Pavilion was situated outside the ceremonial temples and symbolised their passage from life to death and rebirth into the society.

An official holding an open umbrella over his right shoulder stood at the entrance. One at a time, the initiates knelt before the altar of the five ancestors. A masked man brought in a white-and-brown cockerel and swiftly cut off its head, draining the blood into a bowl mixed with sugar and rice wine. Each of the initiates had his middle finger pricked and the blood mixed with this concoction. Drinking from the bowl, they swore the blood oath. Taking a large, flat knife, each laid it on the dead body of the cockerel and swore again the vow of secrecy under pain of punishment and death. Qian was beginning to feel sick and feared he might vomit. His head was full of fumes.

Finally each man, his face smeared with blood, was given a set of rules. Qian felt a desire to giggle crazily as they lined up to have their names entered in the log. It was as if he was back in some mad jungle version of the schoolhouse in his village. When he took hold of the membership certificate and saw attached to it a chit for membership fees, he began to laugh hysterically. Zhen grabbed him and hurried away. Then, suddenly, a long low sound was blown on a bamboo tube, and the ceremony was over.

When Zhen and Qian joined the others in washing their faces and drinking at the water tub, it was past midnight. In the ceremonial halls, the noise had risen, as gambling and drinking had begun again. Many of the initiates had gone to join their new brothers. Zhen and Qian made their way back to the first hall. As they entered, a guard spoke to them and took them to Master Liang.

They again bowed low before the headman. Sang stared at the two young men. One was small and thin; the other was strong and tall, handsome and confident, a man who would please women. He was not sure whether this was what he needed in his house. His first son-in-law had been handsome and charming, and his daughter had been very happy, but not for long. The man had turned out to be a thief and a scoundrel. Perhaps Ah Liang was right: better to go with the smaller one who had a good head for accounts. Well, he would decide later.

'I have heard that you are useful, can read and write. You will both come tomorrow into town. One of my men will fetch you from the opium farm,' he said then dismissed them.

# 16

The band of the Madras Native Regiment was playing in the garden as Robert and Charlotte drew up on the gravel at G.D.'s house. The garden flickered with flames from torches, and the house glowed with the brilliance of Argand lamps.

Robert helped Charlotte from the carriage. He had to admit that his sister looked resplendent tonight. Her new dress cut low across the shoulders was a violet satin which shimmered in the light. White lace loosely framed the lower sleeve. The deep V of the waist emphasised her slenderness. Her hair, for want of expert hands, she had simply rolled up into a chignon and pinned. In any case, she preferred this to the current fashion for ringlets.

The shutters to the whole house were thrown open. The creamy flowers of a great *tembusu* tree gave off their sweet fragrance, and a perfumed breeze wafted over the guests. The sound of the band drifted in and around. Takouhi and George were waiting in the lower hall, greeting their guests. With them was their daughter, Meda. Holding her hand was a pleasant-looking plump man of tallish height, with shoulder-length black hair and dark eyes. This was Tigran, Takouhi's half-brother. Takouhi's dress was a simple, pale green Chinese silk. She did not like the wide skirts of the European ladies, and her silhouette was less voluminous. The close-fitting bodice was green damask. Her hair was tied up in an elaborate manner. Around her neck lay a superb diamond-and-emerald necklace, and she wore long, matching earrings. George was dressed, for once, in European dress: snow-white trousers, waistcoat and a black topcoat. He looked uncomfortable. To Charlotte's enquiries he simply said,

'Takouhi's doing. This clothing is damned hot. While she looks as cool as a waterfall, I feel like I'm about to ignite. By the saints, it's a good job 'tis not often.'

Meda Elizabeth stood by her father's side shyly. She was also dressed charmingly in European fashion, in the same green as her mother, her shiny brown hair in ringlets. She was eleven, and she looked like her mother in every respect except in her fairness of skin and her eyes, which were Coleman's down to the exact shade of hazel–green. She went to school with Mrs Whittle and some of the other young girls. When she spoke in English, she had no trace of her father's accent. With her mother she spoke Javanese and sometimes Malay.

Tigran Manouk spoke softly in Dutch-accented English. For such a powerful and wealthy man he gave off an air of shy diffidence and seemed uncomfortable, particularly with women. She had learned from Takouhi that he was not yet married, although he was now over thirty years of age. Their father had been a difficult and demanding man. After the death of Takouhi's mother he had married the Javanese–Armenian widow of a Dutch colleague. She had been a kind woman and cared for Takouhi, but her frequent miscarriages and illness meant that Takouhi had been raised by her Javanese maidservants. Tigran had been born when Takhoui was fifteen years old. Meeting George had changed her life, and she had been overjoyed to leave Batavia, although not her brother. To Charlotte, Takouhi seemed ageless, and tonight she was undoubtedly the most beautiful woman in the room.

Excited voices caused Charlotte to turn, and she was greeted effusively by Isabel and Isobel da Silva. They, too, looked charming tonight, both in pale blue. They led her to meet their father and mother, who were surrounded by almost their entire family. To Charlotte, this group formed the very picture of life in the South Seas, representing seemingly every possible combination of East and West in hue, shape and dimension.

Charlotte curtsied very low to the governor, who smiled widely. The munshi stood by his side, together with a stately-looking man. She was surprised to realise that this was the temenggong who, at some thirty years of age, was the effective Malay leader in the settlement. He said very little and did not smile. Two fierce-looking men never left his side. They were all dressed magnificently in silk *sarong*s and embroidered jackets. Around the temenggong's head wound, in a fabulous manner, a pale green cloth which shimmered with gold thread.

With them stood two Arab men and, to her great surprise, a small, plump woman dressed in a richly brocaded long skirt and jacket. At her side was a very handsome man, dressed Bugis-style and with earrings in both ears. These people, Lieutenant Sharpe told Charlotte, were four of the richest merchants in Kampong Glam. The woman was Hajie Fatimah; the Bugis prince was her husband. Between them they dominated the shipping that carried thousands of devout Muslims to the Haj in Mecca; they also owned a great deal of land around the sultan's palace. Charlotte was slightly awed by the sense of confidence which Fatimah exuded and her husband's romantic appearance.

Next Mrs Keaseberry took Charlotte to meet Mr Balestier, the American consul, and his wife, Marie. With them was their son, Joseph, a rather gauche young man, but of a pleasant nature. The captains of two American opium clippers in harbour were also present. They rarely saw attractive English ladies and were delighted to meet her. Charlotte, in turn, enjoyed their easy manner and the slow drawl of their accents.

She recalled a conversation with the munshi about his first meeting with Americans: how he had imagined them strangely exotic and found them surprisingly like Englishmen but for their pioneer history.

Charlotte and Robert moved around the different groups in the room; the Europeans and Armenians gathered in conversation near the cool air of the balcony. Charlotte went up to Miss Aratoun, met her parents and renewed her acquaintance, though throughout her conversation none of the family seemed to take their eyes of their hostess or her brother. When Tigran came up, Lilian's mother quickly turned her attention to him, almost pushing Charlotte to one side. Charlotte smiled and left to join Robert in conversation with George.

Mr Coleman was talking to Nanda Pillai and Dr Montgomerie, who was expounding on his favourite topic, the uses and properties of *gutta percha*. He was convinced that this remarkable product could be of use in surgical instruments. He had ascertained that it came from the sap of the *naito* tree, which was plentiful in Sarawak. Mr Coleman was sympathising joshingly with the general indifference to these discoveries in both Calcutta and London. Mr Pillai, George's indispensable contractor, wondered in a gracious and charming manner whether there might be uses for such a product in the building trade. When Mr Mayhew, the secretary to the court, came up to the group, Robert left abruptly, almost rudely, taking Charlotte with him to get some refreshments.

Charlotte had noticed the bad feeling between her brother and Mayhew on several occasions when they were thrown together, but did not understand what lay at the bottom of it. When George sauntered over a few minutes later, she asked him directly. Robert, looking annoyed, left to talk to his two European policemen. It was a subject which irritated him still.

George took Charlotte gently by the arm and led her to a sofa.

'Well, let's see if I can explain it to you simply,' he told her. 'Mayhew is an employee of the East India Company, which, as you know, governs the affairs in India and in the Straits Settlements. He's what's called "covenanted". When the company lost their trade monopoly, they became extremely jealous of their governmental monopoly. All position, honour and emoluments are held as solely and wholly belonging to those in the service of the company. Men, you see, who are appointed at India House in Leadenhall Street. I'm afraid that Mayhew is an example of the weaknesses which a monopoly of power and honour fosters in human nature. Secure in their fortunes and pensions and drawn from a limited sphere, such men as Mayhew have no real spur to urge them to exertion or even thorough attention to their duties. Are you with me so far, Charlotte?'

Charlotte nodded and quietly said, 'Mr Coleman, would you please call me Kitt, for all my friends do.'

Coleman looked her directly in the eyes and bowed slightly. He really was a devilishly attractive man, but she did not, on this occasion, lower her eyes. He smiled slightly.

'Well, Kitt. Then you must please call me George or G.D., whatever you like. I seem to have turned out to be G.D. with the men and George to the women. But I don't mind either.'

They smiled at each other.

'The story continues, for now we come to someone like Robert and even myself. Theoretically, in order to work in Singapore, we should have had the permission of the East India Company. However, they have tended not to bother with that particular rule for some time. So here we came anyway, cumbersomely branded as uncovenanted, and hence unhonoured and badly paid men. Mayhew took Robert's appointment very badly, for he felt the post should have gone to a company man. As it is, your brother is paid one quarter of the salary of the lowest official appointed at India House and half of what would have been offered to a military cadet. On top of it all, though he does all the work, he may only be titled *Deputy* Superintendent of Police, for none of the company men want the precedent of an interloper being created a full superintendent. Do yer follow?'

Charlotte nodded. She was beginning to understand some of the undercurrents she had felt on occasion, particularly on the plain when walking of an evening. Here, where it was common for the town to turn out to enjoy the sea breezes and gossip, she had noticed coolness and snubbings among certain individuals. Mayhew in particular never even looked at Robert or her.

'In my case, I came under me own steam and tried my luck. I was fortunate, but for a very long time I was sometimes obliged to leave the building of my own designs to military types who knew nothing about building or architecture and often could not speak a word of the languages, nor knew the first thing about the men they supervised. Really, it was a quite ludicrous situation, one which left me continually obliged to carry out work on contract while lesser men got government posts.'

He took a deep drink of his dark Porter beer. She could see he had warmed to the subject, and she enjoyed sitting near him in this intimate manner. His voice and lilting Irish accent were musical to the ear.

'Not to bore you too long. I shall finish by telling you how I became Superintendent of Works, finally, after so many years. Having carried out virtually all the major public works in the entire settlement, directing the convicts and opening up new land for development, I was summarily informed that my services were no longer needed and that a permanent position in the government would be given to a young officer of the regiment, Captain Lake. The designs of that gentleman for the jail and battery having been carried out, it was, dare I say to my great pleasure, discovered that the lower part of the jail was useless, for it overflowed with water at high tide, and the embrasures of the battery were blown away at the firing of the first salute.'

He grinned broadly, and Charlotte laughed with delight. He rose then, and in high good humour took her to join Robert and Baba Tan.

The baba was in a group of Chinese men, all merchants in the town. Although she was introduced to them all, she could immediately remember only one, Mr Whampoa. She had heard about him from Robert and Takouhi. His name had been taken from his father's company and birthplace near Canton. He had taken over control of this establishment on the old man's death. She had visited his large emporium on Boat Quay which provisioned the navy. It contained everything a ship could ever need, and behind this merchandise a Noah's Ark of goats, poultry, pigeons and parrots in cages. Whampoa was a rich man in the settlement and had just bought a failed and neglected coffee plantation in Serangoon Road. He spoke of his wish to live there and build a garden in the Chinese fashion. He was young and good-looking, with a queue of lustrous black hair which hung to his waist; she found him utterly charming. She was beginning to think she was becoming obsessed with Chinamen.

Whampoa spoke English very well, and when dinner was called, he accompanied her up the wide staircase to the dining hall.

The tables were set with brilliant white cloth, silver cutlery and candelabra, and French porcelain. Pure white napkins lay at each place, and at each, a dish of fancy breads.

Charlotte could not cease to wonder that just a very short distance from this table lay the impenetrable and tiger-infested jungle. Nor, indeed, could she help but wonder at the extraordinary variety of colour and race of the assembled company, clad in the costumes of so many lands, all at ease and enjoyment.

The dinner was a vast spread to suit any taste. Silver tureens contained mock turtle, mulligatawny, and spicy *laksa* soups, the latter a favourite of Coleman's. The fish course followed, with the delicate flavour of Penang sole and Malay *travelli*. This cleared, there followed joints of sweet Bengal mutton, Chinese capons, Keddah fowls and Sangora ducks, Yorkshire hams, Java potatoes and Malacca vegetables. The next course of rices—yellow, red and white—with spicy curry was accompanied by pungent *sambal*s, Bombay ducks and salted turtle eggs, together with flat spicy breads and crispy Indian ones. Wines, brandy and pale ale were served by the quiet Indian manservants, who were dressed in the finest white calico with scarlet turbans and sashes.

Coleman had confided to Charlotte that these men were all convicted murderers.

'Always take the murderers over the thieves, for they've no interest in me silver, and sure, they're not going to murder me over the dinner now, are they?'

Charlotte was not at all sure when he was joking.

Over champagne came speeches of mutual appreciation. The temenggong made a well-received Malay oration in his rich, deep voice. Governor Bonham stuttered his way through the reply with good humour. Tigran Manouk made a shy but clever speech and Coleman a witty reply, moving effortlessly between Malay and English.

Huge cheeses arrived, and jugs of pale ale. By now most of the guests were somewhat flushed and the level of noise had risen.

The cheeses soon removed, the servants carried in sago and tapioca puddings and silver platters overflowing with mangosteen, mango, pomelo, langsat, rose apple and plaintain. Finally the king of fruits appeared, preceded by its distinctive odour. Mr Whampoa, in high spirit, put a piece of creamy durian in his mouth and urged Charlotte to taste also. This she did with great reluctance and found it delicious. But the smell was not to be borne.

The durian was removed, the odour wafted away, and the dinner broke up. Takoui led the ladies downstairs into the garden for some fresh air. George accompanied the temenggong and his Chinese guests, who were taking their leave. Father Baudrel and Padre Lee also left, together with some older couples. Mr Whampoa had bowed to Charlotte before departing and invited her and Robert to ride one day out to his estate. She was sorry to see him go.

Dancing began with Count Papanti who, with a flourish, led Marie Balestier onto the floor, urging his fledgling students to do likewise. *Avanti*! Coleman threw off his coat and loosened his constricting cravat. He held out his hand first to Evangeline Barbie, who laughed and shook her head, passing his hand to Charlotte. Takouhi had not participated in the waltz lessons and now sat in conversation with Tigran, watching George and Charlotte whirling round the hall. Charlotte noticed that Robert had quickly chosen Miss Crane and felt sorry for her. Really this waltz was an intoxicating thing, and she felt keenly George's hand on her waist as he guided her expertly. She understood, all at once, the foundation of its wicked reputation. Why, a mere movement of his arm and she would be against his body. Crimoney, she thought, get a hold on yourself, Kitt!

When the first dance was over, Charlotte was quickly approached by John Connolly and Lieutenant William Gold of the Madras Regiment. Connolly was a slender Irishman of Coleman's age, with sharp features and a similar ready wit. Coleman and Connolly went hunting together on the outskirts of the town. Lieutenant Gold was an Englishman of good looks and, she thought, fine figure in his dress uniform. She knew they both danced well, for they had all practised together with Senor Papanti. However, as much as to keep these gentlemen waiting as out of solicitude, she selected young Joseph Balestier. To her surprise, he turned out to be an authoritative partner.

The dances had been proceeding for an hour. Gradually the guests departed, until only a few acquaintances remained. Robert and Charlotte, Billy Napier and Willy Lorrain, Reverend and Mrs White, Mr and Mrs da Silva and most of his family, and Captain Scott, who would stay the night. Connolly and Lieutenant Gold had also stayed and continued to engage Charlotte in conversation and urge her to more dances. Tigran Manouk had talked shyly to her in rather halting English but had declined to dance.

At eleven o'clock Coleman addressed the company, mopping his brow.

'Ladies and gentlemen. We must release the band with our thanks. Refreshments will be served upstairs and, to save my poor feet, I believe Miss Manouk is to offer us a rare treat.'

They trooped upstairs. Chatting, they crossed the sitting and dining rooms. The lights were low. The frieze of Greek harps, shamrocks and Irish roses which dressed the high walls and door lintels stood out in relief in the shadowy glow. Breezes wafted around them from the lunettes at the ceiling of the double-roofed house, so cool and perfect for the tropical weather.

They moved to the verandah, where chairs and tables were scattered about. The *punkah* moved to and fro gently overhead. Drinks were served.

Oil lamps and candles were on every table and all around the verandah, casting their flickering light into every corner. At one end of the verandah a group of richly-dressed Javanese musicians were seated on cushions on the floor. In front of them were metal plates strung between decorated wooden holders in various sizes: gongs and drums large and small. Odours of incense hung in the air, and flowers were strewn in and around the small orchestra. When everyone was seated, a beguiling rhythm began, the drums and gongs beating a low theme while the musicians began to strike the metal with soft round sticks, the clear metallic sounds like the stirring of a thousand bells, delicate, mystical. The flutes piped softly, and a man began to sing a haunting counter-melody in a soft, nasal voice. A hypnotic quality enveloped the listeners. From the house, three women stepped out barefoot and began a sensuous, alluring dance. Tied around their jewelled belts hung long, yellow, tasselled scarves. Elaborate gold earrings glowed dully in the light. Their eyes were heavy with black *kohl* and their lips a rich red.

They danced as one, small chained paces, slowly, slowly. Heads moved together in time with the hypnotic music of the orchestra. The jewels in their crowns flashed as they turned. Gems of light kissed the walls. The movement and the music became one, the dancers rising and sinking, turning and stopping to the order of the orchestra. Finally, gradually, the beat began to slow until with infinite slowness it came to a stop. The dancers sank to the floor.

Charlotte had never seen or heard anything so graceful and beguiling. Then Coleman rose and took Takouhi's hand, lifting her gently from the floor. He looked her in the face, and she smiled. He put her hand to his lips. Her guests rose, clapping. Takouhi and the other dancers turned to face the orchestra and, putting their hands together, bowed.

# 17

Qian and Zhen worked alternately at Incheck Sang's godown and Baba Tan's. They began to learn the way the merchants made their money.

The Chinese and Western merchants had an interesting interdependent relationship. Chinese merchants dominated the collection and first processing of the Straits produce brought by the Bugis fleets or by the *chinchews*—Chinese captains who sailed from port to port buying produce that local Chinese secured from the indigenous population. The captain who had brought them from China was involved in this *chinchew* trade with Sang while he waited for the monsoon winds to change.

This they then passed on to the Western merchants for final processing, grading and export. But these Westerners did not deal with the Chinese businesses directly; for this they needed the indispensable skills of the *compradores*, whose knowledge of the local markets and the trustworthiness of prospective Chinese clients was essential. The Peranakan community, with their language skills, their local contacts and the trust of the Englishmen, were the wealthiest *compradores* in Singapore.

The Straits produce received by Tan was in small, unsorted lots, so much of Zhen's day was spent combining and grading the produce for sale to the agency houses. He was amazed at its variety: cloves, mace, nutmeg and pepper, tortoise shell, sugar, gold, shells, bamboo, rattans, grains, ores and metals, beeswax, benjamin, betel nuts, bird's nests, camphor, cassia, coffee, coir, dragon's blood, gambier, indigo, coconut oil, sago, salt, sandalwood, tobacco and opium. Tan showed him how to look up the prices for these articles in the newspaper he had annotated in Chinese, and Zhen and Qian quickly became acquainted with the English names of these products; they learned too the words for 'saleable', 'in demand', 'wanted', 'overstock', the jargon of commerce.

Zhen knew Tan leased property throughout the settlement and had a fleet of five ships. Apart from the godown trading, Tan and Sang also had interests in the gambier and pepper plantations and nutmeg and sago production. They held licences for the opium and grog farms and the gambling dens. Sang was also involved in the prostitution business as headman of the *kongsi*.

After the working day ended they would meet on Boat Quay for a meal at one of the hawker stalls which sprang up as night began to fall.

The peculiarities of the Tan household were always a subject which came up. This locally born Chinese family with its Malay ways was odd beyond anything they had experienced. Neither Qian nor Zhen could understand anything that was said; they spoke a mangled Chinese language mixed up with Malay words. The old clerk in the shop helped translate and, when in doubt, they resorted to writing on a board characters which they could all understand. All except Tan, for, as they discovered, baba merchants like Tan could read virtually no Chinese.

They had, however, quickly understood who had the most influence with the *ang mo* bosses. Tan's godown welcomed English-speaking visitors daily. Tan had even thrown a dinner party for the foreigners in the town on the upper floor of his new godown, which had been designed for him by the foreign architect. It was incredible.

They both understood more clearly now the division of power between the baba Chinese and houses like Sang's. The influence Sang held rested on his vast fortune and his reputation in the settlement, his headship of the *kongsi*, while Tan's stemmed from his mastery of the language of the foreigners. He had the trust of the British through his ability to interpret this South Seas world for them. The foreigners were an ignorant lot, it seemed. They could not speak the language of the vast majority of the population. Keeping them in the dark was so easy it was laughable. Between them, the rich Chinese effectively controlled everything on this island.

One day Zhen and Qian had been told to go together to Baba Tan's large house in Market Street. They had stood waiting at the entrance for some time; then a servant had dismissed them back to their work.

Had they looked up carefully, they would have seen that a small section of the entrance roof had been removed, and through this spyhole a pair of pretty eyes looked down on them. Baba Tan's first daughter contemplated the two men below. From her vantage point she could see their faces quite well as they turned from time to time towards the street and the door and looked up at the ornate ceiling.

Her decision was easy. From the moment she laid eyes on Zhen's face and looked over his figure, which was clad only in loose trousers, she felt a thrill. This one would be her husband. She had seen few men close up, for she had been confined indoors since she had turned twelve years old, but most of the coolies she saw from behind the window screen were thin, sad fellows. She felt a rush of affection for her parents for selecting such a man. The other fellow with him she barely took in. Her eyes feasted on Zhen. She was ready for marriage, ready for family. The stirrings inside her body as she gazed at this man began to overwhelm her, and she could not drag her eyes off him. He would not see her until the marriage night, but she could dream of him until then. She was happy beyond her wildest dreams and ran to tell her father and kiss his hands. Although her mother had sworn her to secrecy, she thought with pleasure of how, when they saw him, her sisters too—all her acquaintance, she was sure—would be jealous of her good fortune.

Zhen and Qian got to know well the crowded little Chinese town of Si Lat Po. Sometimes there was a Chinese opera performance in front of the Cantonese temple on the beach side or at the Teochow temple in Philip Street. A stage would be erected opposite the temple gates so the deities could watch, and the air would ring with the high-pitched whine of the singers' voices and the clashing sounds of the orchestra. The street was always packed with men, clapping and laughing. In the side streets, the gambling dens did a busy trade. At New Year, the streets became a mighty din of exploding firecrackers and beating drums. Lanterns and paper signs, red and gold, adorned every shop, every door. This was when it felt most like home.

Sometimes they listened to the storytellers at the quayside at Bu Jia Tian, the place that never sleeps, where the river opened out into the shape of a carp's belly, a symbol of good fortune. Sitting on a small stool, the taleteller would light an incense stick and put it in a sack of sand. He would begin to weave a tale of old China, heroic deeds, strange doings and hilarious antics. As soon as the incense had burnt down, he stopped. Naturally this occurred at the most interesting part. When the sound of coins had jingled into the cup to his satisfaction, he would begin again. If you sat, you paid, if you stood you didn't.

Fights broke out but stopped as fast as they started. Knifings were not unknown, and sometimes a Malay would run amok, but these incidents were not bothersome enough to worry the vast majority of the coolies. Drinking houses, gambling and opium dens were full most nights, and lines formed outside the *ah ku* houses as men sought escape from their urges, from the airless, cramped sleeping quarters and the monotony of their lives.

Zhen would watch when foreigners appeared on the far bank, hoping for a glimpse of the woman, but she seemed to have disappeared. Nothing beyond the river mouth was visible from the quayside. It seemed to Zhen that this small stretch of river was a thousand miles wide, such was the separation between the Chinese and European towns. Neither he nor Qian had ventured over the bridge or to the other bank since their trip into the jungle.

Sometimes Zhen would visit one of the *ah ku* houses along Hokkien Street. His need for sex had become urgent in the last months. He often found himself thinking of the foreign woman. Her face came to him in dreams. Then he would go to Hong Min, the *ah ku* he had chosen. Her house was relatively clean. He went only to her, hoping to steer clear of disease. He felt sympathy for these poor women who were slaves to the mistress of the house, kidnapped or sold into prostitution for pennies.

Min was a girl from a village near Zhangzhou, whose parents had sold her to the dealer who visited the area every couple of months. She was pretty and was very happy that Zhen, this handsome man, came to her. She would have liked him to take her out of the *ah ku* house, but she knew any talk like this would get her beaten or killed; it had happened to others. Zhen treated her well, was gentle with her but had only friendly feelings for her, she understood. He did not try to kiss her, which she had been glad of in the beginning but soon wished for. He showed her how to use her hand and mouth to satisfy him.

Recently he had begun to realise she no longer served him ritually but truly desired him, and he allowed her to kiss his body and run her tongue over his skin, pleasuring her with his fingers. It heightened his own desire, and he enjoyed giving women pleasure, knowing he was good at it. She often pulled his face down to her breasts, wanting him to run his tongue round her nipples and tempting him to enter her but in this Zhen was very disciplined. He had seen the hideous cankers, the rashes and fevers of the men in his village who came to his father for treatment. One of his uncles had died delirious and deranged. His father had given him ample warnings. From an early age he and his brothers had been given a tea made of various barks and roots, which his father had told him could protect them from these diseases. He had a condom made from gut, but felt so little passion in the wearing of it that he did not bother. Min's mouth did well enough.

In his youth he had been awakened to sex and taught well by the fourth concubine of the local mandarin. She had seen him delivering a prescription of medicinal herbs to the *yamen* when he was fifteen, already well built and good looking. She had arranged for him to be smuggled into her quarters by her young maid, and between the two of them he had received an unexpected and pleasurable education. This had lasted three years, interrupted by his year in the Taoist monastery, and only severed forever when his family's financial ruin had forced them to move into a village in the country. He had missed them both very much and still recalled their last time together and the tearful farewells. For a while he had written poetry about them and fancied himself living a life of sad seclusion far away in the misty mountains. But the harshness of this new life had soon brought him back to reality. The *kongsi* had saved his family from starvation, and he had served it willingly.

Before and after each time with Min he would wash himself with a lotion his father had taught him to make; he made her do so too. Although she had thought it strange at first, she always obeyed his instructions. Every day she drank the tea and chewed the oily seeds he had given her, although they were bitter and distasteful. This was to prevent disease and pregnancy, he had told her. She had always used a pessary and oiled paper and washed assiduously after each encounter, but extra didn't hurt, she agreed. So far it had worked. She had already had one abortion, by massage and herbs, which had been painful and made her very sick. When she had her period or a fever, Zhen brought her herbs. On those occasions, he would often simply lie in her soft arms and caress her. She knew that for many of the men, this was sometimes what they wanted. They often stayed overnight to sleep with her and talk about home—and for this she got a little more money.

Every week she took half her money and sent it home to her parents in the Chinese village through the Teochow money office, which she trusted. She knew she would die in this place and never go home, but her sense of duty was strong. When it all became too much, she would eat opium. When she told Zhen this, he had taken her face in his hands.

'No, do not think this. Harden your heart a little. Become good friends with the mistress and help her. The way out is to become the mistress yourself. I am nothing now, but one day I will have some influence here and you will benefit. I have told the mistress that you are a good girl and to treat you well.'

She had thought this was just the usual talk. The men often boasted of such things. But after each encounter with Zhen, her spirits had risen and she had begun to believe him. With such belief came, she realised, love, and this was a dangerous thing for an *ah ku* whore to have. She hated the filthy mistress of the house, but from Zhen she drew the strength to hide her real feelings. The old mistress liked Zhen and grew sickeningly coquettish in his company. Although she cared nothing for the stupid girl he went with, she had heard through the owner of the brothels that he was a *kongsi* man and had found favour with powerful families here. It was enough for her to keep her temper under control.

Zhen and Qian met one cool evening on the riverside. Qian had news. He was convinced now that they were being considered as marriageable material.

Zhen had been getting the same idea. They had talked to other men in the godown and on the quayside and learned the family situation of the two *towkays*—daughters requiring husbands. Zhen and Qian had discussed it at length over glasses of grog in the drinking houses on Hokkien Street. It was only a matter of time before the proposals came from one direction or another, and they would take them up immediately.

No family, no aid, no women in Si Lat Po for them. Both men knew that only this way could they find wives and wealth in one fell swoop. Their first hand view of how poor coolies struggled with the hardships of life here—a great swarm of men who would never know family, children, home, who would end up broken, addicted to opium, deprived of affection and dead at a young age—had been a stark lesson. Fortune had truly smiled on them.

They had talked about their preferences. Qian favoured marriage into the family of Baba Tan, who seemed an equable man despite all the peculiar habits of the house. Zhen was not sure. He couldn't always understand Baba Tan, but Tan did make an effort to speak more regular Hokkien with him. Sang was a hideous old creature, but even though he was Cantonese, they could speak together easily. Well, it was out of their hands anyway. They could merely wait.

The wait was not long. Two days later Incheck Sang and Baba Tan met at Sang's house. After the usual pleasantries they got down to business.

Tan was slightly anxious and wiped his face with a large handkerchief. Sang eyed him curiously, a long fingernail curled over his lips. As he waited for Sang to speak, Tan thought about his daughter's happy, grateful face. She would make a wonderful wife for this man Zhen, she had told him, and give him many grandsons. Only now had he begun to realise that he might have made a terrible mistake by letting her see this fellow. Sang was always going to get first choice. The words fell like stones upon Tan's ears.

'I have decided to get the tall one, Zhen, for my daughter.'

Tan's heart sank. Before him rose a storm of domestic trouble. His mind was working so hard he felt his brain might explode. It had never occurred to him that the old corpse would choose the man who so resembled the son-in-law who had run off with his money.

Tan had been certain that Qian would be Sang's choice. He had to change the old skeleton's mind somehow, but he had to be careful.

'Really, that is interesting,' Tan said calmly. 'I thought Qian would have been more suitable. A quieter man, more obedient, perhaps. But I am just as well pleased to get him. Zhen seems more willful. May I ask your reasons for this choice? I have other daughters to consider, and your wisdom on this matter would be helpful to me.'

He coughed slightly into his handkerchief at this blatant lie.

Sang eyed him with a rheumy gaze. He was not deceived.

'I may not have long for this world,' he said. 'I need a man in this house, fresh masculine blood. One who can make a grandchild quickly. He is clever, learns fast. He is not like the other bastard son-in-law. I made a mistake with that one, I see it now. You cannot speak clearly with Zhen, but I can. He knows the *kongsi* ways. You have seen him; he is powerful, and his blood will enrich my line. In many ways he reminds me of myself when I was young.'

Tan's eyes narrowed in an effort not to laugh at the vain old fool.

'This Zhen takes risks but is smart with it,' Sang said. 'I will make him an offer that he will find very acceptable. I will make him my heir officially, and immediately and he will take my name.'

It was a lost cause. Baba Tan had never seen Sang so animated. He had made his choice, and Tan knew there was nothing he would be able to say to change the old man's mind. When he left Sang's house, a black cloud followed him up High Street, along North Bridge Road and over the rickety bridge.

Zhen was in the back of the cool, dark godown when Tan came back along Boat Quay. He watched the *towkay* quietly. The man was deep in thought and sat heavily on one of the seats outside. Some decision had been taken, Zhen felt it.

Then the figures of some foreigners, two men and a woman, appeared in silhouette in the door frame. Tan rose and greeted them. Zhen moved slowly forward to the window beside the covered way. As he looked through the shutters he saw the woman's face. It was her. She was looking around, and for a moment she gazed straight at the shutter. He thought they might enter the shop, but within a few minutes they had taken their leave and moved out along the quay. He retreated from the window.

She was beautiful, more than he had remembered, her eyes like the evening sky. Who could he ask about her? Baba Tan, of course, but he didn't know the words, and it might be somewhat dangerous. The old clerk was messing about upstairs, sorting and weighing pepper into small sacks. Zhen ran lightly up to the next floor and, to the old man's shock, grabbed him by the neck and pushed him towards the window. The shutters stood open, and he thrust the fellow's head out of the window. The foreigners had moved only a short distance down the quay and were now talking to some Arab fellow in white robes and another Chinese bloke who went by the name Whampoa.

'Who are they?'

The old clerk looked at him as if he was mad.

'Who are they—the foreigners? Come on, you old fool, you must know.'

'All right, keep your shirt on. Of course I know; they visit here all the time. Let me go.'

Zhen was suddenly ashamed of his roughness with the old man, and let him go with an apology.

'Well, let me see, the Chinese bloke is a Cantonese. Whampoa's his name. And the Arab fellow is called Al Sayed.'

Zhen shook his head impatiently and made a fist. His fleeting remorse had deserted him and he wanted to smack the old fool in the head. He said quietly,

'Not them. The others. The woman.'

The old clerk looked up at him and leered.

'What d'you wanna know for?'

Zhen raised his fist.

'Hao, hao. The older man is that fellow that does all the building stuff round here. His name is Kuliman. The other young one is the police chief, Mah Crow, and I think that is his sister. I don't know her name, but I hear from the Chinese who go to the white men's temple that she is a teacher of their language. They live at the police house round the mouth of the river.'

Letting the old man go, Zhen gazed down the quay at her until he thought his eyes would drop out of his head. He did not like the way that Whampoa was looking at her.

He did not understand this effect that she had on him. Did he love her? Impossible. Love at first sight? Rubbish. Yet he watched them without looking away, until finally the three foreigners left the quayside and he went back to work.

That evening Zhen ate quickly with Qian on the bayside and told him he was visiting Min. Qian was always embarrassed about this. He had started to realise that he might feel more aroused by men than women. The incident with Zhen had simply made him aware of this possibility. He was not concerned about ideas of homosexuality. The pleasures of the cut sleeve were as ancient as China itself.

'In olden times the gay boys,
An Ling and Long Yang.
Fresh, fresh blossom of peach and plum,
Glowing, glowing with a brilliant sheen,
Happy as nine springs
Pliant as branches bent by autumn frost'

Qian was not inclined to any particular religion or philosophy. He supposed he was the usual mixture of bits and pieces: Buddhist, sometimes Taoist, mostly Confucian. And it was this latter, his Confucianist duty to marriage and family, that had him worried. If he was going to marry, certain things would definitely be expected. He would have liked to talk this over with Zhen, but he was afraid. He loved him, but knew that there was no possibility of ... though he often wished it.

Zhen made his way along Market Street and down Battery Road, past the Indian moneylenders on Chulia Street. He had never come this way and felt a certain trepidation as he turned round the big foreigner's house and along the small road down by the fort and on to the river's edge. He settled down on his heels and looked towards the river mouth. From here he could see the police house quite clearly, though all the blinds were down. There was activity visible, as shapes moved to and fro against the light. He imagined her inside the house, inside her room, on her bed, and felt himself becoming aroused. Ashamed for this spying, he stood up and brought himself under control. A soldier on the walls of the fort called out something incomprehensible and waved him away. Zhen moved slowly down the quay.

His mind was sure now. They would meet; it was inevitable. Nature would take its course. The river of life, the eternal pull of *yin* and *yang* in the transcendent Way: this would bring them together. That and perhaps some English lessons. He smiled and, feeling light-hearted, made his way through the thronged streets towards the Thien Hock Keng temple to light some incense and, just for fun, see what the fortune sticks had in store.

# 18

Baba Tan was an unhappy man. He had preferred Zhen over the rather more fey Qian, despite that man's reliability and quiet cleverness. His daughter, he knew, would be miserable. He rued horribly the day he had decided to let her see the two men. His forefathers had known this. A girl should have no say in marriage. She should just obey her father. As he thought this, a vision of his daughter's crumpled, accusatory face rose before him. His wife would silently blame him, for the viewing had been his idea. He hung his head in his hands.

Still, there was a little hope. He had managed to convince Sang to wait until after the Ching Ming Festival, which was only two weeks away.

Baba Tan's parents were buried in the cemetery on the Hill of Teng, in Singapore, near the Hang San Teng temple. The festival was less time-consuming for him than for Sang, whose ancestral tablets were in Malacca. He hoped that the festival would keep the old man away from Singapore long enough to figure out a solution to this marriage problem.

Inchek Sang, by contrast, was a happy man. Seated in his room, on his tiger-skin rug, he was thinking about his decision to make this new man, Zhen, his heir. The pathetic adopted boy would pass down to second son. He had spoken to no one but Tan of his decision yet, not even the prospective bridegroom, but he was confident of the answer he would receive. Zhen was smart enough to know where his best interests lay.

Sang had agreed with the baba to wait until after Ching Ming. It was fitting that this announcement would first be made to his ancestors, and it was a mere two weeks away. Though Sang's ancestors were buried in his village in China, tablets to them were in his house in Malacca. He would

144

travel back there to pay them tribute. His own grave would be here in the cemetery, on the hill, not far from the temple to which he was a major donor. His death tablet would be in his house on the ancestral altar. His will specified that this property was to be kept forever untouched, a temple to his soul. He was considering bringing the tablets of his dead relatives here, too; he would speak to the abbot of the temple in Malacca about it while he was there. He would be travelling to Malacca with his wife and the boy within a few days. There was much to do.

He rose and, locking the door carefully behind him, went across the courtyard. He felt like skipping, his heart was so light. He stopped to admire the bamboo in their pots and the newly budding pink lotus in the small pond. The lotus was the symbol of the eternal cycle of life, of the hope of a spotless spirit rising from a bed of mud; it was the chance of redemption for all his sins through new life. Happiness would re-enter this house as the petals of the budding lotus slowly bloomed into full flower. For the first time in years, a smile came to his lips, revealing his few remaining uneven, yellow teeth.

He entered his office and took out his calligraphy brushes and ink. Once this man Zhen was installed, he could begin to relax, take up the scholarly pursuits he longed for as old age came upon him. He would read the classics, practice again the calligraphy his father had taught him. A tear came to his eye and dropped onto the exquisite ink stone which he had inherited from his father. A man that he had hated in life had, in the long years following his death, gained a place of unexpected affection in his heart. Now, at the prospect of new life here, a grandson perhaps, his eyes welled up.

Turning, he sat at his desk and began to draft the letter of agreement with Baba Tan. Before he left for Malacca he wanted everything clear and in writing. No changes of mind.

Only then did he notice a scroll lying at the side of his desk tied with a red ribbon. Unrolling it, he began to read. His eyes flew open, and he gasped. Suddenly his body felt as it was being tightened in a vice. A searing pain shot across his chest and down his left arm. His face contorted with in agony, and his head jerked. His false queue caught on the horn of the dragon which was carved into the back of his rosewood chair, flew off and landed on the floor. His head dropped with a thump to the desk as his heart beat its last, and the breath leaked from his mouth. His hand fell, and the letter fluttered down, landing delicately on the pile of hair at his feet. His pupils gazed their last on the red-faced statue of Guan Di which stood on his altar.

An hour later his youngest daughter discovered him when she brought him tea in his favourite teapot and cup. Swan Neo put the tray down calmly on the desk and stood over him. She had never liked her father. Her life, and her mother's, had been misery inside these walls. She did not care that he was dead; in fact, she was pleased it would cause pain to the first mother and her daughter. For a moment she felt afraid of the unknown to come, now that this certainty was gone. But the fear passed. Slowly she poured some tea into the cup and sipped it, savouring each drop, her gaze fixed on the old man's staring eyes. Hopefully he is in the first court of hell, staring horrified into the Mirror of Retribution as his life and his sins roll slowly before his eyes. How wonderful the moment when he realises that the next stop is the Lake of Filth and Putrefaction. She smiled, gave him a vicious flick on his dead bony nose then, gathering up the tray, she went to tell her mother.

With no man in the household to deal with this event, Ah Liang was informed. His first reaction was shock and disbelief. But on arrival at his master's house, he saw that all the statues of the deities had been covered with red paper and the great mirror in the hall was shrouded. The servants were draping white cloth over the entrance doors. It was true.

The first wife and daughter were sobbing in the courtyard; the second were nowhere to be seen. He told them to go and prepare the main hall for the coffin's arrival and light incense on the ancestral table. Sang's coffin had been made years before. It was carved from a huge piece of mahogany, coated and recoated seven times with *tung* oil from China until it was a deep black. Ah Liang was not good at this kind of thing, but he knew enough to have already sent for the coffin from Sang's godown, where it was stored. The priest from the temple and the undertaker were on their way, and he had placed a red wax seal across the lock of Sang's strong room.

He touched the old man's hand, which was cold, and said a silent prayer to Amitabha Buddha to care for his friend's soul. He was not a religious man, but this seemed the right thing to do. Sang's bald pate looked so sad a tear came to his eye, and he searched for the queue.

Then he noticed the letter on the floor.

*Father-in-law*, he read. He stopped in shock. A letter from the son-in-law. They had all thought he was dead. *I have repented of my ways and now wish to re-enter the household. By law, I am still married to your eldest daughter and I am sure you will consider her happiness and agree to a meeting.* The letter had come via one of Sang's shops in Medan. The shock of reading it must have caused his death!

The son-in-law must be at the end of his opium-addicted tether to have imagined reconciliation possible, Ah Liang thought. Simply to have revealed himself put him in mortal danger. A glimmer of hate lit in Ah Liang's eyes and his hand curled into a fist. He folded the letter and put it carefully into a pocket inside his jacket.

Sang's left hand was clutching a paper. Ah Liang quickly checked that there was no other correspondence which needed to be hidden and very carefully extricated the paper from between Sang's long fingernails. It was addressed to Baba Tan and began by talking of their agreement about the two men, Zhen and Qian, chosen to be their prospective sons-in-law, their understanding that the man Qian ...

The words ran out. This letter Ah Liang also pocketed.

Gingerly raising Sang's head, he removed the silk cord which held the keys to his strong room and chests and took a last look round. Standing over Sang's body, he bowed, made the peace sign of the brotherhood and then went out quietly and closed the door behind him.

# 19

The group of Europeans filed silently into the Christian cemetery on the low slope of Bukit Larangan. Cholera had come to Singapore. Many of the children at Mrs Whittle's school in the European settlement had fallen ill in the last month. It had been a source of great distress and no little surprise, for illness here was relatively rare. The climate was remarkably healthy for the tropics, and mosquitoes were not such a problem as in Penang or Malacca.

The causes of this particular disease were still a mystery to medical men throughout the Empire, but Dr Montgomerie was amongst those who favoured a theory of waterborne rather than airborne transmission. He had tended cholera victims in India and never caught it himself and, on the basis of what he knew was rather flimsy science, he advocated absolute cleanliness and boiling of water rather than confinement of patients to airless and darkened rooms. He ordered the schools closed and the children kept at home. He suspected contaminated water at the school to be the source and had given Mrs Whittle a stern talking-to about hygiene. She swore that she followed all his instructions.

Young Thomas Hallpike had died yesterday. Mrs Hallpike had taken to her bed. Meda Elizabeth was also ill, but not with cholera. Dr Montgomerie at first suspected malaria, for she had succumbed to severe fever, chills, headache and pain in her legs and joints. But a rash had appeared on her face, and her neck glands were swollen. The doctor was bewildered, but after five days her temperature dropped; she began to sweat profusely, and the crisis seemed to be over. Takouhi had prayed to the Lord at the Armenian church, made offerings to the Javanese gods and somehow they had answered.

Two days later, Meda relapsed. Her temperature rose again and the rash reappeared, not on her face but covering the rest of her body.

The soles of her feet and the palms of her hand were bright red and swollen. Dr Oxford and Dr Montgomerie consulted and concurred that they could do nothing more than note the symptoms. Takouhi talked of taking Meda to Java to consult the *dukun*, the medicine man. Then, suddenly, it was over. Meda's temperature returned to normal, the rash disappeared again and she began to take soup and rice.

Charlotte had spent hours at Meda's bedside, urging Takouhi to take some sleep. Eventually they had slept, exhausted, as Charlotte and Takouhi's Javanese maids nursed the child. The following day Thomas Hallpike had died, and now the small community was mourning the loss of this innocent soul.

The service had been held in St Andrew's Church. Charlotte barely took in the words. She knew Thomas; she thought of his shy smile and his plump little arms around her neck, of him sitting on her lap.

'The Lord is my shepherd
I shall not want
He maketh me to lie down in green pastures
And leads me by still waters ...
I shall fear no evil
For you are with me ...
My cup runneth over ...
Surely goodness and mercy shall follow me all the days of my life
And I will dwell in the house of the Lord forever.'

Charlotte now walked with Takouhi and George as they followed the little coffin, carried in the arms of his father and his uncle, away from the church, along Coleman Street, around the Armenian church and up past the old botanical garden into the grounds of the small cemetery. The bell in the cupola of the Armenian church tolled sadly, and rain clouds gathered as if in sympathy with this passing. Crowds of Chinese, Malay and Indians gathered curiously but silently at the crossroads to watch the spectacle of this European ceremony as it passed slowly across Hill Street.

'The curfew tolls the knell of parting day

The lowing herd winds slowly o'er the lea
The ploughman homeward plods his weary way
And leaves the world to darkness and to me ...

Full many a gem of purest ray serene,
The dark unfathomed caves of ocean bear;
Full many a flower is born to blush unseen,
And waste its sweetness on the desert air ...

The boast of heraldry, the pomp of power,
And all that beauty and all that wealth e'er gave
Awaits alike the inevitable hour
The paths of glory lead but to the grave ...'

The mourners watched as young Thomas was lowered into the ground and the last prayers intoned.

'I am the resurrection and the life, saith the Lord ...
Earth to earth, ashes to ashes, dust to dust ...'

Charlotte shivered, and her tears began to fall. Coleman put a gentle hand on her arm and held tightly to Takouhi's hand. Every family there knew that it could just as easily be one of their own children. Meda's escape filled his mind.

He looked around at the other headstones. They would all be buried here, he was sure, and a feeling of peace descended on him. All together here in the grove of tamalan and banyan trees, it wasn't so bad. He would build their memorials in this place on this lovely island where they had all found such happiness.

He looked down at the woman by his side. An overwhelming feeling of love came over him, and she, as if sensing his emotion, looked into his eyes. Only the propriety and sadness of this occasion stopped him sweeping her into his arms.

As rain began to fall, the mourners dispersed, each throwing a small handful of earth onto the coffin, and Thomas' uncle joined the undertaker in completing the burial. Coleman took Hallpike's arm and, holding an umbrella over him, accompanied the grieving father back to his home on High Street. Takouhi turned to Charlotte.

'Come to my church with me, yes. I say words for little Thomas and all children. Also special words for Meda Elizabeth.'

Charlotte, despite her sadness, was very pleased to be asked. She had yet to go inside the beautiful little church which George had built for the tiny Armenian community.

As they made their way down the hill, Takouhi was silent, but as they entered the grounds of the church, she suddenly began to cry.

'I feel bad thing today. George says I am ... gloomy. Strange word but maybe true. George is not gloomy. He only see light, but I see dark sometimes.'

Charlotte knew that her friend suffered from inexplicable moments of deep sadness and at such times, she would sit with her, reading articles to her from the *Godey's Ladies Book* which Charlotte Keaseberry received from Boston, or light-hearted stories from the newspaper. She had also begun reading to Takouhi from her own small store of novels. They had recently finished *Robinson Crusoe*. Now she was reading one of her own favourites, Miss Austen's *Pride and Prejudice*, which Takouhi also liked better than the one about the men on the island. In this way, reading slowly and explaining words her friend did not understand, she could cause the black mood to eventually dissipate, and Takouhi would find her peaceful and sunny nature again.

Charlotte took her friend's hand, and they entered the church. It was a revelation, small and white, with the doors to each of the three deep porticos thrown open, letting in the rainy air. Charlotte sat in a pew just inside the door and waited whilst Takouhi went before the altar and began quietly to say her prayers. With her exotic looks she might have made a strange sight in a Christian church, even though today she was dressed somberly in European style, her hair drawn back and covered by a lace *mantilla*. Several gentlemen in white robes were also seated. Charlotte recognised Mr Ingergolie, a man she knew from his business in Market Street. She looked around this quiet building.

The outside of the church was a square, but the interior was a complete circle with a semicircular chancel and four small chambers at each corner. Some fifty feet or so above her, she guessed, rose the sloping roof upon which were elevated the eight elegant arches of the bell turret. It was not so grand as Coleman's design for St Andrew's on the plain, but she felt here that it had been a work of particular and purer significance.

As Takouhi rose and made her obeisance to the altar, Charlotte was overwhelmed with the feeling that Coleman had taken most particular care in the design and construction of this church. Then Takouhi joined her, and they sat silently for a moment. Charlotte said a quiet prayer for the soul of poor little Thomas, wherever it might be.

One by one, the men left, nodding to the two women. The rain suddenly began to beat down relentlessly on the roof of the church, falling so thickly beyond the open doors that a curtain of water cut them off from the garden. Only the candles on the altar and around the walls illuminated the interior, but the walls of white *chunam* plaster were so bright that the feeling inside was of glow rather than gloom.

Alone now, and remembering Takouhi's words, Charlotte put her hand on her friend's arm, but Takouhi's mood seemed to have changed. It was clear that, whilst she might find a place for Javanese goddesses in her home, this church nevertheless brought comfort to her, and she smiled at Charlotte.

The Armenian church tolled its bell for the poor little soul of a Protestant boy. It did not seem unfitting, here. Charlotte had even gone once to the sultan mosque in Kampong Glam with Peach and Charlotte Keaseberry, accompanied by the munshi, who was busy translating the Gospels into Malay. It was a bewildering and miraculous tolerance, which Charlotte thought perfectly suited this raw port city, with its bustling and multifarious population.

The rain had almost stopped, and now there fell only the slow drip, drip from the church verandah. The sky had lightened, and shafts of light from the bell turret lent brilliance to the dewy air. Takouhi had taken her to the big Bible in front of the altar, with its strange writing.

'I do not understand this, but I know words of the service in Armenian language. The priest always kind when I come. Priest want me to marry George here, but I think this will not be good idea.'

She stopped, and Charlotte did not press her.

Takouhi looked around the church. 'Armenia merchants and other kind people get money and ask George to build this church. This like home maybe for poor Armenian people who have no country. Here there are not many, but people work hard. This is lovely place. George is very clever man to make so beautiful building.'

Charlotte heard the tenderness in her voice.

'Yes, George is a very clever man, and I think he put a lot of love into this building. Perhaps he did so out of sympathy for the suffering of an oppressed people. I think it was perhaps for love of you.'

Takouhi looked at her and smiled, but said nothing.

# 20

Inchek Sang's body had been placed in the coffin. Two Buddhist monks kept the night vigil, and the house resounded with constant chanting. Sang's son, looking sickly and tired, also obliged to keep vigil, looked as if he were going to collapse at any minute. The first and second wives and their daughters, dressed in black, were seated, their heads covered with sackcloth, wailing loudly and continuously. As soon as Ah Liang had learned of his master's death he had informed the *kongsi*, and notes had immediately been printed and sent to every member ordering them to appear on the day of the funeral to follow the cortège; disobedience would be severely punished. Undoubtedly the mourners would number in the thousands; it would show the *ang mo* what power Incheck Sang had exerted and continued to exert even in death.

Baba Tan greeted the news with undisguised shock. He had known the old boy wasn't so well, but Sang had looked in good health the last time they had met. He and the other Peranakan merchants had put on their mourning clothes and gone to pay their respects to the corpse. As he banged the gong and entered Sang's house, Baba Tan wondered what had been said of their agreement, if anything. After the funeral he would broach the subject delicately with Ah Liang. In the outer courtyard Tan saw that groups of men were gambling. This did not surprise him, for the corpse had to be guarded from evil spirits for several days, and gambling kept everyone awake. Tan entered the courtyard and saw the coffin in the centre, with a huge portrait of Sang to one side. It didn't look much like Sang, Tan thought. It was an ancestor portrait painted many years before, depicting Sang in Ming dynasty robes with a badge of impossibly high rank in the centre of his chest.

Food and offerings had been placed in front of the coffin. The courtyard was thick with incense. Bundles of paper money and ingots were being constantly thrown into the fire contained in a large bronze urn, and smoke swirled thickly. A huge paper palace, complete with models of furniture, servants, horses and carriages awaited its turn. Tan and the others were received by the miserable, dishevelled-looking eldest son, who was lamenting as loudly as he could, though it came out rather as a squeaky whimper. Tan peered quickly into the coffin and bowed to the corpse, which was dressed in robes similar to those in the portrait. A piece of money had been placed between Sang's teeth, as custom decreed. In his right hand there was a willow twig to sweep demons from his path, in his left a fan and a handkerchief. Tan and the others joined briefly in the lamentations.

Tan eyed the son, who looked as if he would be following his father rather quickly. Still, at this moment, he was the eldest son, and as such the heir to Sang's vast fortune. He was about the age of Tan's youngest daughter. An interesting proposition in a couple of years, Tan thought, if the youth lived long enough. He certainly knew absolutely nothing about business and would need a guiding hand.

Ah, but that was all speculation. First things first. The smoke, incense, chanting and wailing all together were starting to give Tan a headache. He quickly lit his bundle of incense offering, placed an envelope of money in the chest watched over by a guard, bowed to the family and withdrew.

Robert was in Governor Bonham's office at the courthouse. They had been informed that Inchek Sang's funeral would take place directly after the Ching Ming Festival and that they should expect large numbers to attend. Ah Liang had smiled when he had spoken to Robert about it: more than ten thousand, he had said. Robert had not believed his ears. Now he and the governor were discussing with Ah Liang how they would deploy their meagre force to keep some sort of order. The cortège would leave from the house in High Street, go right through the town and up to the temple at Tang Heng. There would be fireworks and gongs. As the most important merchant in the settlement, Inchek Sang was to be given a fitting send off, but the governor requested sternly that order be maintained. Ah Liang bowed slightly. Of course, he said, though it might be as well if the police maintained a very low profile.

Leaving the courthouse, Ah Liang hailed a *sampan* and crossed the river to Boat Quay. He made his way through the wares lining the quay and jumbled around the five-foot ways. Having arrived at Baba Tan's godown, he entered into the darkened interior. He saw the old clerk and two other men. The man Zhen was helping stack chests of tea. Ah Liang passed into the back, but Tan was not there. He exited and, speaking quickly to the old man, moved out of the store. Zhen watched him head off in the direction of Baba Tan's mansion on Market Street. He felt a sense of excitement. He knew of Inchek Sang's death; in fact, he had received his summons from the *kongsi* to attend the funeral.

A few days ago, Zhen had spoken to the baba about taking English lessons. The old clerk who was translating looked amazed, but Zhen just prodded him to continue. Ordinarily Baba Tan would have boxed someone's ears for such insolence, but on this occasion he had simply looked thoughtful. He had waved Zhen away and told the clerk to go about his work. Zhen had realised that something was wrong and had said nothing more.

Now Ah Liang knocked on Baba Tan's door and waited on the verandah. Tan arrived a short while later, clearly having woken from a nap. He did not invite Ah Liang inside. It was quite irregular that this underling, no matter who his master was, should bother him at home. He had opened his mouth to tell him off, when suddenly Ah Liang produced a letter from his pocket. He excused himself politely, and Tan, mollified, took the letter and began to read.

It was addressed to him, and Ah Liang explained that it had been in Incheck Sang's hands when he died. Tan's face revealed nothing, but he quickly saw with relief that the matter had not been written down definitively. Thank the great gods, Sang had died before he could write out the agreement.

He looked at Ah Liang. 'What is it you want to know?'

'What does this mean? Did my master mean for this Qian or Zhen to be a husband for his second daughter? I must be the one to fulfill his wishes. His own son is so young. Did you and he have an agreement?'

Baba Tan looked at the letter fixedly for a moment, then at Ah Liang.

'Yes, we had a verbal agreement. He must have been drawing up the written agreement when he died. Blessings be on his soul.'

'Which one did he choose for his daughter, Qian or Zhen?'

Tan did not hesitate for an instant. 'Why, Qian, of course. He is obedient and reliable. Your master preferred him.'

Ah Liang smiled, relieved.

'Yes, of course, he would have chosen that one. The other was too much like the first son-in-law. I must act for him in settling this last matter. I will consult with the matchmaker tomorrow.'

After bowing to Baba Tan, he took his leave.

Tan smiled and went back inside his house. He, too, would act quickly to secure Zhen. He would speak to him today.

# 21

The memory of the attacks on the Chinese Christians had faded. The two men had recovered and were now put to work at the chapel. Charlotte had been asked to help them to learn some English and now devoted two hours a day in the later afternoon at the chapel schoolhouse to teaching them letters and words with some teaching materials prepared by Father Lee. She found she enjoyed this, and within a few days, two older Chinese boys whom Father Baudrel wished to bring on had also joined the class.

Charlotte was glad to be busy. Robert was often away all day. After his birthday celebration he had actually disappeared for two full days, and recently his absences at night had increased. She did not worry too much, for he seemed happy and in better spirits than he had been for a while.

She soon developed a routine. They rose with the gun, took some coffee, and then Robert took a long ride. After breakfast, Charlotte would walk slowly along the seafront and over the little stone bridge to the institution, enjoying the air and waving to the fishing boats. The harbour was never empty; ships continually moved in and out, lining up along the horizon as far as she could see. For three days every week she studied Malay here and helped with the English classes. In the afternoons, when the rain often thundered down, she helped at the chapel school. The evenings were spent with Coleman and Takouhi and young Meda or with Robert's two European policemen, William and Thomas. They were often invited to the da Silva home for musical evenings, for everyone in that large family played an instrument and loved to put on concerts and plays.

Meda Elizabeth and the other children had recovered their health. Captain Scott, who had been forced to take in his niece and nephew for the duration of the outbreak, was volubly relieved to have them return to town. Little Thomas Hallpike had been the only European victim, but Charlotte knew there had been deaths in the Chinese and Malay communities. For the first time it occurred to her that the other communities were in a difficult position when it came to sickness.

She knew there was a Chinese paupers' hospital by the stream between Church Street and Bencoolen Street and seen the wretched state of the coolies who, destroyed by hard work, poverty and opium, inhabited this dilapidated building. She had seen Chinese medicine shops, and Charlotte Keaseberry told her the Malays were very clever with plants for their illnesses. The Indian community appeared to have been spared. The soldiers and convicts were tended by Dr Montgomerie or his assistant, Dr Oxford, in the military hospital in the Sepoy Lines beyond Pearl's Hill, or at the gaol.

Sailors who came ashore wounded or ill were looked after expensively by a new arrival, Dr Little, at his dispensary on Commercial Square or, more generously, by Dr Oxford at the inn in Tavern Street. There was no hospital for civilians. Robert told her that there was often talk in the chamber of commerce of starting one, but somehow no one wanted to come up with the funds. Appeals to the authorities in Bengal fell on deaf ears.

Every Tuesday morning, if the weather was clement and he was not busy, Charlotte and Robert would take out *Sea Gypsy* for an hour or two of sailing. They had learned to sail in Madagascar and had continued in the chilly waters of Scotland. Walking the hills around Aberdeen and sailing with Robert and her cousin, Duncan, had been Charlotte's greatest outdoor pleasure. Here in the tropical warmth it was an even greater joy, whether sailing round Pulau Brani with its stilt villages of *orang laut* or butting along the coast, taking in the colourful Malay kites floating above the plain and the great houses along the beach.

There was the big old da Silva house just before Middle Road, the sultan's elegant new palace, which George had built, and the old attap-covered pagoda-style mosque. The sultan was still absent, but the village around his palaces was always bustling. Here on the beach side was a constant bustle of ship repair, boat-and sail-making using the wood and bark of the glam tree, from which the *kampong* took its name. When the wind turned suddenly, they could hear the clanging of the blacksmith and the noises of the shipwrights. On these Tuesdays they sailed into the bay at Tanjong Rhu and up the Rochor River to the Bugis *kampong* houses built out over the water. Unlike the European town, there were children here in abundance: little brown bodies jumping into the water and calling in Malay, 'hello, hello!'. From September, the mouths of the Rochor and Kallang rivers were filled with the fabulous sight of 300 Bugis Macassar *prahus*. These vessels, with their polished black-and-golden teak hulls, raked stems, and seven colourful sails, made a sight so spectacular that people from the town would leave work and ride out to watch as the great fleet sailed majestically into the bay.

The population of the *kampong* would suddenly swell then by 9,000 men. Their ships carried coffee, gold dust, pearls, spices, fabulous birds and tortoise shell. The Bugis merchants would hawk these wares around the Chinese town for a long time before settling on a sale. They never took money but always bargained for opium, iron, gold thread and piece goods. Charlotte loved the sight of these fierce-looking warriors as they strutted around the town half-dressed, their straight, thick black hair festooned with multi-hued feathers. Their bare, muscular arms were tattooed and bound with leather amulets. Their skin, smooth and hairless, was the colour of burnished copper. Their bodies were strong and compact and their faces handsome, with dark eyes and high cheekbones. Their teeth were black and filed to a point. The sight of a group of these fabulous men bristling with swords, *kris* and machetes gathered around a mild-mannered Chinese merchant was one she was not soon to forget. Though she tried hard, she knew she failed to adequately describe such sights in her letters home to Aunt Jeannie.

In the Bugis season, a fair would spring up on the beach to display and sell the cloth and the *sarongs* which were made all over the islands. Unable to resist the beauty of these garments, Charlotte had taken, like many of her acquaintance, to wearing these cool and pretty clothes at home. She did not quite yet dare to attract the opprobrium of Mrs Keaseberry by 'going native' on the streets of the town, though.

When sailing, however, she wore masculine garb for ease of movement and had had made several pairs of loose trousers and roomy shirts for just this purpose. She loved the waters around Singapore, especially when the sun rising over the crests of the waves turned the sea from slate to green. As it jumped over the horizon, great rays would illuminate the shallows. Then they would drop the sail and watch the bright fish flitting in and out of snowy corals just below the luminous water of the surface. Sometimes, when they had time, they would sail out to an emerald-ringed islet and jump onto the beach.

One day they ventured further round the island to the east. Robert had promised her a surprise. They had sailed alongside the palm-fringed beach at Tanjong Rhu to a place where a great rock jutted out into the sea. Beyond this, Robert said, were the beaches of Katong. He had just received a grant to lease a tract of land along here to begin a coconut plantation.

When they drew up to the shore, she was delighted to find a simple wood-and-attap building on fat stilts, just behind the fringe of palms. An old Malay couple took care of it and lived at the *kampong* down the coast. Standing on the verandah, looking out to sea, it was easy to imagine that there was no one else in the world. She was sorry to leave, but over the next weeks they went often to this place.

One morning Charlotte arrived at the Catholic mission to see Baba Tan in conversation with Father Lee. She had walked slower than usual around the plain, for there was a great hullabaloo as ships were debarking troops and setting up tents. Several cheeky types had whistled and whooped as she went past. She did not mind: they sailed to war. The harbour was crowded with ships. Robert and George were full of news of a great campaign to open up the Chinese ports. These ships were destined for Canton, where they would wage war on the weak Chinese authorities. Day after day new ships arrived, and the Chinese merchants, whether they had misgivings or not on this matter, rushed to fill the orders that such an influx meant.

She was glad to see Baba Tan. After Mr Whampoa, he was her favourite amongst the Chinese merchants who spoke English.

Baba Tan tipped his top hat to her as she approached and smiled broadly. He was happy to see her and delighted to know that she was teaching English to the young Chinese men in Father Lee's class.

'How do you do, baba? So nice to see you.' She curtsied politely, for she knew this charmed him.

'My pleasure also. I am here to discuss some new students for you. Father Lee talks highly of you and of the progress among his students.'

Father Lee smiled at Charlotte.

'Yes, it's true. The baba is enrolling two young men and urgently asking that I not try to turn them also into good Christians. I have told him that if these young men wish to learn about Christianity it is not I who will stop them. He has offered a generous donation to the new church if you will teach them separately from the others, and a handsome salary for you. In view of such generosity, I think we can meet his demands. What do you think, Charlotte?'

'I would be happy to help Baba Tan in any way possible,' she nodded, smiling. 'I know that he is a good friend to us and helps Robert a good deal in his police work.'

They talked a little longer, and it was agreed that these classes could begin after the great funeral of Inchek Sang, for one of the young men was likely to be involved in those proceedings.

The truth was that Baba Tan had not meant at all to get involved with the business of Qian. But when he had put his marriage proposal to Zhen, he had been surprised to be confronted with a man who was most adamant in his terms. Zhen agreed to enter this new Peranakan household and learn its ways, to be a good husband to Tan's daughter, give him grandchildren and learn the business and bring profit to his house. He would take Tan's name and, after his death, carry out the ancestral rites. It was not difficult for Zhen to promise these things, for his elder brother in China would take care of this for their father when his time came.

For all these things he demanded only a certain freedom from restrictions, money to begin his own business in cooperation with his father-in-law, and a house of his own should he wish to take other wives or concubines. In this he was frank with Tan, and the baba realised that he had chosen a rather formidable man for his daughter. He was not displeased; Zhen's requests were bold but not ridiculous. Any man would wish to take concubines; few would settle, like him, for just one wife. Tan began to see what Sang had meant: Zhen had strength and boldness, but it was tempered with a reasonable mind. He would make an excellent merchant. To have these things clear from the start was a good thing.

Zhen's last request also met with Tan's approval. He needed to learn English and wished his good friend Qian to join him. He had heard that the teacher at the Catholic mission house was good with Chinese people. It would be a good idea for him to begin to mingle with the Europeans and follow the example of his future father-in-law. These, after all, were the men he must do business with. Tan had agreed to include Qian until such time as the other man entered Inchek Sang's household. A period of mourning would have to be observed, which might last some time. Until then Qian would work for Ah Liang, who would defray Qian's expenses while he was groomed for marriage to Sang's daughter. Tan was well pleased. It had all worked out for the best, and he felt less guilty about his lie if he helped Qian to come on as well. Sang's weak second son might be worked on by an intelligent man such as Qian to become a decent husband for one of Tan's daughters. An alliance between their two houses would make Tan the richest man in the Straits Settlements.

When Zhen lay down to rest that evening he could not sleep. Truly this island was a land of good fortune for him. Perhaps the legends of the red phoenix were not far fetched after all. A wife and money. Where else could such a thing happen? He wondered what this Tan daughter looked like. He hoped she would be pretty, but it didn't matter. Actually, it might be better if she was plain; he didn't want to feel too much affection for her. He would give her the wedding night of her dreams, this little virgin who had brought him so much luck. It would even be nice to be able to make love freely, not worry about disease. Yes, it might be nice to have a wife. He would get her pregnant right away, and everyone would be delighted. Now that he thought about it, he would be pleased to have a son. Then, if she wasn't too repulsive, he would sleep with her just enough to keep her happy. He had no intention of being locked up in the family home.

And there was the money. Tan had spoken of leasing a shophouse for him, for his new son-in-law would need a place to prepare for the peculiar rituals of the Peranakan marriage, as well as a place of business. Zhen had been allocated a not unreasonable allowance, and after the wedding this would increase. He could send money to his family, help them rise out of their poverty. Once he was established he would send for his younger brothers.

These thoughts occupied him for some time. Then he remembered. He would soon be meeting the violet-eyed Ch'ang O. He sprang from the bed, clapped his hands and danced a little jig, his long queue jumping like a sprite behind his back.

# 22

Qian was happy to go along with the arrangement that Zhen had negotiated. After the period of mourning he would begin his grooming to marry the second daughter of Sang's house. There was a young son and heir who was only eleven, so part of his duties would be to groom this child to take over Sang's large holdings. Ah Liang had spoken to Qian and told him he had been specially chosen by Sang. In the meantime, he left Qian in the hands of the Eurasian clerks, who began to teach him, in a mixture of Malay and halting Chinese, the intricacies of the business.

What he should do on his marriage night lay constantly at the back of Qian's mind. There were young men at some of the whorehouses and, in a moment of intense curiosity and frustration, he had visited one. It had been an explosive revelation. He now knew he had a real problem to deal with but did not know where to turn.

Ah Liang had his hands full, organising the funeral and consulting the hierarchy as to who should replace Sang as grand master. Sang's obvious successor was another rich merchant who had been his number two, but this man had been ill himself and declined the post. After several meetings it was finally agreed that Chen Long, a *kongsi* man from Malacca, who had arrived in Singapore only a year before but had considerable influence and wealth, should be appointed.

Chen Long did not care for the *ang mo* any more than had Sang, though to their face he was friendly and cooperative, knowing the value of such a relationship for commerce. He had a particular dislike for the Catholic Church and its works in converting poor Chinese. Why did these interfering priests not stick with their own kind? The Buddhist priests at the temple didn't go round giving out tracts and preaching to the foreign community. After the funeral was over and his appointment official, he would call a meeting of the higher authorities and put this problem to rights once and for all.

Things were changing in the settlement. The gambier and pepper plantations were less and less profitable as the land was depleted. Opium smuggling decreased the profitability of the opium farm. In any consortium, to buy up the licences offered by the governor every year for the grog, gambling and opium farms, Chen Long would bring huge capital. He had begun to make a considerable fortune in the tin mines on the mainland. If land needed to be cleared over there, he would be of great use. Also he wanted to address the issue of piracy, which plagued not only the British but the Chinese ships as well.

He thought the Malays a useless and lazy race and was annoyed at the *kowtow*ing the British seemed to do to the temenggong and all that rabble at Telok Blangah. His English was good, better than Sang's strangled attempts. He could speak to the governor, and they could work to sort out this piracy thing. For this he knew he needed British cooperation. He had already thought that the newly developed steamships were the thing and was considering buying one himself. Chen Long had other plans, too. One of them included marrying his second daughter to Sang's weakling son and heir. A grandson and hopefully a quick death of the sickly boy would ensure he had his hands well into that fortune before long. Well, all in good time. For now, that could wait.

Zhen became involved in Sang's funeral in the oddest way. A discreet visit from Ah Liang one evening had been a surprise. Since he had been a 'red rod' back in China, he surely knew how to round up and control the crowds who had been ordered to turn out for the funeral. Their main *honggun* was not well; actually he had been severely injured in a knife fight, though Ah Liang did not tell Zhen this. Ah Liang was a bit short on muscle, and the sight of Zhen in full regalia would give them pause.

Zhen had considered this very carefully. As a prospective son-in-law of Baba Tan, he had to be careful what he got up to now. On the other hand, to be seen by the British as having a controlling influence over the *kongsi*, as a man who could keep order, would be to his advantage. Zhen asked Ah Liang to prepare a paper ordering him to attend and give help to Incheck Sang's entourage as a means of keeping order. This he showed to Baba Tan, who, after some initial concerns, considered it not a bad idea at all.

Armed with this paper Tan went to the governor and told him that his new prospective son-in-law was being put in charge of public order by the Ghee Hin Kongsi. Although he was not closely involved with that body he was considered a person able, by his natural authority, to keep the peace, which he had had occasion to do back in China. Bonham had first congratulated Tan, then expressed his delight at the young man's help with the peacekeeping effort. Robert was informed and he, too, was pleased and relieved. It was then arranged that Zhen and Robert would meet, even more desirable, said Baba Tan, since his sister Charlotte had agreed to teach Zhen English.

Robert was more than happy for this arrangement. Perhaps, he suggested, Baba Tan could come to the police office with Zhen tomorrow night to discuss the route and any security arrangements. At the same time, he would have the honour of introducing his sister.

When Zhen heard this news, he bowed to Baba Tan, keeping his face resolutely lowered. Then he turned and busied himself with the stocks of a newly arrived shipment of *chandu* from the farm inland. He drew a deep breath. Soon he returned to Tan's office and began a delicate discussion of his clothes. He was slowly trying to learn Baba Malay and had made some progress, and with him Tan made an effort to speak proper Hokkien.

Zhen had nothing fitting to wear to meet these Europeans, he said. Most of his day was spent half-naked loading bales. Baba Tan nodded. He would find him clothes. After all, he wanted this young man to be very pleasing to his daughter, and a little vanity in that line did not hurt. He was himself, after all, a good-looking man and had kept his physique. His concubine never complained.

All this discussion of physique and clothes turned the baba's mind elsewhere, and he decided to visit his concubine that very evening. First, though, he sent a note to his wife to send round the tailor for Zhen.

# 23

Qian was full of misgivings as Zhen prepared for the meeting he had waited for since arriving in Si Lat Po. He voiced a few, but Zhen eyed him severely, and he shut up. Zhen was nervous, he could tell. He had bathed a long time in the back tub. They had visited the barber, and his face and half of his head were as smooth as glass. Qian was braiding his freshly washed hair and running a red ribbon through it. When he had finished, Zhen began to dress. It was a pleasure, Qian thought, to watch him strip to his undergarment and begin the process of dressing in his shirt and silk coat. He had learned to disguise the erection he often got when he was around his friend, but today, faced with Zhen's semi-naked body, it was proving difficult.

Fortunately Zhen was so preoccupied he noticed nothing. When he had pulled on his high-soled boots, he stood up, and Qian laughed with delight. His friend looked every inch a Prince of Qing, a mandarin of China. Zhen smiled nervously. Then Baba Tan arrived and he, too, laughed at the extraordinary transformation. Secretly he was proud that this handsome and intelligent young man would be his son-in-law; it would give him enormous face.

Tan's personal *sampan* carried them over to the landing stage on the opposite bank. The police house was only a short distance, but as they walked Zhen felt his legs begin to buckle. The Englishman. The girl with the violet eyes. Quietly he said to Tan, 'I do not know how to act with the *ang mo*. You must guide me.'

Baba Tan looked at him and, with a slight smile, said quietly, 'I will speak and shake hands. You will bow when you are introduced, in the Chinese style. They do not expect you to be English. This meeting is so you can recognise Robert Mah Crow, the police chief, and we can agree a route for the funeral cortège. Also, you will meet Xia Lou, his sister, who will be your teacher of English.'

Xia Lou. Her name was Xia Lou. Tan continued to speak, but Zhen understood little else after this revelation. It was lovely, as lovely as her. He searched his mind for the soft sounds of his mother's northern dialect. *Xia*, summer, yes, and dew, *loushui de lou*, summer dew. Xia Lou, yes, perfect. It was as if she had been named for this island, where the dew was warm and where it was perpetual summer. More than ever it seemed that the Way was leading them together. He smiled slightly, relaxed and composed his face into an expressionless mask.

They climbed the steps of the police office. Robert came to the door, and Zhen bowed to him. Baba Tan tipped his hat and shook Robert's hand. They entered a room where some drink and strange-looking food had been laid out and immediately began making plans for the cortège. Although Zhen was somewhat distracted, he tried to forget his possible proximity to this Xia Lou and concentrate on their business. After an hour, the route and security arrangements had been agreed: Zhen would have a patrol of some trusted men to keep order; there would be strict instructions, and the police should keep out of sight unless needed. He showed Robert a drawing of the uniform and regalia he would wear and the flags that would be carried by his men. These had been invented for the occasion and bore no resemblance to the real *kongsi* flags, but they carried one sign which all the members would recognise on the day.

Zhen decided he liked Robert, although the Englishman smiled too much. Perhaps this was the *ang mo* way. In China, if a man smiled too much he was considered effeminate, but Zhen noticed that Baba Tan was completely at ease with them and laughed and smiled more in their company than when he was with the Chinese.

When the negotiations had been completed, Robert offered his guests some Porter beer from the jug on the table. Zhen had never tasted this before but seeing Baba Tan drink his with gusto, he tried a sip. To his astonishment it was delicious and he drank to the bottom of the tankard. However, neither of the Chinamen partook of the strange bread objects on the table. The baba explained they were called 'sandichies', and very popular with the English. Finally Baba Tan rose to take his leave, and Zhen rose with him, his heart sinking. It seemed he would not meet this man's lovely sister, this Xia Lou.

As if reading his thoughts, Robert said, 'Before you go, would you please say hello to my sister?' He opened the door of his office and called her softly.

Zhen heard her move down the hall, the swish of her gown against the floor. It was if all of his senses were heightened, like a hare in the woods. He thought he could hear her breath. Then, suddenly, she appeared in the doorway, as light and lovely as a breeze in the warm night air. He did not notice what she was wearing; he was simply and dumbly transfixed.

Then Robert said something, and he woke and bowed very low. When he straightened up, she was standing just as she had been, her eyes fixed on him.

She advanced slightly into the room and, smiling, curtsied lightly to him. His heart beat so hard he thought it must be heard outside his chest. Robert and Baba Tan were speaking as if from deep under some vast ocean. He stood completely still.

Charlotte knew it was him immediately, the man from the temple, and a deep joy spread over her. He was here, a friend of Baba Tan's; her new student was this man. They would know each other. She hadn't realised how much she had longed to see him again.

He was beyond handsome; he was the most beautiful man she had ever seen, tall and elegant in his silk jacket. She sensed the power of his body beneath his clothes. His face was perfect, his slanting eyes deep and dark. She wanted to go quietly up to him and run her fingertips gently over his full lips, feel his smooth, brown skin. Why was she not outraged at such a thought?

Robert frowned, somewhat taken aback at her stillness, and prompted his sister to greet her new student. He had introduced him to her but she had not taken in a word he had said.

'How do you do?' she said obediently, realising she must recover her poise immediately. She dragged her eyes off the man's face and curtsied also to Baba Tan. Then, smiling again, she apologised for being somewhat tired. She would be delighted to be able to teach English to this new student. A moment later, with every semblance of cool-headedness, she wished them all goodnight and left the room.

Qian was waiting when Zhen returned and quizzed him mercilessly, but Zhen would say little, except that she was lovely. He would talk about it tomorrow. He undressed to his undergarment and lay down on his cot, his mind filled with her. What poetry could he recall to describe her beauty?

'Fair is the pine grove and the mountain stream
That gathers to the valley far below
The black-winged junks on the dim sea reach, adream
The pale blue firmament o'er banks of snow
And her, more fair ...'

He had acted like a stupid country bumpkin, not saying anything. She had been cool, unaffected. He could not bear it. She did not remember him. At their next meeting he would not be so awful. He must learn to be with her. Why was he thinking this way? How could they ever be together in the way he now wanted more than ever? For heaven's sake, she was the sister of the foreign police chief.

The weight of this fact began to sink in. Before he had met her, she was an illusion, a thrilling, erotic dream of a white woman, beyond his experience. Now, she was real. He came thumping down to earth, stood up again and started pacing the floor. Any liaison would be vastly dangerous. It would put his prospective marriage in jeopardy and ruin his chance to save his family in China. Qian was right; he was crazy.

Charlotte, too, was lying on her bed. It was hot, and no breeze stirred the humid air. She rose and bathed slowly, pouring streams of cool water over her hair, and returned to her room. Luckily Robert was out tonight on a patrol round Kampong Glam. She wanted to get outside, go sailing or walk along the sea path, but she knew it was dangerous at night. Instead she went out onto the verandah and sat in the dark; here there was at least a small breeze. She poured a little glass of whisky from a bottle which Robert always had on the table. It seared as it went down her throat, but she had drunk whisky many times before; her grandmother enjoyed it, and it had preceded every meal. The drink relaxed her body, but her mind was in some considerable turmoil. Well, he is beautiful, of course, but he's Chinese. What on earth could come of these feelings? She watched the torchlight and the flickering figures of the soldiers on duty in the fort opposite, gazed at the lights on the ships in the darkened reaches of the harbour.

She took another sip and recalled his face, his parted lips that she had wanted to touch. She thought about what she knew of relations between men and women. More than most, she supposed. From a dictionary of *materia medica* in her grandfather's library she had a pretty good knowledge of human anatomy. As a child on the island, when roaming and playing with the local children, she had seen native men and women together. When she asked, her mother had explained that this was the way people showed their love for one another and how a baby was made. Her mother, a woman of the islands, considered it natural. Now she realised how fortunate she had been in acquiring this information, for in Scotland the subject was taboo.

Her first kiss had been a rather tepid business with Lonnie, a friend of her cousin, Duncan, when she was fourteen. More kisses and fumblings with Lonnie at fifteen. Things had got a bit better at seventeen, when she met Will, the good-looking, thoroughly unsuitable son of a farmer. She had not cared very much for him—he was somewhat arrogant and sure of himself—but boredom and curiosity combined to bring them together. Knowing the consequences, she made sure it all stopped short of losing her virginity, but she had enjoyed their secret meetings. She had learnt some local slang. His erect penis was called a *fearchas*. He had become quite enamoured of her, and she learned quickly how the power of a man's desire could overwhelm him for he often came stickily in her hand. She had not minded, had even licked her fingers once to taste the salty stuff. This act had so inflamed him that, alarmed, she had never done it again. Had it gone on much longer she might well have been in danger of succumbing, so she was glad it came abruptly to an end when he had been sent off to join the navy. How free I was. The thought suddenly came to her. Left to her own devices she had had experiences far beyond those of most young Scottish women.

From eighteen she had been constantly thrown into the company of so-called eligible young men from the Aberdeen gentry, but none had caught her fancy and, thankfully, Aunt Jeannie had successfully defended her from her grandmother's increasingly insistent demands. She had been saved by coming to Singapore, of that she was in no doubt. Here, with no elders to exert pressure, there was no hurry to marry, though she was definitely considered eligible in many quarters and might have her pick of several men. So how on earth could she entertain the idea of a dangerous liaison with a man from a country and culture she knew nothing about? That he felt a powerful attraction to her, she was very sure.

# 24

In Baba Tan's house, another woman was running her hands mentally over Zhen's face and body. Tan's eldest daughter, Noan, was sitting in front of her mirror daydreaming. She was a pretty girl, with deep brown eyes, a button nose and a plump, round face. Except for her skin which was a shade too dark, her looks were perfect. Moon-shaped faces and short noses were the height of Peranakan good looks.

She was brushing her black hair preparing for bed. She had dismissed her maid, an act so unusual that the girl had looked terrified.

Now, putting down her brush, Noan rose and began to take off her *baju panjang*, the long coat all *nonyas* wore over their *sarongs*. Underneath was a bodice which she slowly raised over her head, releasing her breasts. She stood contemplating her image in the mirror, turning to the side and front, pulling her long hair over her chest and flicking it back. She was pleased with what she saw. Her breasts were large and firm, everything to please her new husband. At this thought of Zhen, she raised her hands and touched her nipples, which immediately became erect. Slightly ashamed, she put on her nightdress and removed her *sarong*.

She was not entirely naive. She had married cousins, and she often heard them talking when they didn't know she was around. She knew men liked to touch women's breasts. Since the news of her betrothal had been announced, her mother had begun to talk about what she should expect on her wedding night. Noan knew that they would lie in the same bed together and that her husband would put his 'appendage' into her. That's what her mother had called it: the appendage. How this would happen was something of a mystery. She had seen her little male cousins naked and knew what this appendage was, but how such a little floppy thing could go into her she had no idea. Once this happened, her mother said, it might hurt a little bit and there could be a small amount of blood.

Noan was rather scared of this but her mother reassured her. The sheets would be kept as proof of her maidenhood and the consummation of the marriage. This was all perfectly routine.

Then, her mother said, he would move around until he had finished and put a seed inside her. This seed would grow and eventually become a baby. Noan wanted to ask her mother what it had been like on her first night. She had so many other questions, too, but she did not dare ask. The subject was already embarrassing enough.

She raised her nightdress and took off her underclothes and examined the lower half of her body. She frowned. She was shapely; her waist was small, but she didn't like her ankles which she felt were too thick. She began to touch herself and, raising her leg onto a chair, examined herself in the mirror. With a moue she lowered her nightgown and sat down on the chair. Her mother had told her that it was best to just let her husband do whatever he wanted. Not all women liked it, she said, but it was part of her duties.

She let her mind roam over Zhen's face. She was so lucky to know what her future husband looked like. She had mentioned this to no one. She was sure she would quite like whatever he did because she already knew she wanted to kiss his lips and touch him. At this thought, a little pulse began to throb between her legs. Raising her skirt, she parted her legs a little and contemplated this sensation. It had happened before but, this time, it felt much stronger, and she instinctively put her hand down and began to rub between the lips. This felt very good, and she let out a low moan. Horrified, she stopped. Moving away from the mirror, she went to her small embroidery table and began rather furiously to bead the *mungot kasok*, the shoe face of the extra slippers she was making for her wedding day.

The freedom of her early childhood had ended abruptly at twelve years old. Since then she had spent her days in this house preparing herself for marriage. She had learned how to pound the spices for the hot dishes, bake the *nonya* cakes and become expert at embroidery. She had made exquisitely beaded slippers for her husband-to-be for the exchange of gifts ceremony. She had sewn the phoenixes and peonies, the down-turned bats and the butterflies on the red curtain of the wedding bed. She had just put the finishing touches to the heavily embroidered handkerchief she would carry attached to her ring finger on her wedding day. This would display her skills publicly, and she was proud of her workmanship, which she dedicated to Zhi Nu, the fairy daughter of the Emperor of Heaven and Goddess of the Loom. Noan kept a painted image of Zhi Nu, the weaver maid who spun the silky robes for the heavenly hosts, made the gossamer clouds in the sky and wove the tapestry of the constellations.

She knew exactly how to prepare the *sireh* for her mother and old aunts from the gold-and-lacquer set her mother had been given when she herself had been betrothed to Noan's father. She knew how to take the betel leaf, cut the areca nut, put in the lime paste and fold the quid. She had been permitted to chew since she had turned fifteen but had not much liked it. However, this practice was so central to a *nonya*'s social life that she was given no choice. The men never took *sireh*, which was considered a feminine prerogative, preferring tobacco.

When the old women gathered for games of *cherki* and gossip she was kept busy keeping them supplied with *sireh* and emptying the porcelain spittoons which soon filled up with the red spit which emerged with regularity from their mouths. Many of the older women had stumpy teeth and mouths that looked like they were filled with blood. Some could no longer chew, and for them she had to pound the mixture in a pestle until it was soft. In Peranakan society, white teeth on a woman were considered to be animal-like. Obedience to her mother and constant practice had reconciled her to it, and she was pleased that her mouth and teeth had become stained pink.

Now the marriage for which she had been preparing for the last four years was nearly here. The horoscopes of herself and Zhen had been passed to the *sinseh*, the diviner, and the union had received his blessing. This was a huge hurdle, for nobody dared risk defiance of an unfavourable horoscope. Tan had paid the *sinseh* very well. There would be no obstacle to the marriage. The *sinseh* had chosen auspicious dates for the pre-nuptial rituals, and the wedding itself which was some months away.

The mistress of ceremonies, the *sangkek um*, had been booked. Eventually Noan's mother would choose the various bridal gowns to be worn over the ceremony, which would last twelve days. The *sangkek um* had a large array of richly embroidered and beautiful costumes for this special event. She had jewellery, too, for less well-off families, but Nonya Tan did not need it. Her household had the finest jewels in Singapore.

The bridal room in Tan's house had been selected. The elaborately decorated wedding bed would arrive from China within weeks. Tan's own wedding bed had come from China, and he had ordered his first daughter's when she had turned fifteen.

Noan put aside her beading. As she lay on her bed she began to cry. She had spent years preparing for just this event, but now she felt like a small child, alone and afraid. She turned and buried her head in her pillow.

# 25

The day of Sang's funeral dawned sunny. The promise of such a sumptuous spectacle had brought the entire town out of doors. The route of the funeral cortège had been pasted up all over the town for some days, together with admonitions and orders for a peaceful and respectful procession. Charlotte and most of the Europeans had gathered in the grounds of the Armenian church, for the cortège was due to leave Sang's house on High Street and turn into Hill Street, where it would cross the river at Coleman's newly opened bridge. From here, they would have a splendid view. Father Lee, who was standing near to Charlotte and Takouhi, was very knowledgeable on Chinese customs, which he had studied in his spare time while at the seminary in Penang. He had agreed to explain what was going on.

Charlotte was waiting to see again the man she now knew was called Zhen. Robert had explained his role in the procession, and she thought him even more attractive in this role of peacekeeper but said nothing about it to Robert, for she had determined that the situation required every degree of caution.

High Street and Hill Street were thronged with onlookers of every nationality. Charlotte heard the sound of firecrackers, gongs and drums and the harsh jangle of Chinese instruments. Gradually this noise grew louder, and she could see a great throng of Chinese men moving and throwing ropy bundles of firecrackers. Smoke and the acrid smell of cordite filled the air. Then came two men throwing huge bundles of round pieces of paper into the air and scattering them along the road. This, Father Lee explained, was hell money, used to buy the goodwill of malicious, wandering elves so that they would not molest the wraith of the deceased spirit as it made its way to the grave. Towering above them was the paper image of a grotesque man. As it drew closer, she could see it was being hauled by a dozen men on a carriage. The creature had three eyes, one in the middle of the forehead, and fierce-looking eyebrows of black feathers. Three small standards stuck out from the back of his neck. In his right hand he carried a staff, an ensign of office, and in his left he held out a paper some ten inches square containing the picture of a tiger's head. On either side of the carriage stood two men in masks, armed with spears and clothed in sackcloth, with long, dishevelled hair. These, Father Lee explained, were 'open-the-way' men. They and the image went before the coffin to keep the devils away.

This great image lumbered around the corner, followed by men carrying a series of large white paper lanterns on poles, covered in blue Chinese characters showing the titles Sang had borne in life. Then came at least a hundred standard-bearers of the *kongsi*, led by Ah Liang and another Chinese man. They were dressed in white and carried a black flag with yellow symbols. A sea of flags rose above them like a vast tidal wave. Father Lee pointed out the flags of the Cantonese, Teochow, Hakka and Hainanese. The noise of the band had grown loud, and Charlotte could see the huge drums behind a group of men who Father Lee indicated were the officers of Sang's fleet of junks. A gaily painted and gilded pavilion went before the orchestra, incense pouring out from every side, and the richness of its perfumes filled the air. The band slowly turned the corner with the most raucous noise; Charlotte had to cover her ears. More pavilions, one with a roasted pig and one bearing fruits and cakes, succeeded the musicians. Then came priests and altars. A splendid shrine containing a portrait of Sang was carried by male relatives, then children carrying baskets of flowers.

Charlotte scoured the crowd to catch a glimpse of Zhen. As the shrine turned the corner, she caught sight of a boy and, looming over him, the enormity of the catafalque bearing Sang's coffin. Despite the heat and noise and the vast throng which surrounded him, he was a silent, lonely little figure. This was Sang's only son. Poor child, dressed in sackcloth and looking dishevelled and scared, was doing his best to make a good show of his lamentations, but to Charlotte he just looked exhausted.

Her eyes took in the canopy of white silk which shrouded the coffin, the richness of the coloured embroidery and the great fringe which fell almost to the ground. This vast object was carried on a black wooden dais shouldered by some forty men. After the enormity of the catafalque, the small shapes of the women of Sang's house trailing behind seemed an anticlimax.

His two wives and daughters appeared, dressed similarly in sackcloth and lamenting the misery of losing their lord and master. The younger daughter did not wail, though she walked with her eyes downcast. Charlotte thought her a pretty thing, despite the garments of mourning she was wearing.

Then she glimpsed Zhen through the crowd. He was leading a group of men dressed similarly in white, each with one shoulder bared. They wore armbands on the naked arms, covered in strange characters. All but Zhen carried a pennant painted with symbols.

As they reached the corner she had a clear view of him. Her pulse quickened despite her mental scolding. She thought he might have noticed her, but he looked impassively forward and made no sign of seeing her. Then he was swallowed up by the multitude of men, thousands, she thought, which trailed along behind this procession.

Finally the Europeans grew tired and the group broke up. Coleman took everyone back to his house and gave them drinks. He planned to attend the funeral at the Chinese burial ground on the hill, and they made up a small party, without Takouhi, however, who said she had seen enough. After some discussion, she allowed George to take their daughter; she would meet up with them later for a picnic on Mount Wallich.

So George took Charlotte and Meda Elizabeth, together with John Connolly and Father Lee.

They made their way to the cemetery well ahead of the procession and, leaving the horse and carriage in the care of George's syce, climbed around the hill. Both sides of the wide path were lined with booths selling foodstuffs and drinks and offering entertainments for the gathering crowd. With the jugglers, puppet shows, magicians and other entertainments, the road had the air of a fair rather than a funeral.

A pretty Chinese temple, with its elegant green tiled curving roof and gatehouse stood on the slope. A sound of chanting emanated from over its high walls. Several of George's Indian servants had arrived well before and set out chairs for their party in front of the temple, in the shade of a pair of splendid dragon's claw trees.

The geomancer had chosen a grave site in the north-western corner, a retired part, where the bush had been cleared and a path made for the arrival of the catafalque. The priests, dressed in saffron robes, came out of the temple as the procession arrived and led them to the grave site. The silk covering and flowers were removed, and, to the loud and urgent banging of gongs and cries and shouts, the pallbearers, grunting and streaming with sweat, managed to manoeuvre the heavy black coffin into the gaping hole. Vast quantities of paper gold ingots were burnt at the graveside, sending a pall of smoke into the vault of the sky. The son and the male relatives had taken their places in a ditch dug for them on the lower side of the grave; they continued wailing and shrieking. The women were not present at this part of the ceremony but kept up their lamentations some distance away.

Looking out for another glimpse of Zhen amongst the great crowd, Charlotte suddenly observed Mr Dawson, of whom she had seen little since her arrival. He and several other men were engaged in the distribution of what she could only imagine were Christian tracts and Bibles. When she pointed this out to George, he said wryly,

'They'd be better employed preaching the gospel to their countrymen. There can't be upward of three people in the whole throng who can read. They walk the neighbourhoods, tramp through the interior, board the ships and junks from China, Siam and everywhere. The American missionaries are even more industrious, for they have their own vessel so that the literati of the swamps and backwaters of Borneo and Java might share in the bounty.'

By now the noise was overpowering, and Coleman adjudged it best to depart. They made their way down the hill through the noisy throng, George holding Meda Elizabeth in his arms. Connolly had taken Charlotte's hand so as not to lose her, and Father Lee led the way with the Indian servants and guards, calling out in Chinese to clear a path. They emerged hot and exhausted from the crowd and Charlotte was more than happy to sit back in the carriage.

As the carriages gently climbed near Mount Wallich, Charlotte contemplated the scene. The tree-covered hill, the roofs of the town, the white sandy beach, the sapphire harbour. At this height the wind was strong and cooling and rippled through the branches of the trees like seaweed under clear water.

When they had eaten and drunk everything Takhoui had laid out for the picnic, they began the return journey. Crossing over Coleman's elegant curved seven-arched brick bridge, the carriage turned down High Street and passed in front of Sang's house. A screen bearing Sang's name and age covered the entire doorway. Guards were lined up the length of the fifteen-foot-high wall which surrounded his compound. A delicious smell of roasted pig wafted out into the street, hinting at the funeral meal that was to come.

'By the saints,' said George, 'you've got to admit the Chinese know how to give a man a blazing good sendoff.'

# 26

The *Singapore Free Press* was filled with news of the departure of the forces and vessels of the China expedition for the 'opium war', as it had been termed.

'H.M. *ships-of-war* Wellesley, Cruiser *and* Algerine, *troopship* Rattlesnake *and H.C.* steamer Atalanta, *with sixteen sail of transport vessels, got under way for China, presenting a fine and animated spectacle as they steered out of the roads in three divisions, one of Her Majesty's ships at the head of each.'

Charlotte had watched them leave, sorry for the men she had seen every day for the last few weeks, as they had waited for this departure. Robert had told her that a large number of ships were already in Chinese waters. He was relieved at the disappearance of such a large mob of men, for Chinatown had been unruly and violent every night. There had been stabbings, beatings, drunken attacks on the women in the brothels. Corpses of soldiers and sailors floating in the river were commonplace, for the Chinese reprisals were swift. The army patrols kept some order, but Robert was very glad to see the back of the troops and the fleet.

When most of the warships and steamers had departed, Rear Admiral Elliot, commander in chief of H.M. naval forces east of the Cape, arrived in the *Melville* and landed under a deafening salute from the battery, which had shaken the bungalow and sent all the birds in the jungle wheeling and screeching into the sky. Now, after a mishap involving the seizure of three Chinese junks in the harbour, he too had departed to batter down the forts at Canton.

When Charlotte had discussed this invasion with the munshi, he had told her that none of the Chinese truly believed the English could win.

But to her question Baba Tan had had a quite different response. 'I have never been to China, but I think it is quite a backward country.

Still they bind the feet of their women. It is barbaric. They cannot see the advantages of trade with the world. But the English with the Queen Victoria are enlightened, so they must change their minds.'

She realised then that, unlike the coolies, people like the baba and his family had no emotional ties with China. Despite his looks, customs and dress, his admiration and loyalty essentially rested with the English, and he felt himself to be, as much as any Englishman, one of Queen Victoria's loyal subjects. She found this oddly touching. She liked him very much, and now this strange affection for a land so far away only seemed more endearing.

Zhen and Qian watched as Charlotte approached along the low wall and through the garden of the mission chapel. They had arrived for their first English lesson. Zhen was determined not to make an ass of himself this time, and as she walked through the door, both men rose and bowed to her.

Qian saw what Zhen meant. She was a very lovely woman. He had never seen blue eyes on a woman and couldn't decide whether he liked them or not. When she took off her floppy brimmed hat he saw her hair was a glistening black. She motioned them to sit.

Charlotte, too, was determined to remain cool and collected.

'Hello,' she said. 'Let us begin,' and pointed to the words she had said and the Chinese symbols which Father Lee had written next to them.

Then she passed out papers that Father Lee had printed with Chinese instructions. These said that they would begin with the English alphabet which was at the bottom, and every day would be expected to learn dialogues.

They began with the alphabet pronunciation as she wrote the letters on the board. After this they practiced the dialogues. The word 'hello' was difficult to say, though Zhen understood what it meant. It sounded different in her mouth. He watched as she repeated the word several times and completely lost his concentration. When it came time for him to say a letter or repeat a word, he could hardly speak. Charlotte, too, had difficulty keeping steady, especially when his eyes rested so intently on her mouth. She recovered by concentrating on Qian, who spoke up boldly, enjoying the new sounds his mouth was making.

Finally the hour was up. Father Lee came into the room and spoke briefly to the two men in Chinese. He gave them each a Chinese–English dictionary and showed them how to use it.

After they had gone, Charlotte went outside into the garden and sat down on a bench in a grove of coral trees. She was pleased with her performance, for despite the urge to touch his smooth cheek each time she passed him, she felt she had kept her emotions under control.

She liked his friend, Qian, too, who was willing and clever: his sharp eyes, his little nose, his pointy ears, the high cheekbones of his face. He was not good-looking like Zhen, but she felt his intelligence and dependability. He had wished her goodbye very creditably after just this one lesson.

The two men made their way back to Chinatown. Zhen looked grim and he said not one word. When they reached Monkey Bridge, he stopped abruptly and looked over the shaky parapet into the water. The tide was up and the river full. The wind was blowing stiffly, and even from here they could hear the cracks of the flags on the staff on the hill.

'We stand here between two worlds, theirs and ours. How can we ever be comfortable in theirs? It is impossible.'

Qian knew his friend was not talking about the European and Chinese but about himself and this lady, Xia Lou.

Qian replied steadily, 'We can learn their language, for many before us have done so. So can you, but you are shy before her because you like her. We shall practise together like the Chinese priest says, and with the Chinese Christian boy who speaks English well. It is necessary, you well know, for success in business here. It does not matter what your feelings are for the lady; this knowledge is important.'

They made their way over the bridge, and Zhen turned to his friend.

'I know you are right. I know I should put all ideas about her from my head. This is the difficult part. I do not know if it was a mistake or a good thing that I shall see her every day. Whether it is better that she become familiar or remain a mystery.'

Qian felt somewhat exasperated at his friend. Zhen was a Taoist. They were supposed to have control of their feelings, weren't they? But he said kindly, 'Perhaps after your marriage these feelings will subside.'

Qian put his hand on Zhen's arm. 'Zhen Ah, don't weave nets to catch the wind.'

Over the next few weeks Zhen relaxed in Charlotte's company. He started to understand the strange sounds and remember words.

'Hello, let us begin,' had become second nature to him, and he had learned to write the alphabet and the new words. His calligraphy was not good, but then he thought the language was quite ugly and its writing like chicken scratchings. He was annoyed that Qian seemed to be making much better progress, and to keep up with his friend he started to reread the dialogues and look up words in the dictionary.

Every morning as the first light appeared, he practised the movements of the *tai chi* in a grove of abandoned fruit trees behind Bukit Larangan, letting himself be swept into the slow fluid movements, feeling the *chi*, the vital breath, move around his body, harmonising his mind, body and spirit. Now he could smile at himself. If this was meant to be it would be. Everything was in the non-striving Tao. 'Hold fast enough to quietness, submit to the always-so'. The words of the eternal way.

Sometimes Qian would meet his friend in this grove, watching Zhen in the cool, pale morning light, his half-naked body moving gracefully like a reed in a river as he emptied his mind, arms falling, hands turning, feet stepping light as air in the age-old patterns. He was a thing of golden beauty in this dance of the Tao, the gnarled trees guarding him, leaves rustling on the wind, fluttering to the ground. Qian was always moved. When he finished, Zhen would call Qian, smiling his pleasure at his presence, and show him some movements. Qian was awkward, though, with his limpy leg, and the proximity to Zhen's golden skin pearling with sweat made concentration impossible.

So they would walk round the hill on the old broken-up path to a spring and drink the sweet water, Zhen splashing the sweat from his face and torso, flicking it at Qian, laughing, enjoying the morning and their friendship.

Two or three times a week, Qian, Zhen and the young Chinese Christian, who called himself Matteo, would meet in Baba Tan's godown and practise English. They were curious about this boy and also asked him lots of questions about the mission chapel. This they were forced to do in a mixture of English, which he spoke well, having been raised by the brothers in Penang, and their poor Malay. He could speak Cantonese but read and write only a little. This forced and struggling communication nevertheless meant that they advanced somewhat faster than might have been expected.

Matteo told them that the Christian Chinese were called Hong Kah, a brotherhood, just like the *kongsi* to which they belonged. Their god was just one god, more powerful than all the Chinese gods put together, and the mission helped them with work and education. He gave them some tracts in Chinese.

Zhen thought nothing of it. As a Taoist Zhen believed in no gods, unless nature was a god and the eternal way of nature was a god. He believed only in the quiet internal soul which beat inside himself and the words of the sages, Laozi and especially Zhuangzi. The wisdom of these and other Taoist masters were in the second book he kept with him. The role of Guan Di in his life was a necessity for he was the mascot of the *kongsi*, and Zhen served the *kongsi*. The sages taught to accept what was unavoidable, holding to the middle. Buddhists looked at the senses as windows to sorrow, to be swept away. For Taoists they were the doors to joy, through which the freed soul rushes to mingle with the colours, tones and contours of the universe. Zhen said nothing out of respect for Matteo's youth and limited understanding, but claims to absolute truth were in his mind manifestly ridiculous.

Zhen would say none of this, even had he been able. However, the information about this Christian brotherhood was interesting to Zhen who, since his last encounter with the *kongsi*, had paid his dues but followed Tan's advice to keep a relatively low profile. He had, along with 10,000 men, attended the inauguration ceremony of the newly elected headman, Chen Long, at the fortress out along the Selatar River. Chen Long consulted Zhen on matters of discipline occasionally, and he had helped out at several meetings at the temple. He did not particularly like some of the more sordid activities but this was part of his life in the *kongsi*. He had already agreed with Chen Long that this aspect of his duties would end after his marriage. He knew that Chen Long had a particular dislike of these Hong Kah and was working on a plan to get rid of those Chinamen who worked in the interior and adhered to this sect.

With their eyes watching and their ears listening, the workings of the *kongsi* were constantly under check, and, Long believed, this information was fed back to the white men's police.

Zhen had seen the plans of the interior and the *bangsals* where the men would gather to attack the plantations worked by Hong Kah Chinese. He had also seen that there would be an attack on the makeshift wooden chapel at Bukit Timah, where the Hong Kah brotherhood met for some kind of ceremony.

Zhen had no intention of telling Robert anything about this. He had taken his vows, and if these priests came and made trouble with the Chinese coolies then they should expect problems. After his marriage he would maintain these friendly ties with the *kongsi*, although these would be very low key and consist entirely of law-abiding activities.

Qian's interest in the Hong Kah, unlike Zhen's, extended only as far as the person of Matteo. He had sensed that this young man held tastes similar to his own, but had not yet tested these waters. These Hong Kah seemed very restricted about matters of sex. He still worried about his wedding night.

When the three-month mourning period for Sang had passed, he would immediately be betrothed to Sang's daughter. The Chinese diviner had been consulted, their horoscopes were compatible and the date of the wedding was set.

Baba Tan, true to his word, had selected a shophouse on Chap Sa Hang Au, what the *ang mo* called Circular Road, and Zhen had moved to the upper floor. The day he set foot in this house a feeling of absolute joy pervaded his being. This was his future. He walked about the rooms, which were gradually being furnished Peranakan style with heavy furniture. One of the rooms which gave onto the air well contained an extraordinary bed. He walked around, examining it. Tan had told him it was part of a sale of European furniture from one of the long-departed merchant's houses which he did not use and had lain languishing in his godown. No one cared for it in his household so it might as well serve for Zhen.

It was made of black iron, but so strangely wrought as to be as light as air. Curved scrolls adorned its either end, and he ran his finger around the delicate and sensuous lines of the metal. Above, supported by fluted metal columns, was an open canopy, four curved metal lines leading to a circlet, a small void, holding the whole in one elegant stream. He had never seen such a bed. He felt the truth of the Taoist saying: the utility of the object is in its emptiness. We live in the space created by four walls; we drink from the space created in the cup. Here he felt he could rest in the space created by this bed of air and light.

It was pure joy to have a washing room to himself. He loved this room best of all in the house. It was tiled with blue and white Malacca tiles, with scenes from some Western country place he did not know, where women wore heavy, pointy-toed wooden shoes and strange, curved lace caps. When Tan came to see how the furnishings were going, he told him that this was Holland and these were Dutch girls. Zhen felt sorry for Dutch men.

An old Hokkien servant of Baba Tan's, named Ah Pok, had been appointed to look after his needs. With Ah Pok, Zhen was supposed to practise Baba Malay, but Zhen suspected that Ah Pok had been sent to keep an eye on him as much as anything else. Zhen did not mind; he was still somewhat overcome with his good fortune.

No business would be diverted his way until after the wedding, and the lower floors stood empty, but it did not matter. Here, looking down on the bustling street, he felt for the first time that he could truly make a home here. He thought of his young brothers in China and how he could shower his good fortune over them.

Within a few days, his preparation for the marriage ceremony began. Two men arrived at the house. The first Zhen had met before. He was the *sinseh* who spoke Baba Malay and Hokkien and who had chosen the auspicious marriage dates. With him was a man called the *pak chindek*. Zhang eyed this man suspiciously. He was not a Chinese but a dark-faced Boyanese wearing Malay costume. Zhen had not known what to expect, but it was certainly not this.

The *sinseh* began by congratulating him on the good fortune of his marriage to such an illustrious house. Then he began translating for the *pak chindek*. The wedding date had been chosen: the twelfth day of the eleventh month. The betrothal day would take place ten days before that. This ceremony was called the *lap chai* and involved the exchange of gifts. These gifts would be supplied by the *pak chindek* and would be carried from this house by six elderly ladies from the Baba community, Zhen himself lacking any family here in Singapore. There would be four trays, holding items that would be used in the ceremony: a green wedding gown, diamond rings, pairs of candles. One tray would be lined with red paper and contain a leg of pork, three bottles of rice wine and a bowl of *kueh ee*, small round balls of glutinous rice in a sugary syrup. This would symbolise the whole-hearted joy and sweetness of the new relationship.

Zhen's head was swimming. What had he got himself into? But he had promised Baba Tan he would participate fully in the Peranakan ceremony, and he knew this was very important to his prospective father-in-law. He sat silently.

The *pak chindek* continued with many more details. He finished by saying that soon a tailor would come and measure Zhen for his wedding garments. Two days before the eve of the wedding, he would be prepared by the *pak chindek* for the vowing ceremony.

When they left, Zhen sat staring at the paper the *sinseh* had given him containing the date of the betrothal and his instructions. A feeling of panic flooded his chest. In a few months time he would be locked into this weird family for the rest of his life. No matter what he did, he would be expected to eat their food, share their customs and live in their house. He suddenly felt that he couldn't breathe. He rose and threw back the shutters on the window, but only hot air wafted over him.

He thought of Xia Lou. Seen in every rational light, their relationship was hopeless and dangerous. He had cooled his desire for her, but this encounter with the *sinseh* and the *pak chindek* had rattled him. The thought of never touching her was suddenly inconceivable, yet since the night they had met, she had seemed so aloof. In the classes she was friendly but cool, and he rarely saw her outside of the chapel grounds. He had not seen again the strong reaction she had had in the temple.

In his present state of mind this galled him. Had he lost the power to move her? He had to know. Had to change something, shake something up.

One afternoon a few day's later, after the lesson had ended, he went up to Charlotte. Qian waited at the door until Zhen told him sharply in Chinese to go away and wait for him outside. Qian, with a shake of his head, departed.

Zhen handed Charlotte a small package. 'For you.'

Charlotte looked into his face and then down at his two hands, holding the small package wrapped in rice paper. His proximity made her heart race. For the longest time she had struggled to put this man at the back of her mind, and now he was offering her a gift. She held out both her hands, and he placed the little package gently in them, careful not to touch her skin. She put the gift on the table and began to open it. He stood close beside her, and her hands began to shake a little. It was the reaction Zhen had wanted to see.

Finally she took off the paper and opened the box. Inside was a small but exquisite pearl, as round as the moon. She understood.

'You, you on the ship.'

She looked up, and he nodded. They stood facing each other. Her heart was pounding, and she did not know what to do. He knew that in any other place he would have taken her into his arms and she would have given up all resistance. So he was right. She felt for him as he felt for her. But not now, not yet, not here. They must be careful, and only he could control that. There was too much to lose.

He took a step back. 'I go now.'

She looked stunned, and then, suddenly, with a great effort, she drew herself together. Zhen read this on her face. It was difficult for the *ang mo* to disguise their emotions. Then she did something he had not expected. Putting the pearl back in the box, she took hold of his hand and put the box into it.

'No, thank you.'

She turned on her heel, picked up her hat and left the classroom.

Zhen looked down at the box. What had happened? He could feel the place where she had touched his hand. When he went outside, she had disappeared. Qian was waiting, sitting on the parapet.

'Did you see? Where did she go?'

'Into the chapel. What did you do? She looked very cross.'

'I don't know. I gave her a present. This.' Zhen showed Qian the pearl.

Qian looked at his friend. 'Thunder head, what do you want with this woman? Do you want to seduce her? And then what? You get married to the baba's daughter, and what? She becomes your second wife?'

Qian let out a laugh. 'Your white second wife or perhaps your concubine. Yes, that makes sense. She is sure to accept that. Give you lots of little half-Chinese babies, eh? Her brother, the white police chief, will be delighted.'

Zhen wanted to punch his friend, but instead he pushed past him out of the chapel compound and began to stride along the street. Qian let him go.

Charlotte watched them arguing through the chapel window, her heart pounding. She did not know what to make of this strange act. Why had he given her this present, this reminder of the night they had both arrived in Singapore? The look on his face when he had stepped back! He thought his face was impassive; he was quite good at that. But she had seen the little look of triumph in his eyes. No matter what her feelings were for him—and she knew she was vulnerable—she was not going to make a fool of herself for any man. She was quite angry at this arrogant assumption and began to dislike Zhen a little. After all, what did she know of this man? Absolutely nothing.

She made her way to the parochial house and took a cup of tea with Evangeline. Calmer now, she waited for Father Lee to come in. When he arrived, she explained that she thought the two men Baba Tan had sent might be better in his classes. She had reached a point where her lack of Chinese meant they might not progress. Father Lee was happy to take them on and move some of the younger boys to her class.

They talked a little longer, and Father Lee mentioned that he was going out to visit the chapel at Bukit Timah in a couple of days. Things had been quiet for quite a while, and he was taking some provisions to the young padre who was stationed there. Perhaps she would ask Robert if he could have a couple of peons to accompany him. Charlotte promised to talk to her brother.

Walking back to the bungalow, Charlotte was relieved. The tension which was always floating about whenever she and Zhen met would be over. She was glad to find something she did not like about him. It made everything easier.

Zhen jumped out of the *sampan* and walked rapidly to his new house. Banging the door shut behind him, he threw off his shoes and took the stairs two at a time. He had done something wrong. What? He had offered her a gift. He had not mistaken her emotion, and then something had happened. Before he could think any more, however, there was a knock at the door. It was his teacher of Baba Malay. He felt as if a noose was tightening around his neck.

# 27

Two days later Zhen returned to the chapel, impatient and slightly desperate. He met Qian at the wooden bridge and they walked along North Bridge Road. The day was overcast and cool; grey clouds hung in the sky. Qian sensed his friend's irritable distraction and they walked in silence. Crossing the chapel garden they entered the classroom. Xia Lou was not there. Instead, Matteo greeted them. From now on, he told them, Father Lee would be their teacher, but today he was absent. Zhen's head was in a whirl. Where was Xia Lou?

The hour seemed to drag on interminably. Matteo sensed Zhen's bad temper and left him largely alone. He was, in any case, happy to concentrate on Qian, whom he liked much better.

After the class, Zhen came up to him.

'Woman, Xia Lou, where?' he snarled.

Matteo was trembling, intimidated by Zhen's size, until Qian stepped between them. With effort, Zhen brought his temper under control. Taking hold of Matteo's arm, he led him out of the schoolroom to where one of the Chinese boys was doing some gardening. Zhen knew this boy was Hokkien and he called him over. With the boy translating, Zhen interrogated Matteo.

Father Lee, he said, had gone out to the chapel at Bukit Timah, taking supplies to the Chinese padre. The lady teacher, another boy and two policemen had gone with him. They had left early this morning and were expected back this evening.

Zhen was more than alarmed at this news. The attacks on the Hong Kah farms were due any time now. If they saw the man, Lee, they would be sure to try to kill him, for he was credited with enormous influence over the poor Chinese who worked in the interior. Charlotte would not be spared, of that he was certain. A feeling of panic began to rise in his chest.

Releasing Matteo, he turned to Qian.

'She is in danger. There will be an attack on the chapel, especially if they see the padre.'

Qian could see his friend's rising distress. 'Let's go to her brother, tell him. He will know what to do.'

Zhen did not hesitate. This was not about the brotherhood; this was about her, but he would not betray the *kongsi*. 'Yes, we will tell the brother, but only about the attack on the chapel.'

Qian threw him a look of exasperation.

As they approached the steps to the police office, a large Indian policeman holding a long spear barred their passage.

Qian, catching his breath, said in struggling English, 'Police boss, must speak.'

The *jemadar* looked suspiciously at the two Chinamen. The little one he did not know, but he recognised Zhen from the old miser's funeral.

'Wait.' He held up his hand for emphasis.

He went inside and they heard him talking; then Robert emerged, wiping his mouth. It was lunchtime. He saw Zhen and automatically put out his hand.

'Why, Mr Zhen. Nice to see you again. What's the trouble?'

Zhen stepped forward and dragged the words from his memory.

'You sister, Xia Lou, danger.'

Startled, Robert motioned them inside the office, where Qian explained with great difficulty that they had heard that there would be an attack on the chapel at Bukit Timah.

Robert was seized with horror. He knew Charlotte had gone out there with Father Lee, a Chinese boy and two of his policemen. He had questioned the wisdom of this journey, but she had been more than usually adamant and stubborn. He had had misgivings, but the island had been quiet for a long time, and attacks on the Christian Chinese had stopped. The new headman of the *kongsi* had spoken with him and assured him that things had settled down in the country. Now he was racked with worry and guilt. Why had he let her go?

Qian was dispatched to go to Chen Long. Zhen gave him his instructions: tell the headman about the situation, that it would be counterproductive to kill the foreigners, especially the woman, the police chief's sister. He wrote a note quickly and handed it to his friend. Zhen's opinion as *honggun*. It might carry some weight.

The *jemadar* had been sent for a carriage and two horses. Robert wrote a quick note for the governor telling him the news and sent Aman off to the courthouse. By the time the carriage came round, Bonham had made his way to the police office. He would contact Colonel Murchison, commander of the regiment. A contingent would follow them.

Robert loaded guns and ammunition onto the carriage. Four policemen jumped into the back, and Zhen and Robert sat up front, next to the driver. At a good trot they went round Mount Sophia and out along the road that would take them towards Bukit Timah.

Robert kept his rifle at the ready as the horses raced along the road. Thank heaven Coleman's men had made a good job of building it, for the going was relatively smooth. He had only been out on this road once or twice. The small wooden chapel was about a mile from the crossroad which led to the New Cut.

Zhen was holding on grimly. He did not like these carriages the white men got around in. Though he would not show it, he was fearful of the heavy breath of the horses and their pounding hooves, the bucking and swaying of this vehicle from hell.

They smelt it first. The almost homely odour of burning wood. Then they saw smoke ahead, and flames. The chapel was on fire. Jumping from the carriage, Robert and Zhen ran forward. The body of the Chinese padre was lying across the doorway of the building. He was covered in blood from a deep gash to his head and shoulders. Quickly they lifted him away from the fire and gave him some water. Reviving slightly, he told them that Father Lee, the boy and the woman had been taken into the jungle. The two policemen had run off when they saw the Chinese gang. Having imparted this information with effort, the priest paled and fainted, and Robert feared that he would not survive. Giving him into the charge of one of his men he began calling to the two peons. He was sure they weren't far away, but nobody answered.

Zhen was becoming frantic; he had to find her. Then he noticed the mark on the tree, the three red lines. There was a trail through there!

Taking Robert's arm, he motioned him to follow. Robert took a sword from the carriage and gave it to Zhen. Then, with two pistols in his belt and his rifle cocked, he told him to lead the way. The *jemadar* and two of the peons made up the rear.

They followed the trail markers deeper into the jungle. Then Zhen stopped abruptly; he had heard voices speaking Chinese. Signalling to Robert to make no noise, he advanced quietly. Two men were crouched by the side of the trail in the low bushes. They looked up as Zhen and Robert rushed on them and tried to leap away, howling with fear. Zhen boxed one of them on the ears as Robert held the other.

'Tell me quickly, or you are a dead man. Where is the white woman?' Zhen snarled.

The coolie was terrified. He had seen the gang go by with the Chinese padre, the boy and the woman. He thought they were going to the *bangsal*, about ten minutes from here. Releasing him and telling them both to shut up, Zhen said to Robert,

'Yes, Xia Lou near. *Bangsal* but— umm, er, dog.'

Robert understood. He knew what a *bangsal* was. Zhen meant that there would be dogs to bark an alarm. It would be difficult to approach without raising a racket. There was nothing for it but simply to rush in and see what happened.

With the two coolies in tow, they advanced towards the *bangsal*. They saw two huts ahead in the clearing. As predicted, a pack of four dogs ran out, wildly barking, and rushed towards them. Zhen threw one of the coolies onto two of them and they set about viciously biting him. With his sword he dispatched a third, and Robert shot the fourth. At the sound of the gun the two other dogs gave up their prey and ran off into the jungle.

Two men emerged from one of the huts and Zhen, now in a fury, advanced on them. When they saw the upraised sword, his face and the policemen behind, they took off as fast as their legs would carry them. Zhen flung open the door of the first hut.

A man was cowering in the corner next to Father Lee, who was bound and badly beaten. Zhang picked him up by the scruff of his neck.

'The white woman!' he shouted into the man's dirty blackened face.

The terrified coolie pointed to the jungle.

Dropping him to the floor, Zhen raced in the direction the coolie had pointed. Men were running away from a place behind a huge tree trunk. Zhen's heart was in his throat. It was not a good sign if they had taken her into the jungle. Robert shouted some orders to his men and now took off after Zhen.

Coming round the tree he saw her, lying on the ground, her hands tied above her head to the trunk of a tree. Her hair was a wild and tangled bush covered in dust. Her eyes were closed; her clothes had been ripped and he saw her exposed breasts and thighs. There were black smears on her white skin. Her legs were covered in cuts and bruises, her face smeared with dirt.

Letting out a great roar, he raced up to her. She was barely conscious. Taking his sword he cut her bonds; then taking off his jacket, he wrapped her in it, pulled down her skirt and lifted her from the ground, cradling her gently against him.

Had they raped her? He threw a look of such pain at Robert as the Englishman came into sight that Robert was astounded. He motioned for Zhen to put her down, but Zhen merely shook his head and began carrying her towards the *bangsal*. Robert was surprised and not a little irritated. It was his sister! Who did he think he was, this Chinaman, to ignore his orders?

Then he saw the boy on the other side of the clearing, and almost gagged. The boy's naked body was lying on its side tied hands-to-feet, like a bundle. His throat had been cut, and it was obvious that he had been assaulted horribly, for his lower body was covered in blood. Zhen had taken a step forward, but Robert motioned him to stop. Charlotte must not see this, though he felt sure she must have heard it.

He followed Zhen back to the huts. Here, in the shade of a tree, Zhen lowered her gently to the ground. He took her hands and cut the bamboo cords which had bitten into her skin. He went to get some water, and when he returned Robert was kneeling by her side.

She drank some of the water and opened her eyes with pain as he began washing the raw skin of her wrists. She saw a Chinese head and let out a scream. Zhen looked up into her terrified eyes.

Him! What was going on? Then she saw Robert and let out a

whimper of relief.

As Zhen ripped some cloth from his trousers and began bandaging her wrists, Robert kissed her gently on her forehead.

'Kitt, darling. You're safe now. Don't be frightened. Did they ... hurt you?'

She knew what he meant. Why didn't he just say so? Of course they had *hurt* her. She looked at Zhen, tying up her left wrist, and tears welled up in her eyes. They had rubbed their filthy hands on her breasts and sucked on her mouth, but, she realised, they had not had time to carry out the fullness of their plans. Thanks to Zhen. She had made this journey because she had been angry with him, but he had saved her. She put out a hand and stroked his cheek just once, with infinite tenderness.

'Thank you.'

Zhen looked into her violet eyes. It was as if they were completely alone.

Robert looked on, uncomprehending. What was going on between his sister and this man?

'Kitt, darling. Answer me please,' he said. 'What did they do?'

Charlotte pulled her gaze away from Zhen and looked at her brother. She wiped away her tears and took another drink of water.

'I'm all right, Robbie. But, oh, Robbie, they did something horrible to that poor boy. I could hear his screams, and then he stopped.' She began to sob again.

'Then they all smoked those pipes. I think they had decided to save me for later. My God, Robbie, thank heaven you came in time.'

Charlotte stopped and put her face in her hands, remembering—realising how close she had come. Robert looked grim-faced.

She took a deep breath and said jaggedly, 'They didn't get time to finish their business. Just roughed me up a little. I think we can thank Zhen for that.'

Robert was relieved. He let out a loud sigh. 'Oh, Kitt. Thank heaven. This is bad enough.'

Zhen did not understand what they were saying, but he knew from Robert's expression that she had not been raped. He had arrived in time. He said a silent prayer to all the gods in heaven, in which he did not believe, or whatever it was that had helped him get to her in time. Then he took some more water to her and sat on his heels by her side. She looked at his chest. It was so smooth, and there was a picture there. How odd. She wanted to reach out and touch the bearded face of this fierce-eyed Chinese man, but suddenly she felt too weak to even raise her arm.

Robert and the policemen were tending to Father Lee. All the coolies had disappeared into the jungle, and he wasn't going to start looking for them. He ordered the body of the boy brought from the jungle, and they dug a shallow grave and laid him in it. Father Lee, despite his wounds, gave him the last rites and said a prayer. He was stricken with grief and guilt at the fate of this child.

Zhen picked up Charlotte in his arms. Robert didn't even think of trying to stop him; someone had to carry his sister, and this fellow looked determined that no one else was going to do it.

With Zhen leading the way they retraced their steps. The policeman at the carriage gave a hoot of relief when he saw the group emerge from the jungle path. The two peons got Father Lee into the back beside his compatriot, and then Zhen passed Charlotte to Robert before springing up into the carriage and motioning Robert to pass her back to him. He settled down in the corner, holding her tightly on his lap. She sighed and let her head rest on the face of Guan Di.

They set off at a fast pace and, before long, Robert saw approaching on horseback the familiar figure of Lieutenant Gold in his scarlet jacket, with a platoon of soldiers following. He breathed an audible sigh of relief.

Lieutenant Gold cantered up to the carriage and saw Charlotte: the state of her hair and face, the cotton coolie jacket, the bare chest and the arms around her.

'Miss Macleod, you are safe. Thank the Lord! This is most terrible. Come onto my horse. I will take you quickly to Dr Montgomerie. Unhand her, fellow.'

This last was snarled at Zhen. Charlotte made to get unsteadily to her feet and Zhen rose with her, holding her arm. He did not know what this puffed-up soldier had said, but he didn't like his face or his tone.

'Auch, no need for that tone, William,' said Robert. 'This fellow saved her life. Charlotte, sit down. William, accompany us back to the settlement, please, for we must talk to the colonel and the governor. There is something terrible afoot; I'm sure of it. We must get some protection for the Chinese Christians, or there will be a blood bath.'

William Gold scowled at Zhen and waited until Charlotte had settled. She sat at a distance from Zhen this time, next to the *jemadar*, as they proceeded into town. When they arrived at the outskirts of the settlement, Zhen sprang from the carriage and, without a word, disappeared around Bukit Larangan.

Charlotte watched him go discreetly, her face half-buried in his jacket. William Gold was looking at her intently, and she decided she did not like the lieutenant half as much as she had thought.

# 28

It was Robert's worst nightmare. Over the next three days, wounded and exhausted men poured into the town and made for the Catholic chapel. Stories of bloody murder, looting and burning abounded. The schoolhouse took the worst cases; men were in the chapel and spread out around the garden. Father Baudrel kept a night vigil and prayers were said constantly.

Robert had been to see the governor, but Bonham had not been convinced of the seriousness of the matter. Colonel Murchison would not hear of involving the army: this was a civilian matter. The colonel was a staunch Protestant and did not approve of popish ways, in any case.

Not until six of Robert's Malay policemen died in an ambush did the governor consider the matter with gravity. Within a week hundreds of coolies had come in from the interior. Carroll, the Canadian huntsman, had become a common sight, helping groups to get to the town, telling Robert of farmers murdered, their farms destroyed.

Coleman came to see him. He had given Robert a hundred of his Indian convicts, and the casualties amongst these gallant men had been too high. He would put no more of them in danger. 'Get in the army!' he demanded. Colonel Murchison, however, would not hear of it, and he and Coleman exchanged angry words.

Robert had been to see the Chen Long, who had received him affably and assured him that this was all the work of ruffians and thieves, elements over whom he had no authority. There was little he could do. The trouble was that many people in the Chinese community did not like these Christians and the meddlesome priests who interfered in the time-honoured traditions of China. Robert was as certain as he could be that this elegant and smooth-talking man was behind the attacks, but without proof there was nothing he could do.

Chen Long had called Zhen to give him an account. Zhen had simply told him that the woman was the sister of the police chief and his teacher of English. He had felt it unwise for her to be abused or killed, for that would surely bring about the involvement of the military. As for Father Lee, he had had no control over his rescue with the police chief present. Chen Long had agreed. It was a great pity about the padre, for he was influential with these stupid coolies. The white woman, though. Yes, it was right she should not die, for there would be too much trouble. The government here did nothing so long as trade continued and white men were left untouched.

Robert went to see Charlotte, who looked much better. She had taken a long bath in one of Takouhi's luxurious bathrooms, her Javanese maids gently washing her hair and skin of the detritus and dust of the jungle and the hands and tongues of the foul-smelling men. Dr Montgomerie had bound her cuts and pronounced her well enough. She had slept for almost two whole days. The da Silva girls, Mrs Keaseberry, Miss Aratoun and most of her acquaintance had called and expressed their horror and sympathy. Isobel and Isabel were dying to ask for details but felt restrained by Charlotte Keaseberry's countenance. Takouhi, to set aside any indelicate questions, had assured them later that Charlotte was 'all right'. The men had been interrupted before any truly grave violation could take place. The da Silva twins were vaguely disappointed, but still longed to hear the whole story.

Robert told his sister of the attacks, the numbers of wounded and dying men turning up every day. After he left, Charlotte walked the short distance from Tir Uaidhne to the chapel. She was aghast at the site. Ashen-faced and listless bodies lay over seemingly every inch of the gardens. Hacked and bloody men lay dying in the schoolhouse. Father Baudrel was administering the last rites to one expiring soul. She could hear him intoning the words, see him kissing the cross. The scene at the poor boy's graveside in the jungle came fresh to her mind.

The smell of blood and gore in the heat was overpowering, and she left the room, seeking the fresher air outside. The army had supplied some tents, and these were raised at one corner of the garden. Charlotte could see Evangeline ministering to a group of women.

She was surprised. She had not thought there were any women in the interior. Going up to Evangeline, she kissed her friend and made enquiries. These were slave women, Evangeline explained. The poor things were sold to be whores. Evangeline had tears in her eyes. The evil that men do. But they are safe now; they will come to Christ and be saved in his infinite mercy. *Dieu soit loué*. The women eyed these white women curiously and gulped down the water Evangeline was distributing.

From then on, Charlotte went every day to help Evangeline in treating the wounded and preparing the ever-increasing quantities of food needed to feed them. Mrs Keaseberry and Mrs van Heyde, Miss Aratoun, the twins and many other ladies of the town also volunteered their help, though, Charlotte thought, many of them came merely to gossip and served little purpose. Baba Tan and the other merchants donated sacks of rice, pork and chests of tea. Mrs Shastri gave vegetables, and the Arab merchants had brought cloth for clothes and bandages. Hajie Fatimah came personally to distribute to Father Baudrel the alms that the Muslim community had collected. Dr Oxford and Dr Montgomerie, Charlotte could see, were exhausted. Convicts from the gaol were sent over to help with the cooking and nursing and to stand guard around the walls of the chapel.

In all of this collective concern, Charlotte noted the conspicuous absence of the army, who seemed to stand aloof from this human tragedy. Coleman was most vocal in his criticism. To have left a peaceful and industrious people to cope with such a monstrous event was beyond everything. The police were outnumbered, and the convicts could not be expected to give their lives. He wrote a long editorial in the newspaper. Charlotte had moved back to the police bungalow, and when Lieutenant Gold called to see her, she, too, was quick to tell him what she thought of the whole affair, and he, at least, had the good grace to look somewhat shame-faced.

On Sundays Father Baudrel held an outdoor mass. On one occasion Charlotte was sitting at the back of the garden listening to the hymns when she saw Qian over the low wall. He came up to her.

'Herro, Miss Xia Lou. Want see you well. You well?'

Charlotte nodded. Her mind had turned to Zhen as soon as she had seen his friend.

'I got message. Zhen say prease meet talk him.'

'Yes.' Charlotte's response was instant. 'Where? Qian, now?'

He nodded. She ran to get her hat and joined him. He led her along to the stream by the Chinese paupers' hospital and crossed the bridge. She followed him along the road to Government House. Within a minute, however, he branched off on a broken pathway which led around the base of the hill. They arrived at an old orchard long since abandoned, full of gnarled tree trunks and twisted branches standing like ancient sentinels. Beneath an ancient nutmeg tree, on a stone bench, sat Zhen. He rose as she approached him. As ever, her pulse quickened when she saw him, but since he had saved her she felt much easier in his company.

He took her hands silently in his and gently kissed each white-bandaged wrist. He was apologising for her pain at the hands of his compatriots.

'No, no,' she said. 'Not your fault. You saved me. Thank you.'

She realised he might not understand what she was saying, so she called Qian, who had been standing awkwardly a little distance away, and explained that he would need to help her translate.

Yes, if Zhen agreed.

Zhen made a gesture with his hand and sat on the bench. Charlotte sat next to him. He began to tell her about his love for her. Qian knew the word 'love'. He had looked it up in the dictionary Father Lee had given him, right after the word for 'sex', but that he had not yet found.

Love! Charlotte looked at him. He loved her. Why, yes, of course he loved her, and she loved him. That was what this was. Not a game or some idle curiosity. How simple it all was.

She watched his mouth move as he made the Chinese sounds. She liked the staccato tones of his language and the way it seemed to rise and fall like the undulations of some hilly countryside. His voice was deep and resonant. Putting out a finger, she could not resist touching his full lips. So luscious, she thought. He took her hand in his.

'Marry,' she heard the word. Marriage, marriage. Whose marriage? Ours? Mine, his? What on earth! She looked up at Qian. Zhen had stopped speaking.

'Zhen must marry daughter Baba Tan. Cannot choose. Must marry on twelve day of eleven moon.'

Qian searched his mind and mopped his brow. A little tic started by his left eye. 'December. Zhen must marry.'

Charlotte pulled her hand out of Zhen's. He was getting married? Of course he was. They have arranged marriages just as we do. Why is he telling me this? What does he expect me to say, to do? She looked around the garden. Time seemed to have lost its cadence, and she could see the leaves of the trees, yellowing and wrinkled, fall through the air with infinite slowness, drifting down on the eddies of the invisible breeze. Through a distance she heard him say her name.

Zhen could see the distress on her face, her eyes open wide in shock. A ripple of pain rose in his chest. He had hurt her. Putting out a finger, he turned her face to his.

Charlotte pulled her head back and looked at him accusingly. 'Why, why tell me this? Why?'

Qian could not think straight. A phrase recently learned from Matteo popped into his head. 'Honesty is best policy.'

Charlotte gave a small, slightly hysterical laugh. The ludicrous incongruity of this homily at this moment brought her to her senses. What was she doing with these crazy men in this place?

She stood up to leave. Zhen was alarmed. She could not go, not like this. Not angry, not hating him. In Chinese he could have wooed her, giving this love, this passion for her, poetry and depth. In her language they could not find the words to say this right. It was all coming out tawdry and foolish. The time for words was over.

Zhen took her arm and turned her to face him. 'Not love marry woman. Love Xia Lou. Love you.'

He bent and moved his face closer to hers. 'Love you,' he said fiercely, taking her waist in his hand and pulling her gently against him. She felt his other hand move to her back, his fingers in her hair, on her neck and then her face was against his and he was kissing her. A kiss so deep and soft that, despite everything, she felt herself respond to the touch of his lips on hers, the contours of his body. He held her as if she were made of the most delicate porcelain that he was afraid to drop or crush, strength and softness in one embrace. Her arms went round his neck as if drawn by some invisible chain, and she felt the corded thickness of his queue where it lay upon his neck. A wave of desire swept through her body.

Her arms responded, entwining his neck and head, deepening the kiss. Zhen felt her emotion, felt his own, lifted her from the ground and pulled her closer into him. Floating, she felt liquefied, as if he, like some ancient alchemist, had blended their two base souls into molten gold.

'O Love, O fire! Once he drew
With one long kiss my whole soul thro'
My lips,
As sunlight drinketh dew'

When he finally released her—took his lips from hers with slow reluctance and made them clay again—she drooped weakly onto the stone bench. Zhen fell to his knees in front of her. Bringing his crossed arms to his forehead he gently put his face into her lap in a gesture of submission so completely unexpected it moved her to the core.

Qian, embarrassed and a little jealous, had retreated to the other side of the tree. He had never seen a man kiss a woman like that, and he would have liked to feel Zhen's hard arms around him.

Without thinking, Charlotte put her hands on his head and dropped her face to kiss the place where his queue began, laying her cheek against his naked skin and entwining her fingers in the red-threaded, plaited silkiness of his hair. And so they stayed quietly. A little breeze rustled the leaves of the tree above, which fell in a golden shower over them.

Qian peeped round the tree. It was like an antique painting. To see them sitting so touched his heart, but he did not know where all this would end. He moved through the dried leaves, and Zhen and Charlotte stirred.

'What do you want?' she asked through Qian, her eyes on Zhen.

'To see you, meet you, speak with you,' he said. Qian translated. 'I'll never touch you again if you don't want it. This marriage is nothing. Economic necessity. You must not have pain because of it. All my heart belongs to you.'

All this was difficult for Qian to find the words to explain. She put her hand on Qian's arm, reassuring him. She understood. It was all right. Zhen wanted them to be lovers, one way or another. Marriage with her, impossible. Marriage to the other woman because he was poor. She needed to think about this very carefully, not surrender to the emotions which were swirling around in her.

'Yes, see, speak,' she said quietly. These words he understood. It was enough. He lowered his head in relief.

They parted without another word, and Qian walked back to the chapel with Charlotte. He liked this woman very much, for he felt her heart was pure. He was worried that she would be consumed and destroyed by this passion and love of Zhen's for her. He knew the force of Zhen's character. He was as adept at the *wu wei*, the soft letting-be nature of the Tao, as with its disciplines. If he felt this Xia Lou was his by natural right he would be as the river, pulling her into the flow as effortlessly but relentlessly as a flower petal is carried on the current of a stream.

As he left her at the gate he said, 'Miss Xia Lou, please careful. I your friend. Zhen is dragon, *yang*, but can be *yin*, you understand.'

Charlotte looked at Qian. '*Yang? Yin?*'

'Yes. Chinese people think, all things two but make one. One *yin*, one *yang*.' He clasped his fingers together to show her the unity of these two concepts, for he did not know the words.

Taking a twig he drew the *tai chi* on the ground. She recognised it from one of the temples she had been to or somewhere in the town. He drew the dots in either side of the wavy separation.

'*Yin* in *yang*, *yang* in *yin*. *Yin*, you, soft, water. *Yang*, man, hard. Zhen is fire but can be water.'

When Zhen had taken the decision to kiss Xia Lou, he had been *yang*, fiery and bright, but when he had knelt at her feet, he had surrendered to her *yin* power, soaking it up and turning it to his advantage. Qian felt certain of this. He had put his head in her lap and become liquescent, entering the fissures of her resolve as water fills up the crevices and cracks of a dry riverbed. This was Zhen's power. His ability to be hot light but soak up the cool darkness made him composed under pressure, pliant but disciplined, impulsive but not reckless.

'Careful, please.'

He bowed and left her contemplating the image. Charlotte realised there was so much she did not know. Unfortunately Zhen's mysterious side simply made him more attractive.

Crimoney, Kitt Macleod, I think you're in trouble if he can be fire and water. She thought she might need some of the *yang* stuff if she was to resist him. She could still feel the pressure of his lips on her mouth, the soft strength of his arms around her, the sorcery of his kiss. But Qian's simple explanation had somehow clarified her thoughts. She wanted this kiss again, and probably more, she could not deny it, but if this was his *yang*-ness, his hard fire, then, if this Chinese philosophy were right, she could absorb it too. Smiling, she turned into the gate of the chapel.

Before Governor Bonham felt forced to act, Chen Long called off the attacks. Coolies would think twice before joining this interfering sect. The violence had started to open up old suspicions between Teochew and Hokkien. Peace returned to Singapore.

# 29

The Christian Chinese had largely dispersed. The dead had been buried in a corner of the Christian cemetery on the hill. Of the survivors, some went off to work in the tin mines, some to the islands; others stayed to find work in the town or in the market gardens, but many returned home to China. A few were sent to seminaries in Penang to prepare them for the priesthood. Most of the women had simply vanished from the town, but quite a lot had converted. Father Baudrel hoped they would make good wives for the Chinese Christian faithful who had endured so much. Father Lee had recovered from his beatings. Evangeline returned to her more regular work. Charlotte resumed her teaching of the younger boys, and Zhen and Qian went back to the English lessons.

Over the next weeks Charlotte and Zhen met in the chapel gardens after the lesson for a while before he had to go back to town. On a Sunday, when Robert went to church or disappeared off somewhere, Charlotte would meet Zhen in the orchard in the early morning, for Baba Tan paid little attention to him on that day, which he spent with his family in Kampong Glam. Then they would try to talk about each other.

The first time she went, Zhen had shaken a nutmeg from the old tree and opened up the hard sheath with his knife, revealing the beauty of the shiny black nut and its lacy red mace caul. In her heart she felt that he was like the nut, hard and glowing, and she the delicate enveloping arms of the caul, which she longed to entwine around him. She could never tell him this, but when they looked at the nutmeg together she felt he understood the sentiment. He tried to explain the legends and properties of this spice—how in China it was used in cooking but also in medicine for indigestion and as oil for muscle aches. If you took the right amount it made you euphoric; if you took too much it killed you. So she learned that he knew about medicine and herbs. Sometimes he would bring dried up roots and kernels from the fragrant and pungent Chinese medicine shops in the town and show her something of their use; or he brought pretty spices: star anise and cassia buds.

He discovered she could sail small boats and admired her bravery. She tried to tell him she had had an accident, a blow and deep cut to her arm when the jib had swung back onto her. Miming the word accident, she had pretended to stumble and fall, which had precipitated an actual fall, and he, alarmed, had picked her up, and she had laughed, unhurt, and he had understood and laughed too. They grew easier together and smiled at their constant misunderstandings. Zhen now made a huge effort at learning English and was making rapid improvement. He told her about China, the village where his family lived, the poverty which had forced him to leave.

He had three older brothers, a sister and three younger brothers. He was the second son of his father's third wife. Though he could not articulate this to Charlotte, as a fourth son of a minor wife he had considerable freedoms not enjoyed by his elder brothers, whose duties to the family were greater than his. Charlotte was amazed at the number of wives Chinese men seemed to have. The thought of sharing him with another woman was already gnawing at her. She could not imagine putting up with three or four. Zhen tried to explain his obligation to grow rich and aid his family back home; he did not tell her of his father's addictions, though, for he was ashamed of this stain. Charlotte told him about her island home, the loss of her parents and life in chilly Scotland.

He did not touch her, though he longed to. He would wait, wait for her, half the pleasure in the waiting. He would know when she was ready. It was enough to be together for now. Wanting to touch him, she showed him some dance steps, a half-learned Scottish reel, wishing against reason that he would kiss her again, but he did not. He showed her the movement of the *tai chi*, knowing how graceful and lithe his body looked, enjoying her gaze, waiting, tempting her, turning her, drawing her. Watching him in the morning light as the sun slanted down through the old trees was, for Charlotte, like watching an ethereal and magnificent spirit of the wood.

He gave her a mirrored *pa kua*, the *tai chi* symbol with the eight trigrams, and tried to explain that it would guard her against bad spirits.

She brought a picture book of paintings she had found at the institution library, filled with images of China, and he laughed at the quaintness of these scenes so unlike the heroic landscapes and Taoist paintings of his homeland. 'China not like this,' he said, and Charlotte nodded. Of course China was not like this. For Charlotte, *this man* was China: fabulous, magnificent, the contours of his body the hills and valleys, his eyes filled with the dark rivers and streams of his land.

He took her to Chinatown and tried to teach her how to use chopsticks in a dish of thick noodles. They both ended up laughing at her inadequacy. The shop owner had been astonished to see a white woman in his shop.

Eventually, of course, their relationship came to the notice of Robert and Baba Tan.

'Kitt,' Robert began one day at breakfast, 'people are talking about you and that Zhen. You know he is going to marry the baba's daughter.'

Charlotte looked up at him, displeased at his interference and at the mention of this marriage. 'Are they, Robbie? And what are they saying?'

He recognised the tone in her voice.

'Auch, Kitt, really. I like the fellow and you know I don't like to interfere, but tongues wag.'

'Well, Robbie, let them. There's nothing but friendship there. He saved my life. Why, you should be grateful. He's learning English. I know about the marriage. If it's a problem for you, then tell me, for there's nothing untoward going on.'

Robert had dropped the matter, for he believed his sister, but Charlotte understood she should be more careful. Yet she felt a lightness of spirit when she was with Zhen that was hard to give up.

Baba Tan had spoken with Zhen, too. He liked this young man who would be his son, did not mind that he might be enjoying some premarital fun, but white women were trouble on too many levels. Zhen had simply bowed to him and said, 'Do not be anxious; there is nothing happening there. She was my teacher. I saved her life and feel she is like a sister to me. From her I learn a lot about the white people and their customs. But if you wish it, I will not meet her again.'

'No, no,' Tan had replied, mollified. 'Discretion, though, is required.'

They had been amicable, for Tan did not want to lose this young man who he knew now occupied his eldest daughter's every waking thought. Since the day she had seen him, she had devoted herself to her trousseau with redoubled vigour and attended to her mother and father with a filial piety which bespoke her gratitude. Her joy was so palpable it touched his heart.

Zhen had made such good progress in Baba Malay too and was proving to be a real asset to the company. Of course it was a good thing to get close to the white administrators. So Tan let the matter drop.

In the meantime Qian had been growing increasingly anxious as the day of his own marriage approached. He now knew Sang's business inside and out, and Ah Liang was happy to leave much of the day-to-day running of the company to him.

The two friends met one evening on Boat Quay. Zhen talked to Qian of his growing love for Charlotte. Qian was the only person he could reveal this to, and he was grateful to his friend for his patient understanding. Tonight, though, he sensed Qian was uneasy. He waited for his friend to speak.

When he did, Zhen was taken aback, for it had never crossed his mind that Qian might prefer men.

'*Aiya*, little Qian. This is a problem. Do you fancy me, then, blockhead? Why, by the red face of Guan Di, I believe you do.' He punched Qian lightly on the arm.

'Forget about it. The pleasures of the bitten peach don't interest me, eh.'

He saw Qian wince and was immediately sorry. It had been hard for him to reveal this; Zhen knew that. He did not especially disapprove. The fourth concubine often had a girl or two in her bed, even when he was there, for she liked him to watch them together, and he had enjoyed these romps, sharing himself between them all. Sometimes they were joined by boys, whom she trained in the erotic arts for her master, who enjoyed both sides of the bed. Zhen was not interested in this particular pleasure, but he had known homosexual men back home with whom you could get drunk as easily as the next fellow.

Qian had begun to regret speaking to Zhen, but it was too late now.

'No, thunder boy, I don't fancy you so shut up. But what am I going to do on my damn wedding night? Look. I need the hard body, you know, the dick, all the bits. All that softness and roundness just turns me off.'

Zhen shook his head in disbelief. All the softness and roundness turned him off! *Aiya*, truly he would never understand this kind of passion.

'I don't know what to say. You have to get it up for her once, on the wedding night.'

They went round and round the problem, drinking grog and getting drunk to the point of laughter, but with no answer found.

The next day, Zhen had decided that this was a serious problem for his friend and gave it more dedicated thought. His only solution was that Qian would have to practise on a woman at least a few times before the nuptials. He would have to go to Min and get one of the boys there—do it with them together.

Qian was initially sceptical but in the end, what did he have to lose? Two nights later they met up at the *ah ku* house and waited for Min. When she saw Zhen she was, at first, annoyed. He hadn't been to see her for weeks. He placated her and put a sum of money onto the dresser. He had already paid the old woman, but this would be extra for her.

He explained what was required. Min was not very interested; she wanted time with Zhen. However, she finally agreed and sent for one of the young boys from the *ah ku* house next door. Zhen waited at one of the tea houses for Qian. When he emerged, Qian shook his head. It just hadn't worked.

'*Aiya*, Qian, then I can't do anything more for you. Perhaps you should be honest with your poor new wife. After all, what does she want with an impotent blockhead like you in her bed? Then you can sort out some arrangement with a coolie that she might fancy. She gets some satisfaction at least and possibly a son for the house, and you go your merry way. Make her a good husband in other ways. Be kind to her. I know it sounds radical, but what's the alternative? You need this marriage. From what I've seen of the Sang household, they could do with some happiness.'

Qian knew Zhen was right. There was no other way. He would be useless to her in bed.

Zhen went to thank Min, for he knew she was disappointed that he would not stay. He promised to come back soon, kissed her and departed. He needed a drink. Qian was on his own.

In any case, Zhen was busy. The tailor came to measure him for the wedding suit and other clothes he would need. Many of the gifts that would be taken on the betrothal day had arrived at his house. Suddenly there seemed to be no time to see Charlotte, even at the chapel. He sensed her slight withdrawal. After his lesson, he approached her, trying to engage her but she seemed aloof.

Charlotte, despite her sharpness with Robert, had been trying to decide what to do about her growing closeness to Zhen. Robert was right, of course, tongues would wag, and after all, Zhen was getting married soon. She decided that it would be better to see less of him. John Connolly had called on her many times, and she liked him a great deal. He was something of a younger version of Coleman, and she found him very seductive. John made her laugh; they shared a sense of humour, and he liked to sail also. He had prospects, she knew, and had recently started his own agency house with William Kerr, a new arrival. Lieutenant Gold, too, paid her attendance at parties but she had cooled towards him. He could be prudish and peevish, and she did not think she wanted either quality in a man, nor especially to be the wife of a soldier. John's easy nature was a match for her own, which she knew could be occasionally serious, sometimes grimly determined.

Connolly, as he happily confessed to Coleman, was besotted with her. Coleman was delighted for his friend, for he saw all Charlotte's qualities, her beauty, her inner resolve. She was a woman after his own heart and, were it not wholly owned by Takouhi, he might well have tossed his hat in the ring.

When Zhen first saw Charlotte on the arm of this white man, he thought his brain might explode. John and Charlotte had been visiting the old boy in the big house at Tanjong Tankap and emerged as Zhen was on the quay. He had stood as they approached, right in her line of vision. She had seen him, he knew; he saw her tense, drop the man's arm and say something to him. Abruptly they turned, and the white man hailed a *sampan*, taking them back across the river. Zhen tossed all night.

In the chapel ground the following morning he stepped in front of her and, taking her arm, led her quickly into a grove of trees.

'Who the man?' he demanded.

Charlotte could see his anger. By what right? He was getting married. One kiss, no matter how wonderful, and a few walks didn't mean she belonged to him.

'Well, Zhen, you will marry. Perhaps I will too.'

She said this deliberately to hurt him. The effect was immediate. He was wholly unaccustomed to women resisting him.

'So you marry, eh? My marry no love, you marry no love. What about us?'

He was suddenly sick of this shilly-shallying around.

Charlotte didn't know what to say. What about them? Of course she didn't love John, but this other seemed so hopeless, a fountainhead of endless pain. She found the hard little place where her determination lay.

'We stop.'

Zhen was thunderstruck. Stop seeing each other? End the probability of being lovers, the prospect of which kept him going as all the Peranakan weirdness rained down on him? He thought his heart might stop, and drew a deep breath. He had been certain of her surrender.

He turned and left her. Charlotte watched him go, and now it was her turn to feel wretchedness. She burst into tears, wanting to run after him, throw herself at his feet. Only the prospect of this pursuit in the view of the priests rooted her to the spot.

Zhen returned to the godown in the filthiest of tempers. Very well, so be it. In the evening he visited Min, and for the first time he did not resist. He knew this was the most ridiculous and predictable of responses, but he did not care. She was, at first, delighted but as he got more savage with her she grew afraid of his dark mood. These bloody women who thought they could rule him. It was if he was back in the clutches of the concubines. Finally, as Min began to whimper, he got up, unfinished, threw on his clothes and left, filled with the blackest bile.

Charlotte was not totally taken by surprise when John proposed to her in the garden of Tir Uaidhne. He had told her of his feelings, asked her of hers. She had told him 'care' when he wanted to hear 'love', but he would be satisfied with that for the moment, certain he could make her love him in time. Charlotte was not sure. John was a good-looking man, kind and funny, but how on earth could she marry him and make a life here with Zhen constantly inhabiting her mind—as well as the other side of the river? She had put him off as kindly as she could.

Coleman felt for John, and one day, finding Charlotte alone, he began to plead for his friend.

'Consider, Kitt, he is the very best of men. If there is someone else I understand but if not ...'

Charlotte could not decide how much she should reveal to George. In the end she said nothing. He wanted to show her a house he had picked out for her, he said. Coleman knew he should not pressure her, but he was not sure Charlotte knew at the moment what was best for her. He suspected a love affair of some sort and had heard rumours about the Chinese lad who had helped Robert and saved her life. This was just the sort of romantic stuff that could get inside a girl's head, and though he knew she was more substantial than that, yet it would end badly. The constant pull of the exotic. He knew it, had felt it insanely for Takouhi, still did.

'Kitt, is it the Chinese man?'

Charlotte's eyes flew to his face. 'Oh, George, I don't know what to do. I love him truly, I do, but it's all so hopeless.'

Coleman listened. He felt the truth of her feelings and probably those of the young man. It was an endless story. He did not even know what to say to her, but he could see it was a relief to her to be able to confess it.

He took her in his carriage and they went to look at the houses which were just being finished. As they walked around she felt calmed, soothed by his sense and understanding. He offered her no advice, which was wise, for she knew she could take none at the moment. He showed her the mouldings on the ceilings, the pretty balcony on the first floor, the fancy woodwork, the cool, tiled courtyard. They talked of architecture and decoration. She was glad he was with her and began to feel that yes, she would like to have a house like this for herself, would like to have a husband like George and children of her own.

'Kitt, don't reject John too quickly. He loves you. I know it, for I've never seen him this way.'

'George, if you lost Takouhi, would another do?'

Coleman smiled. 'That is the only argument you could make which stops me in my tracks, my sweet Charlotte.'

They returned to the carriage, and as they drove down Middle Street, Charlotte suddenly spied Robert coming from a house. She called him, and George looked startled. He pulled up the carriage and Robert, looking somewhat shaken, came over to them. She could see the face of a woman at the upper balcony. George's reaction. Robert's face. The young girl. In a flash she understood. Robert had a lover, a native girl whom he kept here.

She looked at Robert, then George. Men could do anything they wanted! Stepping down from the carriage she thanked Coleman coolly, turned her back on her brother and began to walk towards the sea road, needing to clear her mind. Robert mounted his horse and followed.

In truth Charlotte did not really know how she felt about this discovery. She did not blame Robert, certainly. She was annoyed, for she had not thought he had secrets from her. But, she realised, she knew so little of his life here before she had arrived. Had he been very lonely? She suddenly felt her love for him, and as they turned onto High Street, she looked up at him.

Robert dismounted and, handing his horse to one of the peons to take to the stables, he took Charlotte by the hand and looked into her eyes.

'Kitt,' he faltered. She patted him on the hand.

'Well, Robbie, perhaps we should have a talk.'

When he had explained about Shilah, Robert felt unburdened. Charlotte was no longer angry. After all, she had no right, since she herself harboured hidden feelings for a man which she did not yet feel ready to discuss with her brother. Still, she was curious.

'Robbie, do you want to marry this girl? I have seen you often paying attention to Teresa Crane also. What do you intend by it?'

Robert was somewhat taken aback by the directness of this question,

218

for it was one which he tried to avoid addressing even to himself. He ran his hand through his sandy hair. This gesture was one which always meant that Robert was pondering, and she smiled at him with affection. Her brother was a clever and brave policeman, she now knew, but when it came to affairs of the heart he was still a boy. And you still a girl, she thought.

When he had not spoken for several minutes, she added, 'Rob, please we may be honest with each other at least, for we have no other family here.'

'Auch, Kitt the truth is that I cannot possibly marry Shilah. She is a native girl. She understands this, and for the moment we are so very happy. Think of what such a marriage would do to your own prospects, or my own. No, quite impossible. As for Teresa, I like her a good deal. I think that she might make me an excellent wife when the time comes to marry. And connections to the da Silva family do not hurt in this town.' As he said these words he nodded, as if affirming them to himself for the very first time.

'Well, what do you think Miss Crane will make of your native girl then when you are married? Or do you intend to drop her?'

Robert looked startled. 'No, no, of course I don't intend to drop her. Really, the Chinese have by far the best idea about the whole business. They have no qualms about having a wife and keeping other women, and the women do not seem to mind either.'

Charlotte thought that the Chinese women might mind a great deal, but given the status quo and their powerlessness to object, simply resigned themselves. She made this point to Robert, who merely shrugged. Philosophical discussions about human relationships were not his strong suit.

'So what about your Christian beliefs then, Robbie, for you go faithfully off to church on Sunday and say your prayers with prodigious devotion, it seems. I can't imagine that Reverend White would approve of your plans to keep a wife and a harem unless, of course, he is doing likewise.'

Robert smiled at his sister. 'Kitt, don't be silly. Teresa Crane need never know about any of this unless you choose to tell her. If he can afford it, almost every man in the town has a woman, whether he has a wife or not. Life here would just be unbearable otherwise, and this way the native women get a home. Yer must see that.'

Charlotte was not sure she saw that at all, although she remembered the women enslaved in whoredom that she had encountered at the mission. Perhaps this way was better than the other, but she did not say this to Robert. She merely said, 'So, Robbie, what is good for the goose must be good for the gander, must it not? What if I chose to marry and keep a lover as well? Crimoney, Rob, can you image the outrage?'

'Aye, Kitt it's true. But life isn't always fair. For my part, if you chose to do so and it made you happy I would not object. Do not forget our life has made us different to most, but for women choices are still limited. Scandal follows a woman more easily than a man.'

They sat in silence for a while, until Charlotte spoke up. 'Robbie, may I meet Shilah? Would it be all right?'

It was a dilemma, and Robert ran his hands through his hair.

'Well, well,' Charlotte said sensing his thoughts. 'Talk it over with George if you must, but I do not mean any harm. Simply curious, that is all.'

Robert was pleased that his sister had taken it all so calmly, for he knew most women of her age would have been scandalised. He took her hand in his and kissed it gallantly. He had police business to attend to, but for this evening it would wait for a few hours. He poured them a glass of whisky each, and as they watched the light show of the dying sun, he talked to her of his first years in Singapore.

# 30

The Church of Saint Andrew was bedecked with flowers from its portals to the altar. The deep, cool portico was filled with plants. Huge Chinese pots of sea almond with their large, tongue-shaped leaves and sprays of white starry flowers mixed with the green, shiny, plump-ribbed leaves of wild pepper, dotted with stubby white blooms. Orchids trailed the central aisle, bedecking the end of each line of pews. The pillars were wound about with white ribbon. The altar was surrounded by the feathery leaves of fresh green ferns and bunches of long plantain leaves. Today was the day that Jose da Silva was giving his daughter, Julia, in marriage to Lieutenant Benjamin Sharpe of the Madras Native Regiment.

Coleman had received the commission for this church after a series of plans from Calcutta had been rejected for lack of verandahs to shade the body of the church. George's design had twenty-foot-wide verandahs and porticos enclosing carriage roads; there were shady galleries on the upper floor on three sides.

Today the church was full. Every able-bodied member of the European community had turned out in their finery. The Peranakan merchants, too, were in attendance with their wives, dressed richly in their silk *baju panjang* and bedecked in glittering gold and diamond necklaces. The Indians were no less ornately arrayed, with the men in brocade jackets and turbans of every hue, the ladies in multicoloured *sari*s, their dark, lustrous hair arranged in elegant coiffures. The Malays, Javanese, Bugis and Arabs had joined the throng. The Chinese merchants were dressed sombrely but were happy to be there, for a wedding of the white people was an interesting affair. Their wives would want to hear every detail when they returned home. The atmosphere was one of joyous gaiety, for the huge da Silva family and relations were not only popular but made up a good one- third, through birth and marriage, of the European contingent in the town. Everyone present was delighted to see this handsome young couple united in marriage, for their love for each other was so obvious and uplifting that it cast its spell over all present. Children ran around the church, sometimes shushed, sometimes indulged, as the guests waited for the bride's arrival.

Charlotte noticed Miss Crane amongst her large extended family, looking pretty and demure in yellow muslin, her brown hair in ringlets which framed her face. Robert had bowed to her when they had entered the church, and Charlotte would have liked to know what he was thinking.

Meeting Shilah had been surprising. She found herself wondering what this child felt for her brother and, more than she should, about their sexual life together. This girl was young, younger than Charlotte, yet she knew the mysterious world of married love. Takouhi had called on her former servant girl, and Charlotte had been invited along. Robert had spoken to her and Shilah had agreed with some trepidation to meet his sister. Takouhi had told Charlotte of Shilah's childhood. They had sat in the small front sitting room of the rooms she occupied on the second floor of the shophouse. Takouhi gave her a small package of personal items and then asked her to bring some coffee, with which she kept this little house supplied.

Shilah was a pretty girl, with coffee-coloured skin and black eyes. She bobbed a curtsy to Charlotte when Takouhi introduced them. Her English was very good, but other than answering some questions, she had little to say. Charlotte looked around the room. It was furnished well, clearly from George's home, with some English and French furniture. Shilah was dressed in Malay fashion, in a cotton *sarong* and *baju*. Charlotte wondered what she did all day when Robert was not visiting her. For sex, she thought, mentally shaking her head.

Shilah, it transpired, helped teach letters to the children at Mrs Whittle's school, an employment which George had arranged, for Coleman was not sure of Robert's commitment and wanted her to try to make her way in life. Actually, Charlotte was struck with Shilah's lack of shyness and this ability to read and write. Certainly the girl had not looked forward to this meeting, but she was clearly not daunted by it, and Charlotte felt that Robert had perhaps beware. As she grew older, this young woman might develop into a formidable personality who might well view dimly the prospect of Robert's marriage to a Miss Crane or someone similar, especially if and when children came along. Later, when she had talked of this visit to Robert and aired her misgivings, he had simply waved his hand and told her that it was all straight with Shilah: she knew very well that native girls did not marry white men, and that was that. Charlotte could have reminded him of their mother, but she did not.

Charlotte thought the church looked magnificent. The shutters were open on every side, admitting a refreshing breeze over the plain from the sea. Despite this, the *punkahs* were in full flow, and the vault of the roof seemed inhabited by the flapping wings of flying creatures. The din of conversation in twenty languages surrounded her. Charlotte and Takouhi were seated in the third row.

Tigran Manouk was by her side. Charlotte had been surprised at his changed appearance. He had lost weight and grown his hair even longer. He looked a picture of elegance in his black frock coat, tight trousers and snow-white shirt, but there was now something piratical about him in the way he had braided his hair. His eyes looked deeper and darker. She thought he might be wearing *kohl*, as his sister often did, and this thought was provoking and exciting. When she had seen Charlotte on his arm, Lilian Aratoun had practically fainted with barely contained jealousy.

His personal ship had arrived two days before. Charlotte had watched from the verandah as it sailed elegantly into the harbour. It was a beautiful black brig, *Queen of the South*, full sailed, each white sail edged with black, bearing in its centre the emblem of his merchant house, a black Javanese leopard rampant, the emblem repeated in the flags which floated from the top gallants.

Tigran had brought gifts for everyone. She was now wearing on her bodice the beautiful blue diamond-and-silver brooch he had given her, and which had made her gasp. It was a spray of sparkling flowers, the colour so nearly that of her eyes that she had looked at him in amazement. The box in which it had been presented was embossed silver, bearing in jet her monogrammed initials C. M. intertwined, the brooch resting on black velvet. It was magnificent and unexpected. Tigran merely smiled when she protested. Takouhi waved a lazy hand at her friend.

'*Alamah*, goo'ness gracious. Don' be silly-billy. Tigran love to give gift to pretty ladies.'

Takouhi had smiled indulgently at her brother. She would have liked to see him married, knew from his letters of his interest in Charlotte, detected in his changed appearance and the magnificence of his gift a desire for her friend that she had every intention of promoting. He had given his personal jeweller a great deal of trouble finding these stones, of that she had no doubt.

Meda had been invited to be a flower girl today, and over the previous weeks had talked of nothing else. This morning she had woken her mother and father well before the gun, jumping on George and rousing him in a way she did not dare with her mother.

On this morning, George had greeted his daughter by pulling her into bed, kissing and tickling her until, laughing, she squirmed and ran away.

George had turned to Takouhi, kissed her and pulled back the sheet to reveal the black henna tattoo curling sensuously from the triangle of her hair to her breasts, the sight of which always bewitched and aroused him. As she felt George's mood, Takouhi had risen, naked, calling to one of her Javanese maids to get breakfast for Meda. She locked the door and came back to him very slowly, unbraiding her long black hair.

Now she was dressed in dark blue velvet *à la française*, smelling faintly of jasmine and looking happily at Meda Elizabeth, who was standing in a group of little girls by the altar all arrayed in pale blue holding little beribboned baskets full of small silk flowers under Mrs White's watchful eye. They had rehearsed until they knew every move and, at Mrs White's command, they would all move towards the portico and wait for the organ to signal the arrival of the bride. Then they would move down the aisle strewing the flowers before the bride as she progressed towards the altar. They were jiggling with excitement, and it was all Mrs White could do to keep them calm.

Benjamin Sharpe stood amongst a small group of his comrades in regimental red with gold braid. The colonel and other officers occupied several rows, and many of his comrades were at the back of the church waiting to form an honour guard with their swords as the newlyweds emerged. The governor and his men occupied the front seats. George Coleman sat at Takouhi's side, dressed in a grey suit and cravat. Now and again he would lock eyes with Takouhi. Charlotte felt quite warm by the look that passed between them, instantaneously remembering the kiss in the orchard.

Then suddenly Mrs White gave the signal and the children walked quickly down the aisle and waited obediently by the door. The grinder began to bring the barrel organ into life, and the voices of the institution boys rose in song.

'Blessed be the tie that binds
Our hearts in Christian love
The fellowship of kindred minds
Is like to that above.'

The flower girls began a slow progression down the aisle, followed by Jose da Silva and, on his arm, his daughter, Julia, dressed in white muslin, a lacy veil falling from a garland of twisted silken cords covering her chestnut hair. In her hands she carried a bouquet of myrtle with white silken ribbons.

'Before our Father's throne
We pour our ardent prayers
Our fears, our hopes, our aims are one
Our comforts and our cares.'

Charlotte craned to see her and was astounded by her beauty and her obvious joy at this moment. She felt a keen envy. If she wished it, she knew that this wonderful ceremony could be in her future. She had merely to accept the hand of John Connolly, and everything she could want would fall into her arms. Husband, home, children.

She felt Tigran's eyes on her face and turned to him, smiling. Perhaps, she thought playfully, I should marry the richest man in the South Seas and drive Lilian Aratoun mad. He has certainly become extremely attractive.

Tigran took her hand and put it to his lips with a look so shyly smouldering that Charlotte was again taken aback. This idea was clearly not as far from his mind as she had imagined. Then thoughts of Zhen filled her head, and she withdrew her hand from his with a small smile.

> 'We share our mutual woes
> Our mutual burdens bear
> And often for each other flows
> The sympathising tear.'

Meda Elizabeth passed, her face set, carrying out her duties with great seriousness. Charlotte could not resist a smile and touched Takouhi's left hand. George had taken her right hand in his.

> 'When for a while we part
> This thought will soothe our pain
> That we shall still be joined in heart
> And hope to meet again.'

The girls took their places as the bride arrived at the altar, followed by two of her married sisters as matrons of honour.

> 'From sorrow, toil and pain
> And sin we shall be free
> In perfect love and friendship reign
> Through all eternity.
> Amen.'

Despite the cloying sentiments of this hymn, Charlotte was moved listening to the familiar words of the marriage service. When Julia and Benjamin finalised their vows and turned to face the assembled guests, beaming with joy, she felt a small tear come to her eye.

Then the organ began again, and the newlyweds made their way slowly down the aisle to the door to the booming sounds of 'Rock of

Ages', sung by all the Europeans in the church. The foreign contingent clapped, pleased with this quaint ceremony of the white people, the prettiness of the couple affirming their own belief in the bonds of marriage and family.

The wedding reception was a lavish affair, held at the da Silva mansion on Beach Road. As the party wound down, the bride changed her dress and prepared to leave for three days to Robert's house at the beach at Katong. Renting this house for parties and honeymoons had turned into a lucrative prospect for Robert, and he had bought an American four-poster bed from Mr Balestier, and other items of furniture.

The couple left in a craft bedecked with ferns and garlands as the sun set and the band played the regimental song.

Tigran had accompanied Takouhi and Meda home long ago, but Coleman, Charlotte and Robert stayed to watch the boat depart and only turned for home when the sky had darkened and the firebrands were lit. Preceded by a running Indian servant holding aloft a flaming brand, they made their way back in Coleman's carriage along Beach Road to the bungalow. Finally, after a whisky with his friends, Coleman too departed for home, admiring, with a final wink, the lovely jewels on Charlotte's dress.

Robert and Charlotte had retired to bed not more than an hour when they were awakened by a banging at the door. The peon on duty admitted Coleman in a state of unusual agitation.

'Come quickly, Kitt. Takouhi needs you. Meda's taken with fever. At first we thought it was the excitement of the wedding, but she has worsened. Dr Montgomerie is there, but I beg you to come and give comfort to Takouhi.'

Charlotte dressed quickly, and George swung her up onto his horse. Robert would go too, but Coleman said no, not too many people, just Kitt. Gripping George's waist, Charlotte held tightly as Coleman spurred his horse home, swinging her down and jumping from his mount in one swift movement.

Takouhi was with Meda and Dr Montgomerie, who looked up gravely as Charlotte and George entered. Meda's cheeks were flushed, her eyes

227

glitteringly bright and feverish. Charlotte could not believe the change from that afternoon and let out a small cry, rushing to Takouhi's side and wrapping her arms around her. Takouhi seemed strangely calm and put a hand over her friend's. George had dropped into an armchair and sat staring at his daughter.

Charlotte stayed through the night, helping nurse Meda, talking to Takouhi, trying to comfort George. Dr Montgomerie suspected consumption. Sometime in the early morning Meda began to cough. A servant fanned Meda continually, and Takouhi and Charlotte changed the wet towels on her head and body every few minutes, attempting to lower her fever. George sat slumped. Tigran was downstairs, unable to sleep, pacing the floor.

By morning they all looked haggard. Dr Montgomerie had to have hard words with George, for all of them getting sick would not help their daughter.

Coleman began to eat, and Charlotte and Tigran finally prevailed upon Takouhi to take some broth and rice. Meda Elizabeth seemed stable. Dr Montgomerie had given her a mild sleeping draught, and she had fallen into a deep sleep, although her face was still flushed and her breathing shallow.

Takouhi spoke to her brother. She needed him to take them home to Java, up to the plantation house in the cool air of the hills at Buitenzorg, the place 'without a care'. This white medicine was useless; she needed to see the *dukun*, the medicine man. Now Takouhi was far from her Armenian faith, Charlotte realised. She was back in the cradle of her Javanese spirit world. Charlotte understood: in times of trouble she drew comfort from both church and these spirits, but in sickness she believed only in the *jamu*. Tigran nodded.

He was holding his white-trimmed, black tricorn hat in one hand, waiting as Charlotte came to say farewell in the hall. Bowing over her hand, he brought it to his lips, touching her skin lightly, the plaited strands of his hair and their jet beads falling around his face. Despite herself, Charlotte felt a frisson.

'I wait to see you again,' he said quietly and looked directly into her eyes. Placing his hat on his head, he bowed once more, slightly, and dropped her hand before turning to make his ship ready.

When Takouhi told George of her decision, he wanted to forbid it but knew this would mean nothing to her.

'Yes, go to the hills, see the *dukun* if you wish, only make me the promise to come back,' he had agreed.

Takouhi had looked him in the eyes. 'Come back when Meda not sick.'

She said this calmly and with absolute decision, and George was overcome. He knew if Meda died, Takouhi would almost certainly never come back to him. There would be too many spirits in Java holding her there.

'I'll come with you,' George began, but Takouhi put her fingers to his lips.

'Cannot. Do not cry. If I can I come back to you. Not worry. Gods decide. Not you, not me.'

Charlotte was by Meda's bedside when George told her the news. 'God save me, Charlotte, but, if this sweet lass must die, I almost wish she would die here. Then I could bury her with my hands, and Takouhi would stay.'

Charlotte felt his utter anguish. She did not know how to comfort him and stood in the darkened room until she felt Takouhi arrive at her side.

'Go home, Charlotte, thanks to you. Nothing more to do for us. I take Meda to Jawa, make well. Before go tell you. Not worry.'

Takouhi took Charlotte's face in her hands and kissed her on the cheek. Then she stood next to George and took his head in her arms, pressing him to her heart.

Charlotte had never seen her friend so calm, as if all the distress of the last hours had departed and peace had come upon her with this final decision.

It was early morning and raining, the rain of the tropics, dropping straight from the sky like a waterfall, noisy and heavy. Takouhi's carriage arrived under the portico, and Charlotte dropped into its dark interior. She was exhausted, and the thought of this imminent departure caused tears to well. She sobbed for her friend, for Meda, for George, for all the heartache which was to befall them. She could not stop weeping, even when the carriage arrived at the bungalow. She did not wait for the driver to get down with the umbrella, and walked the short distance to the door in the pouring rain, glad of its feel on her face. She waved the driver away and went up onto the verandah of the bungalow.

Azan came out with a sheet, smiling, not understanding, thinking Charlotte had merely got wet. Charlotte was glad. Somewhere life had to be normal.

She changed in her room, listening to the sound of the rain falling on the roof tiles, gurgling off the verandah and swirling furiously round the pylons of the house. From the verandah nothing could be seen. The town, river, islands, jungle, all had disappeared. The harbour was one with the rain, the entire visible world wrapped in a grey watery sheet. She slept, and when she awoke hours later it was still raining.

She thought of him, Zhen, missing him suddenly as if this wall of water might separate them forever.

This thought immediately filled her mind. She cast around for a cloak and a hat. She would have to find him at the godown. He would be there at this hour.

Then one of Robert's peon's came towards her. She hardly recognised him. He held out a note from Robert. Her brother had sent the peon to warn her he was detained. The rain had flooded Kampong Glam by the river, and Robert was needed. He did not know when he would return. She should stay with Takouhi.

Charlotte made up her mind. She went out the back corridor and called Azan over the drumming rain.

'Azan, I go to Mr Coleman's house tonight but first go to Boat Quay. Get a *sampan* to go to godown of Baba Tan. Understand?'

Azan understood. In this drenching rain most of the *sampan*s were crowded together on the far side of the river, but he knew that there were always a few tied up by the landing stage. Why on earth the police chief's sister wanted to go over the river in this weather was beyond him, but he was now so used to the comings and goings of the household he gave it no further thought.

By the time the *sampan* arrived at the police jetty, the rain had lessened slightly and, under the big umbrella, Charlotte got into it, the boat rocking violently. The Indian boatman ferried her quickly through the choppy waters of the estuary into the mouth of the river, where the swells died down. Yelling at the other boatman to get out of the way, he pushed his way through the crowded boats to the steps. The river was high, so it was easy for Charlotte to step up to the quay. The rain had stopped but the low clouds meant that more was to come.

She carefully went under the verandah of the godown and looked inside. It was as dark as a cave, the small glow of oil lamps visible at the back and in the room immediately to the left, where she knew the baba looked over the accounts. He was not in there. There was a young boy crouched inside the door fast asleep, some sort of messenger, she supposed. He was Chinese. How could she make him understand who she wanted? Then, as if by a miracle, she saw Zhen coming through, out of the penumbra into the front of the godown.

'Zhen,' she called, and he looked over to the door. He knew her voice.

Coming onto the verandah, he moved her into the shadows.

'What, why come, you hurt?' His voice filled with alarm, but he was still angry with her.

'See you. I must see you.' Charlotte burst into tears.

Zhen assessed the situation quickly. She had risked the river in this weather. She needed to see him. What for he was not sure, but she was distressed. His fury at her disappeared. They could not talk here; he would take her to his house. It was only a few minutes away. The rain would begin again any minute.

Turning into the doorway, he shook the messenger boy awake.

'Tell the master and the old man I have been called away on *kongsi* business. You understand, blockhead? *Kongsi* business. Be back tomorrow.'

Zhen knew no one would questions this, for Baba Tan had avoided any contact with Chen Long since Chen had become head of the *kongsi* and especially since the attacks on the Catholic Chinese.

Zhen took Charlotte by the hand and led her quickly to his house, hoping Ah Pok was not at home. It was about two o'clock. What was he doing at that time usually? Zhen racked his brains but couldn't remember. He took so little interest in Ah Pok's comings and goings, only grateful to have a servant who did everything for him—including spying, of course.

The bolt was not on the door, but that meant nothing; the bolt was only used at night. At any other time the door was open to all the sundry tailors, knife sharpeners, noodle sellers, pot repairers, dhobi *wallahs*, delivery men and others who seemed to come and go at all hours of the day.

He opened the door and looked inside, could detect no movement and led Charlotte inside and onto the stairs. If Ah Pok was here, he was probably in the kitchen. Quickly he led her up the stairs and peered into the front sitting room. No one. He took her to a chair and motioned her to be quiet, fingers to lips. He ran lightly downstairs and into the kitchen. Then he heard Ah Pok and smiled. He was straining away in the dirt box. Zhen went back down the hall and slammed the front door, walking loudly along the corridor calling his name.

Ah Pok answered from inside the box.

'Listen. There is a meeting here later, people from the *kongsi*. You are a *kongsi* man; you know this will be a private matter. When you've finished up in there, make some tea and noodles for four, and then make yourself scarce. And don't come back until after sun-up tomorrow. Get it?'

Ah Pok made a muffled sound of agreement. He knew better than to argue with Zhen when he had his *honggun* hat on. The fire was stoked and hot water boiling.

Zhen left the kitchen and returned to Charlotte, who now looked calm. She had taken off her cloak and hat and was looking out the window, down to the street, the shutters half-closed. The rain suddenly began again as he went to her side and whispered,

'Not speak. Man here. Go soon.'

They both stood quietly, looking out at the rain. Zhen was puzzled by this meeting. He hoped it meant what he thought, but with Xia Lou he could not be sure. He had never been so hesitant with a woman before.

They watched as Ah Pok hailed the ever-present noodle hawker, who made constant rounds. He came under the verandah, and then there were some footsteps and they heard the door slam. Ah Pok was hurrying up the street towards Kampong Malacca; he had a woman up that way somewhere. Apparently Ah Pok, despite his middle age and his paunch, was something of a ladies' man. Zhen smiled at this thought; he liked Ah Pok.

232

Charlotte looked at his face and saw him smile. She never quite knew what he was thinking. She was suddenly angry at herself for coming like this, yet at the same time so very glad she was here. This was his house. She looked around.

The furniture was an odd mixture of English and Chinese. The tables and chairs were hard, unyielding, inlaid with marble. He noticed her gaze, shrugged.

'Baba Tan give this. I not care.'

'Show me the house?'

He nodded. She had gone from distressed to curious, but he did not mind. She was here, in his house. Cut off by the rain, entirely alone.

He took her downstairs, showed her the kitchen, the red altar of the Kitchen God, the wok and bowls, the chopsticks. Ah Pok had left tea and steaming bowls of noodles. He motioned her to sit at the small table and stools where he ate when he was home with Ah Pok. They were like an old married couple.

She sat and began again to try to use the chopsticks. Hopeless! Zhen took some noodles in a spoon and rolled them deftly, waiting for them to cool, then putting them in her mouth. The sensuousness of this act, the placing of the chopsticks in her mouth, her pink lips closing round them, gave him an immediate and huge erection. He blinked slowly. He had waited so long for this, and still he was not sure.

The noodles were delicious. She had never tasted anything like them. She took the spoon and drank the broth. She was suddenly ravenously hungry. He rolled more noodles and watched her eat. He was not hungry now, except for her. When she finished the bowl she lifted it to her lips and drank to the bottom. Then she noticed he had eaten nothing. His face was a mask.

'You eat?'

'Yes. First tea.'

He poured the tea Ah Pok had made. It was lukewarm, but Charlotte drank it, though she thought it bitter.

She rose and went into the room off the central air well. She was curious about this house and its architecture. The air well was wonderful for it allowed light and air and, at that moment drenching rain, to ventilate the house. Two water jars stood, their contents bubbling over and gurgling down a drain.

Zhen followed her, his bodily control thankfully returning.

They went into the room off the street.

'Shop for me, china um, thing for sick man, maybe, after marry,' he told her. 'Medicine shop' was what he wanted to explain. He frowned at his bad English.

She stiffened. Why had he mentioned the damn marriage? But it was fact. She had to accept it.

'Come.' He took her hand and led her again to the upper floor. They sat on the hard chairs. He wanted to know what had caused her to come.

'Why come, Xia Lou? Why cry?'

Charlotte struggled with words. 'My friend's child sick, go away. I'm very sad, need to see you.'

Zhen watched her. Did she want him to hold her? Comfort her? He had never had such a hard time reading a woman in his life. He was as nervous as a cat, even here in his house. One wrong move, and he felt she would flee, out of his life.

Charlotte sensed his indecision. It was natural, she thought; she didn't even know what she wanted herself, why she had come.

She rose and went to the door of the next room, but it was locked. She turned quizzically to Zhen. He went to a cupboard and returned with a key, unlocking the door. This room, too, overlooked the air well. It had shutters to keep out the rain. It was very dark now, and Zhen stopped her and went back to the cupboard. He took out the lucifers. These were some new white man's invention. Quite useful, but volatile. He had taken some from a store at the godown. They fizzed a lot, but he had learned to light a spill and light the oil lamps that way.

He lit a lamp and brought it into the room. Scents of coconut filled the air. He opened the shutters, then lit another lamp. By the light she could see the strangest assortment of items. Where the other rooms were bare, this one was filled with gorgeous colours and cloths, like Aladdin's Cave. She took the oil lamp and moved around the room, running her fingers over the costumes, embroidered dark silk covered in pink and yellow flowers, clouds and fabulous golden dragons. Not dragons as she knew them, but creatures with deer horns and camel mouths, the body of a snake covered in fish scales, the claws of an eagle. A Chinese dragon. Then came lacquer trays with silver coins, candles and red packets. She saw two diamond rings flash in the light and a woman's green silk dress. She understood. These were his marriage clothes and gifts for the wedding day, for his bride.

Zhen had waited by the door, knowing she would realise. She turned and looked at him.

'Come,' he said. 'Not think about this.'

Charlotte walked out of the room, gave him the oil lamp and went into the corridor; she threw open the shutters to the window and breathed in the rain, which was stopping as the sky suddenly lightened.

Zhen followed behind her, putting the lamps on a table. He touched her lightly first and then firmly turned her to face him; he took one step back, saying nothing, waiting for her decision.

Charlotte thought of her mother, her father, their love so quickly cut off. She thought of her Aunt Jeannie with her spinster's caul; she thought of Robert and Shilah, of George and Takouhi, how precious was their life together, how soon it was coming to an end. Words echoed in her mind:

'Love, all alike no seasons knows, nor clime
Nor hours, days, months, which are the rags of time'

She took the step forward, and Zhen closed his arms around her.

# 31

Zhen took Charlotte's hand and led her to the bedroom. She took in the remarkable iron bed. Netting draped it like a gauzy canopy, one side tied back to the columns. A facet-edged mirrored cupboard stood against the wall on this side. She could see the bed reflected in it, knew that anyone on the bed would be reflected in it, felt a flush of blood to her face. A low table and chairs and a long chest were the only other furniture in the room.

Lifting her onto the edge of the high bed, he separated her legs, pushing the material of her skirt down, and stepped between them. He motioned to her to undo the knotted loops on his jacket. Charlotte was nervous, and her hands trembled as she released the cotton toggles. As the jacket fell loose she could not resist—as he knew she would not—running her hand over the smooth skin of his hard chest, touching the tattooed face.

Taking hold of her lower arms, he moved her hands to his stomach touching the muscles there, then round his waist to the curve of his back and lower, under the edge of his garment, to the muscular swell and deep crevasse of his backside, wanting her get the feel of him on her fingers while he was cloaked from her gaze, so that when she had left him she would not be able to free herself of this touch, his smell, the warmth of his skin. This time with her had come so unexpectedly, and his passion for her was so consuming, that he wanted to burn himself into her heart, to chain her to the wheel of samsara, unquenchable desire returning her to him in an endless cycle from which she could never escape.

Charlotte felt her heart moving and dropped her forehead onto his chest as he led her in this slow, sensual dance around his body. She had seen drawings of Greek gods, and he felt like that, contoured, sculpted but not cold stone. His skin was warm and silken. She let out a sigh of pure pleasure and kissed his chest. He had not moved.

He released her arms. She looked up into his face. He was watching her through half-closed eyes, his lips apart, his teeth lightly clenched, and she saw his emotion. Her nervousness vanished. A languorous vapour of dissipation trailed through her body. She ran her hands up his chest, over his shoulders, down his arms, her fingers detailing every dip and line of his torso, her eyes never leaving his face. She saw the tiny tremble of his lower lip, the dreaminess of his eyes.

Zhen took her right hand and pressed it over his heart and slowly moved the other down his abdomen, under the cloth, moulding her fingers around his erection, holding her there. Charlotte closed her eyes, binding him on her memory. Sounds from the street drifted into the room: muted calls and Chinese voices. The after-rain freshness of the breeze from the well rippled around them, ruffling the netting on the bed. The steady beat of his heart spoke to her hands: remember, remember. She envisioned the coursing of his blood, felt her own rushing in her ears. So they stayed thus, motionless, until clouds obscured the light and darkness crept into the room.

Slowly he released his grip and placed her hands in her lap. He stepped back. Her eyes flew open and met his. In the half-light she watched the dust floating on the air as he pulled off his jacket, letting it drop to the floor. He lit a match. It flared and fizzed, and he quickly held it to the spill. He moved round the room lighting the candles and oil lamps, sandalwood incense. Zhen knew the effect that candle glow playing on his body could have on a woman, and he smiled, enjoying her gaze as he flashed and flickered on the mirror. He took her off the bed, onto the floor.

Charlotte watched, filled with curiosity, as he took from the cupboard a bottle of rice wine and two small porcelain cups. He took a red silk ribbon from the drawer of the mirrored console. Its image doubled and redoubled in the reflection as he delicately tied the two ends around the waists of the two cups. With this drink and this red thread he would bind them together, wed them. Whatever happened in this mortal realm, she would be his wife in the river of the afterlife.

He handed Charlotte a cup and took the other, the thread connecting them. Charlotte had sensed the portent of this ceremony. This was their wedding night, and they would soon consummate their union. These cups symbolised each of them, and the scarlet cord would bind them together. Zhen made a vow to heaven and earth. Charlotte watched him saying the Chinese words.

She wasn't sure what to do. Words from Julia's wedding flew into her mind: 'With this *drink* I thee wed.' It was horrible, but she felt on the verge of a fit of giggles. She knew it was nervousness which had returned, the strangeness of this encounter, the prospect of what was to come, but that did not help. She didn't know the rules. Fortunately at that moment he lifted the drink to his lips, and she followed him. It was mild and delicious, not strong like her grandmother's whisky. She felt as if she could drink a jug of it. Why were the glasses so small? A pleasant heat hit the pit of her stomach. Thank the Lord; the urge to laugh had momentarily passed in the newness of this taste.

He began to undress her, undoing the buttons of her bodice, pushing it off her shoulders. Here, however, he was surprised to be confronted with her corset. He let out a small rumble of bafflement. He had never seen such a garment. He touched her waist, where hard little lines hugged her body, running his fingers up the stays to the swell of her breasts under her camisole, laying his fingers on this fullness, touching the metal hooks which ran down her abdomen. He looked into her eyes. She was smiling at his bewilderment. Slowly he circled her, examining this extraordinary garment, the silken cords criss-crossing her back. Charlotte laughed out loud, a long peal of merriment. The tension drained out of her.

'Corset,' she said.

'Kaw sit,' he repeated, shaking his head.

Taking him by the hand, she led him to a square stool and pointed. He sat, and she spread his legs and stepped in close to him. She undid the top hook. He smiled. She was playing him at his game. A flush of pleasure at her quickness, and he began to release each hook slowly, teasingly, enjoying each little pop. Finally the last hook was released, and he gripped the edges and opened the garment like a book, seeing the outline of her breasts, her nipples erect against the muslin, running his cheek and mouth over her delicately through the cloth, releasing the corset and pulling the short camisole out from her skirt, running his hands up and around her the way he had led hers on him, touching the skin of her breasts with his fingers and palms. His eyes were closed as he traced the map of her body. Charlotte recalled the grabbings and kneadings of her last encounter and could only wonder.

He stood and took the corset from her shoulders and lifted the short camisole over her head, looked at her, his almond-eyed gaze on her breasts, her shoulders, her mouth, her neck. This look made her tremble, and she felt a liquid swell like a rising tide inside her body. Then he picked up the corset again and dressed her in it, liking the look of her in this exotic garment, her soft shape against its hard slats, its silken sides and little ribbons. Sitting again, he moved her between his legs, gripping the two sides of the corset, opening it and pulling her towards his face.

He began to run his tongue around the edge of her nipples, biting lightly, kissing and caressing with his lips and breath the gentle swellings of this so-soft skin, moving around her breasts, not touching the hard little bumps. Teasingly he made her wait for the feel of his mouth on this hardness, could feel her tension. When she swayed slightly he knew, and took first one, then the other, into his mouth, nibbling and suckling.

Charlotte, eyes closed, her hands on his holding her in this delicious prison, gave a deep sigh, felt a looseness in her limbs. Her pulse rose higher. She had no desire to laugh now. These were not the fumblings of Lonnie or Will. She didn't know the rules of this engagement, but he did. The sweet odour of sandalwood and coconut drifted on the air.

Then, suddenly standing, he pushed the tapes of the corset from her shoulders, flinging it off her, and with a low moan took her by the waist turning her back to him, burying his head in her neck, kissing her shoulders, stroking her breasts, running his hand over her soft belly, down under the waistband of her skirt, seeking her, pulling her into him. Charlotte's eyes had flown open at this sudden change of mood, the urgency and hardness of his touch, and then he stopped moving, took his hand from her skirt and wrapped one arm around her waist, the other over her breasts, his hand on her neck, holding her in check. She stayed quietly in this vice-like embrace, feeling the movement of his abdomen on her back, the deepness of his breath on her shoulder. Strangely, she felt no fear. Since the encounter in the jungle, she knew he would never harm her.

Zhen pulled himself under control. He needed to stop, step away from her. Charlotte felt him release her, his breath jagged. She turned to face him. He held up his hand. He couldn't believe it. He had been on the very brink. This had not happened to him since the first months with the fourth concubine. He flooded with joy, felt like falling to her feet in worship. To find intoxicating, exhilarating passion, to forget the mechanical and pointless lovemaking which had become mere physical release, the bliss of it. He took her by the hand and led her to the table, and they sat. This was why poets wrote. The orchid-scented room, the incense-filled curtains, lotus blossoms, perfumed jewels and flowers of fire. He stopped looking at her, spoke to the table, shaking his head, searching for beautiful words, frustrated at this lack of language.

'Sorry Xia Lou. Please wait.'

She had moved him into halls and corridors of magic, and this was all he could manage. He deeply felt its inadequacy.

She nodded, frowning slightly, not truly understanding. When he looked up again, she saw he had regained his composure.

He stood, pulling her from the chair; moving behind her, he began to unpin her hair, letting it drop over her shoulders and back, running his hand over the silky blackness. He moved round her, dropped his mouth to her mouth, kissing her lightly and brushing his lips on her cheeks. Sighing, she reached for him. He lifted her onto the bed, spreading her hair away from her body.

She lay back, watching him. Kneeling either side of her waist, he put the cord of his pants into her hand. She smiled disarmingly at this little game. He felt dizzy and hot. Love, he made a mental note, sapped your will. He breathed himself under control.

Watching his chest rise and fall, her eyes on his, she thought she understood. He wanted to give her this gift of slowness, but it was being compromised by his desire for her. She knew what happened when a man wanted her too much. She didn't want to go home yet. Sitting, she undid the knot, gazing at the bulge underneath the thin cloth, wanting to touch him but unsure of his reaction.

She released the cord and ran the trousers down over his hips. He was wrapped in a cloth, and it was Charlotte's turn to look nonplussed, for she could not see how to undo this garment. She looked up at him, then reached towards him. He grasped her wrists and kissed the faint marks of the ligatures, which had almost disappeared.

'No, Xia Lou. Fast not good, wait.'

He began to undress her unhurriedly, removing her skirt, then her petticoats. At each layer he gave a little laugh. He was surprised by how many clothes a Western woman could support in this hot climate. Finally he came to her pantalettes, with their rim of ruffles on the lower leg. This garment was also intriguing, particularly when he saw that the crotch was open from the waist to the rim of the ruffle. Really, Zhen thought, white women had sexy underwear, that 'kaw sit' thing in particular. He could imagine making love to her in these two garments. Removing this last piece of clothing, he threw it on the floor and, laughing, she joining him. He was calm now and had felt his erection recede.

She was perfect, the perfection of a lover's eyes. Her face was slightly tanned but the skin of her body was like smooth ivory, the triangle of her hair raven black. He saw a scar on her upper arm, remembered her telling him of an accident in a boat. He began to kiss her body with gentle lips, sniffing her aroma, probing with his tongue, caressing with his hands, a touch so light she felt like butterflies had taken possession of her skin.

She wanted to kiss him too, but languidly surrendered to this delicate exploration of her body from neck to toes, watching in the mirror the play of the muscles under his skin as he moved. She entered a floating world of dreamy listlessness, rising and sinking like bubbles on the air. Nothing had prepared her for this drug-like state, and she sighed when he stopped.

He released the loincloth, lay down next to her and took her in his arms, kissing her with his alchemist's kiss. She ran her hands languorously over his chest and back, the smooth skin of his face and head, his thick queue. Turning on his chest he motioned her to mount his waist. His queue descended to below the curve of his backside. She draped herself on him, her hair falling around him like a silken curtain. Still half in dream, she began moving herself against his body, the thickness of his queue, the hardness of him, kissing the muscles of his shoulders, the curve of his arms, smelling him, arms wound under his, gripping his shoulders, licking the sweat from his skin, absorbing his maleness, this Chinese *yang* she had only just discovered. Gone was the dream state; she felt utterly wanton and lascivious. She wanted to melt into his sinew, become every inch of his flesh.

As he felt her reach this place of lust, he moved her off his back and turned her quickly and gently. Now he could do anything with her, but she had aroused him, too, taken him down a corridor of clouds to the dew-edged roof of paradise.

Slow, slow. He held her close, unmoving, face buried in her hair. Breathe, breathe. He moved between the valley of her breasts and pressed her against him. Raising his leg over her hip, he took her hand between his legs and manoeuvred her fingers to the place where he could regain control, pressing firmly. Lying quietly in his arms, the feel of his hardness on her skin, the touch of her fingers helping him in some way she did not fully understand, Charlotte felt a great wave of love for this man and his mastery. She sighed deeply and kissed the rigid muscles of his abdomen very softly. Zhen smiled. She learned so fast, his lovely Xia Lou. He shuddered with the inside release which she had helped him have, light temporarily extinguished.

He wanted her to know this place so that their lovemaking, when they wished it, would be long, textured, full of sensual richness. From ancient texts of the Taoist teachings he had absorbed the lessons of lovemaking with the fourth concubine. They could play the game of clouds and rain only until rain fell. The woman could make a thousand clouds, but once he had released the rain, the game was over. Prolonging her joy and absorbing her *yin* essence would make him stronger, the concubine had said. While he was young, rain storms returned quickly; it did not matter so much, but as he grew older, one cloudburst might be all that was in the sky.

He lifted her head and looked into her eyes. She smiled, and the cool blueness of her eyes trickled over him.

Zhang knew then that he would be able to do this right for them both. Reaching over her to the side of the bed, he took a small bottle and showed it to her. He took out the stopper and put a little on his finger. She sniffed. It smelled of sandalwood and moist earth. Not unpleasant, but she wasn't sure of its purpose. She was sure it had one, for she realised in this bed he controlled everything. If she had only known how many times in the last short while he had come to an utterly unprecedented loss of control, she might have been surprised, perhaps flattered.

She looked at him quizzically.

'Not make baby, not get pox,' Zhen explained.

He was pleased at the way he had remembered this word. He had looked up lots of medical words in the dictionary but could not remember many. This one had been easy.

Charlotte was astounded. What miraculous salve was this that could change the fate of women. Could it be true? She had really not thought this far. But it was too late in any case. She wasn't stopping now. This man was a revelation, more god than any heavenly deity. She had every intention of abandoning herself to him completely. With this body I thee worship, she thought, and suddenly she meant it.

Taking some of the oil on his fingers, he began to touch her with it. Charlotte moaned, as he knew she would.

Crimoney, Kitt Macleod, she thought dazedly. Lucky girl to have married fire and water.

Then thought fled, and only craving came. Zhen, saw her eyes close, her teeth grip her bottom lip. Good, he would not hurt her as he ended her virginity. He had learned how to do this with the fourth concubine's willing maid, under her mistress's expert eye, when he was sixteen.

The fourth concubine had smuggled in young virginal girls destined for miserable concubinage with ancient mandarins, girls who wanted, just once at least, to touch young male skin and feel young male arms. It was easy to fool the old pigs with fake blood, the fourth concubine had told him. These leathery relics were desperate to believe, hoping to prolong their worthless lives by soaking up virgin essences. She had laughed bitterly when she spoke of it. Then they might never come to the girl again, locking her away in the harem to an inescapable life of boredom, cattiness and frustration. She was lucky, she supposed: her master still came to her occasionally, was not so old, could still get it up. She had a daughter, this house and a limited freedom, which was impossible in the *hougong*, the royal harems. But it was a little life.

She liked to watch him from behind her gauzy curtain, drinking wine, and as he gave each girl this gift she would sometimes come to him, pushing the girl away, and take him, still wet from the girl's climax, in her mouth, push him to the edge. Her maid would tie her hands together, for when this drunken mood was on her she could scratch him to a bloody mess. Then he took her roughly, sometimes from the front, often from the back, thrusting into her, the maid oiling and preparing her anus for his entry, which she always wanted in the most violent way, howling with pain as he assaulted her, his blood up and unable to stop. This was, at first, engrossingly intoxicating, but as he matured he had put a stop to it. He knew she needed to feel herself, that pain was a way of somehow affirming her life, but he feared she also sought death in the throes of passion, in his arms. He began to dislike himself. He grew tired of this contract of the flesh, these women's cloistered appetites and increasingly violent erotic obsessions.

He had spent a year in the monastery, meditating and studying the Way, practising the movements of the *tai chi*. Only the fourth concubine's tears and his affection for her had brought him back to her, but on his terms this time. There were no more virgins.

Until this one, this little goddess of pure white jade. He wanted her to know fountains of pleasure. Slowly pushing his fingers, he felt for her hymen, spreading the oil. Using his thumb, rubbing and circling the little pearl on the jade step, he knew she would not feel it as he pushed through the web. There was no blood. She had had no pain. The sounds she was making were not pain. She was slick and wet, but he did not want her to go too fast. He searched with feathery gentleness for her most tender and provoking place. He knew he had found it when she suddenly stiffened and began to shake and move her hips.

He withdrew his fingers. Charlotte moaned in disappointment, but he knew he would find this place again. 'Sh,' he whispered, drawing her to him. She looked up at him, questioning, her face angry. Zhen smiled at her little fury, knowing the reason. He began again to circle and tease her, and she quickly forgave him.

Stimulating and releasing her, he listened to her sounds and watched her face. When her breathing became short and shallow he knew she was near. With the tiniest of movements he brought her to the top, and with deep groans she arched her back; her head jerked, and her essence flowed over his hand. He waited until she had passed through the rushing river of the high uplands, down to the cooler streams of the meadows, floating on the rivulets and looked up at him with languid eyes of wonderment.

Coming between her legs, he placed them around his waist. 'Look,' he said.

She looked at him, engorged with blood, and again reached for him, her mind still half-dimmed from orgasm and desire. Taking a little of the oil, he put it in her hand and let her rub it gently on him, guiding her; he felt the rain clouds gathering.

Lifting her hips, he entered the dark velvet cave in which men for all the ages have sought oblivion. Charlotte felt this smooth thickness like a gentle sliding into her soul, a small white flame in her mind. She let out a cry at the purity of this act of light with a man who felt like silk. He stopped, caressed her face with his lips, listened to her breath.

'Yes, *hao*?' he whispered into her cheek.

For answer she pulled him close, this thief of speech.

He began to move gently, shallow, deep. She abandoned herself to this new sensation, knowing now the flame would grow into a cloud, for she had recently returned from these snowy uplands. Occasionally he stopped and waited, kissing her neck, ears and lips and then began again. She was consumed with this feeling of him in her, all conscious thought gone. She began to move her hips, urging him.

Zhen felt the pendulum of *yin* and *yang*, the divine balance, swing together. Holding her hips in one arm he found again the place which would make her come with him on this cosmic journey. She was holding him desperately now, moaning into his chest, and with a shuddering of her body he felt a gush of hot liquid. It was her *gao chao*, her high tide, a rush of fevered blood, and he flooded into her, together, together, deeply together, souls embedded. Clouds and rain, the eternal and exquisite mystery of the flesh.

'License my roving hands, and let them go
Before, behind, between, above, below.
O my America! my new-found-land,
My kingdom, safeliest when with one man manned,
My mine of precious stones, my empery,
How blest am I in this discovering thee!
To enter in these bonds is to be free;

Then where my hand is set, my seal shall be.'

They lay until he felt her relax. Now he would dot the dragon's eye, seal his mark on her like the calligrapher his work of art. She looked at him, and tears came. They were both bathed in sweat. She could not believe what he had done. What he had made her feel. Was this what love was like? She had had no idea.

He smiled at her and rolled on his back, taking her with him still connected by his slowly waning erection. Straddling him, she felt him grow smaller inside her, the sensuality of liquids dripping. He knew if they wanted he could wait and grow again, begin again without ever parting. She put her hands to his neck, asking him to come up to her and, taking his head in her hands, sobbing quietly, kissed him on his lips, his eyes, his cheeks. He knew she was feeling a great love, a deep gratitude for the way he had opened up her longings and satisfied them. When his young body had matured and he had grown very skilful, the fourth concubine had often cried after a long session of lovemaking. The young girls almost always did. The fourth concubine had been a clever lover, knew more than Charlotte could. But if they were allowed the gift of time he would teach her the art and craft of love. And one thing was very different. He had not loved the fourth concubine. They had played this game a hundred different ways, but he had not loved her. Not like this. This love moved his mind, made him sumptuous and vast, exalted them.

Zhen knew she would kiss him like this as long as he let her, but he suddenly felt the heat of the room, of their conjoined bodies. Gently he gathered her up and moved off the bed. She gave a little whimper as he slipped out of her. Her legs around him, raining kisses over his face and neck, he carried her to the big jar and ladled cool water over them, drenching them from head to toe, drinking and kissing. Then, dropping her feet to the floor, he began slowly to wash them both of the sweat and oil. Light came from the bedroom through the carved porcelain lattice screen halfway up the wall, and she simply watched him, his body moving in the semi-darkness as he went about this strangely mundane yet intensely intimate activity, the smell of coconut-oil soap rising from their skin. She put out her hand to his head, pulling his face down to hers, feeling his wet lips as water dripped from their bodies. This languorous cleansing had made her crave again. She could still feel him inside her. Wanted him there again already. It was incredible.

Motioning her to sit on the cool wet tiles, he gently opened her legs, washing her of the oil and semen seeping from her, cleaning her, scooping water on her, drenching her in this sweet dew, this prime and most northerly of the elements. She leaned back on her elbows. He put down the ladle and smiled at her, a slow, enigmatic smile. She watched him, telling him with her eyes that she did not know what to expect. Parting the wet black hair, he lowered his head and began to run his tongue around her. Charlotte gasped and involuntarily pulled back her hips. Would he always surprise her?

'No?' He looked into her eyes.

'Yes, oh, yes. Sorry, just surprised me that's all. I'm new to this, you know.'

Zhen didn't understand everything she said, but he knew her tone of voice now. The surprising thing about this language of hers was the way words did not always matter. Watching her face and listening to her voice he could detect many messages, although this time he understood most of what she had said.

Pulling her up into his arms, he kissed her, a deep kiss that she fell into as one might sink into a feather bed. Then, lightly, he began to run his tongue around her mouth, sucking and biting the tip of her tongue, her lips. She followed his lead, and soon they were kissing wildly. He picked her up, and she wrapped her legs round his waist. Charlotte, eyes glazed, almost overcome, was biting and licking him. She felt feral. She bit into his neck and he winced, pulling away. Another time he would use this feeling to take her roughly, letting her bite him to blood, but not this time. He knew he could hurt her, bruise her when this mood was on them. But he wanted to let her glimpse into the exquisite rooms of this erotic palace of the flesh which they could explore together, as millions of millions had done for eons before them.

He carried her back to the bedroom. But not to the bed. Slowly he began to turn round and round, calming her, until her hands rested on his queue, her head fell onto his shoulder, her breath returned to normal.

He began to sing a tune full of eastern chords and oriental words which fell on her ear like the patter of soft rain:

'*Xiao baobei, xiao baobei*. Little precious jewel, little treasure.'

It was a lullaby which his mother had sung to him and his brothers. Turning, their shadows flitted on the walls like puppets in the *wayang*. In this slow dance he wanted to show her his joy at their union, which he could not put into words. She was glad that this was the man who had been her first man. Whatever was to come, how could she ever regret this night? With this body I thee worship. Word made flesh. She was calm now; her legs slipped from his waist, and he picked her up in his arms and carried her to the bed.

She was sleepy, he knew, but she could not sleep yet. Eventually they would sleep like the dead, but not yet. Lying on his side next to her, one arm supporting his head, he took her hand in his, bringing the palm to his mouth and kissing it.

'Hello,' he said. 'Let us begin.' This was said with such schoolmasterly gravity, she laughed with delight and woke from her torpor.

He grinned. Zhen could feel a new erection beginning, but that would wait. Dropping her head over the edge of the bed, wet hair trailing the floor, he raised her hips and lowered his face between her legs. The fourth concubine had taught him this skill very well.

# 32

A chorus of songbirds. The old man in the house next door kept singing larks, bubbling thrushes, white-capped bulbuls. Their sweet sounds woke him most mornings. The dawn was not yet up, he could see from the light in the air well. He looked down at the woman cradled against him and remembered the night. She was sleeping deeply, lips parted, her breath making whispery sounds. He looked at her face, the slight downiness of her cheek, the shape of her ear, the curve of her shoulder, the undulations of waist and hips. Lovely, lovely. He ran a finger over his lips, swollen from her kissing and biting, the mark of her little white teeth on his neck, and smiled, luxuriating in the memory. The song of the finch rose, pure and haunting, its lilting call trembling on the air, then gathering energy, bursting into bubbling melody filled with images of Chinese mountain streams and the whispering of pines. The finch was teaching the lark to sing.

The little lark curved into his body. He knew he should leave her alone, that he had done too much last night, but he had felt insatiable, and she had responded to his every call. Callously, almost, he wanted sex with her again today, knowing she would leave him soon, felt his arousal as he experienced the pain of this thought. He cursed himself for not using the balsam on her, caring for her last night, but after the last time, she had fallen asleep immediately, and he too, finally exhausted, had succumbed to the need for rest.

He had a raging thirst and needed to relieve himself. As he left her side, she stirred and turned to where he had been. Gulping water and throwing it over his body, he heard sounds. It was the water cart man filling the two big earthenware jars in the front porch. He and the night-soil collector arrived before the sun, one at the front, the other in the back alley. Was Ah Pok here? Slightly alarmed, Zhen returned to the bedroom. Charlotte was still sleeping, and he threw on his loose trousers, tied the cord, and went to the bottom of the stairs, where he peered back into the kitchen area.

The Indian water carrier was pouring a bucket of water into the jar. He heard the stream and splash, could hear his two buffaloes snuffling outside. Ah Pok did not seem to be here, but he would be back in a few hours. He went to the earth closet and pissed, contemplating his liquid falling through the wooden seat into the bucket, sighing at this relief. It had not been emptied. He threw some soil in and latched down the lid. Collection would be through the hatch at the back.

Two hours, that was all they had. He wanted to make her tea, wedding her again to him in this simple timeless ceremony. He would show her the little buds from the high mountain peaks of his home, full of the flavour of fogs and snow. He would serve her in the tiny cups, watching her drink. Then he would change the sheet to fresh, wash her body in the water, slowly stoke the fire of desire. But the earthenware stove was not lit, and he was not sure where Ah Pok kept the linen. It would take too much time. He let out a low growl of discontent.

Leaning over her, he kissed her on the lips, at first softly then more deeply. She responded sleepily, running her arms round his neck, pulling him down. Remembering. The sheet was stained, sweaty and gluey. Not here. He picked up the little bottle of oil, putting it into her hand, then lifted her and carried her, half-comatose, into the bathroom. He took the bottle and handed her a ladle of water to drink, dropped her feet to the floor and began rinsing her in the cool water, running his hands over her, into her. She protested, moving away from this touch, the inside of her body swollen and painful. She wanted to pee but didn't know how to tell him, was so tired that she just let it run down her leg, shamed, wincing as it burned her raw tissues, then rinsing herself again as gently as she could.

Zhen could see she was hurting, that he was taking her dignity, that she did not want him now. But he did not care. She was woman, and she was his. She would do what he wished. He released the cord of his trousers and let the garment drop wetly to the floor, showed her his virility. Here, he was lord. She would not escape this; it was his will. He sat on the washing stool and sharply motioned her to come, dropping oil on his hands. Charlotte didn't understand this hard-eyed mood that was on him. She obeyed him, slowly, reluctantly. He knew he should stop. Every fibre of his being knew it. This was not the spontaneous flowing of the Tao which had washed over them in the night, bringing joy and peace.

Clean the dark mirror of the mind. Fulfill your purpose without violence, for this is against the Tao. And what is against the Tao will perish. The words of the *Taoteching*. At this moment its wisdom was hidden under the tight, crimped cloak of his lust. He wanted to take her again, even against her will, knowing she would soon be outside his influence, back in her world. Pulling her between his legs, he wrapped his arm around her waist, imprisoning her and put his oily fingers into her. She moaned with pain—no, no—tried to withdraw from him, tried weakly to push his hand away. His fingers still inside her, he locked her between his thighs, pulling her body to his face.

'Please, Zhen, stop.'

Charlotte dropped her head to his. She saw his desire, but physically she could not go on. She knew he understood this but somehow could not give up this need for her.

She held his head against her, willing him to drop his hand. 'Please, please,' she moaned against his skin.

Zhen was squeezed into a tiny place, vines of jealousy and passion all wound round his heart, choking it.

'Please, please,' she whispered. 'I love you.'

Then she kissed him on his head, put her hands on his neck, and he ceased, recognising the words, taking his hand from her, wrapping his arms around her waist, leaning his face against her soft belly, absorbing the power of her *yin*, dark and cool.

She felt his erection against her legs. She loosened his arms and dropped to her knees unsure how to continue, remembering the night, her mouth on him, his mouth on her.

She took him in her hands and touched him with her lips, but they were swollen and painful, and she had no idea what to do. She looked up at him. In the foggy passion of his brain, he gazed at her. Clouds cleared, and he took her head between his hands and began to guide her mouth around him. Yes, this was the way; she was wise. He felt balance

251

return. Why had he lost trust in the Tao? She, child-like, had re-affirmed its truth.

She wanted to please him, grateful for this compromise. She remembered the way he had touched her breasts, the gentleness of his tongue, and began to emulate this, licking and kissing him despite the soreness of her lips, trying to judge the changes of his responses.

Zhen, returned to reason, saw his unfairness. If she were married to him, or his concubine, he would have had years to please her, show her how to please him. This one day was not enough. He drew her head up, looked into her eyes. Then he took her hand and moved it on him. She watched the passing shades of his face. He put her other hand to his testicles. This would make him fly faster, for he knew she was exhausted with sexual games, and he, too, needed to be released from this fleshy tyranny which had suddenly overtaken him.

She knew what he liked now and stroked him, her hand still in his as he moved himself towards release. As he felt on the verge, he ran his hand into her hair, holding her.

'Look, look.' His voice was deep with tension. Look at what I am, look at my *yang* brightness. I am your man. See me, taste me, remember.

Charlotte saw his emotions in the pull of his lips, the grit of his teeth, the rictus smile of orgasm. He let out a deep growl, and she watched this fluid release, aroused by it, wanting to taste him, felt his liquid on her cheeks and lips, like spray from the ocean. The tension drained from his face, and he looked down as the last spasms liberated him. He let go of her hand and ran his finger down her cheek, bending his face to hers, licking her lips clean of himself. Despite the swellings, Charlotte felt blood pound in her ears, inflamed by this gesture, the sight and sounds of his orgasm, his trust in her. She pulled his mouth into a kiss, forgiving him everything. He rose from the stool taking her with him. She took his hand and put it between her legs, urgent.

Zhen knew this ardor was in her mind, temporary, and that if he touched her, pain would wither it. He held her, cupping his hand, waiting for her to relax. This passivity aroused her even more, and she groaned into his mouth. Zhen took his hands away from her, putting them on her cheeks and gently withdrew from the kiss.

'Sh, Sh,' he whispered and pulled her to him, wrapping her close. Charlotte lay against him, knew that it was over, wished now that she had let him do whatever he wanted despite her pain, felt his tenderness, small tears coursing down her cheeks. How could she ever thank this Chinese conjurer who had given her this flawless and incomparable jewel, his selfless patience, his bounteous and immaculate wisdom and generosity? How was it possible for one man to know so much and teach her so quickly? Even with her lack of experience, she knew by instinct that this was rare.

He released her and washed quickly, touching a kiss to his fingers and putting it against her lips. Then, leaving her, he dressed. There were more sounds on the street now, and he pushed open the shutters. The air was fresh and cool. It was still darkish, but the dawn was waiting. The signal gun had not gone off, but he knew it would soon. He would have to take her to the *sampan* quickly. He returned to the bedroom, the scene of their carnal pleasures. How would he sleep here tonight?

She was hooking her corset, crying softly, fingers trembling. She had washed herself, feeling his touch everywhere. Now that it was over, she wanted these hurts, these reminders of him. In the mirror she could see that her lips were bruised and swollen. She fleetingly wondered how she would explain this to Robert, but then suddenly did not care. Zhen went to her and helped her with the buttons of her bodice. Seeing her lips, he brought out the balsam, gently treating them both. These swellings would go down soon, he tried to tell her.

Her hair was wet. Pulling the sheet from the bed, he took the bottom and began to rub, soaking up the water. From a little drawer he took a pommade of perfumed herbs and oil. Rubbing it onto his hands, he began to massage her head and straighten and smooth her hair, running his hands through its length until it lay untangled down her back. Charlotte had stopped crying. The rhythm of his hands in her hair was consoling. Zhen knew he had to comfort her. He could not let her go miserable and despairing, for as far as possible they must conceal this relationship. He sighed. If she had been a Chinese girl or a native girl he would simply have taken her as a second wife, the wife of his heart rather than his head. His father had had four wives and many concubines before the opium devil had shackled and ruined him. But he knew that white men

253

concealed their concubines and kept only one lawful wife. Why, he did not understand, but he knew a white woman would never accept the Chinese arrangement and that outrage would be the response from both sides.

Taking his comb he divided her hair into three and began to plait it, humming the lullaby he had sung to her in the night. He tied the end of the queue with a red ribbon, then turned her towards him.

'Look,' he said, putting their two queues together. For the first time she could smile. How could he make her understand?

'Xia Lou, not sad, please. Meet again but secret.' He put his fingers to his lips to emphasise the word. He knew he sounded idiotic, but what could he do? *Aiya*, this would be so much easier if she were Chinese. Then he would write her poetry, use words which would thrill her, bind her even closer to him.

Charlotte knew what he was trying to say. She must take this night and lock it in her heart. She would jeopardise him, his life and his livelihood, if their affair were made known. Suddenly, her heart lightened. They would meet like this again, and in the meantime she would cocoon these feelings inside her, keeping them only for him.

Zhen took her hand and led her downstairs. At the door he found her hat, and she arranged it on her hair, pulling down the veil. He put her hand to his lips and kissed each of her fingers; then from the pocket of his jacket he took the balsam and put it in her palm, closing her fingers around the jar.

'For hurt, sorry Xia Lou,' he said, nodding. 'Yes? Understand?'

'Yes,' she whispered, putting it into her bag. She looked up at him through the veil. Now at this moment of parting, her resolve wavered.

'I don't want to go,' she said. Not go. He understood, and his heart felt an ache but also a small triumphant pleasure.

'Sh, sh.' He took her in his arms. But there was no time. He did not want her to cry again. Quickly he opened the door, checking the street. Not many people here, but he was sure there were eyes watching the strange sight of a woman in Western clothes in Chinatown at this hour. The gun went off suddenly as they left the building.

It would be better that they not be seen together, but he could not leave her side now. It would not be safe, and he had to see her safely across the river. He held her hand in his, as she followed close behind him. It was dangerous, but for some things it was right to dare danger.

He led her to the quayside, which was already filled with smells of food, voices calling, some of the godowns already open with the Eurasian and Chinese supervisors at work although the sun was not yet over the horizon. He was glad the boatmen were mostly Indian or Malay, not able to chatter and gossip with the Chinese. Hailing the nearest *sampan*, he helped Charlotte into the boat and threw coins at the boatman. She mumbled instructions in Malay and sat looking down, not turning, as the boatman quickly rowed her up the river, round the mouth and disappeared.

Zhen ran back to the house and let himself inside. His brain swirled with ominous rumblings. He had tried to bind her blood to his through this night of passion. In his arms, his bed, he knew she would never stray, but released back to the world of her people, he was not sure.

Charlotte disembarked at the jetty of the police house. She went to her room, throwing off her hat, latching her door, undoing her bodice roughly, unhooking the corset, so hot and hard, dropping her skirt and then, too tired for more, lay down on her bed. She wanted sleep, and Morpheus swept her down into his dark cave. It was midday when she woke, dripping with sweat.

She felt immediately the deep throbbing of the swollen flesh between her legs, where he had been. Her throat was parched, and she went to the water butt, wincing, and quenched her thirst, gulping the water down and letting it course over her hot face, soak her clothes. In her room, naked, she examined herself in the mirror, pulling the queue he had made over her shoulder, touching the red ribbon. Her nipples were sore and red. The swelling on her lips had disappeared, though she still felt the bruising.

'Crimoney, Kitt Mcleod, feels like you've barely survived the Battle of Flodden Field.'

Did all women feel like this on their first time? Surely not. She wished she had someone to ask. The idea of raising this question with Mrs Keaseberry or Mrs van Heyde, perhaps, made her smile.

She sighed and took the jar of balsam from her bag and ran it around her nipples. It felt soothing, but it also brought his face to mind, the feel of his tongue on her skin. How she would get through the next days she did not know.

Scottish resolve, Kitt, she thought and smiled. The words of her grandmother ran in her head. She had not thought of her since her first day in Singapore.

'No matter who your mother was, my poor wee lad was a Macleod. You are of the Clan Macleod, ancient, honourable, courageous, never forget this. Hold fast, that is our devise.'

Suddenly she missed her, the uncompromising, rock-like sureness and strength of her. Her own compass seemed to be as volatile as if she were the tiniest boat on a violent sea. And dear Aunty Jeannie, the softness of her Scottish burr, her gentle understanding: she missed her, too. In this humid and sweaty heat came the memory of the cool mists and granite cliffs of Aberdeen, sailing in the bay, round the headland with Duncan in his skiff, the sharp wind in her face, the sight of Girdleness lighthouse, porpoises, dolphins, eider ducks, skylarks and pipits, the smell of salt fish in the port.

She was no longer a maid. Her mind strayed back to him. She gazed at her reflection in the mirror.

'Hold fast, Kitt.' It was reassuring.

She sat and began to apply the balsam to her swollen skin. She heard the rain begin again heavily.

Then, suddenly, she remembered Meda.

# 33

Robert returned to the police bungalow in the early afternoon. The house was quiet. He called to Charlotte, but there was no answer. Then, rounding the verandah, he saw her seated, looking out over the harbour towards the distant islands. The vault of the sky was high and blue, with white clouds whispering along the horizon, as if rain had never sullied its perfection. She looked small and vulnerable, and his heart went out to her. He knew she was pained by what he was now certain was love for the young Chinaman, Zhen.

Hearing his footsteps, she turned to greet him with a small smile.

He stopped, rooted to the spot. What he had feared had occurred. He had seen that dreamy smile, those languid eyes, when Shilah had woken in his arms.

She had given herself to Zhen. Nothing he could say could change that. And he had no true right. She had understood him. Now he merely wanted her safe.

He walked over to her and kissed her on the forehead, a long and sweet kiss of brotherly affection. She smelled different. Coconut, sandalwood and some other tangy smell. Charlotte put her hand to his face and smiled at him. Beloved Robbie. Then she looked out over the harbour to Tigran's ship, which was coming closer to shore.

'Takouhi is leaving, Robbie. Did you know? Taking Meda to Java to get her well.'

Robert sank onto a chair.

'Auch, I didn't know. When? Oh, poor George.'

Charlotte pointed to the ship. Tigran's launch had set out for shore, its white sails filled with the perfumed breeze, the oars of the men dipping and dripping, dipping and dripping. As it drew closer, she saw it was fitted luxuriously with covers and curtains of dark purple damask, cushions forming a soft bed. It was like a boat from a dream.

> 'The barge she sat in, like a burnished throne,
> Burned on the water; the poop was beaten gold,
> Purple the sail, and so perfumed, that
> The winds were love-sick with them, the oars were silver,
> Which to the tune of flutes kept stroke, and made
> The water which they beat to follow faster,
> As amorous of their strokes.'

But not for love this barge. For woe, the oars beating a dirge.

'I sent Azan to find out. They could not leave while the rain was so heavy. Meda spent an uncomfortable night. She has been coughing. I fear so dreadfully for her. They will be going soon.'

Tears began to run down her cheeks.

'I forgot, Robbie, for a while. How awful. I was ...'

She stopped. Robert said nothing, knowing.

George's majordomo had appeared on the jetty. Chests were loaded into the launch. Charlotte let out a sob and rose, rushing down towards the boat. Robert followed, and they could see George's carriage arriving at the beach side. Then George stepped out, followed by Takouhi. Carrying Meda in his arms, he made his way with the girl's mother across the short stretch of beach and up the steps to the jetty. Two servants arranged Meda on the cushions under the damask roof.

Charlotte went quickly and kissed her. Meda felt so hot.

Takouhi turned to her friend, looked her deeply in the eyes.

'If you need something, write to me. I think you need me. You love man, I know. Tell me if George all right, not sad. Tell about George.'

Charlotte nodded. She would write every day. 'Come back,' she said, feeling the tears jump to her eyes, hugging her friend.

George had taken his place in the launch and now helped Takouhi down. He had spoken to Robert briefly. He would go with them to Batavia and see them safely settled, then return.

All too quickly the launch moved away from shore. Charlotte was sad to her bones. She stood with Robert's arm around her until the boat had been winched onto the ship. The sails filled with wind as it turned towards the south.

The next days were a blur. Charlotte did not go to the chapel. She slept like the dead. She did not go to the Chinese town, either, but sat on the verandah waiting, waiting.

> 'Like a monumental statue set
> In everlasting watch and moveless woe ...'

Robert was worried for his sister, but he was busy and had no time to spend in the day. There were patrols at night.

Then one day Charlotte saw Tigran's ship on the horizon. She recognised its black shape, and she rose, half-dreading the news it carried.

When the launch tied up, Charlotte was at George's side in an instant. Before she could open her mouth he said, 'Tigran has taken them to Buitenzorg. Takouhi has consulted with the *dukun*. She is hopeful, and the air is good up in the hills, not like the air on the coast. It's cool, not hot like here. It will do them good; I'm sure of it.'

George handed her a letter from Takouhi. 'This is for you. If you want to reply, the brig will wait, for there are some other things I must send to them.' He left her, walking across the plain to his house. His face had not expressed the slightest emotion.

Charlotte went onto the verandah and opened the letter.

*Hello Charlotte, lovely sister,*
*I never write letter in English before so sorry if not good. I am happy to come to Jawa. I meet the dukun and he give jamu medicine to Meda. She improve little bit. Tomorrow we go to hills. Tigran has big house there. George not happy we come but here are spirits of my family, spirits of my land. I think he angry. Please you help him, Charlotte.*

*You love one man, not white man, I know. George say not my bloody business but sometimes he is silly-billy. This man marry but not matter. You love this man all your heart like I love George. I not marry George but not matter, I in his heart, he in my heart. This not for one day, one year, for all days, all years. Even he marry hundred million women, not matter. For you same. Then when time come you want leave, not regret.*

*When time come, write. Tigran send ship.*

*Takouhi*


Charlotte kissed the letter. Despite her deepest worry for her child, Takhoui had found the kindness to advise her. Her heart felt suddenly calm. Takouhi was with Meda. She must do everything she could for George.

She sat at her little table and wrote a letter back to Takouhi, thanking her, telling her about Zhen, pouring out her heart, telling her she would care for George, send her news. Then she folded it and sealed it and took it to the launch.

All at once she wanted to see Zhen. It seemed more than a week since they had been together. In her anxiety for Meda, she had lost track of time.

She went along the plain and crossed to the chapel, where Evangeline greeted her with a kiss. Evangeline commented on how thin she looked. She had been worrying too much about Takhoui. Then Charlotte gave her the news, and Evangeline made the sign of the cross, thanking the merciful lord for their safety.

The classes were about to begin. Charlotte waited to see Zhen and Qian arrive, but they did not come. Frowning, she went to consult Father Lee, who was relieved to see her, although he too thought her too thin. 'No, no,' he said, 'they have not come. Today is the marriage of little Qian. It will go on for several days.'

# 34

Zhen had not stopped thinking of Charlotte since he had left her on the river. He knew she had sadness; he had heard through Baba Tan of her friend's departure and the sickness of the child. He should not expect Charlotte's mind to be on him, but after such a night of love, he did. He couldn't help himself.

Qian was busy with preparations for his marriage. The betrothal had taken place. The marriage would be in a few days. Qian had been measured by the tailor; that had supplied a few laughs. They had talked some more about his wedding night, but really there was nothing for him to do about that. Now Zhen was at a loose end. In a return to reasonableness, he decided Charlotte would see him when she was ready and suddenly remembered he had not seen Min since their last, unpleasant encounter.

He made his way to Hokkien Street, stopping only for some food at one of the hawker street stalls. He greeted the old guard at the door of the *ah ku* house and went inside.

The old crone who was the brothel keeper came out from her room to meet him. There had been trouble with the whore he went with, and she wanted to warn him. Zhen's face turned to stone as he listened. Min had been beaten up by a sailor from one of the foreign ships. The policeman had come and arrested him, but Min was not well. The old woman took him down the hall to a room at the back of the building. It was dark and stuffy, and as he opened the door he saw several women lying on cots. The smell was bad, for the buckets were kept in this area, and the odour of opium pervaded the atmosphere. The only window, which gave onto an alley, was shuttered.

He called her name and opened the shutters, throwing a grey light on the interior. What he saw in the light appalled him. Her pretty face was swollen and bruised. He could see marks where the filthy bastard had held her neck. Going to the cot, he took her hand, asking where else she was hurt. She was so glad to see him but could not smile. Her face hurt, and, she showed him, so did her ribs. Opium helped, she tried to tell him.

Zhen knew he needed to get Min out of there. He went quickly back down the corridor and told the old woman to find the *kongsi* man she dealt with, and inform him the *honggun* needed to speak to him. Zhen thought he knew who the man was; he usually hung around the two brothels he was in charge of, gathering a percentage of the girls' wages as protection money. Some protection.

The fellow came at a trot, warily looking inside the door. Zhen grabbed him by the neck, pulled him into the room and slammed him against the wall. The old crone and two customers fled.

'Fucking pig, where were you when the girl was being beaten?'

The man was terrified. He knew who Zhen was, and he started to babble. 'I came as quick as I could. The sailor had already done his work. You can't tell when one of the white men is going to go crazy, especially if they're drunk.'

Keeping him pinned, Zhen put his face up close. The man smelled of grog, opium and sweat.

'Well, I'm taking her out of here. Understand? She's no use to you as a whore, and she's badly hurt. Were you just going to leave her there to rot, pig?'

Zhen wanted to punch the fellow but it wouldn't help Min. The man was nodding wildly.

'Get two men and a litter to carry her. Explain to your bosses what's happened. There's to be no trouble. If they want, they can come and see me, if they fucking dare.'

Zhen knew that taking a woman from the *ah ku* house was risky. Retaliation was usually swift. He could not take her to his house; it would be an affront to the *kongsi* protection men. The only alternative was to take her to the dying house on Chinchew Street. If they thought she was dying, they might let the matter go without too much fuss. No Chinese wanted a dying whore on his hands. Dead souls were better all together in the dying house, where they could be placated during the Festival of

Hungry Ghosts, not hanging around seeking revenge and bringing bad luck.

He let the man go to do his bidding and went back to Min, calling the old crone for water. Min managed to drink a little and began to cry. Zhen did not dare pick her up. She needed a doctor; he feared she had broken bones. He told the old crone to go to the Chinese medicine shop nearby and get the herbalist. This man he knew very well, for they often talked about medicine together. By the time she returned with him, the litter had arrived, and the two men lifted Min gently onto it.

The old crone spat on the ground as they left the house. She was glad to be rid of that little bitch, especially if she was dying. Saved her the trouble of getting her moved.

The dying house was overcrowded, and it, too, was pervaded by the familiar smell of opium fumes. Min was one of only five women in the place. The four others were *ah ku* as well, and one was giving birth to a baby, which she intended to drown as soon as it was born. The old *ah ku* birthing woman was with her.

Zhen's woman could have her cubicle when she had got the job done or when one of the others died, the guardian told him laconically. Min's litter was placed on the floor, and, amid the pregnant woman's groans, the herbalist examined her. She had at least two broken ribs, he told Zhen. Her face was bad, but it would heal. He would make a paste for the face and bind the ribs. Other than that, there was little he could do. She should take opium for the pain. He could send his daughter to take care of her, bring food.

Zhen was grateful and passed him some coins, which he waved away. He did not think, in any case, that this woman had long for the world. He could see by her breathing that there was some internal damage for which he could do nothing. To Zhen's offer of money he said, 'You have given me some good advice from your honourable father's knowledge. We are colleagues.'

The herbalist took a quick look at the pregnant woman; he could see the head of the baby emerging.

'Don't kill it,' the herbalist said. 'I will take it. You nurse for one month. My woman will bring the baby to the brothel for feeding. I will send her to help you.'

The herbalist, Zhen knew, was a devout Buddhist who had at one time been a monk in China.

The old woman looked at him, mouth open.

The *ah ku*, however, did not seem surprised, and even in her pain managed to squeeze out a few words of negotiation between pushes. She'd already done this twice before, both infants dead. With every pregnancy it got easier. What did she want with the filthy coolie pigs' spawn? She had had abortions, but sometimes they didn't work. Fortunately she could keep clients happy right up to the end. Even her belly didn't bother most of the pigs.

'You want, you pay,' she gasped, knowing she would lose income if she must nurse the baby. Men didn't usually like leaky breasts and milky smells. Not that she cared about the men. She and the old mistress would want compensation for the trouble.

The herbalist nodded. He would speak to the whorehouse keeper.

Within minutes the baby was born. By the time the herbalist returned with his medicines, daughter and wife, the cord was cut and the placenta delivered. The birthing woman was cleaning up the mother, tying a cloth on her. The baby was swaddled in a *sarong* still covered in blood and liquids, but crying lustily.

Zhen had never seen the wife before. She was very dark and, he thought, hugely ugly, but she took the baby tenderly, and he saw the goodness of her heart, the pearl inside the shell, and felt ashamed.

The mother of the newborn swung her legs down from the table and, with the birthing woman's help, hobbled away.

Zhen left Min in the cubicle as the herbalist began to care for her, his dark-skinned, almond-eyed daughter seated at his feet.

He went down to the gaol on Canal Street to speak to two men who worked as carpenters. The man who had beaten Min would be inside. Zhen knew there would be little punishment for the white sailor. Beating up a Chinese whore would probably get him a fine paid to the *ah ku* house and he would be back on his ship in no time. It was just another drunken episode in the sleazy life of a man who probably fucked and beat women all over the world. Zhen's eyes narrowed. If the English law wouldn't deal with him, the real law here, *kongsi* law, would. The police would find his body, drugged and drowned, floating in the river; just another hard-drinking, opium-smoking sailor who had lost his footing. With the number of deaths while the English troops were here, no one would pursue the matter.

Suddenly he wanted to see Charlotte. Tomorrow was Qian's wedding day, and he would have to be part of that. Then he would return to the chapel for lessons. Two more nights, and he would be with her. Two more nights. They seemed like years.


Charlotte had taken her class and gone from the chapel disappointed. She walked down the road to Takouhi's house, thinking of her friend, and then turned into Coleman Street, into George's garden. One of the servants told her he was with the horses, and she went around the house and walked over to the big paddock and stables.

George was standing next to his favourite horse, brushing her down with long, smooth strokes. This pretty mare was his pride and joy, bought from the Australian horse dealers in the square at a recent auction.

As Charlotte approached he looked up.

'She's a brumby. They're the wild horses of Australia d'yer know. There's a nice story attached to their name. A Sergeant James Brumby, farrier and farmer in New South Wales, departed one day for other parts, leaving his horses to run wild. When some inquisitive beggar asked the locals who owned them they simply said, "They're Brumby's" and so the name has stuck. They interbred with later stock, so they come in all shapes and sizes. Bit like the people on this island. Isn't she a beauty.'

Charlotte nodded as he stroked her soft black muzzle. The horse really was a lovely creature, pale golden with a pure white mane and tail and a little black mouth.

'Hardy, strong, agile and quick to learn. I'd rather a brumby than any other horse. She's called Matahari. It means "sunrise" in Javanese. Meda named her.'

He leant his forehead against the horse's head and stroked her.

'I was shipwrecked once, yer know. The day was fine, and then, in a blink, there were dark clouds, and suddenly the wind and waves just picked the ship up and threw her into the air, splintering the wood like a hand crumples paper. We were swamped and half-drowned within minutes. From a clear, blue sky.'

> 'The stars be hid that led me to this pain
> Drowned is reason that should me consort,
> And I remain despairing of the port.'

Charlotte put her hand on his arm, and he took it and put it to his cheek. When Robert had left, Charlotte had turned to the healing power of poetry for solace. She was moved by the universal, never-ending power of the words, speaking across generations, bridges between times and places.

> 'Silent as the sleeve-worn stone
> Of casement ledges where the moss has grown
> For all the history of grief
> An empty doorway and a maple leaf ...'

She took George in her arms and said the words which had helped her, and he stared emptily at the ground, listening.

> 'Our two souls, therefore, which are one
> Though I must go, endure not yet
> a breach, but an expansion,
> Like gold to airy thinness beat ...'

After a time he released her and, taking a handkerchief, wiped her eyes.

'Sure, and we're a fine pair.'

Charlotte smiled wanly and took Takouhi's letter from her purse, letting him read it.

'A hundred million women.'

He smiled and thought of her face as he had kissed her goodbye on the quayside. Then he had been angry, not looked back as he boarded the ship. He felt an awful premonition that he would never see her again. Handing Charlotte back the letter, he looked into her eyes and said quietly, 'I don't think I can stay in Singapore, Kitt, my sweet. Without them here it's too bitter. To wake every morning and see her house there opposite my window. If they don't return, I shall have to leave.' He ran his hand through his hair.

'It's hard, for I love this town more than any place on earth. I know it will sound arrogant, but I feel it belongs to me in a strange way, feel like I've nurtured it like a good father, groomed and beautified it like a good mother. But without them both, it would be like there is dust in my mouth and ashes under foot, every street and tree reminding me of what I've lost.'

Charlotte nodded.

'Robert and I shall miss you terribly, but they need you. And Batavia is not so very far away.'

'No, not Batavia. If Meda dies, Takouhi will not come back and will not let me go to her. You don't know her. She is a fatalist. The will of the gods will be hers, too. Takouhi is more Javanese than Armenian and, for the Javanese, life is like a kind of religious experience. There is an acceptance of misfortune which must be dealt with in quietude so that the cloudy waters of life can grow clear again. Fighting against it causes *isin*, imbalance. I would simply keep the waters cloudy for her.'

He brought his hands to his temple, rubbed them, then covered his face. Charlotte did not know what more to say. She could almost see rays of pain like shards of glass emanating from his body. She felt if she spoke or moved he might shatter.

Finally, George dropped his hands, led Matahari to the stable and closed the door.

Then he began to walk towards his house, waving a sorrowful hand at her.

# 35

Qian's wedding day had arrived. He sat in Zhen's house dressed in a long red, embroidered coat and skirt, red shoes on his feet, red hat on his head, looking anxious. It had been decided that, for the occasion, Qian would spend the night with Zhen and depart from there with the retinue to the bride's house. In the absence of male relatives, Zhen was called upon, with the master of ceremonies, to carry out some duties which would normally fall to the father or an uncle. An altar had been set up in the empty downstairs shop area, with the tablets to heaven and earth, the Kitchen God and Qian's ancestors arranged on it. He had kowtowed before it. The engagement contract had not stipulated that Qian take Sang's name. This was not necessary for him since there was a living son, but he had agreed that the first male child would bear Sang's name. Now he sat contemplating the fact that offspring by him would require a miracle.

The *cha-li* (tea presents) had been exchanged and he looked at what remained of the little bridal cakes—one decorated with a phoenix and the other with a dragon—which lay on the table in front of him. These bridal cakes had been distributed to Sang's family and friends as invitations to the marriage. Ah Liang had invited men from the godown and around the town to celebrate on the groom's side. Now Qian had to wait for the procession to the bride's home to begin. The satin-covered blue-and-yellow sedan chair stood ready outside the door.

Zhen came to his side. 'Well, the big day, eh? Let's hope there are no cockups!' He began to laugh. 'What have you decided to do tonight, eh? And by the way, you look ridiculous.'

Qian smiled wanly. 'I dunno. Wait until I see her and make up my mind then. After all, she probably has no idea what to expect from me in any case.'

Zhen shook his head. Poor woman. Stuck with a guy who would never get it up for her. He thought of Charlotte.

Ah Liang came into the room and motioned Qian to come. A small boy, looking terrified, was sitting in the sedan chair, for tradition decreed this was a good omen for future sons. As he settled himself into the sedan chair beside him, Qian patted him on the head. The poor child would never know how useless was his role on this particular day.

The chair was lifted from the ground, and the sudden and raucous noise of fireworks, drums and gongs broke out. The procession set off, crackers going off on every side, followed by two red lanterns swinging from poles, a dancing lion cavorting and snapping and a band of musicians playing as loudly as they could.

Down the street they went, turning into South Bridge Road, following the path by the river to cross New Bridge, then back into High Street, arriving finally at Sang's house. Here Zhen got into some good-natured haggling over the red packets which it was his duty to distribute to Sang's relatives and guests as the surrender price for the bride. When the agreement was finally made, Qian descended from the chair and stepped across the threshold of his new home.

Before the assembled relatives, Qian took a sip of some soup which contained a soft-boiled egg. Breaking the yolk symbolised the breaking of the bride's ties with her family. Of course, no such break would take place in this marriage, and the bridal procession from her home to the groom's would only symbolically be made by going over the river and back.

The bride's red sedan was waiting under the eaves of the gate. Then she appeared, dressed in red from head to toe, a phoenix crown of silver covered in dancing red pom-poms on her head and a thick curtain of glass beads hiding her face.

Qian's first thought was that she was not fat. He could not have borne a woman with big breasts and hips. Zhen craned round the gate to get a glimpse of her but could see nothing. She came out of the door on the back of the good-luck woman, shielded by a red parasol. A woman was throwing rice at the sedan. From the back of the heavily curtained chair hung a sieve to strain off evil and a metallic mirror to reflect light and good luck upon her. The sedan chair set off on its little journey, with firecrackers and other attendants scattering beans in front of her.

Before long the chair was back. The bride dismounted onto a red mat covering the ground and stepped over a saddle which had been placed on the threshold for 'saddle' and 'tranquillity' had the same sound. As she did so, an attendant flashed light on her from a mirror. Now Qian could separate the curtain of beads and take a first look at his future wife.

Swan Neo, from behind her beads, had contemplated him as she entered the room, this male she was offered to like an egg at breakfast. He looked all right. He was slight—she would have preferred a bigger man—but it did not matter, he was not repulsive, and she did not have to care for him. All he had to do was give her a son.

He walked towards her and, hands trembling slightly, separated the curtain and looked at her. She was pretty, he could see. Her face was thin, almost boyish. She had lowered her eyes but now looked directly at him before he let the curtain fall together. This was the man that would change everything in this filthy house, she thought. With the death of her old husband and the arrival of Qian, Sang's first wife's position had altered. With neither husband, son or grandson, she was reduced to a side role. Now it was the daughter of the second wife who would hold sway, especially if a son was born to them. Even without this, Qian would be the man in the house after today.

Zhen could only see her from the back, but she looked slender. His mind flashed to his own marriage and what his bride might look like. He thought of Charlotte, couldn't wait for tomorrow. If she was not at the chapel, he would go by her bungalow and find out what was going on.

The couple now left the room, followed by all the guests, and were conducted to Sang's family altar where they paid homage to heaven and earth and bowed to each other. The marriage was complete. Next they were led to the bridal chamber. Again all the relatives and guests followed them, ribbing them good-heartedly as they both sat on the ornately carved marriage bed covered in red silk pillows and coverlets bearing huge embroidered double happiness characters. Zhen could see Qian looking embarrassed and joined the others in making ribald remarks.

Finally the wedding banquet began in the great hall, all the men seated as dishes of shark's fin soup, pork, chicken, fried vegetables, rice and noodles succeeded each other. The women were eating in another hall towards the back. Servants ran around bringing dishes and taking plates like an army of ants. Zhen knew Ah Pok was helping out in the kitchen.

As the day drew to a close, Qian and his new wife were finally accompanied, once again, to the bridal chamber. This time the bride had removed her phoenix crown and its glassy curtain, and Zhen saw her face for the first time. She was thin and quite pretty, but her skin looked tired. He reflected that she was in for a bit of a shock later on.

Zhen said goodbye and left. He was a little drunk from the rice wine at the banquet. Suddenly, in the midst of nuptials and bridal beds, he couldn't wait any longer to see Charlotte. It was only a short distance down the street to the river. There were other guests leaving and moving towards the river, and he joined them until he saw the police bungalow on his left.

He let the group go on and dropped back. Slipping into the garden of the bungalow, he climbed the back steps from the servants' quarters. Azan came out immediately. Zhen's Malay was quite bad, but he asked to see Miss Mah Crow. Azan eyed him suspiciously but went to the door and called his mistress.

Charlotte's breath quickened when she saw him. How had he dared come? Thank the Lord, Robert was out and there were only two peons on duty in the office. Reassuring Azan, she motioned Zhen to come.

As soon as he got inside, he took her waist and quickly looked into one of the rooms, moving her inside and closing the door.

His lips were on hers in seconds. His arms were on either side of her, holding her against the wall, imprisoning her. She returned his kiss, casting reason to the wind.

Holding her in this kiss, he began to pull up her skirts. Charlotte, at first alarmed, succumbed and pulled up her petticoats, revealing her pantalettes with the long slit. He slid his hand between her legs, into her, still kissing her. As his hand moved, Charlotte started to moan, and then suddenly remembered where she was. She pushed his hand away and pushed down her skirt, put her fingers to her lips. She could hear movements. She was sure Azan or Mo was spying.

Whispering, she told him she would come to his house. His lips tasted of rice wine, and she could see he was a little drunk. She remembered that today was Qian's wedding day.

'Go now. I'll come in half an hour.'

She drew on her hand the Chinese signs for three and ten and minute. Zhen was pleased and understood. He nodded and redrew the characters for thirty on his hand and looked at her fiercely. 'Come,' he meant. 'I can't wait.' As if to underline this longing, he took her once again in his arms, kissing her mouth, her neck, putting her hand against his erection. She felt her legs get weak, basking in his need of her, wanting him.

Then she put her hands on his shoulders, pushing him away from her, smiling. She put her fingers to her lips and opened the door, peeping into the hall. Azan was seated just outside the back door, peeling garlic and trying not to look as if he was peering inside.

Charlotte fixed her hair quickly and in a loud voice thanked Zhen and showed him out through the front door by the river. Zhen was still hard, and he had trouble walking, but he went slowly down to the landing stage and sat for a few minutes before getting a *sampan* across to the quay.

His house was empty. How long Ah Pok would be away Zhen was not sure. Really, Zhen thought, this is so complicated. All he wanted to do was make love to the woman he loved, and it needed all this secrecy. He sighed, remembering the feel of her, anticipating her arrival. When she arrived he would bolt the door. After the last time, he had had a manly chat with Ah Pok and explained the situation. He had a woman. She was a mixed-blood girl, half Chinese, but she dressed in English clothes. She might visit him sometimes. When she did, he would want Ah Pok to disappear for a few hours. If the door was bolted he should stay away until the following morning.

Now Zhen was impatient for Charlotte to arrive, waiting by the open door, watching for her. She had been clever this time. How smart she was. She was wearing a *sarong* and a shawl over her bodice. Her hat was new; he did not recognise it or the veil that covered her face.

Charlotte had left the police house with the *sarong* under her skirt, her hat in a large cotton bag. Once on the other side, she had paid the boatman and walked down by Mr Johnstone's old rickety and cavernous godown, where she knew there were dark corners. Here she had slipped out of her cotton skirt and pushed it into her bag. She wore nothing under the *sarong* or her bodice. She felt utterly bad. She had, to her surprise, become devious, like the wanton island woman her grandmother imagined her mother to be. Just walking through the streets like this made her excited, and she almost ran to Zhen's house.

'Make me mistress to the man I love;
If there be yet another name more free,
More fond than mistress, make me that to thee!
Oh happy state! when souls each other draw,
When love is liberty, and nature, law;
All then is full, possessing, and possess'd.
No craving void left aching in the breast;
Ev'n thought meets thought, ere from the lips it part,
And each warm wish springs mutual from the heart.
This, sure, is bliss (if bliss on earth there be)
And is the lot of this man and me'

He pulled her inside and shot the bolt across the door. He was naked to the waist, his beauty displayed. He pulled off her hat as she threw off her shawl and undid her bodice, showing him her soft skin. He drew her against his chest. She pulled the cord on his trousers, which slithered to the floor. He was ready for her, naked, burning hot, starved, and she looked at him, her eyes glittering, smelling the oil on him. She raised the *sarong*. There was a low stool by the door, and he sat, pulling her. Her legs straddled his hips and she sighed as she sank onto him, reaching for the thick queue on his neck, dropping her mouth to his, possessing and possessed in the dimming light.

# 36

Noan had put the final touches to the embroidered slippers. The red curtain of the bridal bed was complete, covered profusely in embroidered pink peonies, blue and yellow butterflies, flying purple phoenixes, white cranes and pink peaches. The gold-and-red bed of nam wood was carved from canopy to floor with flying bats, double fish, vases, flowers, deer, the eight Taoist immortals, the eight Buddhist symbols and a dozen other animals and plants. The silk curtain was held back with big gold and silver hooks, and small delicate baskets of filigree silver hung from the central post, holding tiny silver pomegranates and Buddha's hand. Other silver hangings of the eternal knot and the *tai chi* surrounded the canopy. Covering this shrine to fertility and wealth was a red silken bedcover and numerous embroidered cushions and bolsters, finished off with exquisitely worked chased-silver pillow plates.

Every inch of the bridal room was covered in carpets of red and gold. A washstand in these same colors stood between the windows, which were covered in thick curtains of white Portuguese lace. The *an chng* bed-blessing ceremony would take place after the betrothal day, which was now only a week away.

Noan looked at the beautiful bed, longing already to be lying next to Zhen, wishing the next three weeks to simply fly away. She had hardly eaten a thing since the wedding date had been fixed, desperate to slim down her legs and bottom, to be appealing to him. She was worried about her period. It had finished only a few days ago. She was now hideously anxious that it might begin again before the wedding night, imagining him repulsed by the sight of her blood, not wanting to touch her.

Her mother came and locked the room. After the betrothal, the whole house would be cleaned from top to bottom meticulously. This room in particular would be utterly spotless for the blessing.

Noan went downstairs with her mother to help the cooks prepare the dishes which her father had ordered. It was time to introduce Zhen to Peranakan cooking. From today, Tan would take lunch with his prospective son-in-law at the godown, introducing him to the dishes he would encounter on his wedding day and thereafter at family meals. That he should enjoy their food was important to Tan, for the spices and tastes of this cuisine were central to the identity of their multi-facetted culture, and he knew the men from China did not always appreciate it. He would begin with something relatively anodyne.

Today Noan was making *chap chye*, bean-thread vermicelli with mushrooms, soya beans, cabbage and garlic. She spooned this dish into the pink, green and yellow *kamcheng* pot covered with peonies and butterflies. In another she poured the *bakwan kepiting*, the soup of pork, fish and crab balls, with garlic and bamboo shoots. She added a covered dish of spicy *sambal*, made from shrimp paste, chillies, salt and sugar. Her mother had let drop that this food might be shared by 'a young man', for she, too, was eagerly looking forward to this union and was happy to see the pleasure in her daughter's eyes.

Noan had paid particular attention to the food and ladled it lovingly, willing Zhen to sense her feelings in the dishes she had prepared. These dishes were tied into a bundle for delivery to the godown. She added fluffy white rice and small, dried fish, black lacquered chopsticks and two bowls, white with blue flowers. She imagined him taking the food with the chopsticks, putting it in his mouth, holding the bowl, and she closed her eyes. Her mother called the delivery boy, and Noan watched as the food left the house, wishing more than anything she could go with it, then flushing at this naughty thought. Then she began to prepare her mother's meal.

Zhen's head was full of Charlotte. He could still taste her on his lips, even as he took up the chopsticks and tried the food from Tan's house. The food was good; he recognised that—even tried the spicy *sambal* to please Tan. It was too hot and sour for him, but he tried not to show it, wanting to please his future father-in-law, happy that he trusted him and was putting no obstacle between him and Xia Lou. For Zhen was in no doubt that Tan knew he was seeing a woman.

Tan was delighted at Zhen's reaction. Actually, he thought the food was especially good today and ate heartily.

He was leaving the woman business alone for the moment. However, he would speak to Zhen as the wedding night approached. It would not do to have Zhen too depleted to fulfill his duties to his daughter. Tan had invested in this man and expected a swift pregnancy.

For the moment, they shared the food and talked of Qian's recent wedding, so quiet, so short, so different from what Zhen could expect. The Peranakan marriage lasted twelve full days, and each day required a different costume. Zhen's were almost complete. All that was left was the preparation of the pair of white silk jackets and trousers cut from the same piece of cloth, which the couple would wear the night of the vowing ceremony and which would be their nuptial garments. This cutting ceremony would take place at Zhen's house directly after the betrothal. The old woman who would cut the cloth had already been selected. She was perfect, Tan confided to Zhen, for her family was intact: husband, son, daughter and grandchildren all alive. It was by no means an easy matter to find such a woman here in Singapore. In fact, he was bringing her from Malacca. Tan still maintained a large house there, where his two old aunts lived. They would all be coming for this happy occasion.

As Tan babbled on happily, Zhen thought about Charlotte. Although he had wanted her to stay, she had not dared, worried that Robert would return. She had left after an hour with slow reluctance, tearing her lips from his, dragging herself away. Then she had come to the godown this morning, ostensibly to see Baba Tan. She was relieved, though to see he was not there. The place was full of coolies loading and unloading the lighters at the front, but Zhen had taken her through to the dark back of the godown amongst the bales of Indian cotton, not caring what the coolies thought. The old man wasn't here, and Tan's chief clerk was at his sago factories upriver. Charlotte had followed him, watching the movement of his naked back, the beads of sweat that gathered in the small of it. He was always half-naked when he worked in the day. How clever the Chinese were not to bother with clothes in this climate.

She had not expected this time, but she was so totally transformed by him now that she thought nothing of pulling up her dress, exposing herself. Do it, do it, here in the dust and dark. He smiled at how shameless she had become, knowing he had created it, liking it, loving her. She climbed up and leaned back on the bale, parting her legs, looking at him through half-closed eyes. He put his fingers to his mouth, sh, then put his mouth to her, and she watched him as he brought her to a sigh, holding his face in her hands, feeling his breath, the sensual movement of his jaw. He pulled her into his arms, kissing and kissing.

'Give me a kisse, and to that kisse a score;
Then to that twenty, add a hundred more;
A thousand to that hundred; so kisse on,
To make that thousand up a million;
Treble that million, and when that is done;
Let's kisse afresh, as when we first begun.'

When he released her, breathless, she told him that she would come in the evening to his house and stay all night.

*Aiya*, Zhen thought, filled with anticipation. There would be time for everything.

Robert had told her he would be spending time with Shilah, so not to expect him. He had looked at her then quite intensely, and she could see he knew. She wondered if Robert had brought it up with George.

'Be careful, Kitt, and use this,' was all he said. He had given her a small bottle, and, to her amazement, she saw it was the same oil Zhen used with her, although Robert's smelled more strongly of oniony earth.

So she had come to Zhen last night, all night, and he had given her food on his chopsticks from all the little plates the hawker had brought, trying to explain each dish, she laughing at his awful English, he laughing too at his awful English, saying the Chinese words, laughing at her awful Chinese. They were joyful at being alone together, anticipating the night to come. Then he made her the good tea, asking her to smell the aroma, share in his pleasure. They had washed each other langorously, taking their time, kissing and touching on the cool wet tiles. Then they had made love and slept and made love again until the gun woke them all too soon. As he kissed her at the door, he held her, lifting her, not wanting her to leave. He did not know when they would meet again.

Tan was still babbling on about the wedding. Then in the doorway appeared Qian. Zhen bowed to Tan and excused himself, thanking him for the delicious meal. He was dying to find out how Qian's wedding night had gone. Tan magnanimously offered to let the two men sit on the verandah for a while. In any case, he felt like a visit to his concubine and, telling his chief clerk he was leaving, he called for his carriage.

After Tan left, the two friends went to the cool, dark interior of the godown. The day was very hot but felt stormy. Sweat trickled off them both, and Zhen removed his jacket. Qian could not help getting an eyeful but now felt strangely unaffected.

Zhen looked his friend in the eye.

'Well, you big girlie, how did it go?'

'Fine. Mind your own business. You're next, eh, thunder head?'

Zhen shook his head and laughed.

'No, you don't. I'll have no problem on the wedding night; don't you worry. My bride will be purring. What about yours?'

Qian reflected on the night of his marriage and the morning after. It had been unexpected, to say the least. They had sat on the bed as the final visitors departed and closed the door.

Neither said a thing for a long time; then suddenly his bride had got down off the bed. She had seen the little tic along his eye, and his passivity had made her bold.

'My name is Swan Neo,' she said. 'When we are together please call me that. What do you want me to call you? I don't want any of this husband or master stuff, except in public.'

Qian had laughed at her boldness. It had broken the tension. She had brought out from a chest some rice wine and two cups. He had no idea how she had got hold of this stuff, and she didn't tell him. In fact, she and her mother had a lucrative small business on the sly, selling their exquisite sewing. Many of the Peranakan daughters were not as adept at embroidery as their mothers boasted to their friends. The *nonyas* supplied the threads and materials and commissioned slippers, handkerchiefs, marriage purses and nuptial embroideries from her, willing to pay good silver for the pleasure of displaying the work to their envious friends, extolling the virtues of their industrious daughters. That they could carry out this business in Sang's house and under the nose of his old bitch of a wife was a source of endless pride to them, as was the money they had stashed away. When she could trust this man she might tell him, but not yet.

Now the rice wine broke the ice, and they began to talk. Her Hokkien was a little old-fashioned. He began to like her. As the evening wore on and they got a little drunk, she removed her jacket, revealing a silk camisole and a thin little body underneath. He took off his jacket too and toyed with telling her, but did not quite dare. And actually, he rather began to think he might like to sleep with her tonight. Finally, half drunk they climbed into bed and, not touching, fell asleep.

Qian did not tell Zhen all of this, but just a little. The next day when she woke, he was still sleeping, and she contemplated his face. Not handsome, but not too ugly, ears too pointy but something mouse-like in the angles of his face. She kept pet mice and smiled at this comparison. He seemed to have a nice temperament, better than her foul father's. Swan Neo knew that his penis should be hard and vaguely what he should do with it. Her mother's experiences with Sang were so distasteful she did not dwell on the subject with her daughter, but she had explained the general idea. She turned and went back to sleep.

Fortunately for Qian, his new wife's back was to him when he woke, and he felt the little tight bones of her buttocks. To his enormous surprise, he felt aroused and after a little contemplation of this fact ran his hand down her body. She woke and turned towards him, waiting, watching with her almond eyes.

It was now or never. Qian began to push his penis into her. He knew it was not every woman's dream, but it was the best he could do. It did not feel disgusting. She let out a little cry and he thought he had hurt her, stopped immediately, seeing drops of blood. He instantly felt a great compassion for this woman, whose life had been so wholly awful in this house, who had given him hope for a decent life. He would make it different.

Qian suddenly realised that he was now officially the eldest male. He could rule this house, Sang's vast empire, even with the presence of the sickly young heir whom he would befriend. The coffers would be open to him; even Ah Liang could do nothing. He felt an overwhelming sense of power and gratitude. He knew he had to do this for her and him, give her a son if he could, cement his place and her status in the house.

She hardly moved, not knowing what to do, and this and this alone enabled him to come to a climax. Had she expressed any sensuality, he was certain he would have withered away like an old root. When he finished, they lay side by side not speaking until the old woman, his new first mother-in-law, came to get the spotted sheet.

'When the time is right, we will come to an arrangement. She is smart, but she needs a little time. I think we can grow into each other,' Qian told Zhen.

Zhen was glad for his friend, sensing in him a new assertiveness.

Qian related to Zhen how he had demanded the keys from Ah Liang before lunch, determined to stamp his authority on the house immediately. He had visited Sang's treasury, discovering the chests and boxes, one of which contained the disgusting and mouldy remnants of dead nails and skin. But the others were more interesting, and he was glad Sang had been such a miser as he ran his hands over the Spanish silver coins, taking a few, laughing, thrilled with his good fortune, the infinite promise of his life to come. Now, he told Zhen, he would send money to his eldest brother, bring out his young brother to work with him, find dowries for his sisters and give his mother peace in her old age. Today, this morning, he had given coins to Swan Neo to get new silks for herself and her mother, sent them shopping in the town, freed them from the gloom of the house.

He had gone to eat with the little son, this new half brother; they had been served by his new wife. He laughed again. How his life had changed in one day.

# 37

The wedding invitations had all been sent. To the Europeans, Tan had sent a red paper invitation embossed in gold. To the rest of the relatives and guests he had sent the traditional *hantar sireh*, the betel-vine leaf wrapped around a slice of areca nut and folded into a neat triangular bundle. These bundles were held in place with sharp sticks and distributed by two old *nonyas* who knew everyone on the island.

The bridal room was finally ready. It had been clean for two days. A new mattress had been added to the bed. Nearby stood a bare, polished wooden table and two chairs, covered in elaborately embroidered silk; there were two footstools of red velvet. Other chairs in the room had white lace coverings with red ribbons tied into bows. The lace at the windows had bows of red velvet formed into the shapes of lotus flowers along their lengths, and the door had a new red velvet curtain. The washstand had acquired a large bowl and jug of white, adorned with phoenix and peonies.

In one corner of the room stood arrayed all Noan's footwear, gleaming with silk and gold thread, beads and satin. A carved teak cupboard stood in another corner, the door ajar to show off the bride's trousseau. There were bolts of silk and fine *batik* cloth, *baju kebaya*, *sarongs* and fine lace undergarments. In front of these were glass and porcelain jars and bottles of perfumes and toiletries from France and England, Java and China.

Incense stood lit in an earthenware pot under the bed, and the room smelled of pandanus leaves, lemon grass and *stanggee*, a pungent incense made from barks. Noan's mother inspected the room, making some minor adjustments. The mistress of ceremonies—the *sangkek um*—now placed gold offering paper under the bed and made a short prayer to the guardian spirit.

A nervous-looking teenage boy came in, dressed in red silk pyjamas.

He had been chosen as a child from a large family in Malacca whose parents were both still living. Under the *sangkek um*'s watchful eye, he rolled back and forth over the mattress three times as a blessing for a first-born male child. His job done, he gleefully accepted a red packet and bolted downstairs.

The house was now in uproar with cleaning and decorating. Baba Tan spent every evening at his concubine's house. Only a week to go until the wedding, and he had ordered a close eye be kept on Zhen. No more women for him until he had done his duty by his daughter.

Zhen felt increasingly powerless as the days drew on, but there was nothing for it. The day the betrothal had taken place it was as if he were already married. The rest was all ceremonial and show. He had not seen Charlotte; at home, eyes were on him all the time now. A second servant had arrived in the house, and this one never went away.

He went to see Min, who had improved. Her pretty face was a mess of scars and bruises, but she was breathing better. She thanked him and begged him not to make her go back to the whorehouse, clutching his arm and sobbing into his sleeve. Zhen considered the matter. Qian had money now. He wouldn't have much until he made some for himself. The allowance would go on, but he wouldn't have access to the coffers which Qian had in his treasury.

When he next saw Qian he asked him directly.

'Buy Min out of the *ah ku* house. I'll use my influence with the *kongsi* men, and if they're paid they'll shut up. Then she can work for you in your new bloody house, you rich bastard. She knows what you like; she could probably get something going for you. And she'd be discreet. If the scars clear up, she'd make someone a decent concubine or third wife or something.'

Qian knew he owed almost everything to Zhen. Without him he would have slaved away on the opium farm until he had dropped dead. But he didn't need Min to get him a boy; that wasn't hard. He didn't want her talking to his new wife. Qian intended to tell Swan Neo eventually that he liked both sides of the bed, but it was too soon. If she got pregnant, maybe. After that, it was none of her business what he did in what was now his own house. He'd slept with her successfully again, and was hopeful. It wasn't very enjoyable, but not too bad. This time had been from behind. It was much easier that way.

'Here's what I'll do,' he told Zhen. 'I'll buy Min out of the house, but I don't want her in mine. What an idea, all the women chattering under one roof. No, I'll shop around to find a man for her, and not here. I'm going to Malacca. Sang has a huge house there and I want to see it. When she's well enough to travel she can come with me. With a bit of a dowry I'm sure we can sort something out. Will that do?'

Zhen was impressed. His friend had grown in stature in the last weeks; he was quick to make decisions, sure of himself. Zhen bowed low to him, his fists clasped above his head as if to an ancient and wise mandarin. Qian laughed.

Now Zhen asked Qian to get Charlotte to come to the orchard. Qian still took lessons at the chapel, but Zhen's had stopped until after the marriage.

Qian shook his head.

'What are you doing? You have to stop this. Your marriage will be in jeopardy, and what will happen to her? Be reasonable, Zhen Ah. We do only what we can without endangering our future. Think of your family back in China. They depend on you.'

His argument was to no avail. Zhen was adamant. He had been told to do some work at Tan's sago factories up river, and these were the least watched of all Tan's properties. From there he could make his way unnoticed to the grove, punting through the swampy river to the path which skirted the hill covered by the trees and jungle growth. He explained that Charlotte would need him. Something was wrong with her friends. So Qian relented and spoke to Charlotte at the chapel and walked with her to the grove as he had before. When he saw her, Zhen thanked Qian and told him to go. Charlotte came into his arms. She took off her hat, and they sat holding hands, not speaking.

'Someone put this bench here,' she said patting it. 'Lovers, maybe, like us, from the past, now all dust.'

Zhen did not understand the words, but heard the soft sadness of her voice.

'My friends are all leaving. You are not mine.'

He understood, drew her head to his shoulder, holding her there, stroking her hair. He searched for words, frustrated once again at his inability to tell her.

'Zhen love Xia Lou, never stop,' he whispered.

Then he straddled the bench, moving her until she sat in his arms and could feel his heartbeat on her back. He closed his eyes, matching his breath to hers, seeking the quietness of the Tao.

Charlotte felt a deep peace descend on her as their breath rose and fell in unison. Her hearing became acute. She could detect the buzz of a distant insect, the sound of a leaf falling through the air, water babbling from the little streams, the pattering crawl of small legs. When he moved, she opened her eyes. Half an hour had passed. It was as if he could perform magic, master time. She took his hand and kissed it.

Then they rose and walked slowly round the old stone path at the base of the hill. Little rills of water came from the hillside, and she cupped her hands drinking, holding water for him. Malay princesses had bathed in the waters of this hill, so it was said. Malay princes had inhabited its wooded glades, and evidence of palaces and temples still lay all about, the *keramat* of Iskandar Shah on its slope, flower strewn. George had told her the story of Parameswara, Javanese prince of Palembang who, fleeing his kingdom, had been made welcome here. He had slain his benefactor and made himself King of Temasek, ancient Singapore. Then he had been forced to flee from here for his treachery and founded the town of Malacca. How lucky he was to have received the support of the Ming Chinese Muslim admiral, Zheng He. How Parameswara had converted to Islam and founded the first Islamic sultanate. The *keramat* was still a place of worship and was kept clean by invisible hands and garlanded by the devout. Bukit Larangan was a place filled with ghosts. Charlotte felt them all around her, in the rustling of the breeze through the tree tops, the tremulous call of the kingfisher, the patterns of the sunlight falling through the branches like the shadowy figures of the *wayang kulit* she had seen at Tir Uaidhne. Shades of the blighted love of Rama and Sita.

The town lay on the other side. He took her face in his hands and kissed her very gently. He left her when she was safely on Hill Street, watching, then disappeared down the track.

Noan sat as the *sangkek um* combed her hair. They said that she could tell if a bride was a virgin during this hair-combing ritual, that if the hairline along the forehead refused to respond to the comb but curled disobediently, then the girl was not innocent. Noan watched anxiously, praying for compliant hair, as the mistress of ceremonies combed the fringe and trimmed it neatly. She was terrified of this hard-eyed woman, who pinched her if she did not respond immediately to what she was told. She dreaded the rehearsal for the wedding ceremony tomorrow, for she knew she would be pinched incessantly. The combing must have gone satisfactorily, for the *sangkek um* did not frown. The fringe was tied in tiny tufts at both sides of her head with white ribbon.

Zhen had been briefed all day on the vowing ceremony tomorrow night and the procession and the rituals of the wedding day. He had a headache. He had been watched incessantly for five days, and he was fed up with it. He wanted to see Charlotte, knowing it was impossible. He went into the cool bathroom and lay down on the floor, ladling water over himself. In two nights he would have to make love to *her*. He would, too, one, two, three. She wouldn't know what had hit her. He wanted her pregnant as quickly as possible. Then for twelve nights he would have to sleep with her, leaving in the morning, returning in the evening under the keen gaze of all the family. He groaned and poured water over his head.

# 38

Takouhi was hopeful. Meda had improved in the cool air of the high slopes of the Buitenzorg hills. Tigran's home here was an elegant double-storey house with a wide verandah, surrounded by trees and flowers and the vast, terraced reaches of the seemingly endless rows of brilliant green tea plants. There was a huge aviary filled with black-and-crimson orioles, and Meda had adopted a pair of scarlet sunbirds which came frequently to the tree near her window.

They were sitting on the old battery at Scandal Point, enjoying the cool evening air, occasionally waving to passers-by. George looked better, rested, Charlotte thought. He was telling them the news from Java. He had ridden over on Matahari, and she stood snuffling by his side, her reins loosely in George's hands. The day had been hot and very humid, but now the breeze was delicious, the tide was high and the water lapped the beach. Stars were appearing. Soon, Charlotte knew, the vault of the sky would be pinpricked with the light of the million stars of the Milky Way. Over the water could be heard the soothing echoes of voices raised in Javanese songs from luggers down the bay.

George, too, was gazing out at this tropical splendour so dear to his heart. Charlotte could almost see what he was thinking. To her he had revealed his deep hope of their return. Takouhi missed him dreadfully; so did his daughter. He had spared her blushes with what followed next, but he had been glad to read it. Takouhi wrote to him in Malay, a language in which she was very expressive.

Robert rose, bidding farewell to George; then he and Charlotte began the walk along the beach back to the bungalow before darkness fell completely. George had lit a cigar and continued his vigil over the Straits.

When they got home, Charlotte went to her room and took out the red paper, sinking onto the chair in front of her mirror. The wedding invitation. Tomorrow was his wedding. Tomorrow night he would be in some other woman's arms. She closed her eyes. Unbearable, don't think. He loved her; what did it matter if he made love to this wife of his. But it did, and she rose, agitated suddenly. He would arouse this other women as he had her, take her down the same scented corridors.

Charlotte started to shake, a black mist enveloping her. Hand trembling, she looked at the paper again. In five days she and Robert were invited to meet the bride and groom. Charlotte was certain as she could be that Zhen did not know about this, but it stood to reason. Baba Tan would have invited all the prominent Europeans in Singapore, proud to show off this auspicious union, his wealth and position.

Robert called to her. Would she take a wee dram? Dear Robert. He knew, and was trying to distract her. Then, suddenly, she was tired, couldn't wrap herself in this cloak of quivering and draining emotion any more.

She took from the cupboard the backgammon set Aunt Jeannie had given her and looked at it. It had become warped in the humidity. She tried to straighten it, pushing the wood against the table, but the invisible moisture had penetrated it, loosening its structure. Did it mind, the wood, being twisted? Or had it merely returned to its natural state before the hand of the carpenter had moulded it? She looked into the mirror, then ran her hand over the smooth surface of the box. It would never be quite the same again, but it would serve. She moved towards the verandah. At this game she always beat Robert.

The time for the *cheo thau* vowing ceremony had arrived. Zhen's head swam with these names which assailed his ears daily. The eleventh hour at night had been selected as auspicious for this most sacred and solemn event, the *pak chindek* had told him. Zhen felt the portent of this time in the pit of his stomach. But retreat was folly, and now it was here. Zhen had been dressed in the white silk garments. As the melancholy strains of the bamboo flute and cymbals of the *seroni* band began, he was led to the space between the altar to his ancestors and the *sam kai* altar to the gods of heaven, earth and the moon. The Boyanese *pak chindek* who had overseen the stringent scrubbing of Zhen's body and hair and the fresh shaving of his head thought the young Tan daughter might very well be pleased with the choice of husband, though he said nothing. Zhen had remained stony-faced throughout the entire process.

The altars were covered in offerings of flowers and tea, carved papaya and red fruits. The two red candles had been lit, and on either end of the *sam kai* altar there were two glass lamps. For the duration of the wedding, Zhen had discovered, a man would be responsible for the flames in these lamps, for if they went out it would be terribly bad luck. On the floor between the altars was a large, round, bamboo tray, and on a red spot in the centre stood a wooden tub, mouth upward, covered in a red cloth. Zhen knew he was supposed to sit on this open tub and had had to stifle a desire to laugh, especially when he thought of his prospective bride doing the same thing at the same moment at Tan's house. Perhaps her arse was so big she couldn't fall in, he thought and had to swallow hard at both the comical and horrible possibilities that this created in his mind.

He recalled the story of the ritual cat his Zen master had told the young men in the monastery.

When the teacher and his disciples began their evening meditiation, the cat that lived in the monastery made such a noise that it distracted them. So the teacher ordered that the cat be tied up during the evening practice. Years later, when the teacher died, the cat continued to be tied up during the meditation session. And when the cat eventually died, another cat was brought to the monastery and tied up. Centuries later, learned descendants of the spiritual teacher wrote scholarly treatises about the religious significance of tying up a cat for meditation practice.

In the presence of half a dozen of Tan's employees, the master of ceremonies and three pageboys, he stepped, at the appointed moment, onto the bamboo tray. The air was heavy with *stanggee* incense.

Noan sat down on the tub without a grimace, although it was thoroughly uncomfortable. She took the *Book of Fate* from the pageboy into her lap as the mistress of ceremonies loosened her hair. A Chinese scale was passed over her head and down to her feet as a reminder to weigh all her actions fairly in life. A Chinese ruler came next, followed by a pair of scissors and a razor, exhorting the exercise of sincerity, good judgement and care. Noan's mother and youngest sisters were now sobbing quietly. Noan, too, had tears running down her cheeks; she was exhausted by the day spent greeting the female guests seated unsmilingly on the hard chairs and the endless rehearsal, the melancholy strains of the *seroni* music in the half-darkness, the flame of the glass lamps bringing the realisation of her passage into her new life.

Zhen wanted to squirm but sat stock still. Finally it was over and, rising, he paid obeisance to the two altars and left the room, his hair hanging loose down his back. When everyone had left, he joined Ah Pok and the other old Malay servant in the kitchen, got out the rice wine and proceeded to get as drunk as he was able. This marriage, which he had embraced as fortunate beyond his dreams, now seemed like a trap.

The next morning, when he was wakened rudely by one of the *pak chindek*'s assistants, he regretted the drinking bout. Really, where was the bloody privacy in this house? He was naked and hot, and the old man was chattering at him in incomprehensible Baba Malay. He rose, growling, and the old man ran out of the room.

The barber again, this time a thorough cleaning up. The razor was sharpened on the leather strop and run rapidly over Zhen's head, down the cheeks, around the neck and between the eyebrows and eyelashes. Pulling back Zhen's head, he scraped his tongue and cleaned the teeth with a sharp wooden stick. Then with small scissors he searched for stray hairs in his nostrils and ears, then cleaned the ears with tweezers. Finally he took his hands, scraped each nail and cuticle and massaged his hands. This ritual complete, he gathered up his tools and left. Now Zhen was again scrubbed and rinsed and sprinkled with scented water. He felt like a pig being prepared for the spit. Finally he was allowed to rest until it came time to dress in the heavy costume. Ah Pok made him some tea and rice, and he threw himself into a chair.

Noan, too, was sitting, for the wedding garments she was wearing were so heavy they made movements hard. She was hot, although the day was cool, and a servant fanned her constantly. The white silk outfit of the previous night had been covered with garments made of thick cotton to absorb sweat, then a rigid outfit of bamboo, over which lay the stiffly embroidered heavy silk skirt and coat. She felt like a trussed-up chicken. Her hair had been dragged into a topknot and pinned with a hundred gold pins, each finished with a floret, giving her the appearance of wearing a crown. The tightness of the hair hurt, and the pins rubbed her scalp. Her mother's heavy gold-and-diamond jewellery covered her chest, hung from her ears, festooned every finger. The last thing to go on would be the crown of gold, covered in little bouncing peonies and phoenixes over a band of the eight Taoist immortals. She could hardly breathe and sat steamily waiting for the groom's arrival. She drank only a little water, for the idea that she might need to urinate was terrifying.

As the procession was announced, her heart started to beat faster. She thought she might faint, and only the *sangkek um*'s fierce looks stopped her. She took some water and calmed down a little. The only blessing was that her period had not started.

Zhen stood behind a pair of six-sided silk lanterns flanked by two young men Tan had chosen to be his companions, followed by the *pak chindek* richly dressed in Malay costume. Qian had been invited to the groom's banquet that afternoon, but he had come down to see this procession and watch as Zhen left his house. First came the wailing band, then two lanterns with his name in characters and two gong beaters banging as loudly as they could. Red tassels and bunting came by, then a severe-looking fellow carrying an open fan, shielded from the sun by a large umbrella carried by a bearer. Qian saw Zhen and tried to catch his eye, but his friend looked straight ahead, impassive.

He wore a short red jacket with a dragon motif and gold border over a long, red-and-gold gown with black-and-gold beaded slippers. Qian wanted to tell him he looked ridiculous. On his head was a black mandarin cap with a brooch of gold and diamonds and a diamond button on the top. He carried a large fan covered in pink phoenixes and peonies. Qian thought he looked like a Mongolian princess and was dying to impart this good news. He raced ahead of the procession desperate to catch Zhen's eye. Finally, as they turned into Market Street, he called his name and Zhen looked at him. Qian mimed small, mincing steps.

From behind his fan Zhen beckoned him with all four fingers, palm upwards, as you would a piece of low scum you'd like to beat, and passed by as impassive as ever. A shallow basket of bamboo stood in the doorway of Tan's mansion, covered with paper flowers. As soon as Zhen stepped over this basket, the fireworks under it were lit and he was ushered forward to the inner courtyard in a deafening hail of explosions.

Behind him the bridges were burning.

Here, eager relatives rushed to sprinkle him with scented water and shower him with saffron-coloured rice. Zhen saw Baba Tan trying to suppress a smile, supposed that the plump, darker woman by his side was his wife. There were the three sisters. He had seen the youngest, for she was only nine and came sometimes with her father to the godown. She was a skinny child, quite plain. The other two were standing by their mother's side, getting a first look at their sister's new husband. The second daughter was lost for words. Zhen was the best-looking man she had ever seen. She was suddenly blackly jealous of Noan. *She* was the pretty one; he should be *her* husband.

Zhen took them in. The second daughter was very pretty, light-skinned and slim, dressed in pink, but she looked rather sour-faced. The third one was pretty too, but short, and her eyes seemed too close together. Doubtless Tan loved them all.

Then he was led through the door and into the main hall. The light grew dimmer.

Noan jumped as she heard the crackers go off, and the mistress of ceremonies rushed to fit her crown and cover her head with a black veil. As she heard the master of ceremonies call that the time had come for bride and groom to meet, the woman helped Noan to her feet and led her out.

Zhen looked at this woman he had contracted to marry. She was short, and in these thick clothes she looked squat. Her head was lowered, and he could see nothing of her face through the veil. Noan kept her eyes down, but she felt his body close to hers, like a furnace, remembering the sight of him so long ago. With the *sangkek um* and the *pak chindek* on either side, they were led slowly upstairs to the bridal chamber. Noan thought her legs might fail her and leaned on her mistress of ceremonies. The guests swarmed like locusts behind them.

In front of all Tan's relatives who had pushed and squeezed themselves into the room, Zhen put out his hands to remove the veil. With the mistress helping, he lifted the black cloth and gazed for the first time on the face of his future wife.

A little pastry, was his first thought. A doughy dumpling covered in white powder. The powder was ominous, probably meant she was dark-skinned. Her lips were full and red, quite pretty. Her eyes were resolutely towards the floor. For the rest it was impossible to tell. His thoughts flew to Charlotte's delicate features and ivory skin. His inner eye began roving around in his memory. Kissing her little white feet as she slid her legs onto his shoulders. Burying his face in her hair. Watching her eyes as she—

He felt a small shove in his side. He was urged, with fierce looks, to sit in one of the embroidered chairs opposite his bride. On the table between them were twelve dishes of food and a pair of burning candles.

Zhen knew what was expected of him, and they both went through the series of movements and gestures symbolic of having a meal together without actually eating anything. For most of the time Noan kept her head modestly bowed, looking only at his mouth, from which she drew a pulse-quickening pleasure. Only once did she look up to see him watching her. He showed nothing in his eyes, and she looked down immediately, disconcerted and trembling slightly.

Then a gasp went up in the room, and Zhen looked at the gathered throng. The candle on the bride's side had gone out, a whiff of air from her sleeve stopping the flame. This meant she would die before her husband.

Her mother put her hand to her mouth. Noan had been taught so carefully to beware of this. The second daughter looked on impassively.

Noan felt tears well up in her eyes. Fortunately the time had come for her to leave the room, and she was escorted out, with the guests all following. Zhen stayed with the *pak chindek* who helped him change his clothes to a light black-and-red silk jacket and trousers. Noan returned briefly and, standing behind Zhen, took a comb and began to symbolically comb his hair as a gesture of serving him. She took in his thick, shiny black queue, the way his shoulders filled his jacket.

Then Zhen was quickly led out of the room. He would return mid-afternoon for lunch alone, while the bride rested and changed into another costume, and then he would change again and pay his respects to the altars and the elders. Normally this would be followed by the bride paying her respects to his family but, since there was no one to pay any respects to, this part had been discreetly dropped, and the groom's dinner was to be held at Tan's. Zhen was heartily sick of it all, but he had made a solemn promise that he would not spoil this day for his benefactor.

Qian came to the dinner, and Zhen was overjoyed to see a face he trusted in this crowd. The dinner went on for hours, dish following dish, all the men drinking heavily. Tan and the older men were absent, for this was the groom's party and it would be followed by the traditional ragging of the bride.

The second daughter could not wait for this part now. Noan must not smile no matter what anyone did. All the young girls hid behind a curtain as the men, drunk and noisy, entered the room. Between her teeth she had an areca nut clenched so as not to laugh, for to laugh would disgrace her husband. Fortunately, she was so exhausted and hot she had not the slightest inclination to laugh. Zhen had drunk a little too much, finally, enjoying the meal and the company of Qian and the other men. From behind the gauzy curtain the second daughter watched Zhen standing in the doorway. He raised his arms behind his head, stretching slightly, watching as the men pranced and mimed in front of his new wife. The second sister saw a flash of taut skin. From behind the curtain she devoured him with her eyes. Finally this noisy display was over, and all the men left, Zhen and Qian half-drunk, arm in arm, returning to his house. In three hours a page would come to him with a red lantern and lead him back to the bridal chamber. Eyes would peep from houses along the way and watch hidden from Tan's windows. Then he would be alone with her for the first time.

# 39

The door closed behind him. His wife was standing in the room, head lowered. She was wearing white silk pyjamas like him. He had followed the swaying red lantern back to Tan's house. The *pak chindek* had taken him to a small room to change and opened a side door to the bridal chamber. Now here he was. Until this moment, he had not realised how much he was dreading this, sure of his mind, his capacities. The hideous thought of failure entered his mind like a worm.

He looked at her from the doorway, a small white figure in a room filled with red. Her hair had been brushed and now hung thickly to her shoulders. The heavy make-up was gone, though her skin was dusted with a thin layer of powder, and she wore some lipstick. She stood, hands by her side, unmoving. Poor thing, he thought. He'd seen so many virgins, and felt weary of them. Xia Lou was the last one he wanted, but now here was another.

He moved to the table, where a French crystal water jug stood and, clanking the lip against the glass, poured and drank. He was dry from the rice wine. He and Qian had continued drinking at his house, and he was still half-drunk. Sitting heavily on the embroidered chair he poured a glass for her. Had to get this started somehow.

'Eh! Come here.'

Noan looked up shyly. He was holding a glass of water, and she went up close to him and took it, sipping it delicately, wanting desperately to touch him but not daring. 'Let your husband do everything, and be quiet' had been her mother's parting words.

He watched her drinking, her eyes lowered. Then he took the glass and put it on the table, released the silk cord at her waist, opening it, looking at her breasts. Not small, like Xia Lou's. Hers fitted perfectly into his hand. This girl's were brown, full. Despite himself, he could see she was firm and luscious. He felt annoyed at himself for wanting to touch her, felt it a betrayal. Suddenly he was annoyed at this girl as well, for tempting him. He was irritated by her passivity and down-turned eyes. He knew his powers; he could change it all, turn her into a creature of love and lust in one night, but he did not want to. He did not want her to dream of him, long for him, expect anything from him. He could not know it was all too late.

Noan stood absolutely still, waiting.

Something dark flapped across Zhen's mind. She was his property, body and soul. She had been raised correctly; he could do whatever he wanted with her. Not like Xia Lou: *she* would never be his like this. He cupped Noan's breasts in his hands, pulling her forward, and began to suckle her, running his tongue over her, burying his face in their soft fullness, his bleary mind not able to control his body's physical reaction, remembering other skin.

She was elated. She pleased him; he wanted her. She had known this would feel good, and it did. She put her hands to his head, and he suddenly stopped, pulling his head away, dropping his hands. Don't touch me, he wanted to scream at her. She tensed as he pulled the cord on the pyjama bottom, letting it slide to the floor, and began to run his hands over her backside. He turned her. He wanted to look at this wife of his. She was shapely, a small waist and swelling hips. Not like Xia Lou's willowy perfection, fitting into his body like Venus in the arms of the moon.

He shook his head. Xia Lou wasn't his wife; this one was. He didn't have to please her; the man who would please her was not in the room. No matter what he did, she was powerless. He put his fingers into the crack of her backside, spreading it, pushing his finger in slightly. She tensed as he knew she would, not expecting this, but made not a sound. He wanted to violate her. Hideous thoughts ran like dirty feet through his mind. But he stopped, shaking his head, clearing it. He was foggy still, he knew. He took another drink of water.

He stood, made her face him. Took off his clothes and let her see him. Any touching she was allowed to do would be controlled by him. He took her hand and put it on his chest over the face of Guan Di, running it down his waist and over his hips onto his half-erect penis.

Noan's heart was beating out of her chest. He was so beautiful, the tattoo on his muscled brown skin unexpected but arousing. He began moving her hand, pulling her head against his chest, squashing her breasts against him, holding her there. Zhen had not the slightest desire to kiss her, though he knew that she was waiting for this.

Then, as he became hard, he swept off the coverlets of the bed and lifted her onto it. He made her lie down and pushed her legs into the air. Little voices entered his mind from far away, whispering, but they were so faint he couldn't make them out.

He pushed himself inside her, feeling the resistance, and then a hot stickiness. His genitals were covered in red, the blood staining the sheet and his brain filled with fire. He began thrusting so hard he was pushing her up the bed, her head trapped against a red silk bolster. He took her arms and pinned them to the mattress. Noan was terrified. She began to cry out, and Zhen's head flew up and he looked into her face for the first time, seeing the terror, enjoying it, looking at her mouth, red lips, pink teeth, red tongue. Blood filled his eyes.

He covered her mouth with his hand, lifted her leg in his arm, trapping her, until with a great groan he came, massively pumping his semen into her to the last drop.

Listening in the dressing room, the *sangkek um* and the *pak chindek* smiled at each other. The marriage had been consummated. If the muffled cries and groans they had heard were anything to go by, both parties had enjoyed themselves. Not many families asked for this service, but when they did, it was always rather titillating. They'd known each other a long time and in younger days had been tempted, in the low light of other dressing rooms, to certain erotic activities. Their job would not end for eleven more days but the bride's parents would be pleased. A grandson was surely on its way. They retired for the night.

The room was dark when he woke, disorientated, stickily hot. The candles had gone out, and the room was airless. He felt for the edge of the bed, banged into silken and metal hangings, swore and dropped off the mattress. He felt sticky on his legs and groin. Then he remembered the night before and felt a hot flush of shame. He groped for the table and found the candle but nothing to light it with. Made his way to the windows and pushed aside the curtains, throwing the shutters open. This room gave onto an air well, and some watery light fell into the room. It was raining. He took a deep breath of this rainy air and went to the other window, opening up the shutters. He looked down at himself. In this light it looked like he was covered in grey sludge, and a slight panic rose in his chest.

He went to the washstand and began rinsing himself, the water turning grey. He couldn't understand what this was and shook his head in bewilderment, brain still befuddled with sleep. Picking up the washbasin, he took it to the window and saw the pink in the water. He put the basin back on the stand and went back to the bed. He could make out her shape huddled against the back wall of the enclosed bed, the woman's side, ensuring she stayed put, he supposed.

He had forgotten her name. Did he ever know it? Climbing on the bed he felt again the stickiness and began to get worried. There was too much blood. He turned her gently and sighed in relief. She was breathing. He stroked her face gently, but she did not wake.

He cast around for something to light a candle, remembered the dressing room, went in there but it was even darker. Throwing on the white pyjamas, he went to the door of the bridal chamber and opened it. A Chinese servant was sleeping rolled up against the door like a log. Zhen felt annoyed. Did they think he was going to run away? He prodded the man awake.

'Bring a lamp. Can't see anything in here. Hurry up!'

The man returned in a minute and handed Zhen the lamp. He knew the household would be informed he was awake, for he was supposed to leave before the sun and return the following evening. This rigmarole for twelve damn days. *Aiya!*

He shut the door and went over to the bed, pulled back the coverlet. He drew a sharp breath. The sheet and the woman's naked body were soaked and caked with red. He had killed her, by all the Eight Immortals, and a great feeling of remorse rose in his chest. Why had he been so rough? He had never done anything like that before to a young girl. He ran his hand over his face.

He put the lamp on the table and pulled her as gently as he could towards the edge of the bed. She opened her eyes slightly, then closed them again. He spread her legs. Blood was seeping out of her. He stepped back, aghast, then ran to the washstand, taking the cloths there and putting them between her legs, stemming the flow. He quickly fashioned a loincloth, grabbed the coverlet and wrapped her in it.

By the time he had finished he heard a knock at the door. It was the *pak chindek*, he knew, to take him home.

He opened the door.

'Get the mother quickly; there's too much blood.'

The Boyanese looked at him uncomprehendingly.

Zhen searched his brain.

'Mother come. Girl sick,' he said in Malay. The man blenched and ran off. Zhen returned to the room, wet a cloth and began rinsing her face. The powder came off stickily. He got a glass of water and lifted her against his shoulder, putting it to her lips. At first it trickled down her chin; then she revived slightly and drank. She opened her eyes.

There he was. That face. She had longed for that face, and he was here. Without thinking she put out her hand and pulled his head down to hers, putting her lips against his. Zhen was surprised, but so glad she was not dead, wanting to apologise, make it up to her somehow for the night, that he let himself be kissed. She put her arms around his neck.

Noan's mother rushed into the room and was embarrassed but pleased to find them. The picture of a loving couple! Her heart was thrilled. She lowered her eyes. As Zhen heard her, he pulled out of the embrace, unthinkingly put his hand to his mouth, wiping off the kiss. He tried to explain.

Noan's mother bowed, asked him to leave, and began examining her daughter, questioning her, looking at the bloody bed.

When she emerged she called Ah Pok to translate into Hokkien, for he was in the house.

Zhen began to apologise, but she bowed her head.

'We are so sorry. Noan has been silly by trying not to bother you. She started her monthly cycle and did not get up to deal with it. It is the most unfortunate timing.'

So that was her name. Noan.

'So she is all right?' Zhen asked.

Noan's mother inclined her head. She had no wish to pursue this subject. The wedding night had been a failure, and it was the silly girl's fault. He had done his duty, very well according to the somewhat salacious reports she had received. It was ominous: first the candle and now this. Bad luck, bad luck. She would go to the temple today. The husband should go away, and the *sinseh* would know how to proceed.

Zhen was taken to the wardrobe room and changed. Within ten minutes he was following the pageboy back to his house.

He ran upstairs, throwing off his clothes, and sat on the bathroom floor, lathering the soap, dousing himself in water, washing himself clean of sweat, blood and this vicious and muddy deed.

He bent and flexed his body to form lotus. Clean the dark mirror of the mind. He relaxed into meditation and contemplated the void.

# 40

'The worst has happened,' he told them. 'She has relapsed. Takouhi has brought in another *dukun,* do you know what the *dukun* is? for heaven's sake he's a bloody witchdoctor for god's sake why did I agree to let her do it eh? why jesus Tigran's with them he's brought the priest from his chapel it's in the grounds of his mansion pretty little building in the Dutch style what was I saying? yes the priest he's an Armenian ha! the priest and the witchdoctor that would be worth seeing eh! poor Meda stuck between the two what were they both thinking anyway she was baptised here in St Andrew's Church the church I built with my own hands, what? yes baptised by me so she's a Protestant for the love of god no? perhaps I should send out the Reverend White to do battle for her soul eh poor little Edward smiting the heathen with his cross of righteousness for my daughter's soul.'

George sank down into a chair putting his face in his hands.

'Her poor little soul. My poor little girl.'

He sat as if suddenly robbed of breath, heartbeat, powerless to move, struck dumb. Charlotte felt hot tears like sharp hooks in her throat: tears for Meda, for George, for herself, for loss and hopeless love, for an unjust and unfeeling God.

Robert rose and went to George's liquor table. He poured half a glass of whisky and, taking one of George's hands, put the glass into it.

George looked up, drank it down in one gulp.

Charlotte moved to his side, took his other hand. 'Is there no hope, George?'

He put her hand to his lips. 'Sweet Kitt. No hope. The letter from Tigran said that she was very sick. The *dukun* is waiting to prepare the *selamatan* if it becomes necessary. It's the feast that's held after— ' He stopped, unable to speak the words.

He rose, and they followed him on to the wide verandah. The evening was drawing in; the sky was filled with faint clouds starting to turn rose. He looked over to Tir Uaidhne.

'I suppose the Javanese ceremony is as good as any. They believe the spirit passes over, yer know, then returns now and again to see if everyone's all right. That's when they hold a feast. The *selamatan* is beautiful; I've been to several. Not sad yer know; happy almost, wishing a safe journey, good luck in the future, as if she had just sailed away on a ship for a visit somewhere.'

He leaned his head against the edge of the opening.

'She won't come back. They hold *selamatan* regularly up to the thousandth day after ... death. Takouhi will be there for them all, well and truly in the world of the spirits. Happy even to be there. Whether she'll think of me, I don't know.'

He stopped, gazing at the window opposite. 'I think I'll sleep in our bed tonight with a few of Meda's things around me.' Turning, he smiled at his friends, went up to Charlotte and hugged her. 'I'm all right now. Ol' Shakespeare said it all, didn't he, eh?'

'There's providence in the fall of a sparrow ...;
If it not be now, yet it will come, the readiness is all ...'

He accompanied them to the door of his house, out under the porte-cochere, calling for his carriage to take them to the bungalow. As they stood waiting, he turned to Robert. 'Robbie, my boy, will you help me do something? I'd like to build a memorial for my two girls, in the cemetery, under the banyan tree. I'll sort it out with White. Then they'll always be with me d' yer see. Can't think of anything else to do.'

He frowned, as if the act of thinking was like moving a leaden weight inside his head, and rubbed his temples.

'I'm a builder, so I'll build something for them. A tangible memory of their brief moment on this earth, a reminder that love is everything. We shouldn't forget, eh, "that all is small, save love, for love is all in all".'

He shook Robert's hand, kissed Charlotte distractedly and left them.

When they got back to the bungalow Robert led his sister to the verandah and poured them both a little whisky.

'Are you all right, Kitt?'

She knew what he meant. 'Yes, Robbie, I'm all right. Don't worry. I know it will have to end, but just not right now. He takes precautions; it's all right. I haven't seen him for weeks in any case.'

Robert put down his glass. He had his own worries, but still, he worried about this as well. Where would it all end?

Baba Tan looked at himself in the long mirror. He had taken special pains with his appearance today, the fifth day of the marriage, the day he would welcome his foreign guests to meet the bride and groom. He took a little of the blackening his wife used to cover her bald forehead and put a few spots on his greying temples. The *nonyas* all had the same problem. Pulling the hair back so severely into the traditional bun always resulted in thinning and baldness. It was one of the reasons he had taken a concubine with thick tresses and made her always wear it loose. If he had ever truly felt any passion for his wife, the site of her bald pate would certainly have withered it. He had not been near her in years and, with the marriage of his daughter, was contemplating taking a second concubine or even another wife.

He ran his hands down his body, over the silk coat. He had grown bored with the first concubine. The thought of grandchildren had unsettled him. He was still young enough to please a woman, make more children. A young woman who inspired him to new passion. That was what he wanted. He had his eye on the third daughter of Baba Tsang by his second concubine, a beautiful Balinese woman. The family had fallen on hard times, for both Tsang and his old first wife were incorrigible gamblers. A price could be arranged. The father had taken some pains to make sure that he had seen her. And why not? He had plenty to offer. Lovely creature, nearly fifteen years old, with a mouth like a bud and eyes like midnight.

He completed his toilette, placed his silk cap on his head and, with a last look, left the room and made his way downstairs. His wife had told him of the wedding night, the unfortunate menstruation. It was bad luck for Zhen. He looked gloomy, and no wonder! He had come every night to eat the special dinners prepared for the couple and sleep with his new wife. Hopefully he was getting some pleasures, even if he had to put off for a while the making of the first grandchild. Birds' nests in syrup, spring chicken with herbs, steamed pigeons, mushrooms and ginseng, herbal soup—tonic food—then a little fondling and a good night's sleep. He'd be ready when Noan was clean again. He must be feeling a little frustrated, though. He'd been getting plenty from that woman of his before the wedding. Tan had often wondered who this woman was. Ah Pok had never seen her, and he didn't like to ask too many questions, alert nosy neighbours. Of course, he was curious. His son-in-law was a virile devil, and Tan had no doubt he could satisfy many women—much like himself. It must be irksome to be so confined. Still, it was not for much longer.

Tan went into the main hall, where the two embroidered chairs and footstools had been set up. After presenting their red packets and paying their respects to him and the other male relatives, the guests would gather here to meet his daughter and her new husband. This was his favourite day: the day the governor and his English guests would honour his family and his position in this society.

He went into the long dining room to inspect the little English cakes, the *kueh* pastries, the elegant English silver tea services, the porcelain tea sets in the English style he had ordered in China, covered in exotic pink flowers the English called 'roses'. These, he thought, were a great success, with their wavy lips and little curved handles. He had asked Miss Mah Crow to find him an example, and she had given him a sketch of a cup and saucer from Mr Kuliman's house. They were not exactly the same, but certainly good enough to impress his guests. He anticipated their surprise with pleasure.

Zhen was at his house. In half an hour he would have to go back to Tan's mansion, submit to yet another inspection, this time from the *ang mo*. He had only this minute begun to think that Xia Lou and her brother might be amongst the guests. Now this idea took hold, and he found himself at the same time desperate to see her and desperate for her not to come.

The time spent locked up with Noan was irksome. He now treated her with kindness, regretting his actions of their first night together. But he had nothing to say to her and, in any case, she spoke absolutely no Hokkien, while his Baba Malay, though improving, served only for the exchange of the most banal of communications. They ate in silence. The bridal chamber had been abandoned until Noan's period was over. It was inauspicious to have menstrual blood in the room during the nuptial period, and it had been scoured, the mattress burned and replaced with a new one. For now they slept in another, similar room which shared the wardrobe chamber. This room had been shut up, and though it had been cleaned, it smelled faintly of mould and damp. When it came time to get into bed, he motioned her to get in and then spent an hour drinking the bottle of rice wine he brought in each evening, staring into space. She watched him silently from the bed, sitting by the flickering candle, the shadow of his arm on the wall rising and falling with each drink, pretending to sleep when he joined her. He slept immediately.

Then she cried quietly to herself. She did not expect him to touch her while she was menstruating, but surely they could kiss. He had not even kissed her once. It was her fault; she wasn't pleasing enough. The assault of the first night had receded in her mind. She had nothing to compare it to. And he had been kind ever since, too kind. He changed in the robing room, not again showing her his body, not wanting to look at hers. Lying next to him, not touching, was exquisite torture, but she did not dare move towards him.

In three or four days she would be clean again. They would return to the bridal chamber. Everything would be different. Her heart lightened a little when she thought of this. And today she could show him off to the foreign guests, this beautiful man who was her husband.

Robert and Charlotte made their way across the bridge in George's little carriage. George had been invited but had declined. Charlotte worried for George. He had lost weight, did nothing but work and refused all attempts by his many friends to join them for evening entertainments.

Now brother and sister rode, not speaking. For his part, Robert was concerned about the effect this meeting would have on his sister. He had begged her not to go; it was not necessary. Any excuse would do. Unwell, indisposed, it didn't matter. But Charlotte knew she needed to see this—needed to see Zhen and this wife, see the woman who would have the right to hold him in her arms forever. She needed to look into his eyes, feel the knife in her heart.

They arrived at Tan's mansion, and his servant took their horse as they crossed the doorstep. Robert deposited his red packet with the chief clerk, who wrote his name in the book. They entered into the inner courtyard, where Baba Tan was talking to the governor. The guests continued to arrive; then Baba Tan opened the doors of the dining room and ushered them inside for refreshments.

Charlotte could hardly concentrate. She smiled emptily at her acquaintance, waiting for the moment, dreading it, wanting it. Tea was served, and the governor complimented Baba Tan on the extraordinary tea service. Bonham was careful not to smile, for the cups were small, with dragon-curled handles and roses that resembled misshapen peonies. From China? Really? Why, it looked so English, he said. Baba Tan beamed.

This tea party seemed interminable to Charlotte. Robert stayed close by her side, and they stood slightly aloof, looking into the inner courtyard, with its pretty lotus pond and pots of delicate bamboo. She should have enjoyed this opportunity to see the wealth and opulence of a Chinese merchant prince's mansion, but all she could do was stare at the golden fish flitting below the surface of the pond and the intricate patterns of the green-and-white Malacca tiles.

Eventually Baba Tan called them to give him the honour of greeting the new bride and groom: his daughter and her husband. The governor left the room first, with his host. He stood in front of the married couple, bowing his head slightly, congratulating them and wishing them great happiness and good fortune in the future. It was a pretty speech despite the stuttering, and when it was over, he took his leave. Now the rest of the guests entered in order of importance. Robert and Charlotte waited, finally approaching the door to the main hall.

As she passed the doorway, her eyes sought him. She could see Mr Erskine, the sitting magistrate, and his new wife, presenting their congratulations. Then she saw them, the young woman in a heavily embroidered gown of pink, blue, and turquoise, covered in jewels, her face round and white, her lips ruby red, eyes lowered, a golden crown on her head.

Zhen was beside her, in dark silk, with the gold-and-silver Chinese dragon on his chest. She remembered seeing it in the room the day she had first walked into his arms. He wore a black mandarin hat, the top studded with a huge diamond. He looked straight ahead, not moving, as each guest passed before him. He had never looked so handsome: regal, a young emperor. Robert gripped his sister's arm and they moved slowly forward.

Zhen saw her. He felt moths fluttering somewhere in the base of his stomach. Her eyes were down, not looking at him. His face impassive, he waited, but Noan had suddenly noticed his hand grip the closed fan he held a little tighter. It was an imperceptible movement to anyone but her. She swivelled her lowered eyes to his face, but saw nothing to explain the movement. The next guest passed, and a pale yellow silk skirt came into view. She saw her husband's hand clench tighter. The skirt stopped in front of her husband, the black trousers of a man in front of her. Words were uttered which she did not understand, and then the skirt dipped slightly and seemed to sway towards the black trousers and departed. Her husband's hand remained clenched. She did not know what to make of this, had not dared to raise her eyes in this company of the *ang mo*.

Charlotte breathed deeply as she left the mansion. She had stood in front of him as Robert paid his compliments and congratulations. Then she had raised her eyes. He was looking at her, his gaze seemingly saying nothing, but knowing him now, she saw the intensity. Remember the words in the orchard, she had thought. They had echoed faintly in the back of her mind. Love, yours: pointless, meaningless words. Then, feeling faint, she had leaned onto Robert's arm, dropped a brief curtsy and Robert had taken her from the room. He had called for the carriage, and they were soon driving away from the mansion.

'A handsome couple, eh Robbie?' Charlotte was eventually able to say.

Robert said nothing.

'Very handsome, don't you think? The bride pretty, the groom manly, eh, Robbie?'

Robert heard the faint note of hysteria in his sister's voice.

'Stop, Kitt. Stop it.'

Charlotte leaned her head on his shoulder and said nothing more. When they arrived at the bungalow, Robert showed her the clothes on her bed, told her to change. The *Sea Gypsy* stood ready, rocking against the jetty. Today they would go out on the sea, far along the coast to the house at Katong, and stay there, the two of them. First they would swim, the way they once had back on their mother's island, the feel of the warm water soothing her cares. He was taking whisky, and they'd talk and get a little drunk, eat fish and walk along the beach, draw solace from the beauty of the island, the curve of the leaning coconut palms, listening to the song of the sea, the white sand. They'd watch the little shells running back and forth with the waves, the crabs popping their heads from watery holes, the kites making lazy circles in the sky. There would be a big driftwood fire, and there would be no one else in the world but them.

# 41

Robert was with George at the Christian cemetery. The pure white twin rotundas were complete, standing together, shining against the dark wood of the banyan tree, the fresh green of the tamelan. George had not wanted his workmen to build them, and apart from preparing the ground on which they stood, he, Robert, John and his old friend, Billy Napier, had put down every brick and spread the thick white *chunam* over them. Now they were sweeping up.

'Fine work, old friends. I thank you; I do indeed.'

They all gathered round and contemplated their handiwork as they drank the ale which George had ordered, brought from the tavern in earthen jars dripping with condensation. Six fluted columns with Ionic scrolls supported a frieze of flowers, and above that rose the curved and nippled domes of the rotunda. George smiled. The rotunda was an ancient and classical monument, a temple to cults of the earth goddess, to fertility, to life, not death. A sacred space, a sky within. There was a reason he had chosen the Ionic order for Tir Uaidhne, a private amusement shared with Takouhi. These two little temples to Meda and Takouhi were his tribute to love. He had buried the tokens—one for his daughter and one for his wife—inside the brickwork, and now as he contemplated them, it was a small soothing balm on his heart.

George seemed to have revived, but all three of these men saw his eyes.

'The heart will break, yet brokenly live on:
Even as a broken mirror, which the glass
In every fragment multiplies; and makes
A thousand images of one that was,
The same, and still the more, the more it breaks;

308

And thus the heart will do which not forsakes,
Living in shattered guise, and still, and cold,
And bloodless, with its sleepless sorrow aches,
Yet withers on till all without is old,
Shewing no visible sign, for such things are untold.'

George went over to the grave of Thomas Hallpike and looked down at it, remembering the day he had stood here with her. Then, together, they moved about the cemetery, contemplating the headstones and reflecting on the brief lives of those who lay there. So many children. Dr Montgomerie's little ones, who had died the same day, two years old and one, Margaret and Robert, next to their tiny brother, dead just two years later. The heartbreak spoken of by those three little graves. Here lay one three years, ten months; there, a child three months; eight years—Charles and Ella, two babies of Jose da Souza; and also his granddaughter, Maria, one year, seven days. It went on and on, the terrible toll.

'Let's talk of graves, of worms and epitaphs.
Make dust our paper and with rainy eyes
Write sorrow on the bosom of the earth.'

He took a long drink of ale.
'Ah, boys. Poor Thomas, Maria, Margaret, all of them, never got to know the joy of love. We should be grateful, aye, we should, for what we get. Takouhi and I had eighteen years, and for most of them we had Meda.' He faltered at the sound of her name and drank.
'Count our blessings, eh? Not for sorrow, these two little temples. *Ad vitam. Ad amor aeternum.*'
He raised his tankard, and they all drank to Thomas, and missed love, and George's two loves, and loss, knowing he would go away too.

When the news had come of Meda's death, George had shut himself up in Tir Uaidhne. Charlotte had gone to the shuttered house, let in by one of Takouhi's young Malay servants. He was dirty and half-dressed, gone the pretty green jacket and white *sarong*. After he closed the door, he ran off, and in the dusty half-light she climbed the staircase to the bedroom.

'Black Melancholy sits and round her throws
A death-like silence and a dread repose
Her gloomy presence saddens all the scene
Shades every flower, darkens ev'ry green'

She felt it in the house: black melancholy, a miasmic vapour trailing on the air. She opened the door to the bedroom. Airless, it smelled cloyingly of jasmine incense. He lay curled on their big bed, behind the mosquito netting, unmoving. When she went up to the bed, she saw that he was asleep, a bottle of whisky by the bedside, a book open on a pillow. Gaunt, unshaven, his head resting on Takouhi's silken gown, one of Meda's little English dolls held loosely in his hand. She lay down by his side. She was as utterly miserable as he, although she knew she had no right to compare his enduring love, his dreadful loss, to her brief encounter. Yet both seemed monumentally important.

The faint and haunting chords of the *gamelan* seemed to echo round the empty house, but she knew these sounds were inside her head.

She slept, and when George woke, befuddled, he imagined Takouhi had returned and took her in his arms. She woke then and held onto him, and he realised.

'I'm leaving, Kitt.'

'I know, George. You have to go.'

'Will you be all right?'

'Yes, I will, George. I think I must go too, soon, to Takouhi. Would that be all right, do you think? Will you not come with me?'

'No, Kitt. I cannot. It could never be the same between us. But will you tell me if she's well and where Meda is buried? Tell her about the temples on the hill. Perhaps lovers a hundred years from now will stop and gaze at them and wonder what they mean, kiss against them in the dusk. Ask her *dukun* to guide their spirits there to meet up with me one day. That'd be a comfort.'

'Yes, I will, though I'm certain she will return. She needs time.'

She took his head in her arms, and they lay awhile together as shadows moved around the room.

Finally she sat up and took up the book on the pillow, opened at the page he had been reading:

'For hearts so touch'd, so pierc'd, so lost as mine.
Ere such a soul regains its peaceful state,
How often must it love, how often hate!
How often hope, despair, resent, regret,
Conceal, disdain—do all things but forget.
But let Heav'n seize it, all at once 'tis fir'd;
Not touch'd but rapt; not wakened, but inspir'd!
Oh come! oh teach me nature to subdue,
Renounce my love, my life, myself—and you.

How happy is the blameless vestal's lot!
The world forgetting, by the world forgot.
Eternal sunshine of the spotless mind!'

The impassioned plea of Eloise to erase Abelard from her memory. 'Desires compos'd, affections ever ev'n', the spotless mind of emptiness.

'Would you cut them from your remembrance, George? As if they'd never been?'

'Sometimes, when the longing is strong. When I think of sweet Meda and in what shades she might lie.'

He sat up now too, against the pillow.

'She would not want it though. "Silly-billy, George," she'd say. But the Javanese are the most gentle people, locked into eternal rhythms, accepting what we white fools cannot. As if we can change the way of the world.'

He stopped for a moment, then continued. 'Plato said that death is not the worst that can happen to men. It is either a dreamless sleep or else a passing to another place where all the dead are, the poets and heroes, wise men of old, children, lovers. Either way it is not a loss but a gain.'

He paused, then looked at Charlotte. 'Of course, you might find all the long-departed, pale and pompous governors of the East India Company, and that would not be such a blessing.'

Charlotte smiled. 'And their wives.'

They both laughed.

'When will you go, George?'

'When I've found a tenant for me house. Not Tir Uaidhne, not this one. I don't want anyone living here. Put things in store, lend Matahari to Robert. I might go to Europe, cultivate meself, do the tour. A thousand miles or one, what does it matter if she won't be with me anymore?'

He moved away and sat up.

At the mention of Tir Uaidhne, Charlotte suddenly remembered that she had never had an answer about the name written large across its portal.

'George, may I ask about Tir Uaidhne? What does it mean? I asked once before, but you never told me, and Takouhi didn't feel able to explain properly.'

George rose and got off the bed, offering her his hand.

'I'm as dry as a nun's cupboard. Pardon the vulgarity. And I surely smell like Father Flaherty's goat as well. Come, we'll get some coffee, and I'll tell you the story.'

He smiled at her, and they went down to the kitchen.

When she left George, she walked down Coleman Street to the Armenian church and sat inside. It was always so peaceful inside this lovely building, and she felt close to Takouhi here, able to reach her through a mist of Javanese spirituality. Alamah, she heard her say, don' be silly-billy, for goo'ness sake.

Charlotte smiled, lit a candle for Meda's sweet soul and leant her head against the back of the pew, filled with the futility of it all, remembering her voice: '*Bonjour. Comment allez-vous?*'

The wedding was over and this was the first time Zhen had been free. He was in his house. The shop was being fitted. Tan was passing over some of his business to his new son-in-law, and Zhen was also using part of the shophouse for Chinese medicine. The final night of the wedding he and Noan had moved back into the bridal chamber. Her period was over. This time he had lain next to her when she got into the bed. He had decided that he would have sex with her regularly until she got pregnant, but quickly, no lingering around. Zhen knew he would have to sleep in this house until that time. Tan would not bother him after that. He would be freer to come and go.

Noan lay still as he moved on her. She did not know if he wanted her to touch him, so she lay passively, scared he would repeat the rough intensity of the first night.

Zhen finished as quickly as possible that first time. The second time, though, he began to like the feel of her soft and full brown body and had begun to touch her gently. He realised, despite everything he had told himself, he could not lie with a woman, any woman, without using his skills to arouse her. Without her response, it made everything too ugly. The third time, Noan had begun to react, happy beyond anything that Zhen allowed himself to be touched.

Now, weeks later he had grown sick of her. He could see she adored him. She could not hide it in the way she served him food, poured him tea, turned her body to his each night, desperate to touch, be touched. She sought his lips, but this he could not bear. There was no passion in this lovemaking with her. Her red mouth repelled him, and her cloying attentiveness had begun to irritate. He needed to see Charlotte. Since his marriage, she had not once come to Boat Quay.

Tan, by contrast, was delighted. In the morning, at the breakfast table the two men shared, he could see his daughter's happiness. She served her father and husband with devotion. Nothing was too much. Zhen only had to raise his head for Noan to run to his side, waiting to answer any call. He certainly had a way with women, for all the daughters got slightly giggly when he was in their presence. He could see that it might be time to look for a husband for his second daughter, for the marriage of her sister seemed to have unsettled her. She was not yet fifteen, but after her birthday he would start to look around. Zhen had been a good choice. As soon as a pregnancy was announced, Tan intended to settle a sum of money on him for his new business.

The second daughter was more unsettled than her father could have imagined. She had developed a black hatred for Noan, envious every night when she and her husband closed the door to the bridal chamber. She had taken to creeping into the robing room after her mother went to bed and listening to the noises they made. She heard her sister's soft moans and his deep voice, and trembled with the intensity of her feelings. She could not help thinking about what she knew: if something happened to a wife, it was not uncommon for a man to marry a sister.

# 42

Zhen fairly skipped across the bridge and along North Bridge Road. Qian had trouble keeping up and had to call him to slow down. Zhen smiled and stopped, waiting for his friend. They were going to the school at the Catholic chapel. Today he would see Charlotte after so long. He would ask her to meet him at his house tonight.

He saw her as they turned in the gate; she was standing with Father Lee. Her loveliness was a rediscovery, a moment of Zen enlightenment; he felt his whole being falling instantaneously in love with her again.

When she turned to face them, she did not smile. They bowed to her, and she bobbed a curtsy and then turned abruptly and went into the chapel to teach the younger boys. Zhen was dumbfounded. He had seen her eyes the day of the wedding reception, seen her faltering, knew she was badly affected. It had occupied his thoughts every night as he drank the rice wine and willed the silly girl in the bed to go to sleep.

He could not wait for the lesson to end and bowed quickly to Father Lee and left the classroom, going to the chapel before she could leave. As she came out of the little room next to the sacristy, he called her quietly. She looked at him with such impassive coldness he felt it pierce him like a needle. She made her way down the outer aisle to avoid him, but he quickly cut her off near the door to the side garden. He pushed the door open and, taking her hand, pulled her through. On this side there were several groves of trees, and he knew that once inside one of them, they would not be seen from the chapel.

She tried to pull her hand out of his, but he was not about to let her go. Charlotte knew she should cry out, but this touch on her hand had shaken her resolve—this sad, crumbly thing she called 'resolve'. She let herself be led into the wood. He put her against the trunk of a tree, taking her waist in his hands, sinking to his knees, imploring her soundlessly to take his head in her hands, forgive him.

She looked down at him. Why did he always know how to turn her mood? Had he tried to kiss her she would have slapped him but this passivity squeezed resistance out of her.

'Please, Xia Lou.'

She put a hand on his head, touching his hair, and he pulled himself into her, holding his face against her dress. 'Zhen, I cannot go on like this. It will kill me.'

He rose then and took her hand, putting it to his lips. 'Yes, we talk about this. Please, Xia Lou, come my house tonight?'

Charlotte sighed. If she went to his house, she knew there would be little talking. Qian had been right. Zhen was a river, and she was simply swept along when she was alone with him, powerless to resist.

She had made up her mind to leave. George had found a tenant for his house, auctioned off some things, stored others. He stayed in Tir Uaidhne now. Charlotte had gone every day at dusk with George to the cupolas, putting flowers under their domes, lighting incense, both of them finding peace in this quiet, green place. They sat near the young banyan tree which was entwining itself in and around the tamelan so that the leaves of both drooped gracefully to the ground together. The tamelan was just beginning to put out its flowers; they covered it in a haze of lilac buds. George read a poem to her which he had received from one of the American clipper captains, an American Indian funeral chant, the captain had said, and it had given his mind an unexpected comfort:

'Do not stand at my grave and weep
I am not there. I do not sleep.

I am a thousand winds that blow,
I am the diamond glints on snow,
I am the sunlight on ripened grain,
I am the gentle autumn's rain.

When you awaken in the morning's hush,
I am the swift uplifting rush
Of quiet birds in circled flight,

I am the soft starshine at night.

Do no stand at my grave and cry,
I am not there. I did not die.'

Yes, she had said, and felt its strange consoling power. For all the history of grief an empty doorway. She was relieved that George had accepted his daughter's death now, moved through the empty doorway and found somewhere on the other side to ease his heart.

George's passage was booked. As soon as she had said farewell to him, she would write to Takouhi.

Thinking of this, she said firmly, 'Zhen, no. I cannot come.'

He looked at her, stricken to the heart. His emotion was so visible on his face—a face which rarely showed expression—that she could not help herself. She moved into his arms, put her head against his chest, holding him. It would always be like this, she knew, for as long as she stayed in Singapore.

'All right,' she relented, 'tonight.'

He kissed her hand, holding it against his cheek, loving her, amazed that three words could take him from the blackest cave to the wide, blue sky.

When Charlotte got home, she opened the little box with the nutmegs she had collected on each visit to the orchard. They had withered now, lost their black-and-red brilliance, but the scent was so potent it conjured up images of him on the air.

She put the box away and went out to the verandah, looking down past the fort to the Chinese town. Robert was not at home, and she knew that if she left him a note, he would not be concerned for her.

Azan brought her some rice, curry and tea, and she sat, quietly, watching the sun go down. She thought of Robert's house at Katong and wished she could have spent a night with Zhen, there by the sea, only the birds to hear them sighing.

One of the *pantuns* the munshi had given her came to mind:

'Last night, about the moon I dreamt

And tumbling nuts of coco palm
Last night with you in dreams I spent
And pillowed lay upon your arm'

Then she suddenly recalled another:

'Twere better not in dreams to trust
For where are dreams when comes the morn?'

Yes, thought Charlotte. Where are dreams when comes the morn? Taking a slip of paper she wrote a note to Robert.

As she crossed the river, the light left the sky, and she saw the moon, full and bright. The moon. She could never escape it, and so she could never escape the memory of him.

He was waiting for her by the door and smiled, lifting her inside and throwing the bolt.

# 43

The entire town seemed to have turned out to wish George farewell. Bonham had held a banquet in his honour at Government House, a splendid affair, for he was truly sorry to see Coleman depart. They had known and liked each other these twenty years. Every person of any importance had come from all over the settlement. From the hill they had looked down on the town and harbour, every ship, every boat, every road, every house lit with a profusion of lamps and flaming torches, so that George might see what he had built.

Boat Quay was ablaze with yellow lamps and scarlet lanterns. Now fireworks began, their myriad colours fizzing and whizzing, exploding on the night air. The Chinese community had spared no expense in their wish to honour the man who had worked so tirelessly for them and built them their elegant palaces of trade. It was a sight so beautiful that even the governor had a small tear in his eye, remembering Coleman's time with him when they had both been so much younger. He had watched George build this town into the Queen of the East. George was touched, and could not, for once, find anything sardonic or witty to say.

The barque *Midlothian* awaited him, and thousands of people had gathered on the plain, the band of the Madras Regiment and all the officers lined up to offer the salute. All the boats from the river, decorated with a rainbow of fluttering flags, had come out and in lines three deep from the jetty to the ship formed a guard of honour for the cutter which would carry George to the barque. Bands had formed on the different boats, playing Malay, Javanese and Chinese music, so that a general cacophony filled the air.

The night before George had said farewell to Robert and Charlotte, John and Billy and several of his other close friends in a quiet way in the sitting room of Tir Uaidhne, sharing memories, recalling good times. For

John Connolly it was a double heartbreak, for he was sure that Charlotte, too, meant to go.

Today it took George two hours to shake the hands of everyone who had gathered, and he was overcome with this rousing farewell. Then George smiled and waved and got into the cutter. As it pulled away from the jetty, the regimental band began to play. When he passed, the boatmen cheered and banged their oars, almost drowning them out. Gongs banged, guns and firecrackers went off. The uproar was deafening. As the anchor was raised and the barque turned to depart, Colonel Murchison gave the order and the eleven cannon at the fort boomed a salute. A mighty cheer went up from the town. Charlotte strained to see her friend, watching long after the town had returned to its occupations and the ship was a mere smudge on the horizon.

From the rocks below the fort, Zhen watched the ship. He knew that Charlotte's friend was leaving today and felt sad for her. Baba Tan was amongst those who regretted this man's departure, so Zhen presumed he must have been a good fellow. He respected Baba Tan's opinions of others, for he had found a deep affection for his father-in-law which far surpassed that for his daughter.

His spirits were light, for his last meeting with Xia Lou had been passionate beyond his wildest dreams. In the morning, she had woken him with kisses and made love to him langorously, half asleep still, moving her body on his. She had come to him again two days later; he could not believe his good fortune. She had promised to come again, but two weeks had passed. He was impatient about this, but so busy now, too, with his new business, and there would now be celebrations in the Tan house. This morning Noan had shyly told him that she was pregnant, and he was so delighted that he had taken her in his arms and held her, knowing that now he could safely leave her alone. With his obligation fulfilled, his sleeping outside the Tan mansion would find no objection. The only problem in the house was the second daughter. He had said nothing, but she had come to him one evening, finding him in the robing room, and, like a shameless minx, had lifted her *sarong* and put his hand between her legs. He had stopped her and pushed her out of the room, but he knew he must be sure never to be alone with her.

Charlotte finally turned and went into the bungalow. In her room she sat looking at her reflection in the mirror. Then, taking pen and paper, she began to write to Takouhi.

When Robert came home that afternoon, she told him she was leaving. Robert felt a little guilty at his relief. The visits to Zhen had become too frequent. John Connolly had been to see him, asking about Charlotte's whereabouts on certain evenings. Robert had not known what to say, had lied as best he could, but he knew this could not go on.

'Robbie, will you tell him after I've left? I cannot bear to say goodbye, and he will surely be half-crazed and may do something we would all regret.'

'Aye, Kitt, I will. It's the best course of action. When things have settled down and you feel calmer, come back, eh, for I shall sorely miss you.'

Tan was so pleased with Zhen's news that he had left the godown and gone home immediately. He called Noan to him, and she had bowed to him, smiling. This was a splendid day, Tan thought. A grandchild on the way, and the negotiations almost complete for the second concubine. He thought he might bring this one into the house, for he did not want to be out and about at all hours of the night every time he wanted to lie with her. His wife would just have to put up with it. Anyway, she'd have enough to do with the grandchild. To make things even better, he had a prospective husband for the second daughter lined up, for Zhen had recommended a young coolie working in one of the European godowns.

Zhen had not seen Charlotte for weeks. She no longer taught at the chapel. Father Lee said she had been indisposed, which turned out to mean sick. Alarmed, he had gone to the police house, but she was not there, and the brother had rather stonily told him that his sister was better, thank you. Then, one day at the godown, he saw Robert talking to his father-in-law. Robert had heard the news of the grandchild and come to congratulate Tan. Zhen moved towards the small office and listened.

'Yes, that's right. I'm surprised you've heard.'

Tan said he had heard rumours about Robert's sister departing from John Connolly, who had appeared distraught. Obviously the man had some inclinations in that direction. He liked Charlotte, expressed his sadness but did not dare ask more.

Robert left then, rather annoyed at John's ill-thought-out comments. It was all very well having designs on his sister, but he ought to keep his tongue inside his head. Charlotte had seemed better recently. She had been quite low for a while, but Robert assumed that it was as much sickness of the heart as of any other part of her.

As he moved along the quay over the canal bridge, he was astonished to be confronted with the man who was responsible for this heartsickness.

'Can I speak to you?' Zhen demanded.

Robert pursed his lips. Really the fellow had done quite enough mischief. He would have liked to put a fist in his face, but still he was the baba's son-in-law and might one day, who knows, be useful as a contact in the secret societies. Robert's policing instincts got the better of him and he asked, 'What is it?'

'Sister leave Singapore?'

Well, he certainly came straight to the point. What a cheek; none of his business. Well, perhaps it was, in a warped kind of way. And he had saved her life. Robert knew he should say nothing, had promised Charlotte only to speak to the fellow after she had left, but, well, here Zhen was, asking him a direct question.

'Aye, yes. My sister is leaving Singapore soon.'

If Robert had expected a reaction, he was disappointed. Zhen's face was impassive. Really, he thought, you could never tell what these Orientals were thinking. Made them hard to deal with, especially the ones from China.

Without a word Zhen bowed, turned and disappeared down a small lane leading to Circular Road.

Extraordinary. Perhaps if Charlotte knew how little he cared, it might do her good, thought Robert, angry for her, wishing now he had never agreed to the whole thing. Women were terribly vulnerable to blackguards like this. He should have seen that, taken better care of her. But at bottom Robert knew he would never have been able to impose authority on his sister.

Zhen walked along Circular Road to South Bridge Road and turned past the gaol, then went as far as the Indian temple, his mind a complete blank. He stopped, a feeling of desperation coming over him. He turned and began to walk back the way he had come. Clouds scudded overhead, casting darkness on the ground as they passed over the sun.

Tan had not seen Zhen depart, and only when he called for him did one of the coolies tell him he had gone down the quay. Putting on his black top hat, he went outside and gazed the length of the promenade towards the bridge, but there was so much traffic and activity there that he couldn't see anything. Then, just as Tan was about to turn back into the godown, he saw him. Zhen was in a *sampan* which was sculling quickly down river. What by all the gods was his son-in-law doing on the river?

He watched as Zhen got out at the landing and walked quickly along the bank and disappeared towards the European town. Tan could not understand what Zhen was doing and, curious now, began to walk along the quay towards the fort. As he got to Tanjong Tangkap, he stopped. Now he could see Zhen in conversation with a fellow at the police office. Suddenly Tan's mind began to make connections. Miss Mah Crow was leaving, and Zhen was at the police office, suddenly disturbed. Could it be— ?

All at once, Tan knew it. The woman Zhen had been seeing all this time was Miss Mah Crow! The devil!

Tan was not especially annoyed. Rather, he was impressed at this young man's prowess. Tan had sometimes wondered what it would be like with a white woman. Well, carrying on with Miss Mah Crow and getting his daughter pregnant! He certainly had energy. Still, it was probably just as well that the sister was leaving. That could have become very complicated. He would have had to put a stop to it at once. He continued to watch until Zhen abruptly turned and walked around the police office, and Tan lost sight of him going along High Street.

The man had said Miss Mah Crow was at her friend's house, Miss Mah Nuk. Zhen was confused. He thought the friend had left with the sick child. He walked until he saw the white house, which looked completely deserted. He went into the garden and under the huge porte-cochere. The white men had amazing buildings, was his first thought. Every one a palace. One day he would like a house like this. Build it for her.

A bolt of lightning fizzed and crackled across the sky. A great roll of thunder boomed overhead, and he ducked involuntarily. Zhen sensed a bad squall and knew the boats out on the harbour would be turning tail and racing to the river mouth before they became deluged by the storm. Certainly by now Tan would be wondering where he was, but he did not care. He'd given the blasted man a grandchild.

He could see a dense black cloud rising from behind the distant islands and quickly overspreading the sky.

The door to the mansion was locked, and he began to circumnavigate the building. He heard a clack of shutters closing. Someone was inside. Convinced it was Charlotte, he went to the back of the building and found a door slightly ajar. As the first drops of rain fell, he went inside. It was dark, but he could make out a corridor. This led to a storeroom and kitchen area.

He continued deeper into the house and came to a tiled hallway. Several rooms led off this hallway, and he peered inside each of them. There was furniture, stores of some sort, but no living person. Now he came to the large main entrance hallway and looked up the great height to the chandelier. There was a room off to one side, where the door stood open and he could see light. Going quickly across the hall, he pushed the door open and saw her.

She was packing some of Takouhi's china into a wooden chest. Tigran was coming personally in his ship to take her to Batavia. With Takouhi's welcoming response to her letter had come a request to bring with her personal items and gifts from George. Charlotte hoped against hope that when time had passed, Takouhi would return to him.

Hearing the movement in the doorway, Charlotte turned.

She was so surprised to see him standing there that she almost dropped the little crystal vase she was wrapping.

He crossed the room and took the vase out of her hand, throwing it to one side. She heard the glass shattering as it crashed onto the tiled floor. He swept her into his arms and went out into the hall. He said not one word, and she suddenly didn't care what happened. She dropped her head on to his shoulder.

He went up the marble staircase and onto the long landing. There he found a big room with a huge bed standing in the middle of it. The shutters let in a little watery light. Zhen moved through the gauzy netting and lay her down. Lightning and thunder sizzled and rippled across the sky, and the rain began, blotting out all sound but its own watery lament.

# 44

The *Queen of the South* stood waiting in the harbour. It was not yet dawn, and the sun was still below the horizon like a tiger waiting to pounce on the day. She and Robert had watched as it sailed closer, threading through the squat Siamese craft, half square-rigs, half junks, the sleek English vessels and the long-prowed Sumatran ships. Charlotte could see the oculus, the eye, large, black and white, keeping a close watch on the steely cobalt of the deep ocean. She was certain that Tigran was on board.

The anchor fell into the sea. She felt the splash she could not hear, and her heart sank down with it to the depths. The hour had come. She could already see the cutter being swung out over the sea, ready for lowering, quivering, as if impatient to be where she was waiting.

She had made her brief farewells to her acquaintances. She was on a visit to Takouhi, to pay honour to Meda's resting place. Miss Aratoun had smiled coldly and wished her Godspeed. Mrs Keaseberry had been sad, liking this young woman with whom she had spent many hours in conversation. Charlotte, too, was sad to leave this other Charlotte, for Mrs Keaseberry had been ill, and in the tropics lives were precarious.

The da Silva girls had cried briefly, then asked her to write with all the news of Batavia. Charlotte realised how little she had seen of these women over the last weeks and months. Her greatest sorrow was leaving Evangeline, and she had made promises of rapid return she was not sure she could keep.

There was a knock at the door, and Robert went out. For ten days Zhen had watched, knowing this ship and its purpose.

Every day he had searched in his mind for wisdoms to deal with this hand of ice creeping round his heart, the bleak and passionless future which lay ahead without her.

'Double curtains hang deep in the room of Never Grieve
She lies down, and moment by moment the cool evening lengthens
The lifetime he shared with the goddess was always a dream
No young man ever in the little maid's house
The wind and waves know no pity for the frail pond-chestnut's
branches
In the moon and the dew who can sweeten the scentless cassia
leaves?
We tell ourselves all love is foolishness—
And still disappointment is a lucid madness'

Now he confronted her. 'This ship take you? You want this? Leave
me?'

She nodded, head down, unable to look at him.

'Come back?'

Charlotte shook her head, not trusting her voice.

He took her hand and kissed the palm. The feel of his lips, at this
parting, was not soft but like sand. Then he put a box into her hand. She
could see that it was the one he had given her at the chapel. When was
that? Ten lifetimes ago?

She opened it, and there was the pearl. He had made it into a
necklace. It lay under a delicate, latticed silver mount shaped like the
upturned eaves of a Chinese temple roof, on an entwined rope of red silk
threads. The pearl was perfectly round, like the moon. She took it from
the box and held it in her hand, and then he took it and turned her so he
could put it round her neck. It felt light as it lay on her skin. A touch as
light as him. As he tied the silk ribbon, his thoughts were bitter.

'The East wind sighs, the fine rains come,
Beyond the pool of water lilies, the noise of faint thunder.
A gold toad gnaws at the lock. Open it. Burn the incense,
A tiger of jade pulls the rope. Draw from the well and escape,
Chia's daughter peeped through the screen when Han the clerk was
young,
The goddess of the river left her pillow for the Great Prince of Wei,
Never let your heart open with the Spring flowers,

One inch of love is an inch of ashes.'

'One inch of love is an inch of ashes.'

She did not understand the Chinese words but heard the harshness of his voice.

She faced him and saw that his eyes were narrow, angry. He knew he should find tenderness, but he could find none, only a cold burning, the words of the *Taoteching* echoing dimly: 'The deeper the love the higher the cost, the bigger the treasure the greater the loss. Seek restraint and contentment.' It was wisdom he could not find. Maybe only withered old men could find it, and he was angry at these dead philosophers, at her, at everything.

'One inch of love is an inch of ashes.'

At the jetty, the launch had arrived, its purple covering floating in the breeze. Tigran had made a royal barge for her, as he had for his sister. Azan was helping load the chests and cases which had stood ready, waiting for this journey. Tigran had waited on the ship, and she knew he had not wanted to hurry her, wanted to let her make her farewells. Perhaps Takouhi had told him about Zhen.

Out there, in the harbour, they both knew, the boat stood ready now. Zhen had wanted to kiss her, but abruptly he could not bear it, furious, filled with a cold hard wish to smash everything.

He turned. She put her hand on his arm. He shook it off and let out a roar of anguish. She caught his hand as he moved away. He stopped, wanting to strike her, but when their eyes met, he felt turned to stone.

She moved to him and put her hand to his cheek, pulling him to her face, holding him quietly. He tried to hold on to his anger, fearful of what would rush in to take its place when it had gone.

But he could not, and he held her fast, releasing her only as he heard Robert come into the room.

She took his hand, laying a scroll of paper tied with a red ribbon into the palm. He looked perplexed, holding it. Then, as Robert came to his sister's side, he went down the verandah and disappeared.

Charlotte put her hand to her cheek, where his had been, then to her throat and touched the pearl. She took a breath and straightened her back.

From the rocks under the fort, Zhen watched the black brig turn slowly towards the south. Suddenly the slack sails stretched on the rigging, hearing the call of their mistress, the wind. In a breath she commanded, and with a snap they obeyed. The ship moved swiftly away.

He gasped. Tears sprang to his eyes. He remembered Qian's words. He had tried to weave a net to catch the wind. Then she was gone.

He looked down at the paper in his hand, opened it, read the black characters painted there. He gazed at the far horizon. Tears remained, but bitterness flew away.

The wind tasted blue, of brine and foamy swells, and the sea looked like her eyes as red threads crept up the sky.